D1648845

CONFLICT
OF
INTEREST

OTHER BOOKS AND BOOKS ON CASSETTE/CD
BY CLAIR POULSON:

I'll Find You

Relentless

Lost and Found

CONFLICT OF INTEREST

a novel

CLAIR POULSON

Covenant Communications, Inc.

Covenant

Cover image by Mel Curtis © 2003 PhotoDisc Collection/Getty Images

Cover design copyrighted 2003 by Covenant Communications, Inc.

Published by Covenant Communications, Inc.
American Fork, Utah

Copyright © 2003 by Clair Poulson
All rights reserved. No part of this book may be reproduced in any format or in any medium without the written permission of the publisher, Covenant Communications, Inc., P.O. Box 416, American Fork, UT 84003. The views expressed herein are the responsibility of the author and do not necessarily represent the position of Covenant Communications, Inc.

This is a work of fiction. The characters, names, incidents, places, and dialogue are products of the author's imagination, and are not to be construed as real.

Printed in Canada
First Printing: May 2003

10 09 08 07 06 05 04 03   10 9 8 7 6 5 4 3 2 1

ISBN 1-59156-209-0

Library of Congress Cataloging-in-Publication Data

Poulson, Clair.
    Conflict of interest : a novel / Clair Poulson.
        p. cm.
    ISBN 1-59156-209-0 (alk. paper)
    1. Attorney and client--Fiction. 2. Public prosecutors--Fiction. 3. Widowers--Fiction. 4. Utah--Fiction. I. Title
    PS3566.0812C66 2003
    813'.54--dc21   2002041772

Dedication
To Doug Horrocks, my chief deputy when I served as sheriff. Doug was a great help to me during those years and has remained a loyal friend and confidant since. I am forever indebted to him.

Acknowledgements
I wish to thank those attorneys and judges whose advice and technical help made this book possible. They are too numerous to name, but they know who they are. To each of you, I appreciate your friendship and help.

PROLOGUE

If one had to choose when to die, this Friday evening in late September would have been a beautiful choice.

Yet dying was the furthest thing from Jennifer Sterling's mind. She gazed out the screen door at the sunset that filled the low western sky with fiery clouds, tinting those hovering higher in several shades of pink. A slight breeze stirred the wind chimes on the deck, evoking a sweet melody from them. She drew a deep breath, drinking in the pleasant scent of the afternoon's light rain that still lingered in the cool air. It had been a lovely day. And it was a beautiful evening. Too beautiful, perhaps, considering the unpleasant task ahead of Jennifer—a task that might render the day's conclusion dark and unsettling, rather than the perfect close it hinted at now.

She turned from the window as darkness settled in, a sinking feeling of despair in her heart as she thought of what she must say when Rob returned tonight. And surely he would be home soon. She had a confession to make to him, and it would be one of the hardest things she'd ever had to do. She really did love Rob, and she knew he adored her. Why she'd let herself spend time alone with another man, especially when she knew that man was attracted to her, seemed both strange and foolish to her now.

Perhaps it was because she'd had certain expectations when she married Rob. He came from a wealthy and prominent family, so it was only natural that she'd expected him to lavish her with the finer things that money could buy. But he had rejected his father's business in order to become a cop, and his father had basically disowned him for it. What he had now in the way of possessions were bought with his meager salary, and now that he was in law school, the only money he had was from student loans and what little he made working a few shifts as a reserve deputy. They had been pretty much surviving on her salary as a legal secretary, and that wasn't much.

She'd begun to flirt with Dan partly because she was lonely. Rob spent long hours at school and at the library studying. She missed him when she was home alone in the evenings, and she resented his being gone so much, but she knew that was no excuse for flirting and spending time alone with another man. Oh, it had seemed innocent at first. She hadn't really done anything but have lunch and dinner with Dan a few times. And he'd seemed like such a nice guy, his attentions no more noticeable than what she was used to.

As a former Miss Utah, Jennifer had been admired by many men. The fact that she had chosen and married Rob had not stopped her admirers. Dan, she had thought, was simply one of those. She had enjoyed his company, but after a while she realized that she was attracted to him. That was when she started to think about what she was doing.

Now, as she reflected, Jennifer realized that she had not been faithful to her marriage covenants. She remembered complaining to Dan about how Rob spent so much time away from home in the evenings. She'd even whined about being scared because she was alone so much wondering if she really *was* alone.

Dan offered to come over and spend those disturbing times with her, but she'd quickly redirected the conversation, telling him that she'd be fine as long as she stayed near a flashlight and a phone at all times. "But can you get to them quickly enough?" he'd asked.

"Oh, yes. We keep a flashlight in the kitchen cupboard near the back door. It's small, but it's bright. And I keep the cell phone by my side."

"Use it if you need me," he said, and she'd promised she would.

They talked about a number of things when they went out. Dan often kidded her about going to church, and now, as she reflected, she realized that spending time with him and listening to him had adversely affected her activity in the Church. Rob had been hurt, maybe even a little angry, when she'd insisted that she was just too tired to get up on Sunday mornings lately. The truth was, she didn't want to go. That was what her association with Dan was doing to her. She had finally made up her mind that morning, when Rob left early for school without even giving her a kiss, that it was time to change all that.

* * *

Martin Ligorni got very excited as he watched Jennifer moving around the living room. She cleaned and straightened things up, the motions of her body a work in perfection. She was so lovely to watch. He'd talked to her as often as possible over the years, and he loved her voice too. He was sure she'd been impressed by his as well—he'd seen it in her eyes. He had such a smooth and melodious voice, even if he did say so himself. He also loved the way Jennifer moved, the way she smiled and the way she flipped her gorgeous blond hair from her eyes. As he watched now, he memorized the way she crossed her legs when she sat on the recliner for a few minutes to watch TV. Every move she made caused him to love her all the more.

Jennifer got up and walked into the kitchen. Martin had to hurry around to a different window. When he peeked into the kitchen, Jennifer was just pulling a glass from the cupboard next to the back door. She left the door to the cupboard ajar when she stepped to the sink to fill her glass with water. Martin strained to see if anything valuable was in the cupboard, not that anything more valuable than Jennifer herself graced the house. She drank about half the glass, set it down, then returned to the cupboard. She picked up a flashlight from the cupboard, opened the back door, and began shining it into the yard. Martin dropped down, hiding himself. *What is she doing?* he wondered. Had he made too much noise?

But a moment later he heard the door close, and he again peeked into the kitchen window. She had just put the flashlight back in its place and then checked the back door and locked it. After that she returned to the living room. He hurried as fast as his chubby legs would carry him back to the main living room window.

Martin suddenly became angry, his thin lips quivering as Jennifer walked to the mantel and took down the large framed picture of her and Rob on their wedding day.

What right did she have to choose Rob Sterling over him? Martin had loved her since the time in high school that he'd been assigned a seat next to her in a math class. He'd helped her a little with her math because she wasn't very good at it. But even after that it was all he could do to get her to notice him. It was Rob's money—his family's money—Martin thought, that made her marry him. She didn't love Rob, she just loved his money. *Well, when I, Martin Ligorni, get to be a successful lawyer, I'll have plenty of money,* he reminded himself. He could provide Jennifer with the lifestyle she wanted.

But Martin became increasingly frustrated as his lovely Jennifer traced her fingers over Rob's profile in the portrait. It was making him furious. All she had to do was get the guts to leave Rob. Martin would take her in anytime. He'd seen her toying with the idea over the months, could see it in her behavior. He loved her, and he'd be better to her than Rob. He wouldn't leave her alone almost every night like Rob did.

Martin was suddenly forced to turn away from the window and drop behind Jennifer's shrubs when he saw headlights turn onto the street. His visits to see Jennifer had to remain his little secret until he was ready to tell her himself, to present what he had to offer.

As Martin thought about the months he'd spent getting to know Jennifer, he still couldn't believe the coincidence that had occurred when he and Rob ended up in law school together. It was so convenient to be able to come here when Rob was studying late. *And tonight . . .* Martin smiled to himself as he waited for the car to pass. Tonight Rob would be real late, at least Martin hoped he would, since Martin had arranged it so that he could watch Jennifer for several hours.

He stood up and peeked back in the window. What he saw made his blood run cold with the anger born of betrayal. Jennifer was kissing the picture of Rob! *How could she?* he wondered. He turned away, too angry to watch anymore. She'd just ruined his whole night. Fuming, he walked away from the house and back to his car. *What is the matter with her?* Martin wondered as he hoisted his heavy, pear-shaped body into the driver's seat. Why couldn't she see that she was meant for him? He shook his thick jowls in disgust. She *was* meant only for him. Rob had forfeited his right to her months ago.

* * *

Jennifer put the picture back on the mantel. When Rob came home, it would be him that she kissed, not his picture. She knew he was angry with her. He'd never said a word, but just a couple of days ago he'd come into the firm, and she'd been alone with Dan in his office. The way he'd looked at Dan, and then the way he'd looked at her, had frightened her. And she knew that Rob could get very angry. He didn't lose his temper often, but when he did it wasn't pretty.

Tonight, before she admitted her guilt, she would kiss Rob the way only she could, give him a good dinner, and tell him how much she loved him. Then maybe he'd forgive her when she confessed, and they could get their marriage back to the way it had been before she'd started entertaining another man.

Jennifer sat down again. The TV was still blaring, and for several minutes she watched it. But she wasn't interested in the show that was on. She could only think and worry. She had to make things okay with Rob again. She just had to. She picked up the remote and shut the TV off. Then she sat staring at the black screen as she recalled the confrontation she'd had with Dan.

"I'm sorry," she'd begun, after following him into his office that morning and shutting his door, "that I let you think I was interested in you romantically. I never intended for things to go this far."

"What are you talking about?" Dan had asked, his dark blue eyes narrowing and his handsome face scowling. "Surely you're not trying to say that you don't intend to go to lunch with me today?"

"That's right, Dan," she'd told him. "Not today, not any day. And no more dinners when Rob's at night classes. I'm sorry, but I love Rob, and this isn't fair to him. And it's not fair to you either, Dan. You told me yourself that we'd have to be careful because Ralph Hacking had come down on you once before for dating a married woman. You need to think about your job and what might happen to you if we were seen together. "

Dan had exploded. "I'll worry about my job, that's not your problem. Anyway, Ralph can't afford to lose me. And let me remind you, Jennifer, that I'm a very successful attorney, a partner, as you well know, in a prestigious firm. I can do a lot for your career. I already have, if you will recall. Dan suddenly calmed down. You can't play games with me—with my heart—and expect me not to hurt. Or strike out at the cause of that pain."

His words were so scripted, so calm and practiced, that they scared her. She suddenly felt like she couldn't trust him. "I know that," she said slowly, carefully. "And I appreciate what you've done for me." Maybe that was part of the reason, she admitted, that she'd spent the time with Dan that she had. He could, and already had, given her greater status among the other women in the office, and she and Rob had needed the money.

"You'd better appreciate it," he'd thundered, and Jennifer suddenly wondered what it had been about Dan that had attracted her. He was certainly not attractive now. "I'll forget what you just told me. I'll consider it your age," Dan said as he smoothed the lines in his face and painted on an artificial smile. "Be ready at one. I have an appointment and can't go to lunch until then."

"Dan," she'd tried again. "I mean it. I don't want to lose Rob. And that's exactly what will happen if you and I continue to have lunch together. You saw him when he came in here the other day. He gets jealous."

"Let him be jealous. He certainly can't offer you what I can."

"Dan, you don't seem to understand. Rob is the most important part of my life. I sort of forgot that, but when I got to thinking of what it would be like if I lost him, I realized that he means more to me than anything else."

Dan stared at her as if she'd lost her mind. "He has nothing, Jennifer. His parents don't even want anything to do with him. Can't you see why? He'll never amount to anything. I'll be surprised if he even makes it through law school. He was cut out to be a cop—officer friendly—and that's all he'll ever be."

Jennifer hadn't left her position in front of Dan's closed door. She'd turned then and grabbed the doorknob angrily. "He was an excellent officer, Dan," she said impulsively. "And there's nothing wrong with being a cop. Thanks for all you've done for me, and I really did enjoy your company, but I can't let it go on." She'd opened the door and left Dan glowering at his desk.

Late that afternoon he'd come by her little cubicle. "How about dinner tonight? You can tell Rob you had to work late," he said with one of his winning smiles. *Is he crazy?* she wondered.

She'd looked up and said quietly but firmly, so no one else would hear, "Dan, I mean it. Rob wouldn't like it if he knew you were pressing me to go out with you even after I've made it perfectly clear that I don't want it to happen again."

"You're a flirt, Jennifer. You can't help yourself," he'd observed. Then the dark side of Dan came out again as he said, "You'd better think this over seriously, my dear. There are other girls who could do your job, you know."

Jennifer later decided she should have left well enough alone after that threat on her position in the firm, but instead she'd lost it. "I've made up my mind, Dan. I intend to tell Rob everything when he gets home tonight. I love him, and I intend to prove it to him."

Dan had snorted contemptuously. "You'd do well to rethink that. I don't give up at the toss of a hat, as you well know. You can't just blow me off this easily." Even now, sitting in the safety of her living room, she could still see the look in his eye when he'd said that. He was a man who was used to getting what he wanted, and it was clear that he wanted her.

Jennifer turned on the television again. She didn't want to think about Dan anymore. She hoped Rob would get here soon, and she prayed that he'd forgive her. She also hoped he wouldn't get too angry with her or with Dan. Rob's anger was one of the reasons he'd decided to leave law enforcement. Facing stressful situations nightly, he was afraid he'd do something he'd regret to some criminal whose tongue flapped too much. The idea of practicing law had always appealed to him, and he had decided, with Jennifer's blessing, to go to law school. And he was doing very well. He had just started his second year a few weeks ago.

The minutes dragged by as Jennifer watched the television. It was almost nine. Rob had promised to be home by then. She wasn't really aware of the movie she was watching; her mind was filled with regret and foreboding. The wind chimes sent their tune through the screen door, a little louder than they had been just minutes ago, and they had an unpleasant harshness to them. *The wind must be picking up*, she thought. Perhaps it would rain again. Thunder cracked in the distance. A chill touched Jennifer's bare arms and she hugged them to her chest. Suddenly a bright flash of lightning lit the room, followed by a louder crash of thunder and a rush of fierce wind.

Rain began to pelt the roof as the wind howled a warning. Jennifer shivered and stood up. She couldn't imagine how such a lovely evening could turn to such a horrible one so quickly.

Jennifer thought she heard a key turning in the back door. *Oh finally, Rob's home*, she thought with both excitement and apprehension.

There was another terrible thunderbolt. The lights flickered, then went out, plunging the house into darkness. Unsettled, Jennifer tried to make her way through the living room in the sudden oppressive blackness. A gust of wind suddenly blew through the house, and she wondered if Rob had forgotten to close the door. There was a crash as something blew over just a few feet in front of her. Judging by the sound it made, it was almost certainly the lightweight floor lamp just inside the door that separated the living room from the kitchen. Jennifer stood still, listening, her heart pumping frantically.

She thought she heard the sound of shuffling feet. *Rob must be finding his way in the darkness*, she decided. But that was silly. He could just grab the flashlight, or had she, as distracted as she was tonight, put it in the wrong place after she'd used it to check the backyard? Maybe she'd laid it on the counter when she went to lock the door. And now he couldn't find it. Something else seemed strange though, she thought. She was sure she'd heard the key turning, and yet she didn't remember hearing Rob's car pull into the driveway.

As if you can hear anything with the thunder crashing, she chastised herself with nervous humor. She stood in the middle of the room, frozen suddenly with unreasonable fear. Another minute passed, and she was sure she heard the door banging, followed by the shuffling again. She was puzzled at Rob's behavior. Maybe he was trying to figure out what had happened to the lights and was attempting to get them back on again. Then there was another crash, not loud, but just a few feet away. It was followed immediately by a grunt.

There's someone in the house with me! Her thoughts began rushing in panic. She hoped desperately it was Rob and that he wasn't angry. A flashlight flicked on, shot a beam across the room, and stopped on her face, blinding her. "Oh, there you are," a familiar voice said. Jennifer jumped in fright. The tone of his voice sent shivers up her spine. "Jennifer, we've got to talk," he said. "I don't want to hurt you if I don't have to."

Jennifer nodded dumbly. *What in the world is he doing?* she wondered in fright. She took a step back, unable to form words. Surely he wasn't capable of violence, not the kind she felt filling the air around her. The flashlight wavered, and the shuffling started again. Just then a lightning flash lit the room illuminating a hazy image of Martin Ligorni's glowering face in a mirror to her left. She screamed just as the intruder stumbled over something that was lying on the floor. *It must have been the lamp,* she thought. He fell, came quickly to his feet, and bumped into the arm of the sofa, lunging forward. The last thing Jennifer Sterling ever saw was a bright flash of light coming at her from where the sofa sat. She never even heard the sound of the shot that struck her frantically beating heart and took her life.

"Jennifer, are you all right? Jennifer—" The voice became frantic. "I didn't mean to shoot. Jennifer!"

Jennifer didn't move.

The lightning flashed again, and Martin Ligorni's face was no longer reflected in the glass.

CHAPTER ONE

Rob Sterling rose wearily to his feet when the bailiff called the court into session. These past weeks had been a nightmare he never could have imagined. His beautiful young wife was dead. And he had been arrested and charged with her death.

He'd retained Raul Garcia, a defense attorney who was a lifelong friend and a man he fully trusted. When he told Raul that he hadn't killed Jennifer, he was sure that Raul believed him. And if Raul believed him, perhaps he could persuade others to believe him as well. Raul promised to do his best for Rob, and Rob knew he would— Raul was that kind of friend.

But when the district attorney informed the court that his office would seek the death penalty, the judge had insisted that another attorney take over Rob's defense. Raul, though he was a good attorney, was not experienced in defending homicide cases.

After some courtroom wrangling, the judge, the Honorable James F. Horton, announced that he was going to appoint someone certified to handle capital cases—homicides that carried the death penalty—to defend Rob. He'd called Rob and his attorney into court that morning to announce who the new counsel would be.

"I have appointed Dan Smathers of the firm Hacking, Kirkwood, and Smathers to handle your defense, Mr. Sterling. Mr. Smathers is well qualified, and I'm certain he will do the best he can for you," Judge Horton said.

"Thank you, Your Honor," Rob mumbled.

"Mr. Garcia, you may assist Mr. Smathers in the defendant's case," Judge Horton then told Rob's attorney, "but Dan must take the lead. This is a serious case, and the court is obligated to see that Mr. Sterling gets the best representation available to him."

"I'll leave it up to Rob," Raul said, glancing at his client. "We'll talk it over with Mr. Smathers."

The judge then called forward Dan, who was sitting in the galley. "Your experience speaks for itself," he told Dan after he had joined Rob and Raul at the table.

Dan nodded and then said, "Your Honor, if I might address the court."

"Go ahead," the judge said.

Dan considered for a moment how he might phrase his objections to the dilemma that had been thrust upon him. His romantic involvement with Jennifer Sterling, since she was the victim in this case, was certainly enough grounds to change the judge's mind about appointing him. On the other hand, it would be extremely perilous to his career to reveal his involvement with Jennifer; it would cause him all kinds of trouble with his partners in the firm. He knew that they all frowned upon partners having relationships with married women—it would hurt the firm's credibility in the community, which in turn meant less income for all of them.

Finally, he simply stammered, "I . . . I'm awfully busy with other cases. As I told you on the phone this morning, I'm not sure I have the time to devote to the case that it needs. I'd really rather you appoint someone else."

The judge frowned. "There are plenty of good attorneys in your firm that can carry some of your other cases. This is to be your first priority."

"But, Your Honor," Dan began again. "I really—"

The judge cut him off. "You are appointed, Mr. Smathers. Now get to work."

Dan nearly scowled. *I should never have threatened that stupid girl!* he chastised himself. Sexual harassment wasn't exactly something companies swept under the rug anymore. Rob was also angry, but at the judge almost as much as at Dan. It appeared that Dan wasn't overly enthusiastic about defending him, and Rob suspected that he knew why. This was the man he'd seen Jennifer flirting with, and if that became public knowledge, it could damage Dan's reputation and that of his firm. Even though he knew that Dan Smathers was a talented defense attorney, he would rather have had his fate in the hands of someone he liked and trusted. But Rob knew old Judge Horton. It would have been futile to ask him to reconsider, and the last thing Rob wanted to do was tarnish his deceased wife's reputation. He'd just have to take his chances. Though he would insist that Raul stay on the case, even if it took every dime he had to keep him there.

* * *

Salt Lake County had been well served for nearly six years by District Attorney William Montgomery. In his late fifties, silver-haired and silver-tongued, William had proven to be a relentless crime fighter. He'd recruited some top talent to aid him in prosecuting. Among the most aggressive was a young woman from New Jersey. At thirty-one, Haley Gordon had already distinguished herself with several high-profile cases she had fought and won against some of the best defense attorneys in the state. Most notably, she'd recently won a rape conviction against none other than Dan Smathers's wealthy client. It had clearly unnerved Dan to lose; it wasn't something he did very often.

It was that fairly recent case, as much as anything else, that led William to choose Haley to prosecute the highly publicized murder case against Rob Sterling. He invited her into his office and waited until she'd taken a seat to give her the assignment.

Haley smoothed her long, jet-black hair while waiting for William to speak. He eyed her appreciatively for a moment. She was a striking young woman. Clear brown skin, intelligent black eyes, and an elegant face accented her perfectly dressed, tall, lithe figure. But William knew that she was a lot more than just a beautiful woman. He was satisfied that she was the best attorney in the office to turn loose on Rob Sterling and Dan Smathers. She was a tough prosecutor—at times even more intense than seemed necessary—and she took no pity on any criminal who fell in her path. William badly wanted a conviction on this case, he reflected, and if anyone could get it, it would be Haley.

William knew that life had been tough for Haley, and that's what had shaped her current strengths in prosecuting criminals. She'd risen from poverty and oppression to become a successful attorney. She showed little sympathy to those who used their backgrounds as an excuse for their behavior. And because she had ascended from an environment from which failure was not uncommon, she had proven to William that she would work harder than ever to convict those who had been given every opportunity in life to succeed and yet still turned to crime. That would certainly include people like Rob Sterling, William speculated, since Rob came from a prominent family. They were wealthy, influential, and privileged. And though he would never let Haley know this, they had also contributed heavily to men he'd opposed in his political career. This victory would be personal on many levels.

"I have an assignment for you," William began, smiling at his rising star.

Haley waited expectantly. It was unusual to be called into the boss's office to be assigned a case. It must be a big one. She hoped it was, anyway.

"I'd like you to take on the Rob Sterling homicide prosecution," the district attorney said. He was not disappointed in the reaction he got from Haley.

"I'd love to!" she exclaimed. She'd never tried a high-profile murder case before.

William slid a thick file across his wide oak desk. "Here's the file. Get to know it well. You'll be up against Dan Smathers."

Haley's smile deepened. "I know Mr. Smathers," she said.

"Yes, you've beaten him before. But this is a much bigger case. And I want a conviction, Haley," William said. "We're going to be scrutinized on this one. A former Miss Utah is the victim. A cop, the son of wealth and privilege, is the defendant. The press is already making a big deal out of this case."

William watched Haley's face as he said that, and her frown was all he needed to see. She was going to go after rich, hypocritical Mr. Sterling. "Leave no stones unturned," he told her.

"I'll do my best," she said. "And I'll get familiar with the case today. Is the evidence good?"

"Mostly circumstantial," William answered, "but solid. Just a couple of things missing."

"Like what?" Haley asked.

"Weapon and motive," her boss said. "We need to know and prove why Rob Sterling did it. From everything we've heard, he loved her and was good to her. He had everything going for him. In addition to a beautiful young wife he had a good record as a cop and was near the top of his class at law school. His family had money. There's got to be a reason he killed his wife. And the weapon is somewhere. Find them."

"I'll get right on it," she promised.

"Oh, and he is an active member of your church." That was the one thing that bothered William about giving this case to Haley. He knew that she'd been converted to the LDS church shortly after coming to Utah. He hoped that wouldn't deter her. He personally despised the hypocrisy of men like Sterling, and in his mind, her church was full of them. Personally, he thought himself above religious superstition.

"He also has a temper," Haley said, thinking back to a case she'd prosecuted a couple of years ago when she was still fairly new in the office. Rob Sterling had been the arresting officer. She narrowed her eyes thoughtfully, trying to recall what it was that made her remember his temper.

William already had her answer. "He sometimes said things to defendants that made it possible for people like Dan Smathers to blow smoke to a jury. I think he did it in one of your cases," he said. "He does have a temper."

That was it. Rob had gotten angry at a drunk driver and made some verbal threats to him about what might happen if he didn't try to perform the field sobriety tests Rob had requested. The man had been mouthy, even vulgar, but the defense had nearly succeeded in convincing the jury that the defendant had only failed the tests because he was so frightened of the officer. After all, Rob Sterling was tall, strong, and imposing. Haley had been able to save the case, but barely. She'd shown that although he'd threatened, he had never been accused of using excessive force in his career. And that particular night, he'd not been any more threatening to the defendant than the man was toward Rob. Fortunately, she had evidence of that. Rob's camera had been running, and the whole incident had been caught on tape.

Afterward, Rob had apologized to her for making her work more difficult, and she'd come to respect him. But the apparent intensity of his temper had left an impression. "He never actually assaulted any suspects," she told her boss, knowing it would make her current assignment easier if he had.

"He has a good record as a cop. And lots of people have bad tempers—doesn't make them bad people," William Montgomery said with a smile as he rose and shoved the file the rest of the way across his imposing desk. "But Rob Sterling is a killer now. We need to find out why he became one. Sergeant Rex Thomas of the sheriff's department is your case officer. And if you need help from one of the other attorneys in the office, all you need to do is ask. But keep me informed. I want this guy, Haley. His kind makes a bad name for the rest of us."

As she left the office, Haley wondered why the district attorney was so intent on winning this case. Then she remembered the talk around the office. It was all timing. He was probably going to make a run for state attorney general. A clear conviction of a man from such a prominent and wealthy family could prove to his voters that he was beyond bribery and the wrong influence. This trial could be what it took to propel him to state attorney general. Well, he'd been good to her. She'd see what she could do to help.

* * *

Not everyone believed Rob was guilty of taking the life of his young wife. Rob's sister, a close friend of Jennifer's before Rob and Jennifer met, and an even closer one afterward, knew that her brother would never do such a thing. Tasha Andrews was closer to the couple than anyone else in the world. She simply couldn't accept what the press was saying about Rob.

Her eyes filled to nearly bursting as she watched her big brother struggle with his emotions. She faced him through glass at the county jail, and never had she seen a sadder sight than Rob. He'd been ostracized by their parents when he'd chosen to become a Mormon years ago, and that was on top of their disapproval of his becoming a cop for a while. Then when he'd permanently decided not to be part of the family business, they'd practically disowned him. And now to think that he was charged with killing the woman he'd loved and relied on to get him through the difficulty of losing his family just didn't seem possible.

Tasha missed Jennifer herself, but the depth of pain in his eyes revealed how much he'd been mourning for Jennifer, and he was troubled and distracted by every incident relating to her death. He rubbed his hand across his face. "It just doesn't make sense," he told Tasha. "Nobody could possibly have had a reason for doing that to her. It must have been a case of mistaken identity. You know, the wrong house or something."

Tasha agreed. "Somehow we've got to find out who the guilty person is," she said. "We've got to clear you and get you out of here so you can return to a normal life."

"Oh, that hardly matters right now. I don't care much about myself anymore," he said sadly. "What do I have to go back to? Jennifer is what mattered in my life, and she's gone."

"Snap out of it, Rob," Tasha said firmly. She couldn't just sit by and watch Rob give up. "You've got a lot to live for."

Rob shook his head. "Be practical, Tasha. My old department and all the others in the area are convinced I'm guilty. No one will even look for anyone else. I'm it, don't you see that?"

"Then we'll just have to hire someone else to help us," Tasha said stubbornly.

"With what?" Rob asked. "Everything I have will be going to my attorneys. I can't afford more help."

Tasha shook her head and said, "I'll talk to Dad. Surely he can't let his anger at you—"

"Please don't, Tasha," Rob said. "Anyway, he wouldn't help. You and I both know that. His name is on the line now, and that's all he's ever cared about."

"I guess," Tasha agreed. "But the press is certainly playing it up big, the fact that you are who you are."

"That's what the press does," Rob growled in frustration. "And that will only make Dad more determined to throw me to the wolves."

"Okay, I know you're right, but Jim and I'll help," she offered. "We've talked about this, Rob. We have some money saved. We'll help out."

"You can't do that, Tasha," he said. "This isn't your problem."

"You're my brother! I love you, and it is my problem," she retorted. "I'll talk to Raul Garcia. Maybe he'll know of a private investigator we can hire."

"You don't have to do this, Sis," Rob said.

"But I'm going to. We'll find the real killer, Rob. I promise." Tasha wished she felt even half as hopeful as she was trying to sound. But Rob needed positive support right now, and she was going to see that he got it. "And we'll keep praying for you."

* * *

Had Ralph Hacking known that his partner had been trying to win the affection of Jennifer Sterling, he would have personally talked to the judge and gotten Dan taken off the case; he would also have dealt firmly with Dan for such a serious indiscretion. Dan had always liked women. He'd even been married and divorced three times. But he was usually discreet. To Ralph's knowledge, Dan had never dated anyone from within the firm, but he had been seen in public with a married woman, and that had caused no small stir among some of their clients. However, Ralph was under the impression that Dan had learned his lesson; so Ralph had no idea that Dan might have a conflict in the Sterling defense, and he therefore simply refused to intervene when Dan asked him to help get him off the case.

"But I just don't feel good about this one," Dan said lamely.

"That isn't enough reason to turn down a defense case, if this were one where you even had a choice," Ralph said. "And it sounds like you don't."

"But if you'd talk to old Judge Horton, maybe he'd reconsider," Dan pleaded.

"Hey, he's my age," Ralph said with an attempt at humor. "Remember, he and I went to law school together."

But Dan was in no mood to be humored.

"Give me one good reason. Just one," Ralph said, "and I'll see what I can do for you."

"He killed a girl that worked for our firm," Dan said with sudden anger. "He should have to pay."

"Hey, what's this?" Ralph asked. "She didn't work for you personally. And I've never known you to be emotionally involved with any case."

"I know, but he's guilty, Ralph," Dan said with as much conviction as possible.

"They almost always are, but you've never let that stop you before," the senior partner said with raised eyebrows. There was a mildly uncomfortable pause, then, "One *good* reason," Ralph reminded him.

Dan slowly shook his head. He was stuck with the case. "Okay, I guess you win," he conceded bitterly. "But if I have to defend him, then I can't work with that fool Raul Garcia. I want him off the case." Dan couldn't work with a man who believed in Rob's innocence. Especially if the man was Rob's close friend.

Ralph shook his head. "That's your client's call. You know that, Dan. Anyway, I've heard Raul is really very smart. He's just not experienced in these kinds of cases. You'll have to make do. Now get to work, Dan. I'll see that your other cases are covered."

That was what worried Dan. Raul might be too smart. And that wouldn't do at all. Raul had to be removed from the case one way or another.

* * *

Tasha was frustrated. She'd tried for several hours before she finally caught up with Raul Garcia on the phone. They met in his rather humble office in West Valley City the next morning. The first thing she said to him was, "Rob is innocent. You do believe that, don't you?"

"Of course I do. Rob and I go back a long way," he said. "But the evidence is overwhelming." Raul thought about his best friend, trying to imagine how Rob had ever come to such an awful place.

Raul and Rob had been friends since high school. They'd played basketball on the same team, they'd gone to church together, they'd double dated, they'd camped and fished together. They'd been practically inseparable until their missions. And they'd done a lot of things together since then. Rob had been the best man at Raul's wedding. And when Rob finally got married, Raul had returned the favor.

So it was only natural that Rob turned to his best friend when he got in trouble. And Raul wanted to help him, but no one was more aware than Raul of his lack of experience in the type of criminal defense work Rob needed now.

Suddenly a thought struck Raul with such force that he jerked his head up and stared at Tasha. "Someone wants Rob convicted. He must have been framed." Tasha stared back. Though she couldn't imagine who would want to frame Rob for anything, it did seem like the only answer.

"So what do we do now?" she asked slowly. "We've got to prove his innocence."

Raul looked thoughtfully at the ceiling. "Ever watch Perry Mason?" he asked.

"Old reruns, yes," Tasha said impatiently. "What does that have to do with Rob?"

"The only sure way to save Rob, I'm afraid, is to find the person who actually shot Jennifer. That's what Perry Mason was famous for."

"Can we hire someone to help us?" Tasha asked. "You know, a private investigator."

"We can, but it won't be cheap," Raul warned.

"Whatever it takes, we've got to do it," Tasha said with determination. "Rob's my brother."

"I'll get on it," Raul said, rising to his feet. "He's also my friend."

CHAPTER TWO

Raul felt uneasy as he stepped from his car, dropped a quarter in the meter, and turned to the tall office building that housed the downtown offices of Hacking, Kirkwood, and Smathers. He knew that Dan Smathers was very good, but he also knew that Dan was arrogant and self-serving. Working with him was not going to be easy.

After meeting with Rob's sister, Raul had almost begun searching for a good private investigator but had thought better of it. The last thing he needed right now was to ignore his co-counsel and make the working relationship any worse than it already was.

A few minutes later, he was waiting in the reception area of a plush suite of law offices that made his look cheap, which, he admitted to himself with a wry grin, they were. After fifteen minutes, Raul asked the receptionist what the delay was. She smiled at him and said, "Dan is busy at the moment. He'll see you as soon as he can."

"Now would be helpful," Raul said impatiently. "He and I are supposed to be working the same case."

"The Sterling matter?" she asked. "Dan didn't say he had another firm involved."

"I was hired by the defendant," Raul said. "And I need to discuss this case with Dan. I'm also busy and have other work waiting."

"I'll check with him. I'm sure he'll want to see you as soon as he can free himself."

Raul was not sure of any such thing, but he wisely said nothing more except to thank the young lady before returning to his seat. He was afraid he might wear the seat out as he nervously fidgeted while he waited. Twenty minutes later the receptionist finally said, "Mr. Garcia, Mr. Smathers will see you now."

Raul Garcia felt like a client rather than co-counsel as he was ushered into Dan's office. "Have a seat, Raul," he was told brusquely.

After he was seated, Raul came quickly to the point. "I've had a conversation with Rob's sister today. We both feel like we need an investigator working for us. I have a fellow in mind, but I just wanted to let you know before I went ahead."

"What in the world do we need an investigator for?" Dan asked. "Waste of good money."

"Well, we thought—" Raul began.

But Dan broke in quickly. "Let's get one thing straight right now, Raul. I'm lead counsel here, and you'll do what I ask you to do, nothing more. And for right now, I have things well in hand. I'll let you know when I need some errands run."

"That's not quite how I see it," Raul said, rising to his feet. "I don't work for you, and I don't run errands."

"To the contrary, that's exactly how it will be," Dan said, coming to his feet as well and starting around his desk. "I'll be in touch if I need you."

Raul had been dismissed, but he wasn't ready to leave. "Just a minute!" he said angrily. "You and I need to go over a few things. Rob's life is in our hands, and we need to discuss exactly what our current position is and where we go from here."

"Our position is that I am looking for legal loopholes. I'm best suited to do that. There's not a lot more we can do."

Raul stared at Dan, shock and disgust written across his usually pleasant features. He collected himself and addressed Dan in an even, measured tone. "I disagree. I believe that Rob is innocent of this crime. His best defense is to find out who really killed his wife." There was a smirk of contempt on Dan's face. "And we can't do that looking for legal loopholes," Raul added hotly.

Dan stepped close, pointed a finger in Raul's face and said, "You might just as well face it now, Mr. Garcia. My client is guilty. We'll provide him the best defense we can despite that," Dan said angrily. "Now if you'll find your way out, I'll try to get some work done here."

"*My* client is innocent," Raul almost shouted. "What kind of counsel are you if you go on the presumption of guilt before you've even had time to examine the case?"

"I know what the evidence is," Dan countered. "The state has an excellent case, and I'm sure it'll get better. But I'll find some way to upset it for them. Now you are excused, and don't you do anything until I give you the word, or so help me, I'll see that the judge gets you removed from this case."

"I'm being paid by Rob Sterling," Raul said as he opened the door and stepped through. "And I'll give him the best assistance I'm capable of. And you'd better do the same."

Before Dan Smathers could say anything else, Raul slammed the door behind him and stormed out. By the time he'd reached the ground floor and was leaving the building, Raul had forced himself to calm down. What Dan Smathers was up to was a mystery. Despite his personality, he had a reputation for fighting for his clients. His weak reference to loopholes didn't sound like much to Raul. What it did sound like was that, for some unexplainable reason, Dan had no intention of providing a sound defense for Rob, nor did he intend to let Raul do so.

Well, Raul decided with determination, he'd see about that. A few hours later, a tough retired cop turned private investigator had a check from Raul in his pocket as a retainer for his services. He'd known Rob when they were both officers and agreed to see what he could do to help clear him.

"Be discreet," Raul said as the two shook hands at the door. "My co-counsel doesn't know I'm bringing you on board."

"And who is co-counsel?" crusty Sperry Collier asked.

"Dan Smathers," Raul said, watching closely for any reaction Sperry might give.

He needn't have watched closely. Sperry's face darkened and he said a word that wasn't in Raul's vocabulary, followed by, "Why in the world would you team up with that man? I wouldn't trust him for a minute."

Raul explained how Dan had come to be appointed and Sperry simply shook his head. "Be careful. He'll stab you right in the back if he can. And I will, as you say, be discreet."

* * *

The cars on the street below Haley's fourth-floor office moved smoothly as she stared down at them. But even though she was watching them, her mind was on Rob Sterling. She had just completed reading the full report of Detective Rex Thomas. As the district attorney had told her, the case was good, maybe even too good. And that was bothering her. Rob was not stupid. She'd already checked with the law school at the University of Utah and found that he was near the top of his class.

Why, she wondered, *would he not cover his tracks better?* As she thought about her question, a fire truck, siren wailing and lights flashing, came into view on the street below. Cars cleared to the side as it made its way eastward. One car, however, seemed oblivious to the truck until it drove right up behind the car and blared its horn. The car swerved to the side, narrowly missing a collision with a blue truck that had come to a complete stop.

The driver had panicked. Suddenly Haley had the answer to her question. Rob Sterling had killed and then panicked. That explained why he'd left evidence against himself. Relieved to have made a little progress on her puzzle, she returned to her desk and the photographs she had carefully laid out a few minutes before.

Most of them were of the crime scene, but she paid little attention to them. She was going with Sergeant Thomas and his partner, Detective Kurt Palmer, to Rob's house in an hour. She'd memorized the layout of the house and the area of the crime from the photos and diagrams in the file. But right now she was more interested in the faces that lay before her. Jennifer Sterling—young, pretty, intelligent—smiled up at her from several poses. Haley picked up one of the photos of Jennifer and studied it carefully. There was nothing in her face that suggested a motive that might lead Rob to take her life. Haley tapped her finger on her desk. Jennifer was very good-looking and several years younger than Rob. *Could that have caused a problem in their marriage?* she wondered. *Or did Jennifer perhaps flirt with younger men?* That too was possible, but neither scenario, if they were even true, provided much of a motive. Besides, Rob wasn't too old to be attractive to the young woman.

As Haley laid the picture of the smiling young woman down, she knew that in her own face, if she were to look at it now, she would see sadness, anger, and determination. Jennifer's killer would not go unpunished.

She next picked up two photographs of Rob Sterling. She held one in each hand as she studied his face. She was looking for deceit, hatred, cruelty—evil of any kind. But as hard as she tried, the face was as she'd known the man personally. She could see intelligence, honesty, goodness.

There was nothing there to indicate why Rob would commit such a terrible crime. She laid the photos down, pushed herself back from her desk, and rose to her feet.

She paced her small office for several minutes before sitting at her desk again. When she did, she gathered up the photos and returned them to the envelope that had held them and then placed them in the file. She did not look at his face again as she did so. That innocent-looking yet guilty face would have to stay there in the darkness of the envelope. She could have no sympathy for a man who would do what he'd done.

An hour later, Haley followed the two detectives into the well-kept and orderly yard of Rob and Jennifer Sterling's house. She was totally focused after the twenty-minute ride with the two detectives, during which time they recited what they had seen when they arrived at the home that night. They'd described a panicked call from Rob reporting that he had just found his wife dead in their living room, and he'd been visibly upset when they arrived.

Panicked, Haley reminded herself. The two veteran officers had confirmed her feelings.

"The power had been off, according to neighbors," Rex said as they approached the back door. "It was on again when we got here."

"Just this house or more?" Haley asked.

"The whole area had lost power. As you recall, a sudden fierce storm had hit the area. Time of death, according to the medical examiner, fit the time of the storm. We checked with the National Weather Service as well as neighbors," Kurt explained.

"But Rob claimed the lights were on when he got home?" she asked. Both officers confirmed that he had told them the house was lit up.

Haley reached the door. She stopped and examined it closely. "It was locked when Rob got here. At least that's what he told us. He said he'd come to this door, tried it, found it locked, and then went around front. He used the front-door key from the ring on his car keys to get in the front. He claimed he doesn't usually do that as the back is more convenient," Sergeant Thomas said over her right shoulder.

"You found the ring of keys for the back door on the kitchen counter," Haley said, recalling that fact from the report.

"That's right, but Rob told us he usually kept that small ring of keys in his car, in the pocket beside the driver's door. He kept the keys to the back door and his shed," Rex said as he pointed to a small metal shed in the corner of the backyard, "and a couple of other ones on that ring."

"You asked him if he'd used them to open the house when he came home, is that correct?" she asked as she reached for the door and opened it.

"That's right, and he said he hadn't because when he went to get them to let himself into the house, they weren't in the car. He claims he thought he might have left them in the door the last time he locked it, so he went to the back door first, hoping to find them. When they weren't there, he went around to the front door," Kurt explained.

"He told us that he didn't take any more time looking for them before going in the house because he was late, and he knew his wife would be worried," Rex added. "He says that the only thing he can figure is that he might have accidentally dropped them on the sidewalk. He claims that if he did, it would explain how the killer got in. He might have spotted them there on the ground and used them instead of forcing his way in."

Haley thought about the keys. "Rob's fingerprints were found on the key that fit this door?" she asked. She already knew that the slightly smudged prints of his right index finger and thumb were found on opposite sides of the key. What she really wanted was more information. She got it.

Detective Palmer said, "We found no other prints but his on any of the keys."

Haley was thinking ahead, thinking of the cross-examination Dan Smathers would give these two officers. What might he ask them then? She tried one question out. "Could the key have been inserted and turned in the lock without disturbing the prints you found? In other words, could someone else have used the keys and opened the door without disturbing Rob's prints?"

Sergeant Thomas pulled a set of keys from his own pocket. "The ring was about this size," he said, holding it up for her to see clearly. "It's very unlikely, but yes, if someone took his time, he might manage to work the key into the lock by holding onto the ring only and wedging his thumb in like this, causing the desired key to stand out straight as it were inserted. Then all a person would have to do would be to turn the key by using only the ring." Rex had demonstrated as he talked by putting his thumb into the key ring and forcing the nail of his thumb tightly against the back edge of the key. "Definitely unlikely, but possible," he concluded.

A small chink had just been broken loose from the evidence she had to work with, and Dan Smathers would find it. "What about prints on the ring itself?" she asked.

"Nothing," Sergeant Thomas answered.

"Okay, so Rob's only explanation for how they got from his car, where he usually keeps them, to the kitchen was that he might have dropped them in front of the back door. The theoretical killer might have found them, used them to open the door, and then dropped them on the counter after getting inside?" Haley asked.

"That's it," Rex agreed. "He says he knows he didn't leave them on the kitchen counter. We haven't asked him more since that night because his lawyer, Raul Garcia, told him not to answer any more questions. Of course, he'd have come to his senses pretty soon anyway. He was an excellent officer."

"And a traitor to the uniform," Kurt said with what sounded to Haley like hurt mixed with disgust in his voice.

The two men looked at each other. Then Rex said softly, but with an undertone of bitterness, "It hurts when a fellow officer does something like this."

Haley nodded. She understood how they felt. An officer gone bad would be a bitter betrayal. She stepped inside, giving her eyes a few moments to adjust to the darker lighting in the kitchen. She stood and studied the room intently for two or three minutes. The two detectives stood crowded in the doorway behind her, waiting.

Finally, she spoke. "This light switch . . . ?" She pointed to the one beside the door.

"Partial prints. We could identify both Rob's and Jennifer's. There were no others," Detective Palmer said.

"And the keys?"

"We found them right there." Kurt pointed to a spot near the edge of the counter to Haley's right.

They proceeded through the kitchen. The floor lamp was standing beside the doorway that separated the kitchen from the living room. "Exactly where was this lamp when you got here?" Haley asked.

The officers showed her where it had been lying and explained that it had few prints. Again, only those belonging to Jennifer and Rob Sterling were present.

"Do we have any idea how this lamp got knocked over?" she asked.

"Probably by Rob, although he says it was lying on the floor when he came in. There was some very hard wind that night, but the windows and doors were all closed when we got here, and they were closed when the defendant got here, according to his statement. So I think we can rule out the wind as the culprit," the sergeant explained. "Rob knocked it over himself, possibly after the shooting."

"And the flashlight. Where was it?" Haley asked.

She already knew that it had only Rob and Jennifer Sterling's prints on it, and that Rob said they kept it in a kitchen cupboard. "He claimed there would be no reason for him to have used it that night, because the lights were on when he got here," Kurt said.

It seemed strange to Haley that Rob would deny bringing the keys into the house or getting the flashlight from the cupboard. It seemed to her it would be in his best interest to say that he had used both items. But his denial would be good evidence, hard for the defense team to get around since they were both found in the house, in places he claimed they shouldn't be. She really wondered what would happen if and when Rob got on the stand and she had a chance to question him about that. She found herself looking forward to it.

For the next hour, Haley personally examined the physical evidence still remaining in the living room—the chalked outline showing the position of Jennifer's body, blood spatters that indicated that the fatal bullet was fired from an area near the edge of the couch, and the way a large chair had been disturbed slightly when Jennifer fell.

When Haley had gone over it all, she analyzed what she had learned. The pistol, a 9mm, had been fired from about the level of the arm of the sofa. The assailant was either sitting and holding the pistol in or near his lap, or else he had been kneeling on the floor and shooting across the arm of the sofa. Both scenarios seemed strange. Then an alarming thought occurred to her. She voiced it aloud. "The shooter could have been carrying the gun, stumbled . . ." Haley looked around. "Say over the lamp, and fallen against the couch, causing the gun to discharge accidentally."

But Rex Thomas argued with that theory. "We already know that Rob had to have knocked the lamp over," Sergeant Thomas reminded her. "It seems unlikely that he would then have tripped over it too. Or, he might have knocked it over after the shooting. And remember, he did have the flashlight, despite what he says."

"But why sit down on the couch or kneel beside it?" Haley asked.

"Our guess is that he was sitting on the sofa and that she was sitting in the chair. They argued, she got up, he pulled the gun and shot her."

"That's possible," she said. But in her mind, she was left with another troubling question that didn't have a satisfactory answer. Haley didn't like the doubts that were beginning to clutter her mind. There weren't any of them that were very serious when considered alone, but added together, it could give a sharp defense attorney something to help cast reasonable doubt into the minds of jurors. She had to be very thorough.

"Rob was still a reserve officer. So he must have a pistol," she said.

"Yes, but it's not a 9mm," Kurt said. "However, we've learned from men he used to work with that he once carried a 9mm off-duty weapon—his own."

"And where is it?" she asked.

"We don't know. He claims to have sold it when he enrolled in law school. However, the fellow he says bought it from him has left the state, and we can't locate him," Rex said.

"Very convenient," Haley observed. "So he might have thrown it away before you got here?"

"Anything's possible, but that's most likely what happened," Kurt agreed.

"Was the area around and on the sofa vacuumed by the lab people?" she asked.

"It was, and they found fibers that matched clothing of both the defendant and his wife," Sergeant Thomas said. "There are other fibers they couldn't identify, but that's to be expected. Many people have probably been in the house and in that area of the room. We'd have to have another suspect and something of his or hers to compare it to."

"Meaning the defense would have to name someone else and demand that a comparison be made," Detective Palmer added. "That isn't likely to happen."

"You never know," Haley said. "Dan Smathers will be trying to come up with someone besides his client. That's his job, you know. And our job is to be as thorough as we can."

* * *

That was exactly what Dan Smathers was thinking about the work he was doing. He couldn't be too thorough. And he was indeed trying to cover all his bases. He smiled to himself. He really was an intelligent man, and he'd see to it that no one outwitted him.

CHAPTER THREE

Haley was surprised the next morning when she got a call from Dan Smathers's secretary. "He'd like to meet you in his office at ten this morning," she said.

"I'll be there," Haley responded as she looked at her watch. It was now almost nine. She didn't have much time.

Ten minutes later, she got another call. This one really surprised her. "Counselor, this is Detective Sperry Collier. I'm a private investigator. I need to speak with you in confidence as soon as possible."

"About what?" she asked.

"I'd sooner not say right now," he answered. "But it's very important."

"Who are you working for?" she asked.

"Miss Gordon, really, you don't think I'd tell you that do you?" She could feel his smile over the phone. "Please, would eleven be all right?"

"I have a ten o'clock appointment," she said. "Would noon work? You could buy me lunch," she suggested, intrigued by his call. *Could Dan Smathers have hired him?* Haley wondered. *He must have. Maybe I'll ask him.*

"Who's your appointment with?" the detective suddenly asked.

"Another attorney," she said evasively. "I'd really rather not say who." She smiled to herself. "You see, two can play this game."

"Dan Smathers?" he asked, though the levity in his tone was gone now, and only a gruff voice replaced it, one filled with what sounded like contempt.

"Detective Collier," Haley said very seriously, "what business is it of yours who I'm meeting with?"

"None, possibly, but please, if you do see Smathers, don't tell him I contacted you."

It sounded like he was begging. How very strange. And how intriguing. Perhaps this man could help her with her case. Maybe she wouldn't say anything to Dan about this call. "I'll keep our little date secret," she promised. "Meet me at my office at noon. We can walk to lunch from here."

"Thanks," the private eye said and the phone disconnected.

This was a morning for surprises. Dan Smathers was very cordial as he invited her into his office. She hadn't even had to wait. That was not his usual style. Then the big surprise came when he went directly to what he had summoned her for.

"I'd like to propose a settlement to the Rob Sterling matter," he said.

Haley was shocked. So early in the process and the offer of a deal? Rob must have decided there was no point in going on denying his guilt. Furthermore, if a skilled attorney like Dan Smathers was trying to deal away a case this quickly, even he must know he couldn't possibly win, in which case, it might be best to move ahead with the trial. But she should at least listen, so she said calmly, "What exactly do you have in mind?"

"Don't get me wrong, this case will be an easy win for the defense. There are some huge holes and some technical errors in the state's case," he said.

"I don't think so," Haley countered. "But tell me what you have in mind."

"You really don't want to go up against me in court on this one," Dan said, his ego simply too large to allow him to back down. "But I have to think of my client and his wishes. We'll take a manslaughter. Rob will plead straight up to it and save everybody time."

"Manslaughter!" Haley responded with a snort. "Not a chance. You know we have a solid case. Good try, but you'll have to do a lot better than that."

"Okay," Dan said with a sly grin. "We'll accept second-degree murder. That keeps Rob alive. He's ready to accept that. And anyway, you can't prove it was premeditated."

Suddenly Haley felt trapped. Dan might well be right. "I'll have to run this by the district attorney himself," she said. "But if that's what your client wants, it is within the realm of possibility."

Haley hated even saying that; she relished the chance of going before a jury against Dan Smathers again. She'd love to beat him on a case that had received so much publicity, but she knew that she also had a duty to the people, and she had to consider this offer carefully. "No possibility of parole?" she asked, feeling that she would more likely convince William Montgomery if she could guarantee that Rob would never see freedom again.

Dan creased his brow thoughtfully, even closed his dark blue eyes for a moment. Finally, his eyes still closed, he spoke slowly. "I'll have to get back to my client on that, but I'm quite certain he'll accept it."

"I'll be in touch soon," Haley said.

* * *

Jail was having its effect on Rob. He was already beginning to look pale. His bright green eyes were faded, and his light brown hair, normally combed meticulously, was ruffled and unkempt. *He's giving up hope,* Tasha thought as she sat down and watched him through the glass of the visiting room. "Rob, are you doing okay?" she asked tenderly. Her heart was so full of anguish for the big brother who had always watched out for her that she thought it might burst. No one could watch out for him here.

"I'm all right," he told her. "This isn't exactly a fun place to be. I've sent lots of people to this place over the years, and guys in here know it. I'm not the most popular inmate in the jail."

For some reason, the thought of Rob having enemies inside the jail had never occurred to her, and she was suddenly more frightened for him than ever. "Rob, we've got to do something," she said desperately.

"Like what?" Rob said with a hopeless shrug. "I have the best counsel available, or at least that's what I'm supposed to believe," he finished with a touch of sarcasm. "And the officers in here are watching out for me the best they can. It doesn't matter anyway. I've lost everything worth living for."

Tasha began to cry at the sight of tears forming in her big brother's eyes. She wiped hers away and tried to be brave for him. "Raul hired Sperry Collier. He's an investigator. He says he'll do everything he can for you," she told Rob.

"I remember Sperry. Good man. He was a good cop too," Rob said. "But I can't afford him, I told you that before."

"We'll help. We've got to find who did this to Jennifer. And we will," she assured him.

Rob didn't know what to say. It was such a sacrifice for Tasha and Jim. "Thanks," he said, choking on his emotions. "I'll pay you back if I ever get out of here," he finally conceded when he had control again. Then he asked, "How did you get Dan Smathers to agree to this?"

"He didn't. Raul and I decided on our own," Tasha informed him.

Rob was suddenly suspicious. "Did Raul even consult Dan?" he asked. "He needs to work with him, not against him."

Tasha sighed. "That's exactly how Raul felt."

"Felt?" Rob asked. "Did the two of them have a disagreement?"

"I take it Dan hasn't said anything to you about what he told Raul," Tasha said.

"I haven't seen or talked to Dan since we left the courtroom the day he was appointed."

"You've got to be kidding. How can he plan a defense for you if he isn't even consulting you?" Tasha was alarmed. She didn't like or trust Dan Smathers, especially since Raul told her that Dan had admitted that he believed Rob was guilty.

"I've wondered the same thing," Rob said, but then he shrugged his shoulders and slumped forward slightly in his chair. That alone was a bad sign of the deteriorating state of Rob's spirits. He usually kept his six-foot-five frame erect, even when he was sitting in a chair. "It doesn't matter anyway. We'll just have to trust that he knows what he's doing."

Maybe you will, big brother, Tasha thought to herself, *but I won't rest until I see you out of here. And Dan Smathers isn't going to be a part of it.*

* * *

Raul Garcia stood politely as Haley entered the waiting area near her office. She was a beautiful woman, her clear brown skin glowing and her long black hair falling about her shoulders in natural waves. At five feet and ten inches they were the same height, but with heels on, Haley made him feel slightly shorter. Raul laughed at his budding insecurity. He was used to being *shorter*. Rob towered several inches above him—especially when they played ball.

"Raul," Haley said pleasantly, breaking him out of his reverie. "It's good to see you again. Are you and your family enjoying the new home?"

Raul had lived in Haley's ward when she was baptized, and he had been her home teacher for a few months. They had developed a firm mutual respect for one another. But then he'd moved to a new house, out of both her ward and her stake, and they had lost contact.

"We love it," he said. "There's more room for the kids to play. I even have a computer room."

"Well, it's certainly good to see you again. Tell your wife I said hello," Haley said with a warm smile.

"I'll do that," Raul promised.

"Thanks. Now, what can I do for you, Raul?"

"I believe you're having lunch with Sperry Collier. I thought it wouldn't hurt if I joined the two of you. Do you mind?"

"Actually, I'm sorry, Raul, but I'm afraid I do," she said bluntly. "I don't even know what Sperry wants, and I'm not sure he'd want you there." She paused for a moment, watching Raul's face with dawning realization. "Unless, of course, you know what it's about and if he doesn't mind."

"I talked to him and he welcomed it."

"What about Dan Smathers? Why isn't he here?" she asked. "This is about Rob Sterling, is it not?"

Raul simply nodded. "Sperry will be along anytime. I'll just sit here and wait."

"You'll do nothing of the sort," Haley said with a smile. "Come into my office. There's something I should discuss with you before your private investigator comes."

Haley watched Raul for any sign of denial that Sperry was *his* investigator. She decided it was quite clear that the one was employed by the other, and she signaled for Raul to follow her.

In her office a few moments later, she invited Raul to sit. He hadn't yet done so when his cell phone rang. He pulled it from his jacket pocket and glanced at it. Then, embarrassed, he said, "Do you mind if I answer this? I'll step back into the hallway."

"Quite all right," Haley agreed. "Just come back in as soon as you've finished the call."

"Raul," Tasha said over the phone as soon as he was alone. "I'm worried about Rob."

"So am I, but is this something new?" he asked as he detected fear in her voice.

"I just came from the jail. He's really despondent. He didn't even attempt to comb his hair before he came into the visiting room."

That was strange for Rob. He was an incredibly meticulous person, and he was especially self-conscious about managing his naturally unruly hair. But Raul let Tasha continue, sensing there was more to come.

"I think he might be in danger."

"From whom?" Raul asked.

"Other inmates," she said.

"Yes, I suppose that's a possibility, but I'm sure they're keeping a close eye on Rob. I think he'll be fine," Raul reassured her, wishing he actually believed that himself.

"I don't know, Raul. And I'm so angry! Rob hasn't even heard from Dan Smathers since he was appointed to help you," she vented.

"Actually, he's made it very clear that *I'm* to assist *him*," Raul said dryly.

"You've got to do something," she insisted.

"I am. I'm about to meet with a very important person, and we'll talk about this. Also, I'll go see Rob myself as soon as I'm through with the meeting," he assured her. "Now be calm and I'll get back with you."

Haley Gordon smiled as Raul entered her office again. She pointed to a chair and he took it. "I hope that wasn't an emergency," she said, referring to the phone call.

"Oh, that. No, just someone as concerned as I am over Rob Sterling's plight. That's what Sperry and I want to talk to you about," he revealed.

"That's odd," she said. "I didn't realize you were acquainted with Rob."

"We're more than acquainted, Haley," he said, his face very serious. "He and I have been best friends all of our lives. I'm the one who got Rob interested in the Church when we were just teenagers. My dad baptized him. We played ball together and well, we practically lived at one another's homes. Actually, we spent more time at mine than his. His folks didn't approve of me because my family didn't have a lot of money and because they felt like I'd taken Rob from them by introducing him to the Church. I think they even blame me for his decision not to be part of their business empire. He didn't care so much about the money as he did living the kind of life he wanted. And maybe it was because of his association with me that he felt that way. My family didn't have much, but we were always happy. You couldn't say that for Rob's family."

"What about Tasha?" Haley asked. "Is she still close to the family?"

"Not really, but for different reasons. She's never joined the Church, but she's a really decent and honest woman. As far as her folks are concerned, though, she's a fool for marrying a man they didn't think was good enough, so they more or less cut her off financially," Raul explained. "But at least they still talk to her. They act like they don't even know Rob's alive."

"That's terrible," Haley said sadly.

"It is." Raul paused. "But anyway, Rob and I have always been close. We were even best man at each other's weddings. I was the one who planted the seeds in Rob's mind about becoming a lawyer."

"I had no idea," she said, but it explained why a good, honest man like Raul would be willing to work in defense of someone accused of such a cold and calculated crime. "Do you want to tell me what it is you need to talk about?" she asked.

"No, we'll wait until Sperry joins us." Raul forced a smile he didn't have his heart in. "He tells me he's buying lunch. Which means I'm buying."

"So he *is* working for you." Haley let her suspicions be known.

"He is, but I would really appreciate if you wouldn't let Dan Smathers know."

"You're hiring help behind his back?" Haley asked. She was a little alarmed for Raul, but she had to admit she wasn't surprised knowing what kind of a man Smathers was. After all, Raul and Dan were as different in their approach to the law as they were people.

"That's just the problem. He basically won't let me do anything, and I was retained by Rob personally," Raul complained. "But even worse, Dan's not doing anything, and I can't sit back and let Rob suffer because of an attorney who doesn't care about him as a person."

Haley pointed an accusing finger at Raul. "Now that's not true. Surely you're aware of the offer Dan has extended to me on Rob's behalf."

"Offer?" Raul asked, clearly puzzled. Haley suddenly had a sinking feeling in the pit of her stomach.

"Yes, offer. I just came from Dan's office. Rob asked Dan to talk to me and tell me that he would be willing to plead guilty to second-degree murder," she said.

That news catapulted Raul out of his chair. "He did no such thing!" Raul shouted angrily. "Rob would have told me."

"Calm down, Raul," Haley said, forcing herself to remain seated in the face of Raul's uncommonly explosive reaction.

"How can I calm down? My co-counsel is lying, feeding my best friend to the wolves, and you expect me to calm down?"

"Sit down, Raul, please," she said firmly.

Just then the intercom came alive. "Miss Gordon, a Mr. Sperry Collier is here to see you. He says he has a lunch appointment."

Haley glanced at Raul, who was finally approaching his chair again. Raul nodded, and she said, "Have him come in, please."

Sperry entered and saw Raul, who was still standing, his dark face purple with rage. "Mr. Garcia," he said. "I see you beat me here." And then without waiting for a reply from Raul, he extended a large, calloused hand across Haley's desk. "I'm Sperry Collier," he said. "It looks like Raul got here ahead of me, and I judge that you two aren't getting along marvelously."

"We're fine, Mr. Collier. Raul and I are old friends. Please sit down and I'll explain what has Raul so upset," Haley said as she looked Sperry over with an appraising eye. He was at least sixty, stocky, but in good shape for a man of that age. His pale green eyes were piercing and serious. He didn't look like a man who did a lot of kidding around. But she had a feeling he was good at what he did. And if Raul trusted him, he must be honest.

Sperry sat where she signaled, and Raul did the same. Then Haley addressed the investigator. "I just delivered a bit of news to Raul and he doesn't seem pleased with it."

Raul spoke right up. "Dan has offered to plead Rob to second-degree murder. Says it's what Rob wants. But Rob's sister just came from the jail, and she told me on the phone that Rob hasn't seen or spoken to Smathers since he was appointed."

The pain in Haley's stomach got worse. Dan had lied to her. His client knew nothing of the offer. Or else these men were lying, and she knew Raul well enough to know that he wouldn't lie even if it was in his best interest to do so. Or maybe Rob himself had lied to his sister, but Raul didn't seem to think that was the case. So she had to wonder what Dan Smathers was up to.

"Are you both ready for lunch?" Sperry asked gamely. "There's more you need to know, Miss Gordon."

Haley wasn't at all sure she wanted to know more. But she knew she had to listen. So she rose to her feet. "I'll eat, but I'll buy my own lunch," she announced. "Let's go."

Not another word was spoken about Rob Sterling's case until their lunch was on the table. Small talk had taken up most of the time. All three participants had become nervous and guarded, most notably Haley. It had occurred to her these past few minutes that the case she'd been given to prosecute could well be one of the most important cases she would ever handle. She could possibly have the life of an innocent man in her hands, and she would have to be on guard constantly so she wouldn't make any mistakes. Rob Sterling was not only from an important family, but his best friend, a man she personally held in high regard, clearly believed he was innocent. Her whole future, as well as Rob's, could well hang in the balance of how she handled this case.

It was Detective Sperry Collier that finally brought the conversation back to the case that consumed all three of their thoughts. "There is something that I learned last night that has me very concerned," he said. "I know it's highly irregular to go to the prosecutor with this information, but I don't see how you can do your job if you don't know what I've learned."

"As long as you don't breach client confidentiality," Haley said since she couldn't think of any other response.

Raul spoke up. "Our client doesn't know this, I don't think. Then again," he began, looking with sudden alarm at Sperry, "if he does . . ."

Sperry was a shrewd man, and he grasped the same insight that had just occurred to Raul. They had both been concerned only with what to do about an attorney who they believed was being deceptive and jeopardizing Rob's life. They had come to Haley hoping she would help them convince Judge Horton that Dan Smathers simply couldn't be allowed to continue on this case. But both suddenly knew that if they revealed what Sperry had learned, they might be handing the shrewd young prosecutor something that was missing in the state's case: motive. And that they simply couldn't do.

Haley, for her part, couldn't fail to see the troubled looks that passed between the two men. And her own concern was heightened. They clearly believed in the innocence of their client. Knowing they were both honest men, she found her own doubts growing.

Raul and Sperry both fumbled for words. It was Raul that finally said, "I think we've wasted your time, Miss Gordon. I'm sorry."

"I'm sorry too," she said. "Are you sure you can't tell me what it is that's bothering the two of you?"

"I'm afraid we can't," Sperry said.

"What we wanted," Raul added, "was your help in getting Dan Smathers off this case. But we both just realized that what Sperry learned we really can't share with you. But I will say this much, Haley, we don't trust Dan Smathers, and that makes it hard to have to work with him. We better just enjoy lunch. I'll pay for yours after causing you so much trouble."

Conversation during the meal's remainder was sporadic and had nothing to do with the case. Each was somewhat preoccupied with troubled thoughts. And each had doubts growing in their minds. Different kinds of doubts, but pertinent ones. Haley was wondering more and more about Rob Sterling and the case against him. She needed more evidence, and hoped Rex and Kurt were busy finding it. Raul was concerned about what Dan Smathers, whatever his motives might be, would do to further jeopardize the case and send Rob to prison, or worse still, to his death. Sperry was worried about the information he'd learned. He needed to be absolutely sure it was true. He'd thought it was, but now he couldn't help but wonder.

CHAPTER FOUR

One of the most plush and noticeable offices in Salt Lake City was not the ideal setting for meeting with certain clients. Dan had such a meeting that afternoon, and the man he was to have a serious discussion with had been instructed never to set foot in or even near the offices of Hacking, Kirkwood, and Smathers.

However, as the man was not the client this time—in fact the roles had been reversed—avoiding the office would not be a problem. The man Dan Smathers would be conversing with did not have a conventional office. Though every meeting place was private, obscure, and continually changing, the man was paid well for the work he did. Dan was now one of his clients, but he'd once been a client of Dan's, and through Dan's considerable courtroom savvy and questionable out-of-courtroom tactics, Dan had cleared him of a heinous crime of which he was guilty. The two were now allies. And if either ever betrayed the other, the civility of the courtroom would not settle their dispute. Each man had a healthy respect for the other's ruthlessness, fear of the other's callousness, and secrets about one another that served as effective two-way blackmail. They also harbored a distinct dislike of each other. Neither had a desire to associate in any way outside of the clandestine activities that brought them together from time to time.

This afternoon was one of those times. A significant amount of money passed from Dan to his contact, and explicit orders were given—orders that could not be revoked once Dan gave the man the signal to proceed. Everything hinged on the district attorney's answer to his proposed deal to end the Rob Sterling case.

* * *

Two more meetings were to take place that afternoon. Haley
Gordon was to be present at both of them. The first would begin in
just a few minutes in the spacious and elegant office of the district
attorney. Regardless of the outcome of that meeting, the second
would take place in her own office. She'd invited Detective Sergeant
Rex Thomas and Detective Kurt Palmer to come up at three that
afternoon. All she told them was that there was a specific line of
investigation she wanted them to follow up on.

For the past twenty minutes Haley had done nothing but sit at
her desk and think. She was barely into this case and already it was
troubling her more than any case she'd ever dealt with, and the
strange thing was that she honestly wasn't sure why. After a great deal
of thought, she finally concluded that it was a lot of little things that
bugged her. Foremost on her mind was a strong curiosity about what
it was that Sperry Collier had discovered—why it had seemed so
important to him and Raul that they felt they needed to bring it to
her attention, only to suddenly decide they couldn't do it.

That was what she had the two detectives coming to meet with
her about. She'd drop that little mystery in their laps and see what
they could dig up. And the strange, possibly even unethical, behavior
of Dan Smathers was eating at her. Now, just moments before she was
to meet with her boss, she was torn over whether to tell him what she
knew of Dan's questionable behavior or simply pose the question of
Dan's offer and leave it at that.

She hadn't come to a decision on that question when she walked
into William's office and sat opposite him, his large desk separating
them. "How is the case against Rob Sterling coming?" he asked after
only the smallest amount of chitchat.

"That's what I'm here to discuss," she told him.

"Ah, I thought that might be the case. How can I help you?" he
asked as he sat back and folded his arms across his chest. His eyes
never left Haley's face, and she felt herself squirming.

"I had a meeting with Dan Smathers this morning," she began.

"And he pumped you for information?" William speculated.

"Actually, no. He simply told me he had a deal worked out that his client was in favor of. He wants us to consider it."

"A deal already?" William asked, unfolding his arms and leaning forward. "I don't think we're interested in deals. But tell me about it anyway."

"He said Rob would plead guilty to second-degree murder," Haley said.

The slightest flicker crossed the district attorney's face, and Haley couldn't fail to see a look in his eyes that told her he was not pleased. But he said nothing, so she went on. "I told him I would only discuss it with you if it included a provision for no possibility of parole. He agreed and said he was quite certain his client would go along with that."

William sat in the same position for a full minute or more, his eyes boring into his young prosecutor's face. Finally he spoke. "I suspect that you've heard that I'm considering a run for the state attorney general's office."

She nodded that she had.

"I intend to win," he said. "And when I do, I want you there with me. But first you've got to get the death penalty for Rob Sterling. We've got to make a statement. There will be no deals, Haley, and you can tell Mr. Smathers that."

He sat back and crossed his arms again. Haley felt more uncomfortable by the minute. She'd love to be an assistant attorney general. But she also had to resolve the doubts that had been creeping into her mind about Rob Sterling. She almost mentioned the weaknesses she'd discovered in the case, but once again Mr. Montgomery's eyes stared hard into hers, his message clear, and she changed her mind. "Whatever it takes to win, you do it," he said. "Don't let that snake Smathers gain one foot of ground on you. Now get back to work."

He didn't say it curtly, but his message to Haley was clear. Victory in this case was crucial to his upcoming campaign; it was crucial to her future as a prosecutor.

Haley's next meeting was not nearly as tense. Haley explained what had happened earlier and the importance of not letting anyone know about the fact that their former colleague, Sperry Collier, was working for the defense. Then she said, "I want you to find out what

Detective Collier found out. It will almost certainly have something to do with Dan Smathers, and it could well help our case. Be discreet, but thorough."

"How do we go about it?" Sergeant Thomas asked.

"I don't know, Sergeant. I'm a lawyer. You two are the investigators." She smiled as she spoke. "However, if I were to hazard any guesses as to how you might begin, I'd guess that it would be helpful to find out who Collier's been talking to. But you'll know best."

They took her teasing and her confidence in them in stride. "We'll see what we can find out," she was told.

After they'd left, she picked up the phone and called Dan's office again. He'd been out when she'd returned from meeting with the district attorney, but that had changed now. "He just walked in," she was informed.

Dan only kept her waiting for a minute or two. When he came on the line, he seemed in a good mood. "Have you made a decision, Counselor?" he asked.

"I met with Mr. Montgomery a few minutes ago. He said there would be no deals. So I guess you and I have our work cut out."

The good mood vanished from the phone line. "You can't win, Miss Gordon. I'm sorry for such a foolish decision," he said. Before she could offer any further comment, he hung up.

And he made another call.

* * *

Rob watched his lifelong friend through the glass. He felt terrible that Raul Garcia had to be enmeshed in such an ugly case. He trusted him like he trusted no one else, but he'd never wish the stress Raul was facing on anyone. Raul was like the brother he'd never had. Estranged from his parents, and with Jennifer now gone, there were only two people left in the world that he was really close to—Tasha and Raul. And his situation had brought both of them unspeakable pain. He wished he could relieve them of it.

"I pray for you," he told Raul. "I don't know what else to do." He was too emotionally worn out even to be angry anymore.

"You need to be praying for yourself," Raul said. "I'm fine."

"This isn't fair to you," Rob persisted. "Raul, you know that I love you like a brother."

"The same's true here, but we could never fool anybody. A short Hispanic and a tall Caucasian," he said with an attempt at humor.

The joke fell flat when Rob didn't even crack a smile. Rob was not in the mood to be humorous right now. "Raul, I mean it. I'm causing you a lot of trouble. You don't have to help me anymore. Dan Smathers is as sharp as they come. Let's leave it up to him."

"I thought we'd decided that I was to stay on," Raul said, a hurt look in his dark brown eyes.

"We had, but it isn't fair to you," Rob said.

"That may be true, but what's happened to you isn't fair either," Raul reminded him. "We are like brothers. You said it yourself. And the Savior said that we must be our brother's keeper. I couldn't sleep at night if I wasn't doing everything I could to help you, *brother*. So that's how it's going to be."

Rob rubbed his eyes. There wasn't a better man in the world than Raul. He'd tried to free Raul of the pain of what Rob had to admit could be a losing cause, but he was immensely grateful that Raul refused to leave him on his own. "Thank you," he said softly.

"You're welcome," Raul responded. "Now, let me tell you what's been happening, and you'll see why I couldn't leave you alone in the hands of Dan Smathers even if I wanted to."

"I haven't talked to him at all," Rob said. "I assume he's been doing something."

"You assume correctly," Raul agreed. "I spoke with Haley Gordon earlier today. She's the young woman who's been assigned to prosecute you."

"I hear she's become really good," Rob said. "I worked with her once. She saved my case for me then. You know how I used to struggle with keeping my temper. She's good, and I never even dreamed she'd be my worst enemy one day."

"I don't believe she is, Rob. How much do you know about her?"

"Practically nothing. She's intelligent, beautiful, and ambitious. And it seems like I remember hearing that she'd joined the Church, but I could be mistaken about that."

"You're not mistaken at all. She is LDS now. I was her home teacher from the time she joined the Church until my family and I moved into our new home," Raul said.

"You never told me that," Rob said. "You must know her pretty well then."

"I do. And she's something of a miracle. She comes from an impoverished background," Raul said.

"Really? That's really something considering where she is now. How much of a miracle?"

"More than you can imagine," Raul went on. "Her father was white and a criminal, and Haley told me that he was a serious alcoholic besides being a petty thief. He was in his twenties when he married her mother who was a sixteen-year-old African American girl. The marriage only lasted three or four years, then her father split. Her mother raised her the best she could until she was about eight. Then her mother got really ill."

"What happened to her then?" Rob asked.

"Her father showed up and for a couple of years she was shuffled back and forth between the two of them. Then her mother died and she was raised by her father and an assortment of women until she couldn't take it anymore and ran away at sixteen. Haley's been on her own from then on."

"Seems unlikely that she'd ever even finish high school," Rob observed, "let alone become a lawyer. How did all that happen?"

"She somehow managed to put herself through the last two years of high school. She must have done well, because she was recruited by a big university, got scholarships, worked jobs, and so forth. Then she went on to law school. The fact that she did all that is evidence of her intelligence and drive," Raul said. "Although she plays it all down. She says it was luck."

"Sounds like she's something else," Rob said. "I had no idea she'd had such challenges."

"Yeah, but she came through it. It's made her ambitious, and she's relentless in the courtroom, but she's also honest and just . . . plain good," Raul concluded.

"And I'm afraid she's the enemy," Rob said.

"I guess, in a way, that's true. She is your prosecutor. But let me tell you about what she and I talked about today," Raul said. Rob nodded, and Raul went on. "She met with Dan Smathers, at his place and at his invitation."

Rob's eyebrows rose, and his green eyes narrowed. He rubbed a hand absently through his hair, but he said nothing.

Raul said, "He offered to plead you guilty to second-degree murder with no possibility of parole."

Rob's face fell. He stammered for a moment. "He did what?" he finally managed to say.

"Exactly what I just told you."

"But he hasn't said a word to me. I thought those kinds of things had to be approved by a defendant," Rob said. His despondency was lifting and his anger was coming slowly to the surface.

Raul was glad to see it. Rob had to be willing to fight for himself. "Dan told Miss Gordon that he had your approval. She was going to talk to the district attorney this afternoon and see if he would agree to the terms Dan spelled out for her."

Both of Rob's fists came down hard on the counter in front of him. "Never!" he exclaimed. "I would never agree to that. I'm innocent, Raul! I would never have hurt Jennifer for any reason. I loved her. You know that, Raul. She wouldn't want me to lie either." He paused, rubbing his mussed hair some more. Then he said, "If they want to execute me, let them do it, but I will never admit to something I didn't do, nor will I ever agree to life in prison. I'd much rather be dead." Raul looked at Rob in surprise and concern. He looked at Raul then as the anger slowly drained away. "I didn't really mean that. But life in prison . . . You won't let them do that to me, will you?"

"They can't make a deal without your consent," Raul said. "Besides, I'm glad to see a fighting spirit in you. Don't worry, you would have to stand before the judge and say that you're guilty. As long as you refuse to do that, no amount of dealing between attorneys can make you plead otherwise."

"Good. Because I'll never do it. Jennifer would never forgive me."

"I'm glad to see that you and I agree," Raul said.

"But what about the district attorney? He can't make me do it, and why would he even try?"

"Have you heard about his ambitions?" Raul asked in frustration. When Rob simply gave him an inquiring look, Raul finished in disgust, "Word around the Bar is that he intends to run for attorney general. I may be wrong, but I get the feeling that your case is important to him, Rob. A victory in a high-profile case like yours would go a long way with the voters."

"Why is it so high profile?" Rob asked. "I'm not anybody."

"Actually you are. You married one of the most beautiful women in the state, a former Miss Utah, you know. But the papers have made a big deal about your parents. They are some of the most prominent people in the state. And they're politically active."

"And they have nothing to do with me, Raul. You know that."

"The press isn't interested in that. They have painted you as a both a cop—a protector of the community—and a rich man who married a beautiful, younger woman and then wasn't apparently satisfied with the marriage," Raul explained. "Add to that the fact that you're an active Mormon, and it really gets people's attention. A lot of people take pleasure in seeing hypocrites and liars brought down. You're news, Rob," Raul summarized. "And news makes politicians scramble for position. I can just see William Montgomery bragging that his office convicted a rich and privileged hypocrite who murdered a girl who both loved and trusted him." Raul shuddered as he spoke, but he felt that Rob needed to hear what he'd just said.

Rob dropped his head into his hands. Raul waited until his friend looked back up. Then he said, "We'll win this thing, not just for your sake, Rob, but for Jennifer's too. But we've both got to be willing to fight."

* * *

Fixing dinner simply didn't appeal to Haley tonight. She was an excellent cook, and even though she lived alone, she usually took delight in concocting a superb meal. But the day had not been an easy one. Haley was simply drained. So she stopped at a restaurant on the way home and ate a slow but relaxing meal. She consciously pushed the day's activities from her mind. But it didn't last long.

On the drive home, she began mulling over the case again. And she became depressed. She wished she'd never heard of Rob Sterling. He made the things most precious to her since her conversion seem degraded and misused. It angered her. How could anyone who was active in the Church intentionally hurt an innocent person?

And then, unbidden and unwelcome, came still a worse thought to her troubled mind than any of the others this confusing day had thrown at her.

What if Rob Sterling *was* innocent and she sent him to his death? She went over and over what she'd learned about his disturbing case. She found some solace in the evidence that pointed to Rob's guilt. *But still,* she thought, *what if?*

She hadn't been home more than thirty minutes before the doorbell rang, and she opened it to the smiling faces of her home teachers. *Maybe they'll help me feel better,* she thought as she invited them in.

CHAPTER FIVE

As the two men, both high priests in her ward, visited with Haley, she felt the tension of her day melt away. They were restoring her faith in the kind of man the gospel could produce. They were both married men, had families, and loved the Lord, and they took their assignment to watch over Haley very seriously. They'd come to know her well, and she felt totally at ease in their presence. They were always willing to come at a moment's notice if she wanted a blessing. She tried not to be a burden, but she also let them do their duty when she needed their help, though that wasn't very often.

The older of the two men, John Murray, sensed that there was a certain uneasiness about Haley tonight. She'd seemed a little worried and almost overly glad to see them when she opened the door. And she seemed hesitant for them to leave. Finally, he asked, "Is there anything we can do for you, Haley? You seemed rather uptight when we came. Is it something you'd like to talk about?"

Brother Murray was like the father she'd like to have had. His children were raised and gone from home, but she knew they visited often. He and his wife were such good people. He'd served as bishop before she joined the Church, and she still felt a special strength about him. "It's just my job," she said.

Both men nodded, and Brother Murray said, "I read in the paper that you've been assigned to prosecute the murder case of that young woman—the former Miss Utah. Is it a tough case?"

"I thought it would be easy," she admitted. "But I've found that it isn't going to be any fun at all." She smiled and tried to convey the impression that it wasn't that big of a deal.

But John Murray could tell it was weighing heavily on her, so he tried again to prompt her to open up. "Rob Sterling comes from money and wealth, according to the press. There was quite a bit of publicity when he married the young woman and a lot more now that he's accused of killing her. What would make a man like him do such a thing?" he asked.

She hesitated and said, "We don't know that yet," suddenly thinking that maybe she didn't want to talk about this tonight after all, and wondering how to politely change the subject.

"No motive?" he asked. "But there had to have been something. You know, unfaithful wife, or deeply rooted psychological problems. Or perhaps it was really just an accident. Is that possible?"

Haley was about to respond when his last comment got her thinking. *The bullet from about the height of the couch. The fallen lamp. What if it was an accident?* she thought. *What if Rob hadn't meant to kill her at all? What if he'd been carrying a loaded gun in his hand . . . and . . . and . . . and what?*

"I hadn't thought of that," she said as she noticed both men watching her expectantly. "I'll look into that angle."

"It would be horrible if an innocent man were convicted," Mike Spacer, the younger home teacher, said thoughtfully.

That statement hit her right in the pit of the stomach. She was a prosecutor, but did she have a duty to seek conviction no matter what? Or did she have the right to have reasonable doubt of her own to look more closely at a case such as this one?

She knew the answer to that question, but she also knew the answer that William Montgomery would give. He expected a conviction, nothing less. And if she didn't produce, she knew that it would be hard to ever get a decent assignment again.

"It's quite a compliment, getting assigned to prosecute such a widely publicized case as this one. The district attorney must have a lot of confidence in your ability and in your judgment. I'd sure hate to be in your shoes." John smiled and Haley said nothing. She could tell that he had something on his mind, and she was no longer in a hurry to change the subject. She wanted to hear whatever it was that he was coming around to.

Brother Murray turned to his companion. "Ever serve on a jury, Mike?"

"Never have," Mike answered. "I've been called but never actually had to sit as a juror. I don't think I'd like to either."

"I have a couple of times," he said, still looking at Mike, but giving Haley the distinct impression that it was her that should be paying close attention, as she was almost certain she might gain some wisdom from what he was going to say. "I agonized over the decision in both cases. One involved a woman charged with robbing a bank. She was young and pretty and had a baby. She swore that she didn't have anything to do with the robbery. The evidence said otherwise. All eight of us were convinced she was lying, that the police were right. We voted to convict her, and she went to prison. But I've never forgotten the look on her face when the verdict was read."

John looked back at Haley. "I wasn't positive she did it, just almost. That term you legal people use—reasonable doubt—I suspect that it's a standard that's applied a little differently in every juror's mind. Every judge too, for that matter. I don't think I had a reasonable doubt, but I wondered if she really didn't do it. I've always hoped I wasn't wrong."

He looked back at his companion. "Ever felt like that, Mike?"

"With the kids I have," Mike said with a grin.

John looked back at Haley. "I really don't envy you, Haley. You're not a judge, but you have to make judgments. It must be hard."

She nodded. His long speech probably seemed like idle conversation to Mike Spacer, but it was loaded and Haley knew it. "It's hard," she said. "There are so many pressures."

"That's one thing about being a juror. Both sides, the prosecution and the defense, argue their position, but when the case is given to the jurors, no one but them debates it." John was talking right to Mike again, and Mike was listening with interest, but Haley knew he was on to her problem. "But Haley here," he said, a slight twinkle in his eye, "she has a boss to account to, and police officers that think she should present a case a certain way. You know, lots of pressure. And she has to be able to discern the truth the best she can and then present it to the jury."

Brother Murray turned back to Haley again. "Maybe I'm wrong, but I'll bet you have superiors who put pressure on you, even when they aren't as familiar with the facts as you are."

Bull's-eye! Haley thought, a relieved smile lighting up her face.

"I guess the only way a body could find their way through that mess would be to ask the Lord." Suddenly he glanced at his watch. "I've rambled enough," he said to Mike, his point to Haley made. "We better have prayer and let Haley relax for the rest of the evening. I don't suppose her work will be any easier tomorrow."

Haley asked Brother Murray to offer a prayer before they left. It was exactly what she needed. He prayed that she would be blessed with the gift of discernment, with wisdom, and with the courage to stand up for what she knew was right.

It seemed like a simple prayer, but Haley felt the power of it, and she was grateful. She needed all the help she could get. She knew things were going to get harder as the days and weeks passed. And after the men left, she sat with her head in her hands. If she were a juror and had the evidence before her now, she'd have reasonable doubt. She wasn't convinced that Rob was guilty. And she wasn't positive he wasn't. She simply didn't know. Was it an accident, and if so, why didn't Rob simply say so? But if he wasn't the one who killed Jennifer, who was?

The preliminary hearing was coming up in a couple of weeks. She didn't have to meet the burden of proving Rob's guilt at that point, but she did have to do everything she could to convince Judge Horton to bind him over to stand trial. She had to have a lot more evidence, and it would have to be good before she could honestly stand in that courtroom and call Rob a killer.

Two days later, Sergeant Thomas entered Haley's office. He seemed excited. "We have your motive for the Sterling murder," Rex said. "And we also know why Raul Garcia wants Dan Smathers off the case."

"It better be good," she said. Rex gave her a puzzled look. He and Kurt thought it was a pretty open-and-shut case.

"Let's have it," she said, trying to sound more enthused and put his mind at ease.

"It appears that Dan Smathers might have been seeing Jennifer Sterling," Rex said flatly.

It took a moment for her to assimilate that information. Then she was jolted into action. "I need proof, Detective. Solid proof. And if it's there, Raul Garcia is right. Dan Smathers has to be off the case."

"I suppose so, Miss Gordon," Rex agreed, "but it also seems to me that if Rob doesn't care enough to prevent the man who was trying to steal his wife from defending him, then why should we care? Makes your job easier."

"Makes my job harder!" Haley said louder than she'd intended, but Rex's reaction had made her angry. "I'm sworn to uphold the law, and even though it's my job to present evidence for the state, it's also my moral duty to see that fairness exists. And to have Dan represent Rob under these circumstances is not fair. Furthermore, doesn't it make you wonder why Rob wouldn't object to Dan's . . ." She trailed off as it became clear to her.

"Okay, sorry, Counselor, I didn't mean to offend you," Rex said defensively. "But consider this. You now have the oldest motive in the book: jealousy. And Rob would be the last person to make an issue of the appointment of the very man he'd killed his wife over. If he states why he doesn't think it's fair, he'd have admitted his motive on the record of the court!"

"Okay, you're right, but like I said a moment ago, I need proof. Bring me witnesses that saw Dan and Jennifer together, for starters, and bring me evidence that Rob knew about it. Also, I need to know what your source of this alleged relationship is," she said.

"Same as Sperry Collier's," Rex said. "Another secretary working in the same firm as Jennifer saw them talking together several times. Says Dan often took Jennifer to lunch, and she even claims she saw them in a restaurant one night. Jennifer didn't work for Dan at all, and yet she was often with him in his office with a closed door."

"That's it?" Haley asked.

"Pretty much," Rex responded. "They seemed secretive, she told me, and she could tell by the way Dan looked at her that he was infatuated. Her word, not mine," he clarified.

Haley shook her head, her long black hair sliding over her shoulders. Then she ran a hand through it. "Dan Smathers has been married and divorced three times," she said thoughtfully and with some disgust. "That tells a lot right there."

"We thought we'd start interviewing Rob's associates now," Detective Thomas said. "Fellow law students at the U, professors, other officers. We'll find out when he last worked a shift and with whom."

"Good," Haley said. "Get right on it. This could mean a delay in the prelim if Dan gets booted."

"We'll get started this afternoon," Rex promised.

"Oh, Detective," Haley said as he was leaving. He turned around. "Thanks for the good work."

He left with a smile on his face. Haley Gordon was a cut above the rest, he thought.

* * *

Raul left the jail in a huff. He'd just gone in to see Rob and found that his friend had been severely beaten the night before. He was recovering all right, but to make matters worse, an officer told him they were considering asking the district attorney to bring additional charges against Rob for assaulting another prisoner. Raul had had enough. He was on his way now to see the sheriff, and he wanted a full investigation and report. He'd only been able to talk briefly to Rob, but his friend told him that he'd been jumped by five inmates. He admitted to fighting back defending himself and breaking one of their jaws, and that was what the proposed charges were over.

"I thought he was being protected," Raul practically hollered to the sheriff a few minutes later.

"As did I," the sheriff agreed. "But you do realize it's difficult, Rob having been an officer and all."

"And still is. He's a reserve."

"Not any longer," the sheriff said. "I couldn't keep him on my active reserve roster under the circumstances."

I can't believe this is happening! Raul thought in amazement. "I would suggest there be no charges filed against Rob on this matter," Raul said ominously.

"Charges? Who said anything about that?"

"One of the jailers," Raul said. "And this type of violence against my client had better not reoccur."

Raul was assured that it wouldn't, and he left, fully prepared to begin work on a lawsuit the next day. The sheriff had been cautioned and proper precautions had not been taken.

Back at his office, Raul had a message to call Haley Gordon. "It's urgent," his secretary told him.

He dialed immediately. He wanted to let her know about the problem at the jail. Rob wasn't injured badly this time, but it could be a lot worse if it happened again. When Haley came on the line, he said, "Good afternoon, Haley. Have you heard from the jail?"

She hadn't and wondered why she should. "Rob's been attacked, assaulted," he told her.

"Oh no, I'll call the sheriff," she said.

"That would be good. I just came from there, but we've got to see that this doesn't happen again," he told her. "And since you'll find out anyway, Rob did fight back. It was five on one, but he managed to break the jaw of one of the inmates. The sheriff assured me they wouldn't be seeking charges against him, although I was told differently at the jail."

Haley's head was swimming. She couldn't imagine how five inmates had been allowed to get to Rob. That was serious. She didn't even have to ask Raul if a suit would be pending. That was a given. "I'm sorry about this, Raul," she said, and he could tell she meant it. When she spoke again she said, "About the matter I called you for, I think we should meet."

"In the morning?" Raul asked.

Haley looked at her watch. It was getting late. "At 9 A.M.," she suggested.

"I'll see you then," he agreed.

* * *

Just before going to bed, Haley got a call from a young lawyer by the name of Nat Turley that she'd met a couple of times at Bar functions. She'd also seen him once at a multistake singles fireside. They'd spoken to each other for a few minutes that night. He'd seemed nice, but she wondered what he could be calling about, and she was surprised when he asked her out.

Haley hadn't dated much the past few years. She'd had chances and turned them down because she simply didn't care for the types of men she seemed to attract.

Since joining the Church, she'd gone to some singles activities but found that she still didn't meet men who wanted to take her out—nice men, the kind she'd love to date. She'd been told they probably didn't dare ask her because she had an air of self-sufficiency. Some women had suggested she work on that, as she always scared the good ones away. But Haley didn't know how to "work on" acting needy, and she wasn't going to pretend to be someone she wasn't.

She first thought she should turn Nat down, since she didn't know him all that well. But she decided after a moment's consideration that she needed and deserved some diversion. *Why not Nat?* she wondered. After all, she'd spoken to him at a church function, and he wasn't much older than she was. So she accepted a dinner date for the next Friday evening.

The next morning, after a long and restless night, she went to the office early. She had several matters she could attend to before her meeting with Raul Garcia. Her mail was already there, and she took a moment to scan through it.

All else was forgotten as one letter left her with a bad feeling in her gut.

There was no return address, but her name spelled incorrectly and the address of the district attorney's office were spelled out in letters cut from a magazine. She didn't even want to know what it contained. It was so frightening. Almost certain that it was a threat of some kind, she finally forced herself to open it, but not until she'd slipped on a pair of gloves. She didn't want to destroy fingerprints or any other evidence it might contain.

Inside was a short note. It was also prepared from letters painstakingly cut out of a glossy magazine and pasted to a sheet of paper. It said simply,

> *Hey, black lady, you better find a way to lose the case against Rob Sterling. You win, you die! This will be your only warning.*

District Attorney William Montgomery was just coming in when she went in search of him. Her hands still gloved and shaking, she showed him the letter. "Blowing smoke!" he bellowed. "That killer Sterling has to be behind it. Pay it no mind."

Easy for him to say, she thought. It wasn't his life that was threatened. She'd give it to the police department. She would also show it to Raul Garcia when he came in. Even though he was an adversary in this case, the soft-spoken, gentle man was also a good friend.

She turned back to her office, shaken as much by her boss's lack of sympathy and support as by the letter itself. She almost jumped when he called her name as she was stepping through her door. "Haley, I mean it now. You can't let that letter shake you. That's what it was intended to do. You're a good attorney. Just stay focused and win that case."

Haley forced a smile, nodded, and continued into her office. William probably meant that as both an apology for his abruptness and a signal of his support. But she also took it as a warning that she had better win this case or else she would reap the wrath of the district attorney.

* * *

Rob nursed his injuries. He'd known it would be dangerous for him in here, but five on one? It didn't make sense. And then he had a terrible thought. What if there was a correctional officer who wanted to see him hurt or dead? That seemed so unlikely, but it was possible. He knew he'd have to watch out for himself.

He continued to ponder his situation. Something was going on. Why was someone so determined to frame him? It was a nightmare that haunted him by day and woke him sweating in the night. He reviewed what clues he had. He'd been betrayed by the attorney the court had appointed. That was as disturbing as the possibility of being in the care of a corrupt officer. What chance did he have if his own counsel was determined to sell him out? And he further wondered why Dan had done what he had. It made no sense, unless . . . Rob slammed his head with his hand as, side by side, his mind suddenly placed Dan's hesitancy to take the case with the day he'd seen Dan and Jennifer together. Was Jennifer more involved with Dan than Rob had thought? The idea sickened him.

Rob pushed past that thought, trying to ignore the hurt, in an attempt to logically determine what was going on. If that dark possibility did exist, could Dan be afraid that if Rob knew what was going on and went free that he'd go after Dan? Or maybe he was doing everything possible to keep Rob behind bars in case anything about Jennifer and Dan did come out—he could use Rob as a smokescreen to divert attention from the matter. Or if Rob's reputation were destroyed, he could argue effectively that Rob was an untrustworthy criminal who was trying to escape his own punishment by planting reasonable doubt in the minds of jurors trying to make them consider that anyone other than Rob would have had an interest in hurting Jennifer. The possible reasons for Dan's strange behavior suddenly seemed as vast as the ocean—any one of them a fatal blow to Dan's career and reputation. Only one thing was certain now: Rob would not trust Dan Smathers. He'd double-check with Raul on everything he was told by the man. He was most grateful that Raul had insisted that he stay on the case, but he didn't have much to offer Raul in terms of solving the mystery.

Another thought occupied Rob's mind. It had to do with his prosecutor, Haley Gordon. He respected her a great deal. Would she try to convict him even if she could be shown that there were huge holes in her case? Somehow, he didn't believe she would.

CHAPTER SIX

Raul was over a half hour late and was quite shaken when he entered Haley's office. He was not so distraught, however, that he failed to recognize the same about her. After apologizing for his tardiness, he said, "Something's the matter, something other than what you called me about last night. Care to share it with me?"

To Haley's dismay, tears filled her eyes and she choked up. *Why can't William Montgomery be more like Raul?* she thought to herself. Sympathy, though at times embarrassing, was often the best remedy for a shock like she'd just received. She was grateful that Raul cared, but she also wondered if he'd received a similar threat, by the way he was acting.

"I guess it would be okay to tell you what just happened," she said thoughtfully, hoping there wouldn't be anything unethical about showing the threatening letter to an opposing attorney.

"Please do, then we can talk about the other matter you have on your mind," Raul said.

"And maybe we could also discuss what's upsetting you this morning," she said.

"It shows, huh?"

"Apparently we're neither of us as good at hiding our feelings as we might have thought," she agreed as she reached into a desk drawer, pulled out her gloves, and put them on.

"Gloves?" Raul said, baffled.

"I don't want to destroy any evidence," she replied as she retrieved the letter. She laid both the envelope and the letter on the far edge of her desk and said, "Pull your chair up here. But don't touch them."

Raul nodded. Haley watched him closely. A dark shadow crossed his face and he creased his brow. He stared at the threatening document long enough that she figured he must have read it two or three times. When he looked up, he said, "One thing I can promise you, Haley, is that this didn't come from my client or anyone he might have influenced."

"I didn't say it did," she said mildly, remembering the harsh words of her boss when he read it.

Raul went on, seeming intent on making his point. "Like I told you before, Rob and I grew up together. He's more like a brother than a friend. Rob's got his faults, but they're not big ones. He's a good and honest man. He simply isn't capable of this type of trash. I know you have some damaging evidence, and as soon as you get it to my co-counsel I hope I get a chance to look at it," Raul said. "It simply isn't possible that he could have ever done such a thing. If you knew him well, like I do, you'd agree with me," he added with a degree of conviction that was unsettling to her. Especially in light of the doubts she'd been having.

Haley had two questions come to mind as a result of what Raul had just said. She considered for a moment which to ask first. She decided to wait on the most crucial one, the one about Jennifer Sterling possibly seeing Dan in the days before her death. She wasn't ready for that discussion yet.

So instead she asked, "Why wouldn't you get to see the evidence that I send to Dan?"

Raul reached into his pocket and pulled out a folded piece of paper. She immediately thought she was right that he'd received a threat as well. But why would he receive one since he supported Rob's release? They were adversaries in this case.

"You can handle this without those gloves," he said, and she quickly put the threatening note away and pulled her gloves off. Then he handed his letter to her and said, "This is more than a threat, it's an action."

She'd already discovered that the letter was from the Office of Professional Conduct of the Utah State Bar. That was the arm of the Bar that investigated attorneys accused of wrongdoing. The Office of Professional Conduct could, if it found sufficient evidence after an investigation, begin proceedings in the district court that could ultimately result in the lawyer being disbarred.

"This was faxed to you this morning," she noted. "They must consider it urgent."

"Read on," he said with a slight quiver in his voice.

She read the entire document before she looked up. "They're serious?" she asked. A stupid question, she knew, but the allegations outlined in the letter she'd just read didn't sound at all like something the man sitting across the desk from her would do.

"Quite serious," he said. "I have to make a written response. What can I say to them? I'm not guilty of any of the things they've listed. If they aren't satisfied, I suppose I could be suspended pending further investigation. If whoever is behind this pack of lies can convince them that I did what I'm accused of, I will be disbarred."

"Oh, Raul, I'm so sorry. Who could possibly be behind this?" she asked.

Raul looked down at his hands and mumbled, "I only wish I knew."

Haley was heartbroken for Raul. He was a loyal friend and a good and decent man. She knew he hadn't done the things that had been reported to the Bar. It just wasn't possible. She then remembered that he had said that very same thing about Rob. She simply didn't know what to believe.

"I'm in a terrible situation," he told Haley. *But not as terrible as Rob's going to be in once I'm off the case,* he thought.

"Have faith, Raul," she said sincerely. "That's what we've both got to do." When he gave her a weak smile, she decided to change the subject. "Now, let's talk about what I asked you to come for. The detectives that are working this case for me found something very disturbing."

"Oh, good," Raul answered sarcastically. "We both need more disturbing news."

Haley smiled. He smiled too, then he said, "Okay, shoot."

"You probably already know this," she said. "They found a young woman, a secretary in the same office where Jennifer Sterling worked, who claims Jennifer was secretly seeing Dan Smathers."

Raul nodded. "That was what I couldn't tell you the other day. So if it's true, you have motive established."

"That's right," she agreed. Now she could ask the question she'd postponed. "You said Rob wasn't capable of taking the life of another person. Does this change your thinking at all? Could Rob, in your opinion, kill in a fit of jealous rage?"

Raul shook his head in mock rebuke. "You know I couldn't say yes even if it were true, which it's not. He is no more capable of such an act than you or I."

"Well, that point will have to wait for another day for debate," Haley said. "The problem we face now is what you intended to discuss with me the other day. Do we have enough to approach Judge Horton and attempt to persuade him to pull Dan Smathers off the case? With your status as a practicing attorney in question, Rob simply has no chance of a good defense if Dan Smathers was in fact seeing Rob's wife."

"My concern exactly," Raul said. "And for Rob's sake, I'm scared to death."

"That is if I do my job well and put my own life in jeopardy," Haley said lightly. Neither of them laughed.

"Sperry has been following that angle further," Raul said. "I'm sure your guys will learn what he has, but it'll take time that shouldn't be wasted. I'll save them some footwork, if you don't mind."

Haley welcomed the information, whatever it was. If she questioned it, which she probably wouldn't, she'd just have Rex and Kurt follow up, and that wouldn't take long. So she asked Raul to proceed, sliding a yellow pad in front of her and grabbing a pen to take notes as Raul talked.

"This is what he's learned as of last night. The secretary—Ann Denton is her name—saw Dan and Jennifer go into his office together a few times, even though she didn't do any work for him. She also knows they went to lunch together on occasion. She believes they also went to dinner in the evening at times, but could only say she saw them at a restaurant once. However, when Sperry pressed her, she admitted that she'd really only seen them leave the office together at lunch time. But that happens from time to time with attorneys and secretaries. Although it's usually because they have work to complete, and that couldn't have been the case with Jennifer and Dan. Ms. Denton also admitted that she could have been mistaken about the dinner date. She didn't go in the restaurant herself. And even though she could see Dan's face, she only saw Jennifer from the back. But she added that she's sure Dan took Jennifer out other times."

"Sounds like she might just be a little gossip," Haley remarked.

"A jealous one," Raul said. "She admitted that she found Dan attractive. And when Sperry asked if she'd ever talked with Jennifer about it, she said she hadn't because Jennifer was a married woman and thought way too much of herself. There may have been more, but the gist of it is, Ann was jealous. That makes her a poor witness. We'd go right down the tubes with Judge Horton if we tried to use that. Oh, and this Ann Denton also said that Dan and Jennifer talked the day of Jennifer's death. It looked like they'd been arguing when they came out of his office. But she couldn't be sure."

"Interesting," Haley said. *Was there really motive?* she wondered. *Or has Ann Denton made most of her story up?* "Is there more?" she asked.

"Oh yes," Raul said. "Sperry's done a great deal of sleuthing. He found a law student, one who's not doing too well and could be jealous of Rob this time, who says he saw Jennifer with another man at Ruby River Steak House one night not long ago. The student's name is Martin Ligorni."

"Did he identify the man Jennifer was with?" she asked as she made notes. "And how sure was he that it was Jennifer?"

"He was positive it was Jennifer, or at least that's what he claims," Raul said. "As to the other man, he never saw his face. But the description, which he could only give from having seen the man from the back, could fit Dan."

"Or several thousand other men?" Haley asked.

"Exactly. But it couldn't have been Rob if his description is right. And the fellow declined to even speculate on who it might have been."

Haley drew a deep breath and then exhaled slowly. "Is that all?"

"Yes. But Sperry was going to talk to Ruby River employees last night. So there may be more. I'll let you know as soon as I hear from him," Raul promised. He continued even as his cell phone rang and he began to fish it from a pocket. "But so far we have nothing we can really take to Judge Horton, do you agree?"

"I'm afraid so," she said as Raul looked at his cell phone to see where his call was coming from.

"My office," he said and answered his phone.

From the look that developed on Raul's face, Haley knew he wasn't getting good news. He took a pen out and jotted a number down on the back of his hand and then disconnected. "Judge Horton wants me to call," he said.

"If you'd like me to step out," she began.

"No, let's see what he wants."

Haley was only getting half of the conversation, but she was certain she knew what Judge Horton was telling Raul Garcia. And after he had completed his call, he said to Haley, "I'm off the case until I'm cleared by the Bar," he said. "Dan Smathers has Rob's future in his hands now."

* * *

Dan Smathers also got a call from Judge Horton, and he was elated. "Dan, you've got the case of Rob Sterling all to yourself. Raul Garcia is no longer co-counsel."

"Did he quit? He was actually quite a bit of help," Dan lied.

"No, I ordered him off. He has a serious complaint that's just been lodged with the Bar. I can't let him continue with a cloud like that over his head," the judge said.

"I'm sorry to hear it, and very surprised," Dan said, offering two lies in one sentence. "Raul seems like a very honest and conscientious lawyer," he added, almost gleefully.

"You can work the case alone, Dan," Judge Horton went on, "or you can pick someone else to work with you."

"I'll handle it," Dan said confidently. "I'll miss Raul's involvement, but I don't think I'll need help, at least not until we get closer to trial, if it goes that far."

"You'll need to let your client know," the old judge added. "I told Raul that if he gets cleared of the allegations anytime soon, and if Rob Sterling wants him to, he can come back on the case."

"That's not—" Dan began confidently but cut himself short. "That's good," he corrected himself. "I'd welcome him back."

It was probably more accurate to say he'd make certain Raul never practiced law again.

Dan smiled to himself after hanging up the phone. Things were going nicely so far.

* * *

It was true that Haley now had a motive for her case against Rob, *if* Ann Denton could be believed. That should have made her feel better, but it didn't. What she'd learned today could also provide a motive for someone else.

Against her better judgment, Haley pulled out the pictures in the case file that was now sitting on her desk. She'd been adding notes and comments to the file, but she wanted to look at the pictures again. The ones she wanted were upside down. She turned them over and studied the face of Rob Sterling in an attempt to examine again who he was in light of all she now knew about this case. She scrutinized it in search of a hint of something evil in his eyes, or something suspect in the set of his jaw. She even studied his posture in another photo. Was there a slouch that might betray a flaw in his character?

She could find nothing that would in any way help her case. Then, after failing at that attempt, she looked at him as a man rather than a criminal. It was not such an amazing thing, she concluded, that a former Miss Utah would fall in love with what Haley saw in this picture.

Then another thought came. She really needed to see Rob Sterling again in person. Surely then she could find the fatal faults that lay beneath his appealing and innocent-looking exterior. Troubled at her line of thinking, Haley rose from her desk and began to pace. How could she ever do justice to the state's case with the doubts she was experiencing? Perhaps she'd better march right up the hallway to William Montgomery's office and ask to have someone else take over for her.

She actually put the file neatly back together and was headed for her door before she seriously considered what the district attorney's reaction might be. She could be out of a job before she left his office, and he might well prevent her from getting another good one in the state again. One didn't just quit cases with this district attorney. Not without compelling reasons—ones that could easily be substantiated.

What did she have? A growing feeling that Rob might not be guilty. That would go nowhere with the district attorney. He considered Rob guilty and didn't want to hear otherwise. Even if she pointed out the weaknesses in her case, Mr. Montgomery would scoff at them.

Then there was only one thing she could do: start looking for more evidence against Rob Sterling. For starters, she could call Sergeant Thomas, show him the letter, and see if there was any way it could be traced to Rob. After all, the logical person to send a threat like that was the one person whose life was on the line, and Haley held that line.

That decided, she made the call to the detective, then opened the file and aggressively started through the case once more. If Rob Sterling had killed his wife, Haley Gordon would prove it!

Her secretary buzzed her. "Haley, there is a group of kids here to see you."

"Kids?" she asked, wondering if she'd forgotten an appointment. But she'd remember if some kids were coming to see her. That wasn't something that happened on a regular basis . . . unless it was a group of students on a field trip. Maybe someone else had made the appointment with a school class and forgotten to tell her. Well, if so, she'd have to make this fast.

"Yes. Boys and girls," the secretary said. "They're probably about twelve or thirteen years old, and there are about ten of them. And they are determined to talk to you."

"Is their teacher with them?" Haley asked.

"No teacher, just the kids."

Haley had a soft spot for youth. "Send them in," she said wearily.

"Oh, Miss Gordon, they say they need to talk to you about their Sunday School teacher."

"What?" Haley asked.

"Their teacher. Rob Sterling."

CHAPTER SEVEN

Haley met the young people as they came through her door. They were all dressed neatly and seemed like really great kids. But there was something strange about them. Not a single one of them was smiling, and that wasn't like kids. These young people were much too sober— angry even.

"Hi, I'm Haley Gordon," she said with a smile, extending her hand to the boy who was closest to her and seemed to be the one in charge. "I'm an assistant district attorney."

The young man held his hand out and took hers. She noted that his palm was sweaty and his hand was trembling a little. "We need to talk to you," he said. The others nodded in support and closed rank by huddling around him.

Haley closed the door to her office and then retreated to her desk, but she leaned against the front edge of it. She couldn't sit if the kids couldn't, and she didn't have chairs enough for all of them. "Okay, I'm listening," she said. "What did you need to talk to me about?" In dismay, Haley noted that her own palms were sweaty and she was trembling ever so slightly. She'd never been uncomfortable in the presence of young people, especially ones the age of these kids. But she was uncomfortable now.

"Are you the one that's trying to get our teacher convicted of murder?" the boy asked bluntly. His face could have been chiseled from granite. In fact, all ten faces could have been.

"And your teacher is?" she asked, knowing full well what the answer was.

"Brother Sterling." Haley was surprised at her reaction to his simple choice of words. It wasn't Rob, or Mr. Sterling, or Rob Sterling. His tone conveyed love and respect.

"I see," she said. "Well, in answer to your question, I have been assigned by Mr. Montgomery, the district attorney, to prosecute the case against Mr. Sterling."

"He didn't do anything wrong," the boy said. "You gotta quit trying to make it look like he did."

They may have been first- and second-year teens, but Haley felt like she was up against some of the toughest adversaries she'd ever faced. "It's my job," she said patiently, "to look at all the evidence the police gather in any case I'm assigned and then present it to a jury. That's what I plan to do in this case. Then it's the job of the jurors to decide whether Rob is innocent or guilty."

The boy shook his head, and to Haley's dismay, his eyes were getting wet. "He didn't do it," he said. "He would never do anything like that. Don't you understand, Miss Gordon? He's a great guy. He's our Sunday School teacher."

Haley was without words. Would the kids she taught in her own Sunday School be as supportive of her as this boy and his friends were of Rob? Her students were a little older, but she genuinely cared for them. Did Rob feel the same about these young people? He must, by the way they were acting. It took a lot of courage to do what they were doing.

A young girl, very pretty with long flaxen hair, spoke next. "Sister Sterling was nice. We liked her too. We don't know why anyone would do that to her. It's so awful." She began to cry.

A third student, another boy, took over. "Somebody else did it," he stated with such conviction that Haley was near tears herself. The others nodded their support.

Then other students spoke up, all stating their convictions that some terrible person had done the awful thing to Jennifer, and that they were trying to do an awful thing to Rob, too. *Couldn't she see that?* they all wanted to know.

These kids were hurting. They were sincere. They were for real. And they truly loved Rob Sterling. And once again, the thought crossed the stage of Haley's mind. *Could it really have been someone else? Could someone have framed Rob? Could that someone be . . .* Haley mentally slapped herself. She couldn't go on and accuse anyone of anything without evidence. But the persistent thought wouldn't go away.

"Miss Gordon." She looked down. It was the first spokesman again. "Are you a Mormon?"

"I am," she said. "I joined the Church about two years ago."

"Then you should know that Brother Sterling didn't do it."

Haley smiled, and then looked at all the young people, so intense, so frightened, but so convinced. "If Rob Sterling is innocent," she began, "then I will find it out. And if he's not, you young people must accept it, as must I."

Another girl spoke up. She was short, a little heavy, and spoke slowly, her speech slightly affected by some defect she must have been born with. Haley's heart instantly went out to her. "Please, Miss Gordon, pray about Brother Sterling. Heavenly Father will let you know he didn't do it. He let me know. You've got to help him."

"I'll try to do that," she heard herself promise. "But you all have to promise something to me in return."

They all looked at her suspiciously. She could see the relief that came over them all when she said, "You need to pray for me, to help me help him."

If William Montgomery could have seen and heard what had just taken place in the office of his young star prosecutor, it wouldn't be her office much longer. She had just committed to helping Rob Sterling. Not that it was wrong, for she should have been seeking nothing but the truth of the matter from the get-go. But her job had just become a lot more difficult; the district attorney wasn't so concerned with the truth right now, and her future as an attorney was in jeopardy. But she couldn't help what she'd just done. Her doubts over the guilt of Rob Sterling were becoming stronger than her belief that he was guilty. She still intended to follow the resolve she'd made just before the young people came in. She would work hard to find out if Rob had sent the note, or had it sent, and whether he was guilty of a terrible crime. But she would work just as hard to find out if he was innocent.

* * *

Raul Garcia, accompanied by Detective Sperry Collier, had just broken the bad news to Rob. But the reaction had not been exactly what he'd expected. Rob was angry, but not because his own defense was in jeopardy. He was angry because his best friend had been unfairly accused of something he hadn't done. They were both in similar situations now, but Rob's was still far worse. However, Raul wasn't sure his friend understood that, the way he went on about how unfair it was that someone was victimizing Raul.

"You're probably the intended victim in all of this, Rob," Raul said wearily.

"Don't you worry about me," Rob said, and then he looked directly at the private investigator. "You get busy and clear Raul's name. "I'll sell my house if I have to, Sperry, but I'll pay you to help Raul. His problem comes first now. Anyway, I'm sure that whoever killed my wife is behind this. You find him and maybe you can save us both. But regardless, you've got to clear Raul."

"We'll do our best," Sperry said.

"Even though I can't represent you in court," Raul said, "I can still work to clear you. And I will."

Sperry spoke again. "Are you going to tell him about the letter to Miss Gordon?"

"What letter?" Rob asked.

Raul explained and Rob seemed more devastated than ever. "It was meant to appear that I was behind it," he said as he dropped his head into his hands. "I'd never do that."

"But someone did," the tough PI said. "And along with all my other digging, I intend to trace that one down too. And when I do, I suspect it'll be from the same source as the complaint to the Bar against Raul."

"Now, about your little problem in the jail here," Raul said. "I met with the sheriff. He says they'll tighten up security for you. And he assures me that no further charges are coming out of this incident against you. But as a precaution, I've begun to prepare a lawsuit."

"I'd rather you didn't do that, Raul," Rob said. "The sheriff's been good to me. Even when I told him that I was quitting to go to law school, he offered to keep me on as a reserve. I don't feel good about suing him. You can't do it anyway, can you? The judge won't let you."

"The judge can't do anything about me suing in your behalf. It's not part of your defense, and it will be in a federal court. As long as I don't get disbarred, I'll represent you on that matter, unless, of course, you fire me."

"Well, I don't want to fire you, but I also don't feel like suing the sheriff. None of this is his fault," Rob persisted. But he wondered whose fault it was. He was becoming more convinced all the time that a correctional officer was somehow involved. And if so, the sheriff wouldn't be able to protect him unless he fired the officer. And that would never happen unless someone came forward to accuse the officer.

He said none of this to Raul, but Raul was having the same thoughts and tried to reason with him. "Sperry and I can't do much of anything to find out who's behind the assault without a lawsuit."

"Why not?" Rob asked, knowing full well what Raul and Sperry were thinking and agreeing with them even before they said it.

"Because no one in here will want to talk to us, I'm afraid," Sperry said. "They'd have no reason to and we'd get no cooperation."

"However, if we sue, we can force depositions," Raul pointed out. "Anyone we ask to talk to us must do so, and they'll do it under oath. It's the only way that I can see to get to the bottom of it."

"It's a good strategy," Sperry agreed.

After several more minutes, Rob finally relented. "Go ahead then," he said, "but only until we find out what's happening. Eventually I want the suit dropped."

After leaving Rob at the jail, Sperry and Raul went over what had to be done. They listed the many different directions the investigation now had to go. First, they had to find out if what the young secretary, Ann Denton, had told them was true. That was one part of the case they weren't telling Rob about just yet. Second, they needed to find out if Jennifer had been seen with any other man, as Martin Ligorni claimed, and if so, who that man was. Third, they needed to find out who was behind Rob's assault. Fourth, they needed to find out who had made the complaint against Raul to the Bar. Fifth, they needed to find out who was threatening the assistant district attorney. And finally, they had to find out who the real killer was.

They both paused after making the list. It sounded more like the work fifteen or twenty men could tackle, not just two.

* * *

Haley made a similar list as she ate dinner that night. The bulk of the evidence still pointed toward Rob Sterling, but it was all circumstantial—nothing that would prove guilt beyond a reasonable doubt. And her doubts about his guilt were growing by the hour. She also didn't have any committed help. The two detectives who were working for her were convinced of Rob's guilt. The threatening letter had made both of them angry, and they swore they'd find out who Rob had hired to send it to her. So Haley didn't dare share her doubts with them. They had some loyalty to her, but it was professional. If they thought she was getting soft, their true loyalties would come first. If she said too much to them, it would probably get back to William Montgomery, and she'd be through, not just with this case, but with her entire law career.

But she had to use them, she realized. There was nothing more she could do. She just needed to point them in the right direction, and when they found evidence it could be in Rob's favor, and she'd do with that what she could when the time came. In the meantime, she had a lot of work to do on the case in preparation for the upcoming preliminary hearing.

Haley worked long, hard hours. She got home with only twenty minutes to get ready for her date with Nat Turley on Friday night. She found that she actually looked forward to seeing him again. He had seemed quite nice. She just hoped she hadn't let herself in for a long and boring evening instead of the diversion she needed and wanted. He was late only by five minutes but it gave her time to be ready when he got there, so she didn't need to make excuses for not being ready on time.

She answered the door and smiled at the tall blond who was standing there. "Sorry I'm late, Haley," he said. "I had a hard time getting away from the office."

She understood fully, but didn't say so. "You look like you're all ready," he said, his clear blue eyes shining.

Nat really was very nice looking. And he seemed like such a gentleman. He opened the door to his Jaguar for her, lifted her skirt into the car when it trailed, and then shut the door gently. He smiled at her again when he climbed in himself.

"Nice car," she said.

"Thanks, I've worked hard for it."

They had a good evening, and dinner was excellent—more expensive than she'd ever buy for herself, but it was really nice. Nat didn't bore her with talk about himself, something she'd worried about. He asked her only questions about herself, and she answered them openly. None of them were really personal things.

She had to probe Nat with questions to learn anything about him. He told her that he practiced business law and that he enjoyed it, that he'd gotten his law degree from BYU, his father was a surgeon, he was the third of five children, and he'd served a mission in South America. As a result he spoke fluent Spanish. That was about it. It wasn't much to go on, but she enjoyed his easy manner regardless.

He left her at the door to her apartment, promising to call again. She thanked him and said she'd like that. And for the first time in several nights, Haley Gordon had something good to think about when she went to bed. *Who knows?* she thought. *Maybe Nat is someone I could get to like.* She fell asleep with a smile on her face for the first time in days.

* * *

From the shadows behind her apartment, another man had watched as the couple conversed beneath her porch light. For a long time after the blond man had driven away in his gold Jaguar, he watched the apartment. He had a message to deliver to the woman, and then he'd leave. But he also thought about the gold Jaguar. He'd really like to get his hands on that car. Maybe he would sometime. Yeah, that wasn't such a bad idea. He would do that.

And sometime, he'd also like to get his hands on that woman. She was a real fox. Maybe he'd take her for a ride in the Jaguar. But right now, he was being paid quite well to do a job. A little romance, his twisted style of romance, could wait. He'd learned to be patient in prison.

It was after midnight that he delivered his message. It was tied to a rock and sailed right through the window of her bedroom.

* * *

Haley didn't know if it was the sound of breaking glass or the rock striking her leg that woke her. But she came up with a start, her heart heaving within her chest. She reached for the lamp, then thought better of it as her head quickly cleared. She might be a target for whoever was out there.

Haley rolled quietly off the far side of her bed and reached for the phone. At his insistence she'd memorized Sergeant Thomas's home phone number after he'd read the threatening letter. He answered on the first ring. "Hello," he said, not sounding the least groggy. *He must be used to getting awakened in the night like this,* she thought.

"Sergeant, this is Haley Gordon," she began.

"What's happened?" he asked before she could say more. She told him, and he said, "Stay put. I'll be right over. I'll send a patrol unit too. There'll be a city unit close, I'm sure."

"Thanks, I haven't looked at the rock. I didn't think I should turn on the lights," she said, her voice breaking with fear.

"Don't touch it. I'm on my way," he said, and the connection was cut.

Sergeant Thomas was good to his word. There was not one, but two police cars there within a couple of minutes, and while two officers began a quick search of the area outside the apartments where Haley lived, the others came to her door. Sergeant Thomas was only ten minutes behind them. The city officers saw but didn't touch the rock with the attached note, leaving that for the detective and their own lab people, who were on the way.

Rex Thomas read the note, handling it with surgical gloves so as not to destroy any prints that might be on it. He read the note out loud. "Pretty lady, I'm watching you," was all it said. She couldn't have been more frightened if it went on for pages.

The note was scrawled in longhand with a pencil. It looked like the writing of a five year old, or a very uneducated adult. More likely, it was the purposefully disguised work of a man intelligent enough that he would be hard to catch.

Hours later—after the cops were gone and she'd been assured that someone would be sitting outside her apartment for the rest of the night—Haley went back to bed.

But she didn't sleep.

CHAPTER EIGHT

The crowd had thinned at the Ruby River Steakhouse on 700 East when Sperry Collier went in. He was hoping to find at least one or two of the same people on duty as had been there the night Jennifer Sterling had eaten dinner there. He was hungry, so he ordered a meal and studied the waiters and waitresses while he waited. Long years of observing people had helped him develop an uncanny ability to make reasonably accurate judgments about various personality characteristics. Right now he was looking for someone who might be easily persuaded to speak with him.

He found what he was looking for in a young man with slicked-back hair, heavy eyebrows, and a large gold earring. He looked tired, and something about him told Sperry he needed money—he probably worked there most nights of the week. He was a good bet. The young man passed close by as he waited on his assigned tables. Without being too obvious, Sperry managed to read the young man's name tag. The next time he came past empty-handed, Sperry said, "Hey, Ruben, when you're not too busy, slip back here. You and I need to talk."

Ruben looked at him in surprise. It never ceased to amuse Sperry how often people who wore name tags were surprised to be called by name. Ruben was no exception. "Do I know you?" he asked.

"Think for a minute," Sperry said, and a shadow crossed Ruben's face. "Don't be too long. It's not that busy in here."

The young man went on, but before he disappeared from Sperry's view, he'd looked back three times. Five minutes later, he came out, walked directly to Sperry's table, and slipped in opposite him. "I can't remember where we met before," he said nervously.

"Think some more," Sperry said as he pulled out a picture of Jennifer Sterling and laid it on the table in front of Ruben. "I know you know who this woman is."

Ruben studied the picture for only a moment, then he said, "She used to be Miss Utah. She was killed recently. But I've never met her."

"Ruben," Sperry said softly, his voice conveying disappointment. "You must not remember me or you wouldn't lie. You should know that you don't lie to me. This woman was in here and you waited on her, remember?"

"I don't think so . . ." Ruben began.

"She was with someone, a man. Does that help you remember?"

Ruben squinted his eyes, as if deep in thought. Sperry laid a fifty-dollar bill in front of him and waited while the young man studied the money and then shoved it in his shirt pocket, looking around as if afraid someone might see him. "I know you've got to get back to work, and I'm not here to cause you trouble, although you know I can," Sperry said darkly. "Now think."

Sperry knew the waiter would not remember him—they'd never met before. But he had the young man's undivided attention. "I . . . I know," Ruben admitted, and Sperry wondered what he'd done to make him act so guilty. "What do you need to know?"

"Who she was with that night," Sperry said.

The young man squinted again and unconsciously pulled on his gold earring. Sperry waited. He was quite sure the young man knew something. "I don't know who he was."

"Was it this man?" Sperry asked as he laid a picture beside Jennifer's.

Ruben studied it for a moment before saying, "No, it wasn't him."

Sperry didn't say anything more at the moment. He simply waited while Ruben squirmed. After a few more seconds, he laid down a second photograph. "How about this man?"

"Yeah, that was him," Ruben said almost instantly.

"Are you sure?"

"That was the guy," Ruben said as he started to slide from the table.

"Not so fast." Sperry stopped him. "You may have to testify in court. You need to be certain."

"It was that guy," Ruben said. "I'm positive."

Sperry laid down the picture of a third man. "I think it was this guy," Sperry said.

But Ruben's mind was made up. "No, it was this one," he said touching the picture he'd already identified.

"Good, you've been a help. I just need one more thing for now," Sperry said, effectively stopping Ruben in his second attempt at getting away. "I need to know who else was working the night these two were in here."

"Uh, that was several weeks ago."

"Think," Sperry said.

Ruben hesitated, then named several names. One of them was Cindy, the young woman who was waiting on Sperry that evening. "Thanks, Ruben. Maybe next time I come in you won't have so much trouble remembering me. You already know I won't forget you."

Ruben nodded. "I'll remember," he said and started to slide again.

"Oh, Ruben," Sperry said, "have you ever seen this lady here with either of these two other men? Not the night I asked about, but some other time."

"Never," Ruben answered. "I only saw her that one time, and she was with the guy in the sports shirt. I've never seen either of the guys in suits."

After Ruben had made good his escape with Sperry's fifty-dollar bill in his pocket, Sperry picked up the photographs. Even though it seemed crazy to trust a young man with that many secrets, he was almost certain Ruben had told the truth. The first picture, that of Raul Garcia, he put back in his pocket. He'd used that picture only to gauge Ruben's honesty. He looked at the others for a minute, then put them back in the pocket of his jacket, shaking his head and picking up his fork.

When his waitress came, she asked, "Is your steak to your satisfaction?"

"Just right," he said.

"Could you use a refill of your drink?" she asked.

"Please," he said.

When she returned, he'd laid the pictures of Jennifer, the man in the sports shirt, and the one in a suit who was not Raul on the edge of the table. She sat the soft drink in front of Sperry. He watched as her eyes darted to the pictures, then away, and finally back again. "Could you tell me which ones you've seen in here?" he asked, showing her his ID and smiling pleasantly.

She hesitated. "You may have waited on her and one of these men a few weeks ago," Sperry added. She nodded, then placed a finger on the picture of the man in the sports shirt. "Are you sure?" he asked, smiling again.

"I'm sure," Cindy responded, her own smile a nervous one.

"Have you ever seen the other man in here?" he asked. "This one in the suit."

He looked straight into Cindy's eyes. She flinched, then said, "Yes, I'm sure I have."

"With Jennifer Sterling?" he asked.

"No, not with her," she answered. "She only came in here with him." Cindy's eyes were troubled. "I can't believe anyone would kill her. She was really nice."

"Even him?" Sperry asked, pointing now to the picture of the man in the sports shirt.

"Especially not him!" Cindy exclaimed. "He was very gentle with her all night."

"Thank you, Cindy," he said as he picked up the picture of Dan Smathers in his expensive suit and put it in his pocket. Cindy had moved away by the time he picked up the other pictures, the one of Jennifer Sterling and the one of Rob Sterling in a sports shirt.

The law student had lied to the two detectives from the sheriff's department. The question that now had to be answered was why he'd lied.

Perhaps Rob Sterling could shed some light on that. But it would be the next day before he could see Rob. He'd visit the jail on Sunday afternoon.

* * *

Haley was nervous as she faced the young men and women of her Sunday School class. She'd never experienced this feeling with these kids before, but she suddenly felt very responsible for them—for teaching them correct principles and for her role as an example. She knew it was because of the visit of Rob Sterling's class. They'd taught her how much her influence could affect the kids she taught. She struggled with her lesson at first, but after a few minutes she finally felt at ease. However, when the class period ended, Bonnie Coffman, the bishop's young daughter, lingered after the others had left.

"That was a good lesson," Bonnie said.

"Thank you, Bonnie," Haley said. "I don't feel like I did very well today."

"You always do well," Bonnie said, absently fussing with her short brown hair. "I can't believe how much you know about the scriptures after being a member of the Church for only a couple of years."

"I have to study hard for these lessons," Haley admitted. "I learn far more than any of you kids do."

"Well, I'm learning a lot," Bonnie said.

Haley picked up her books as Bonnie continued to linger. "Are you okay?" the young girl asked as Haley reached for the light switch.

"Sure, I'm fine," Haley answered quickly.

"Oh, okay."

Haley opened the classroom door and held it for Bonnie. But Bonnie didn't move. "Why did you ask me that question?" Haley prodded, quite certain that the bishop's fifteen-year-old daughter had something specific on her mind.

"I heard about your window," Bonnie admitted, her face suddenly crimson. "Why would somebody throw something through your window?"

Haley smiled at Bonnie. She didn't want the girl to worry. "Probably just a prank," she said.

Bonnie shook her head. "I'd be so scared," she said. "Somebody won't hurt you, will they?"

"No, I don't think so. You can quit worrying now, but thanks for your concern. The window will be fixed tomorrow."

Bonnie's color began to return, but she still looked very serious. "My mother said you could stay with us for a few days if you needed to. We have a basement apartment in our house."

"Thank you, Bonnie. But that won't be necessary."

And yet Haley found a certain comfort in knowing there was someplace she could go if she had to. But surely she wouldn't have to, would she?

* * *

When Sperry arrived at the jail, he was told that Rob already had visitors and that he'd have to come back another day. He produced identity and asked the officer if the other visitors were Tasha and Jim Andrews. Surprised, the officer said they were. Sperry then said, "Tell them I'm here and need to visit with both of them as well as Rob."

The officer did as Sperry requested, and when he returned, he invited him back to the visiting area. Tasha was glad to see him and introduced him to her husband. "This isn't a social visit," he said, "and what I have won't take long, but I really need to talk to Rob. Thanks for having the officer let me come back here with you."

Jim Andrews said, "We knew when he mentioned your name that it must be important."

"I'll be quick so you folks can continue your visit," Sperry promised. Then he turned to Rob. "How are things in there?" he asked.

"As good as can be expected," Rob said. "Do you have any good news?"

"I wish I did," the detective said. "What I came for is information. What can you tell me about a fellow law student of yours by the name of Martin Ligorni?"

Rob was puzzled. "Ligorni, huh? What does he have to do with my case?"

"Maybe nothing," Sperry said evasively. "His name came up in some of my inquiries. Do you know him well?"

"Not really," Rob said. "I've spoken to him, but that's about all. He's sort of a loner. He's toward the bottom of the class. Seems lazy to me."

"Describe him," Sperry said. "I want to know him when I see him."

"He's only about five foot five or so, but he must weigh over two hundred pounds," Rob said. "Strange-looking duck, too. His hair is very dark brown, but he's bald halfway back. The rest of his hair is combed back and he keeps it in a short ponytail. His eyes are small, dark, and set close together. Reminds me of a mouse. He has thin lips and thick jowls. His facial hair isn't very thick, but he still tries to wear a paintbrush beard. It's small and pointed but doesn't have many hairs in it. You ever see him, you won't soon forget him."

"You ever have words with him, you know, a disagreement of any kind?" Sperry asked.

"Not that I can think of. He's not the kind of guy I'd have much to do with. I wonder how he ever got into law school, and I can imagine the kind of clients he'll have if he ever makes it through," Rob said. "What's he done, anyway?"

"Well, not much, but he doesn't seem to like you, according to a report I got," Sperry said. "Did he ever say anything to you about Jennifer?"

Rob thought for a minute. "Now that you mention it, I do remember one thing. We sort of bumped as we left class one day. He said something about how did I ever get such an attractive young wife. I told him I was just lucky. I don't remember exactly what he said after that. It was something about her being Miss Utah. I never really gave it much thought. I'm always getting comments about that."

"He didn't seem sullen or angry or anything?" Sperry asked.

"No more than usual. Like I told you, he's really sort of a loner. I've never seen him smile, so maybe you could say he's always sullen. I figured he was just trying to make conversation," Rob said. "I wouldn't worry much about him."

But Sperry did worry about him. He planned to make a visit to Mr. Martin Ligorni. Something just didn't seem right. The man had lied and Sperry wanted to know why.

* * *

Later that Sunday afternoon, as Haley sat alone in her living room, she felt vulnerable. The curtains in her front room window were open, and she could see the street that passed in front of the apartments. She knew she was getting paranoid when she thought she saw the same car pass by several times with a large black man at the wheel. She finally shut the curtains. She couldn't let anyone or anything get to her.

After dark, she looked outside once more, parting the curtains very slightly. A black man was just disappearing past a van that was parked near her car. She shivered. She didn't recognize him, but she knew that wasn't something that would normally bother her. She didn't know very many of the other tenants. And she certainly didn't know their friends.

She checked the locks on her doors and went into the bedroom. The apartment manager had boarded the window up until the glass could be replaced. The darkness of the window was disconcerting, but she tried to shut out the worry. Everything would be okay. And the police would keep an eye on her apartment, she'd been promised. *I'm just overreacting,* she thought.

Haley was dog tired, and when she finally fell asleep, she slept soundly. And by morning, she was feeling rested at last and much more at ease—until she went to her car and found a note beneath her windshield wiper. Hands suddenly shaking, she took it by one edge and shook it open.

Sleep well, pretty lady?

It was the same childish handwriting as the note that had accompanied the rock through her window.

* * *

After reporting to Sergeant Thomas the latest incident of what Haley figured was a campaign of terror against her, Haley received a call from Raul Garcia. "Heard about the window," he said. "You'd better be careful, Haley. I don't like the way things are going for you."

"I'm not terribly pleased myself," she admitted. Then she told him about the morning's note on her car.

"Have you talked to Montgomery about this?" he asked. "He needs to know."

"He'll say to forget it," Haley said with a bitterness she was surprised to feel. But she was feeling it. All her boss wanted was a high-profile victory no matter who it hurt. "I'll just let it go for now. Anything new with your problem?" she asked.

"I got a copy of the complaint against me. I've never heard of the guy who made it. Claims he was a client of mine, but I'd remember if he was."

"That can be easily enough proven," Haley said. "You'd have a record of it if you'd represented him. So would a court somewhere."

"That's the problem. They could say that I destroyed the case file since he's claiming I never filed his case for him with the court. It's part of his complaint to the Bar," Raul told her.

"What kind of case was it supposed to be?" she asked.

"He claims he was fired by an employer for reasons of race. He's Hispanic, and he says that's why he came to me, but he also says that I kept putting him off."

"That doesn't sound that terrible so far. There must be more than that," Haley speculated.

"I'm afraid so. He says he has a witness who can prove that his former employer paid me a large sum of money just to bury the case," Raul said.

"Does he name the witness?" Haley asked.

"No, but he says he can and will, and that the witness will testify."

"What about the employer you were supposed to sue? Surely he can be reached," Haley suggested.

"That's another problem. Seems it's one of these outfits that sets up shop, works people by phone, scams them, then gets lost. The company had an office in Murray. That's where the complainant says he worked for them," Raul said. "Sperry did some checking. Seems the state received several dozen complaints against them, but the company vanished. Now the guy who's after me is saying if I'd acted when I was asked to, they'd have been stopped before they got away."

"If I were you, Raul, I'd invite someone from the Office of Professional Conduct to come to your office right now and look at your files, including your electronic ones. And they could talk to your secretary. She'd remember him if you'd ever taken him as a client. Maybe you can end it all right there," she suggested, wishing her own problem could be as easily resolved as his.

"Good idea," he suggested. "I'll get on that right now."

"Good luck, Raul. And keep in touch."

"Oh, Haley, I forgot to tell you what I actually called about," he said. "Sperry went to that Ruby River Steakhouse over on Seventh East. He spoke to some people there. Jennifer was in there with a man all right, but the man was Rob. The ones Sperry talked to hadn't seen her with Dan Smathers. He's going to talk to the law student that reported it. I'll let you know what he finds out."

Haley was upset as she hung the phone up. A witness that could have strengthened motive, who could have reinforced Ann Denton's statement, was lying or mistaken. And Ann's information was suspect. Her case was getting weaker, not stronger. And she also wondered, with some anger beginning to fester, why the detectives that first heard the story from the law student hadn't bothered to check out his story. They could as easily have discovered the information as Sperry Collier had. She was rather afraid that they were so convinced of Rob's guilt they weren't being thorough.

Haley grabbed her briefcase and headed out. But her secretary called to her as she passed her desk. "Haley," she said, "there's another call for you. Would you like me to get a number and have him call back?"

"Who is it?" Haley asked.

"He says he's a friend of yours, Nat Turley."

Haley turned and headed back to her office. "Transfer his call to me," she said, her heart beating just a little faster at the prospect of talking to Nat.

"Haley," he said as soon as she'd answered. "I heard what happened. Are you all right?" His voice was full of concern, and it made Haley feel much better about things, just knowing someone who wasn't part of the case cared.

"I'm fine," she said. "It was frightening, but as I think back on it, I guess it's just one of those things that happen."

"It is not one of those things that happen!" Nat exclaimed. "It's a despicable criminal act. Someone is trying to frighten you."

"Well, it won't work," Haley said bravely, trying to shrug off the fear she felt each time she thought of the previous night's events. "I'll do what I have to do."

"I know you will," he said. "Hey, I haven't got long, I'm due in court. But I just had to check on you. Do you need help fixing the window?"

"Oh no, the apartment manager has arranged to have it replaced," she said. "But thanks anyway."

"I'm here if you need me," he said. "And let me know if anything like that happens again. I'm really quite concerned about you."

"Actually," she said slowly, wondering if she really should mention the second note. But there was no reason to make him worry.

"What, Haley?" Nat asked.

The concern in his voice was so genuine that she couldn't help herself. "There was another note under my windshield this morning," she said.

"Haley! We've got to do something about this!" he exclaimed. "Have you called the cops?"

"I have, and no, I don't think there's anything we can do, but thanks for offering," Haley said. She was touched more than she wanted to admit.

"Well, besides offering to be your bodyguard," he joked, "I'd love to have dinner with you again. Would you have time tomorrow night?" he asked.

Suddenly, Nat's company seemed like just what she needed. "I'd love to, Nat," she said.

"Pick you up at seven then," he said cheerfully.

"It's a date," she agreed. And as she again left her office, the day seemed brighter. She scarcely knew Nat Turley, but she looked forward to spending another couple of hours with him.

As she passed her secretary's desk this time, the young woman looked up and smiled before saying, "Nice guy?"

"Yeah, he is," Haley answered. "Really nice."

"I see," the secretary said knowingly.

"Don't start any rumors," Haley answered with a laugh.

"I won't," the young woman agreed. "But he did sound like quite a guy when I talked to him. He was really concerned about you."

* * *

A few moments later, William Montgomery received an expected call. "I just talked to Haley," Nat Turley told him. "She seems fine to me. A little scared after the rock incident, but she seems game. I'm worried though. The note this morning seems to be establishing a pattern."

"What note?" William asked. "She didn't say anything to me about another note."

"I guess she doesn't want you to worry," Nat said. "She'll be okay."

"Good. Did you make another date with her?" William asked.

"I did. Tomorrow night," he said. "I better stay pretty close to her I think."

"Great, you do that. But pump her a little more after this," William ordered. "I want to make sure she's right on top of this matter of the Sterling murder. She's a great young prosecutor, but I worry a little that she could get sidetracked with these threats. That worries me. This case is important. We can't afford to lose it."

"I'll keep you informed," Nat said, even as a twinge of guilt began to pester him. He'd accepted this little assignment as a favor to a man who'd been really good to him, a man whose advice had been timely when Nat was struggling as a new attorney. And he admired William as an attorney. But now, Nat wasn't so sure of himself. He felt like a spy, and that wasn't something he wanted to continue, as he'd found that Haley Gordon was someone he could grow fond of. But he'd made a promise, and Nat Turley kept his promises.

* * *

William Montgomery sat thinking after Nat's call. He'd assigned Haley Gordon to the Sterling case because she was one of his most aggressive and bright prosecutors. The fact that she was a woman hadn't in any way affected his decision. Now he wondered if he should have considered it. But how was he to know that Rob Sterling would resort to terrorizing her from his jail cell?

He cursed beneath his breath. Sterling was already charged with a capital crime. There was nothing worse he could be charged with. And yet William wanted to bring more charges against him—teach him a lesson and impress the voting public at the same time.

Maybe he could think of something. There was the matter of the assault against another inmate, but that one was weak. He couldn't bring a charge that might evoke sympathy for Rob. No, he'd have to wait. Maybe something would come along, proof that he was in fact behind the terror campaign. *Yes, that might work,* he thought. In the meantime, it irked him that Haley was being distracted. She was good, but unless she kept her mind on the case and did everything she could to get a conviction, he would have to make a change. She could be removed from the case if his move for the attorney general's office was threatened.

CHAPTER NINE

Rob's description of the law student Martin Ligorni couldn't have been more accurate. Detective Sperry Collier had no trouble spotting him as he came from class that afternoon. He could have intercepted him and spoken with him at anytime after that, but Sperry wanted to find out where he lived and confront him in his own apartment. A lot could be learned about a person from how they lived—even something as simple as how they decorated their apartment.

So Sperry chose to follow him. He had to wait while Martin made a short stop at the library. Then he waited again while he gassed up his car. But finally he followed him to a large apartment complex clear over in Kearns. He waited while Martin went into his apartment and then approached the door himself.

He knocked and waited. When Martin opened the door, it was only just a crack. He could barely see the man's mousy eyes peering out at him. "I don't talk to salesmen," Martin said and began to shove the door closed.

But Sperry's foot was in the way. "You and I have something to talk about," Sperry said. "So either let me in now, or I'll come back with a warrant and an army."

The weight of the short man inside leaned heavier against the door. "I don't even know you," Martin said. "Now go away or I'll call the cops."

"Go ahead and call. I'll wait," Sperry said as he finally showed some ID to the young law student. "Perhaps they'll send Detectives Thomas and Palmer. Of course, they'll be coming anyway, as soon as they find that you lied to them. You'd better talk to me if you know what's good for you."

"Go away," Martin said, his voice getting high and pinched. "I don't have to talk to you."

"Actually, you should. You've involved yourself in the case of Jennifer Sterling's death, and if not before, you'll be talking on the witness stand at Rob's preliminary hearing, which is just a few days away."

The pressure against the door eased up, and Sperry shoved. Martin stumbled back and the door flew open. At the same time, Sperry's mouth fell open as he found himself staring at a life-size picture of Jennifer Sterling on the far wall. A black X had been drawn through her face. Before Martin could recover, Sperry stepped inside. There were more pictures on the wall of the small studio apartment. All were various poses of the former Miss Utah. And each had a black X drawn through her face.

Indeed, Sperry had been right. A lot could be learned about a man from where he lived. But this was not what he'd had in mind. Martin began to recover and rushed toward Sperry, his chubby arms churning. Sperry simply stepped aside and threw a brawny arm around Martin's neck. The young man struggled briefly, but he was no match for the veteran detective.

Once Martin was subdued, Sperry called Haley's office. As soon as the call had been transferred and her voice came on the line, Sperry said, "Miss Gordon, I'm at the apartment of Martin Ligorni. I think it would be good if you and your detectives came here at once. Mr. Ligorni may have something to tell you." He gave her the address.

"I'll be right there," she promised.

"We'll be waiting."

* * *

Haley dialed Sergeant Thomas's cell phone. When he answered, she said, "Meet me at Martin Ligorni's apartment." She passed on the address. Then she added. "I'm on my way there now."

"But we're about to talk to someone we think can help us discover who was behind the threat against you," he said. "Can Ligorni wait?"

Haley was suddenly torn. She had no idea what she was going to learn at Martin Ligorni's apartment, but if the detectives were in fact close to finding out who was threatening her and why, that was critical.

She made a quick decision. "I'll go to Ligorni's myself and see what Detective Collier wants," she said to Rex.

"Collier!" Sergeant Thomas snorted. "He's working for the other side, Counselor, or have you forgotten which side is which?"

"We are after the truth, Sergeant," she said coldly. "And don't you forget it. I'll be in touch."

Haley was so angry that she didn't even bother calling Sergeant Thomas back when she found another note on her windshield. She snatched it off, whipped it open and read,

Wake up, lady. You're being dumb.

She shuddered. Haley glanced nervously around her, then opened her car door, threw the note on the seat, and climbed in. Angry, scared, and determined, she tore her way through city traffic, determined to get to Kearns as quickly as she could.

* * *

Rex Thomas was also upset. He couldn't imagine what Haley Gordon was up to. She had no business talking to Sperry Collier. He'd been an excellent detective in his day, but he was working for the wrong people now as far as Rex was concerned. And that made anything he dug up subject to question. He already knew what Martin Ligorni had to say, and though it was weak, when coupled with Ann Denton's story it did provide something of a motive for the prosecution to use against Rob. Then he had a troubling thought and wondered if Haley Gordon was giving in to the threat. Was she trying to discredit her own case? That was something to think about.

In the meantime, he and Kurt were pulling up outside a house in south Salt Lake. He didn't share his concerns with his partner. That could wait. They had a man to talk to who might know something about the note to Haley. It was critical they find who was trying to undercut the prosecution, especially now that Haley seemed to be caving in herself.

It had taken all day and a number of interviews with different informants before they'd found anything. But when they did, it had sounded promising. The man who opened the door must have been expecting a friend, because as soon as he saw Rex with the shield in his hand, he tried to shut it. But Rex had already seen a large bong just ten feet inside the door, and he wasn't about to step back. He now had probable cause to enter. He heard the back door bang and shouted to his partner, "Cover the back!"

Ten minutes later, other officers were on the scene and both suspects were in custody. Later, after only a cursory search of those areas in plain view, enough heroin, cocaine, marijuana, and methamphetamine were found to bring felony charges against the pair. Rex saw to it that the process was underway to obtain a search warrant for the rest of the house and that the two men were off to jail. Then he said to his partner, "These two won't be going anywhere for a while, and we can get back to them later. It should be easier to make them talk now that we have something to charge them with. I think we better get out to Martin Ligorni's house and find out what our prosecutor is up to."

When they arrived at the law student's apartment, they found Haley, Sperry Collier, and Martin Ligorni just leaving the apartment. The relief on Haley's face was clear when she spotted the pair of officers. She was obviously under a great deal of stress, and Rex felt sorry for her, but he still wondered what she was doing here.

"You need to take a look inside this man's apartment," Haley said in greeting the two.

Rex looked at Martin. "Any objections?" he asked.

A much subdued Martin simply mumbled, "Go ahead. I haven't committed any crimes."

What Sergeant Thomas and Detective Palmer saw moments later gave them both the chills. "This is but the tip of the iceberg," Haley said after they'd both looked closely at the pictures of Jennifer Sterling plastered all over Martin's studio apartment.

She led them into his bathroom where there were more, then asked Martin to show them what he had stored in various drawers in the tiny apartment. A few minutes later, they loaded a whining Martin into their car. Detective Palmer got in with him. Sergeant Thomas closed the door and led Haley and Sperry a few steps away, out of earshot. "We'll question him when we get him to the office. In the meantime, we'll have someone come and take pictures of this place." He then turned to Detective Collier. "Thanks Sperry. This case has suddenly taken on a whole new look. If you'd like to be there when we question this worm, you're more than welcome."

Sperry didn't hesitate. He was almost certain that Martin Ligorni had a lot of explaining to do, and in the explaining, Rob Sterling could very well be cleared of murder. Ligorni might have had a motive—a much stronger one than anything the prosecution had against Rob and he knew Haley Gordon realized that. He also felt confident that both detectives also realized they practically had a new investigation on their hands.

Before Rex Thomas returned to his car, Haley said, "I got another note. I'm afraid I wasn't too careful with it, but I suppose you'd better take it."

Rex just shook his head as he read the latest note. "We've got two more suspects at the jail waiting to be questioned. We may soon learn a lot more about this," he said, waving the note toward her. Then he explained what had happened earlier, and Haley actually found herself breathing a sigh of relief. The threat against her life had hung over her like a cloud, hampering her ability to think clearly. If they could arrest the person behind that, she could get on with her work without all the worry.

Haley even allowed herself to hope that Martin would confess to the murder and that she would be relieved of the task of proving the guilt of a man whose guilt she doubted.

* * *

Earlier that day an investigator from the Office of Professional Conduct found something that caused Raul Garcia to slump in his chair and bury his face in his hands. Raul's devoted secretary had burst into tears.

"And you both still maintain you've never handled a case for one José Ramirez?" the investigator asked smugly as he clung possessively to a file he'd retrieved from one of their filing cabinets.

"It can't be," the secretary moaned. "It just can't be."

"But the social security number, the address, the birth date, and the telephone number of Mr. Ramirez are all right here in this file."

Raul looked up. "Would you please be more careful about fingerprints. You're contaminating evidence, you know."

"Of course," he said curtly. "We'll want to make sure none of yours are smudged, or those of this young woman."

"I can assure you, ours won't be there. We've never seen that file before," Raul insisted hopelessly.

"I will, of course, need to take this file," the man said.

"We would like a copy first," Raul said forcefully. "I'd like the chance to study this. It's obviously been planted here."

The investigator laughed. "Good try," he said. "We already know there's an electronic file as well, and it required a password to create that information."

Raul knew all that, as did his secretary. He also knew that he had never met José Ramirez and that the man had never been his client. He pulled on a pair of surgical gloves and handed his secretary and the investigator a pair also. For the next few minutes they copied all the documents in the file.

Raul noted some interesting things, but he decided he'd already said too much. So he didn't point out that there were no handwritten documents in the file. That was unheard of in his office. He always took notes, and he always included them in the client's file. He also noted that nothing bore his signature. That too was unusual. But he'd save that information for later.

"I'll need a copy of the electronic file as well," the investigator said.

Raul nodded his consent, and his secretary quickly copied the file to a disk and handed it over.

After the investigator left, Raul turned to his secretary. "We've had a break-in here. Someone figured out your password, and someone took the time to create these files."

He glanced at the windows. "It had to have taken place at night, and whoever did it would have closed the blinds in the outer office, shut the door to your office, and turned on equipment. There could well be prints all over the room. We need to have this place processed, but I don't suppose the police will be very likely to do it. We're not going to get a lot of sympathy right now."

"Raul, what's going on here?" the secretary asked. "Why would anyone go to so much trouble to get your license withdrawn? Who's behind this?"

"I have a pretty good idea," he said, "but until I have proof, I'd better not say. Now, let's see if we can get Sperry Collier to come over. He should be able to check the place for fingerprints."

Raul dialed the number of the investigator's cell phone and got no response. "He must have his phone turned off," he said. Then he tried the office. When Sperry's secretary answered, Raul asked her where Sperry was.

"He's with those two detectives that are working for Haley Gordon," she said. "They're involved in some interviews at the jail and will be for some time I suspect."

"Who are they interviewing?" Raul asked.

"I don't know, but it has to do with the Rob Sterling matter," she told him.

Raul glanced at his watch. It was getting late. "Tell him I called and that I'll need to have him come tomorrow and fingerprint my office."

"I don't know if he does that kind of work," she said.

"Well, give him the message. It needs to be done. Maybe he can help me figure out who can do it if he can't."

After hanging up, Raul said to his secretary, "Let's lock up and leave everything like it is. I don't want to mess up any evidence. We don't have any cases that can't wait until after we get the place dusted for prints."

"Okay, I'll log off my computer," she said.

"Do that," he agreed, "but first, I'd like you to back up all the files onto CDs and take them with you. And I'll also take this file home," he added, showing her the one they'd just copied. "There are a lot of problems with it, and I'd like time to really look it over closely."

"But why copy everything? I've already got it all backed up," she said.

"Of course you do," he said sheepishly. "Just take the CDs home, then, or better yet, I will." The young woman looked at him like he'd lost his mind. "I know," he said. "It sounds silly, but if someone could get in here once and break into our computer, they could do it again. It's not likely, but just in case, I'd like the backup record out of here."

As one further precaution, Raul took several files out of one of the filing cabinets. "I think I'll take a few of these home," he said. "I'd just like to make a few comparisons tonight with this one."

* * *

Martin Ligorni wouldn't budge on his testimony, which was that he didn't know anything about the murder of Jennifer Sterling, although he did admit that he'd been in love with her for years and that it was unfair that Rob had taken her away from him. His obsession was disturbing to the officers. He'd kept every picture and every article about the former Miss Utah that he'd ever found. They dated back to when the two of them had gone to high school together.

It was significant to the officers that Martin had developed such hatred toward Rob Sterling. If Martin was going to murder someone, the most likely choice for a sick mind like his would have been Rob Sterling, not the woman he professed to love. And yet they couldn't overlook him. It was possible that he might have gotten angry and shot her just to keep Rob from having her or something deranged like that.

When they asked Martin why he'd put a black X on the face of every one of the dozens of photos he had, he'd replied in a choked voice, "Because she's dead." To him that was logical. It was also more evidence of a potential mental imbalance.

He also stuck to his story that he'd seen Jennifer in the Ruby River Steakhouse and that it had not been Rob with her. "I'd know her husband anywhere," he'd insisted, which made sense. Yet it wasn't in line with what the witnesses at the steakhouse remembered.

Sperry kept his feelings to himself, but he was convinced that there was something Martin was hiding, something important. He made a mental note to pursue that further.

The deputies finally gave up on Martin Ligorni and turned their attention to the men they'd arrested for drug offenses. Things went a little better there. Besides a large amount of drugs, the police, when executing the search warrant that evening, had found the magazine that had once contained the words and letters that were used to fashion the threatening note to Haley Gordon. One of the men admitted to being the author of the first letter when his prints were found plastered all over the magazine.

Sergeant Thomas then pressed him about why he'd sent the letter. "Do you know Rob Sterling?" he asked.

"No," was the reply.

"Then why did you threaten Miss Gordon? Were you paid to do it?" Rex asked.

"Yes."

"By who?"

"I don't know," the suspect answered. "I never met the guy. We only talked on the phone and he left the money for me in my car."

"So you don't know who you were working for?" Rex Thomas asked.

"I didn't say that," the suspect said. "I only told you that I didn't meet the man that contacted me and delivered my money. He told me who he was working for."

"And who was that?" Rex asked.

Before the answer was made, Sperry Collier knew what it would be.

"An inmate in the jail. Rob Sterling."

"And you'll testify to that?" Sergeant Thomas asked.

"I guess I'll have to now," was the answer.

"And Rob Sterling is also the person who wanted you to continue to leave threatening notes where Miss Gordon would find them?" Rex asked.

"I don't know anything about any other notes," was the response.

"You mean to tell me you didn't throw a rock through her window with a note attached to it?"

"Nope, not me."

The two officers exchanged glances with Detective Collier. "That'll be easy enough to prove," Detective Palmer said. "We'll simply take handwriting samples and have them compared at the lab."

"Take them," the suspect said. "I'm telling you the truth. I've told you everything I've done."

And with a sinking heart, but renewed determination, Detective Collier believed the suspect had spoken what he believed was the truth. What Sperry didn't believe was that Rob Sterling was the silent man behind the whole plot. But it was apparent that the deputies believed Rob was their man, and that part of their investigation was now back on track.

* * *

Haley got home just after dark. She had just stuck her key in the lock when she noticed a movement on the street. There was a man standing in the shadows. He was watching her. She was sure of it and she began to tremble. The men Rex and Kurt were questioning at the jail were both dark-complected, but the man she'd become convinced was stalking her was even darker than that.

She entered her door. The mail was on the floor where it had landed after the postman had pushed it through her mail slot. She shut the door and then bent to pick up the mail. She froze when she saw that the top piece of mail was not mail at all. It was another note.

Her hands were shaking so badly she could hardly pick it up. She didn't even attempt to shake it open until she'd sat down at her kitchen table. When she did, the note was scrawled in what was now familiar handwriting. It read,

Lady, you don't learn so good. Do you want to die?

Haley called Rex's cell phone. He answered at once. "Detective Thomas," Haley said quickly, knowing that she couldn't disguise the fear in her voice, and not even trying, "there's someone watching me. And there was another note stuffed through my mail slot today."

"What did the note say?" Rex asked.

She read it, and he said, "Stay put. I'm coming over."

* * *

That night there was a fire in another part of town. It destroyed part of an office complex. All of the offices suffered some damage, but only one was a complete loss. It was the law office of Raul Garcia.

CHAPTER TEN

Word of the office-complex fire spread quickly. Haley heard about it when she entered her office at eight, but she was so upset she didn't make the connection. She'd slept reasonably well during the night, but once again she was shaken when she found a sheet of paper on the driver's seat of her car. She knew she'd locked the car, and it was still locked when she went to get in it that morning. Someone had somehow broken in, left the note, and locked it behind them.

She'd thought about calling the police, but decided against it. Whoever was doing this to her was too smart to leave prints. Sergeant Thomas had already checked other notes, and they were clean. This note was the shortest she'd received, but it added to her growing apprehension. It said simply,

> *I'm here lady.*

Haley, after hearing from one of the secretaries about the fire, dismissed it from her mind, entered her office, shut the door, sat at her desk, and silently sobbed. Then she took a moment to pray. She'd found great comfort in prayer over the past couple of years, and today was no exception. She soon felt better and began to quickly scan her mail. She hadn't finished it before her secretary announced that she had a visitor.

"Good morning," an extremely attractive woman of about thirty-five said as she entered Haley's office and extended her hand. "I'm Trista Zippeta."

"Haley Gordon. How can I help you this morning?" Haley asked.

"I'm sorry I didn't come sooner," the woman said as she invited herself to a chair and sat down. "There's something I must tell you."

Haley sat down herself, hoping whatever this was wouldn't take long, but fearing it would. She looked directly at Trista. She was a beautiful creature in an artificial sort of way, with long, dark eyelashes, short black hair, and purple fingernails an inch long. "What is this about?" Haley asked as she tried to make eye contact with a pair of the darkest green eyes she'd ever seen. But Trista's eyes kept moving, never for a moment settling on Haley's face.

"This is a terrible thing," the woman finally began, her eyes roving in sharp jerks about the office. Haley said nothing, hoping the woman would say whatever she had on her mind and leave. She went on, "Miss Gordon, my ex-husband was seeing Rob Sterling's wife before her death."

Haley sat up sharply. "Do you have proof?" she asked, trying to hide her shock.

"Of course I do," Trista said as her eyes continued to flit about the room. "Rob knew too."

"Okay," Haley said, trying to catch her breath at this startling news. "What proof do you have? I mean, I'll need testimony in court from you, so you'll need to be specific with me now."

"My ex admitted it to me," Trista said.

"That seems a little strange," Haley commented, wondering how much of this woman's words might actually hold some truth.

"It's true," Trista said, not a flicker of annoyance over Haley's doubt showing on her face or in her voice. "We have that kind of relationship. I tell him who I'm dating, and he does the same with me. We're still friends actually. We just couldn't live together."

Haley supposed that could be true. She made a note on her yellow pad as Trista continued. "As for Rob, he knew all right. I told him. And if he says he doesn't remember me, he's lying."

"You told him yourself?" Haley asked, astonished again. "Why would you bother to do that if you and your ex-husband have such an open relationship?"

"Because Jennifer Sterling was a married woman. I don't care who he sees as long as they're single. But married women, that's where I draw the line," the woman said indignantly. "It's just not right."

"It's certainly not," Haley agreed. "How did Mr. Sterling react to what you told him?"

"Oh, he was murderous!" Trista said. "I've never seen anyone so angry. I was afraid he might hurt my ex, and I was wishing I hadn't said anything then."

Haley waited as the green eyes flicked past her face. She was getting annoyed. The lines about Rob were *too* perfect. But she held her tongue. Someone with an agenda may have penned the woman's script. Finally, Trista said, "I was actually relieved when I figured out that his anger was toward his wife, not my ex. He said something quite terrible about his wife and how she just didn't seem content with him anymore."

"He said that?" Haley asked.

"Oh, yes, and much more. He told me he'd stop her from running around if it was the last thing he ever did. He assured me that I needn't worry about Jake seeing his Jennifer anymore. He said he'd take care of the problem once and for all."

Haley waited again, resisting the urge to roll her eyeballs. When Trista seemed to have nothing more to say, she finally asked, "Is there anything else?"

"No, nothing. But I'll testify to what Rob said. And my ex will testify too. He's so angry at Rob for murdering that poor little girl," Trista said, her long lashes closing slowly over her flickering eyes as if in pain. "It's such a terrible thing."

"I'll need your address, the spelling of your name, your ex-husband's name, his address, and so forth," Haley said.

She got it all and the vixen rose to her feet and glided from the room, leaving only the strong scent of her perfume in her wake. *She'd be a terrible witness,* Haley thought, *but if she's telling the truth, a very strong motive has been revealed.* It should be the kind of thing that would make a prosecutor sing with joy, but Haley felt no joy, only loss and confusion. She had to talk with Jake Zippeta. No, she'd send Sergeant Thomas to talk to him, and she'd do it now.

She called Rex's cell number. He answered immediately. "Haley," he said, "can you believe that about Raul Garcia's office?"

"What about it?" she asked. Then it hit her. *The fire.* "Oh, no, was his one of those that burned?" she asked.

"More than that, I'm afraid," Rex said. "It appears the fire started in his office. It's a total loss."

Haley moaned. It was too much. Anyone connected with this case was being hurt. She said so to Rex. "I'm connected and I'm fine," he countered, "and so's my partner. And Dan Smathers hasn't been hurt. Anyway, it appears that Raul may have started the fire himself."

"No!" Haley protested. "Why would he do that?"

"It's quite logical really," Sergeant Thomas said. "The Office of Professional Conduct sent a man to look into the complaint lodged against Raul. He found the file that Raul said didn't exist. Raul claims now that he wanted the place fingerprinted, although he never called the police and made such a request."

"Why would he want it fingerprinted?" Haley asked, her mind literally whirling.

"Raul claims that someone broke in and planted evidence," Rex explained. "That's not very likely, but he'd like us to believe it."

"At this point I think there isn't such a thing as *unlikely,*" Haley said sourly. Far too many bizarre things were occurring.

"Raul might have all the reason in the world to be lying. The file that he claimed never existed was found in his office. So he now conveniently insists that someone burned his office so a close examination and collection of evidence couldn't happen."

"That makes sense," Haley said.

"Yes, but let me tell you what makes more sense," Rex countered. "Raul might have burned it himself so he could claim someone didn't want evidence found that would back up his story. The arson investigation team found that the fire was started with gasoline that was poured inside the office. Yet the outside door was locked when the fire actually began. The remnants of the lock prove that. They also found remnants of a simple fuse, the kind used to light dynamite, that had been lit and led to where the gasoline had been poured on the floor. It would have given Raul time to leave and lock the door behind him before the fire started. They're talking about charging him with arson."

"The district attorney's office will have to decide that," Haley reminded him sternly. "I think this needs to be looked into very carefully."

"Whose side are you on?" Rex suddenly asked Haley, a touch of anger in his voice.

She gripped the phone then said, "I'm on the side of truth, Sergeant, always the side of truth. And that's where you should be. Now, let's get to why I called you. There's something I need you to do."

She went on and explained about Trista and Jake Zippeta. "Would you find Jake and get a statement from him? This could be crucial," she concluded.

"Yeah, sure," Rex said slowly. "Hey, Miss Gordon, I'm sorry. I was out of line just now. You're right, it's truth we want, no matter how it affects our case. You've obviously just found the one piece of evidence that could nail this case together for us. I judged you unfairly."

"It's okay," Haley said, but she didn't believe this would nail anything together. Trista simply wasn't believable. But again, what motive would she have for lying about her ex-husband and Jennifer Sterling? *What does she have to gain?* Haley wondered, tapping her pencil on her desk.

An hour later, William Montgomery summoned Haley to his office. "I want a complete rundown on how your case is coming right now," he said in a businesslike tone. "I'm hearing that you may not be doing too well, and I'm concerned."

"I'm working as hard as I can," she said defensively. "This is a complex case, and all the things that are going on aren't making it any easier. But I'm giving it the best I have."

"Good girl, Haley. Now don't worry about that threat," he said, obviously relieved.

"Threats," she corrected him mildly.

"There have been more?" the district attorney asked.

Haley then revealed to him the series of notes that followed the one thrown with a rock through her window. As she spoke he watched her with what actually looked like sympathy. When she finished, he said, "I'm so sorry, Haley. Maybe I should take you off the case."

That was not what she wanted at this point. Give this case to the wrong prosecutor and Rob Sterling could be convicted even though he might well be innocent. She had to—for Rob's sake and for the sake of the truth—stay a part of this case.

"That won't be necessary, Mr. Montgomery," she said. "I can handle it."

"That's the way. This is all bluff, this note stuff. Just Rob Sterling trying to warn you off. You've got him running scared. Don't let it worry you, Haley. Just go after him for all you're worth. Now tell me exactly what we have to date."

Haley walked him through the evidence, keeping her opinions to herself. His heavy eyebrows dipped ominously when she told him about the law student, Martin Ligorni. Then they raised when she told him the young man's story. "Sick kid," he said. "But obviously we can forget about him. He has nothing to do with the case."

Haley didn't agree, although she wasn't sure what it was that still bothered her about Martin Ligorni. She continued with her narration, and Montgomery was almost ecstatic when she got to the latest developments, the story told her by Trista Zippeta. "That's the clincher," Montgomery said with a clenched fist and a grin. "You're doing good work."

She stood to leave, but he stopped her when he said, "Too bad about that poor fool Raul Garcia. Makes you wonder how a man like that ever passed the bar exam. We'll probably be filing arson charges against him before the day's over."

Haley held her breath, afraid to say a word for fear it would be the wrong thing and anger the district attorney. She had to stay on this case no matter what. He seemed not to notice anything amiss in her reaction however, and he said, "I'll be publicly announcing my candidacy for attorney general at a press conference tomorrow. I'm going to talk about how my office fights crime with every tool at our disposal. The case against Rob Sterling is proof that we go after anyone who breaks the law—no matter who they are."

Haley got the point. She was sickened by the whole thing. To her the truth was what mattered, and that was what she intended to ferret out, despite the threats against her and despite the jeopardy it might place her career in.

The next summons Haley received was from the office of Judge James F. Horton. It came just before noon by way of a clerk of his court. Haley was to be in his courtroom at one o'clock sharp. When she asked the clerk what it was about, she was told that the defense had a motion to make; she was to be there since she was the prosecutor. Haley wondered what Dan Smathers was up to now. She trusted him like she trusted a snake.

However, when the appointed hour rolled around, she was sitting at the prosecution table across from Dan Smathers. She leaned over and whispered to him, "What's this all about, Dan?"

He shrugged his shoulders. To her surprise, he said, "I have no idea. The judge just told me to be here. I thought you were behind it."

A moment later, Rob Sterling was brought into the room and led to the defense table where he was seated beside Dan. Rob ignored Dan and looked over at Haley, nodding an unemotional acknowledgment of her presence. His eyes stayed on hers for several seconds. A sadness that wrenched her heart was revealed in his intelligent green eyes. Strangely, her heart beat faster. Then a smile that did not extend to his eyes crossed his face ever so briefly and he looked away.

Any doubts that might have been planted by Trista Zippeta vanished. Haley had just looked into the eyes of an innocent man. She knew it in her heart. She'd prayed, as Rob's students had asked, and what she felt now was the Spirit. She was sure of it. All the things that were happening around her, to her, to Raul, were being orchestrated by someone who was both unethical and brilliant. She suddenly felt very small and very weak, almost swallowed up in events she could not control but which someone else both could and was. She offered a silent prayer for strength.

The judge entered and they all stood. He sat and they all sat. Then, without preamble, he said, "Mr. Sterling, you have made a most serious and foolish request of this court in the form of a letter that came today. Would you like to explain?"

Haley looked over at Dan who was clearly ignorant of what his client had requested of the judge. Rob spoke clearly, his voice strong and determined. She watched him, his broad shoulders squared, his strong, square chin held high.

"Your Honor," he began. "I feel that it would be in my best interest to represent myself in this case. And I know that I have that right."

"This is foolishness, Mr. Sterling. A year of law school doesn't qualify you for even a simple case, let alone one as complex and serious as your own," Judge Horton said sternly. "I have provided you with the best defense counsel this state has to offer for a case such as yours. You should be grateful."

"I am grateful to you," Rob said with a graciousness that surprised Haley almost as much as his request. "But I don't believe that Mr. Smathers has my best interest at heart. However, I do. And I insist that I defend myself."

The judge's stern eyes turned slightly and caught Dan's. "Mr. Smathers, have you done anything to undermine your standing with this defendant?"

"I have not," Dan lied with a straight face. "I'm working very hard, just as you asked. I didn't want the case, as you well remember, Your Honor, but now that I've got it, I think I should continue. Mr. Sterling needs me; he just doesn't understand the difficulties that come with a case of this magnitude like I do."

"I agree, Counselor," the judge said.

Once again his gaze shifted. "Mr. Sterling, I think you should reconsider your request. Dan Smathers will give you the best defense you can possibly get."

"With all due respect, Your Honor," Rob replied, "this is not a request. It's my right. I will defend myself. I wanted Raul Garcia, but someone has succeeded in discrediting him. He would have done a good job for me, but absent him, I'm my own next choice—incompetent as I may be."

Haley watched Rob in fascination. He was angry; she could see it in the way the veins stood out in his neck, and in the set of his jaw. But he was also in complete control of himself. She couldn't help but admire him. And she also couldn't help but wonder why Rob hadn't told the judge of the plea offer Dan made without his consent. Maybe he just didn't want to stir up more controversy at the moment. She didn't blame him if that were the case.

The judge tried once more. When Rob didn't relent, Judge Horton said, "Very well, you may represent yourself." It was clear he was perturbed. "But you will be assisted by Mr. Smathers," he finished. "Mr. Smathers, you are assigned as backup counsel. You are to advise him and do everything you would ordinarily do, but the final word in how his defense is presented is up to Mr. Sterling." It was obvious Judge Horton was finished with the nonsense before him and intended to get on with his day. "And Mr. Sterling, I would strongly suggest you listen to Mr. Smathers." The judge rapped his gavel, stood, and hurried out so fast the bailiff barely had time to request everyone stand.

After he was gone, Dan said to Rob, "There's an old saying: 'He who represents himself has a fool for a client.' And you are the biggest fool I've ever met. However, I'll do as the court has ordered. You would do well to take my advice when I give it." He turned to Haley. "Looks like you've been given a break, Miss Gordon. You could never win this one against me. And in the end, I'll see that you lose anyway." Then he left, the tension in the room palpably lifting.

Haley had never seen such arrogance. Her eyes again met Rob's, and something passed between them, a subtle but warm emotion. She felt a twist in her gut and a wrenching of her heart. He was innocent—she knew it. And she would proceed until his innocence could be established. She felt so sorry for him. She tried to control her feelings as she met his gaze. There was goodness there, intelligence, and courage. She wanted to help him. She had to help him.

She rose, picked up her briefcase, which had remained closed during the length of the short hearing, and headed for the door. She looked back once more before she walked through it. Rob was on his feet, a deputy at each arm. He glanced at her, smiled once more, another mirthless smile, and turned away. She felt like the weight of the world was on her shoulders. And indeed it was. His life was in her hands. She knew it, and she knew he knew it. And somehow, she felt that was exactly what Rob Sterling wanted.

CHAPTER ELEVEN

Sea-blue eyes were intriguing to Haley. They always had been. Perhaps it was because the reflected ones she'd looked into every day of her life were so dark, almost black. Haley had her mother's eyes, which she was very familiar with. Her father, whom she'd never had much of a relationship with, was blue-eyed, and the memory of his eyes had always haunted her.

This evening, sitting across from Nat Turley in another nice restaurant, she couldn't keep her eyes from swimming in those beautiful blue eyes of his. And he seemed equally fascinated by her dark ones. They conversed lazily, and Haley found herself relaxing with Nat in a way she never had on any other date. And this was only their second time out. She hoped there would be more.

Even when talk slowly turned to her difficult prosecution of the Sterling case, she felt at ease at first. But she began to stiffen when Nat's questions started to unearth more than her surface feelings about the case. He was strangely persistent, but his concern seemed sincere, and Haley felt it a strange coincidence that such a wonderful man should so suddenly come into her life right when she was involved in the most stressful work she'd ever had and needed the support. A thought suddenly troubled her. She'd always been suspicious of coincidences. After a while, she'd usually back off and attempt to find a reason for one. More often than not, especially in her work as a prosecutor, a reason would emerge, and then it was coincidence no longer.

But she couldn't imagine that Nat entering her life at this time was anything other than a coincidence. Well, a blessing perhaps, for blessings, since she'd joined the Church, were something that explained certain kinds of coincidences and made them acceptable. Yes, he seemed like a blessing right now, as he certainly had the ability to take her mind off her worries. But talking with him about Rob Sterling's prosecution brought her back to the stress she was going through. She preferred not to have to deal with that stress while they were together. Surely he'd understand.

"Let's not talk about my work, Nat," she said. "I'd rather not think about it tonight. It's so good of you to give me a break from my worries."

There was only the slightest flicker of emotion across his face before he spoke, and she figured the passing expression to be of no significance. "Whatever you like, Haley," he said. "I guess I shouldn't let my curiosity get in the way. I enjoy the work I do, but it doesn't have the same glamour and excitement that yours does."

"I don't know if I'd call it glamorous right now," she said. "It's more like frightening."

"Haley," Nat said, his wonderful blue eyes growing wide with concern, "Has something else happened?"

She reached across the table and put a hand over his. "Let's not talk about it," she said. "It's really no big deal."

"But I'm concerned about you, Haley," he said. "I enjoy your company, and I was hoping we could see a lot more of each other. And I . . . well . . . I couldn't stand it if you got hurt."

"I'll be okay," she said. "It's all bluff. And I won't let it get to me." She knew she was sounding much tougher than she felt, but she wanted to get off the subject now. Fears that had receded this past hour with Nat were rapidly resurfacing. "Please, let's talk about something else."

Haley was mildly annoyed when Nat still persisted. "Perhaps you should get off this case," he suggested.

"That's what my stalker wants," she said firmly. "And I won't do it."

"But the threats," he reminded her.

"Please," she begged. *Why won't he let the subject drop?* she wondered.

"Maybe one of the men in the office would be less vulnerable to the kind of intimidation—" Nat didn't finish his sentence when he realized that it was anger that was flashing from those beautiful dark eyes across the table. Haley jerked her hand back, knocking a glass of water over.

Abruptly, she stood as tears filled her eyes. She looked as though she was about to walk out on him, and he was suddenly angry at his own stupid persistence. His first response was guilt and concern for her feelings. But his second was of the district attorney. He'd never learn anything about how she really felt about her case if she refused to see him again. He had to calm her down. "Hey, Haley," he said softly, standing up beside her. "I'm sorry, I didn't mean to be so persistent. But I worry about you."

"Please don't," she said sharply. "I need to visit the ladies' room. I'll be back." She strode off without another word.

Nat sat down and began sopping up the water, hoping she really would come back. He had her glass filled again and then sat thinking as he waited. He realized that he did have something substantial to report to William Montgomery the next morning. Haley, he was quite certain, was deeply shaken by the threats on her life. She'd spoken of bluff, but she was the one bluffing. She couldn't possibly be up to the quality of prosecution that William was expecting of her. He wondered if he should tell the district attorney and was concerned over what that would do to Haley. At the same time, William had reminded him that there was an important place for a sharp attorney with his experience and skills in the attorney general's office. Not everything in the attorney general's office had to do with criminal law; there was a place for good business attorneys, and the idea appealed to Nat. It hadn't exactly been an offer of a job, but it was clear that William was more or less making a promise, *if* Nat delivered as expected now.

A few minutes later, Haley appeared, and Nat stood up, watching her as she approached. To his surprise, he felt something flutter inside, and it was accompanied by a shortness of breath. She was a stunningly beautiful woman. She was also intelligent and gentle and brave . . . Suddenly he realized that she actually did mean something to him. He had in reality worried about her these past few days, but it had been sort of paternal, because he knew she was a good person and vulnerable. And she was also a woman, and he despised men who hurt women. Nat felt guilty again, more guilty than he had when he'd last spoken to William. Now, as he smiled at Haley and she returned his smile, he had to admit that he'd been hurting her, and further, that he cared about what happened to her for reasons he never suspected would come into play when William first called him and asked for a favor.

"I'm sorry," he said genuinely, even as he knew that he still had to carry out his promise to the district attorney. There was so much at stake. His future. Her safety. William's future. Nat really was sorry he'd hurt her, and in a way, he was sorry he'd made the promise he had to William. And yet in another way, he was glad he had. Someone needed to look out for this beautiful lady.

Haley sensed only the sincerity of his apology. "No, I'm sorry," she told him. "I'm way too sensitive. And I'm ready to finish eating," she added, flashing him a bright smile. "And thanks for cleaning up the mess I made. I do embarrassing things like that from time to time."

She'd thought about her behavior as she paced the ladies' room floor. She had no right to expect him not to wonder and worry. And once again she'd found that it felt good, once she thought through things, to have a man actually care so much about her feelings and her safety. She hoped she hadn't destroyed what could have been a beautiful relationship with a good man. She hadn't had many opportunities like this with a man of his character, and she was actually grateful for this chance. She didn't want to blow it.

The same easy atmosphere was impossible to restore during the rest of the meal, but it came close. Nat didn't say one more word about Haley's work or the danger she was in. And they lingered at the table for a long time after the meal was over. Later, after arriving in front of her apartment, Haley asked, "Are you in a hurry, Nat?"

"No, not at all," he replied.

"Could we just go for a walk?" she asked almost timidly. She was not at all ready to be alone again. And he was so comforting to be with. "It's such a beautiful night," she added. Indeed it was. It was cool but clear, and a full moon hung in the sky overhead. *Perhaps it's a sign, a romantic one,* she thought wistfully—though jokingly at the same time.

Nat took her hand in his as he helped her from his car. Without a word, they turned together and walked up the street. For over an hour they strolled. They spoke very little, each immersed in thought.

At one point they stopped at an intersection and she turned toward him, looking into his eyes dreamily. She couldn't see the blue in the subdued light of only the moon and a nearby streetlight, but she liked what she could see. His face was strong and handsome and caring. His blond hair was slightly disheveled. He put his arms around her and pulled her close. She put hers around him and laid her head against his shoulder. She felt so safe in his arms.

Nat hadn't intended to kiss Haley. Nor had Haley intended to kiss Nat. It just happened. But it lingered, and as it ended, she sank contentedly against his chest and felt even more sheltered. The light had changed, and it changed again, but they just stood there in silence until it shined green once more, then Haley pulled away reluctantly.

"Thanks, Nat," she said.

"Anytime," he responded, and despite the mission he was on, he knew that he meant it. Suddenly shame flooded over him.

But Haley was unaware of his shame. She walked close to him as they slowly covered the last few blocks back to her apartment. At the door, she sighed, hesitating to let go of his hand. Then, as naturally as before, he circled her waist with one arm, squeezed the hand he was holding, then circled her waist with the other. Again, he drew her to him, and their lips met, and Haley felt something inside of her that she'd never experienced before. It was good, and it was sweet. She closed her eyes as the kiss lingered.

When she finally opened them as their lips drew apart, she glanced beyond him.

The romantic haze she was looking through cleared and Haley could barely suppress a scream. There, across the street, standing in the dark shadow of a large elm was a large black man. There was no question that he was watching them. She stiffened and clung desperately to Nat. "Haley, what is it?" he asked in alarm.

"We're—we're being watched," she stammered.

Nat let go of her and spun around. As he did so, the man eased behind the tree. "Where?" he asked. "I don't see anyone."

Haley pointed. "He was beside that tree. He slipped behind it. He knows I saw him."

"Have you seen him before?" Nat demanded.

"Yes, at least I think so," she began.

But before she could tell him that she wasn't sure if it was the same man every time, Nat interrupted. "You think so?" he asked. "But you're not sure?"

"Someone has been watching me," she said firmly, feeling that he was doubting her. If only he'd turned quicker, or if she hadn't panicked giving away the fact that she'd spotted him. "I'm sorry, Nat. Maybe I'm just too jumpy."

"Let's go across the street and see," Nat suggested.

"No," she protested, instinctively drawing back toward her door while clinging tightly to Nat's arm.

"You stay, I'll be right back," he said, his eyes full of determination. Before she could protest further, Nat shook free of Haley's hands and whirled, darting down the sidewalk from her door and across the street. Haley stood frozen as he ran, praying that the man behind the tree wouldn't pull a knife or a gun.

Nat reached the tree, slowed down, approached it slowly, and spoke. "Whoever you are, come out where I can see you."

There was no answer. Nat suddenly didn't feel as brave as he had only moments before. But he knew Haley was watching him and what she thought of him had begun to matter, so he forced himself to walk around the tree, his fists balled up, ready to fight if he had to.

He didn't have to. There was no one there. Was Haley so shaken up she was seeing things? He began to wonder. But as he walked back toward her, he resolved not to say that to her. In reality, he'd taken his eyes off the tree for a few moments before running over. The man could have left in that time. *But still . . .*

Haley was tense as Nat took hold of her hand. "You shouldn't have done that, Nat," she scolded mildly. "He could have been armed."

"I doubt it. But you make sure your doors are locked. I think we scared him off though," Nat assured her. *If he was ever there,* he thought.

Haley was reluctant to let Nat leave. She knew the man was watching her, stalking her, threatening her. It was terrifying. For a few moments she continued to cling to him on the doorstep and tried to gain reassurance from his gaze. But finally he kissed her lightly on the forehead, let go of her hand, and said, "I'll stand here until you have your door locked."

"Thanks for everything, Nat," she said, her voice still unsteady. "I'm sorry I spoiled everything tonight. Will I see you again?"

"You'd better believe it," he said with a chuckle. "A herd of wild horses couldn't keep me away."

Feeling better, she let herself into her apartment, and after shutting the door and locking it, she moved to the window and watched him as he walked to his gold Jaguar. Her heart skipped lightly as he stopped after opening his door and waved to her. She waved back, and a moment later he drove away.

Another moment later, a dark man stepped from behind the elm tree and waved back at her. Haley nearly fainted. She realized he must have just gone behind the house across the street.

When she called the police moments later, they said they'd send a car around. She felt better after that, but if they didn't catch the man or put a stop to his behavior, she was going to have to move for a while.

* * *

Rob was sitting alone in his cell, reading, when a correctional officer walked toward him. Rob looked up. The man whispered. "Hey, Sterling, come here a minute."

Rob sat his book down and moved to the front of his cell, wondering what the man was being so secretive about. "What's up?" he asked.

"You didn't have to kill her," the man hissed softly. "You could have shared her first."

Rob would have punched the man if he could have done so. But he was standing too far back. Rob's fist was clenched, and his face was burning. The officer leaned forward, still out of the range of Rob's fist, and taunted him. "Yeah, that's it, Sterling. Try hitting an officer. That'll help your cause. You filthy scum."

Amazingly, Rob's anger actually began to subside at the taunting. This man was an idiot and an animal. But he clearly seemed to think that Rob was deserving of his insults. Rob turned away and went back to his book. The officer laughed softly. "Coward," he whispered.

Rob couldn't help but marvel at the man's ignorance. *Who's the coward here?* he thought. The officer hadn't even spoken loud enough for anyone to hear him. Of course, that was so he could deny it if it ever came up. *How could anyone be so heartless?* Rob wondered angrily.

Then he thought about Jennifer. No one knew how much he missed her. Nor did they know how he'd suspected her of being at least a little unfaithful to him. But he felt awful now that he'd been angry with her. He hadn't even kissed her that last day when he left early for school. *How can I ever forgive myself for that?* he reflected somberly.

He also had to admit that he'd continued to have doubts about her after her death. But he'd had a lot of time to think in jail, and he'd spent a great deal of it in prayer. He was no longer angry with her. A feeling of peace had come over him one night as he was praying about Jennifer. As he remembered it now, the same feeling again descended upon him. Whatever she might have done, he was convinced that she'd repented and that the Lord knew her mind. Somehow he felt secure about his eternal relationship with her. No one could take that away from him. No matter what else they did to him, they could never take his love for her, or the knowledge he now had of her love.

Rob began to read again and kept at it for several minutes. Then he stopped. His mind was no longer on his book. As he'd read, he'd really only been seeing words while his thoughts had returned to the correctional officer. And they were suspicious thoughts. Rob couldn't help but wonder if this man, and maybe others like him, were behind the beating he'd received.

Then an even worse thought occurred to him. Someone had been sending threats purported to have originated with him. *Could it be an officer?* he wondered. Was this man actually jealous of him? Rob had married a fairly well-known young woman, someone a lot of men might covet. Perhaps he'd just spoken to one who had, he concluded. Rob knew that there had to be a way to find out if this man was out to destroy his chance for a fair trial.

Rob laid his book down and began to think about other inmates he'd become acquainted with. Though his exposure to others was limited, he was not entirely isolated. And not all of the inmates had displayed animosity toward him. Perhaps one or two of them could be persuaded to be extra ears and eyes for him. He fell asleep that night thinking of who he might approach the next day.

As he slept he dreamed of the woman whose job it was to prosecute him. In his dream she was his greatest ally.

* * *

Haley's mind had been so active that she'd taken hours to get to sleep. She was both disturbed and elated; she'd found a man who was giving her a chance at a relationship she wanted more than she'd been willing to admit, but she was also both angry at and afraid of another man who continued to stalk her. When she had finally fallen asleep, she'd slept soundly, as she was exhausted. But now she was awakened by a faint tapping sound, and it took her a minute to orient herself.

The tapping had stopped. Then it started again. She looked toward the newly replaced window. A large black face leered at her through the glass. She fought a wave of dizziness and tried to get a better look as she slid her hand toward her phone. Then she realized the face was obscured by a clear nylon stocking. The nose was flattened, the eyes almost hidden, the long black hair flat and messy, the lips wide and flat and curved into a terrifying smile.

Then a hand came up. She flinched, but the man simply waved then ducked beneath the window and disappeared. *Where are the police when you need them?* she wondered as she first picked up the phone then set it back down. She was going to get a reputation if she wasn't careful. She'd already called once tonight. She slipped silently into her living room and parted the curtains she'd closed after seeing her stalker earlier. A police car cruised slowly by. She thought again about the phone, but didn't act on her thought. The man would be gone by now. They'd never be able to find him. He wasn't about to let himself get caught.

Feeling at least some security knowing there were police in the neighborhood, Haley returned to her bedroom. But she didn't lay down there. She simply drew her blinds, then gathered up her pillows and returned to her living room where she spent the rest of a long and sleepless night on her sofa.

CHAPTER TWELVE

When the phone rang Haley was just stepping out of the shower. She wrapped a towel around herself and hurried for the phone, glancing at a clock as she did so. She was a little late and hadn't had any breakfast yet. Maybe she'd have to skip it this morning, she thought as she picked up the phone.

She didn't even get to say hello. A raspy voice said, "Sleep well, pretty lady?" And the phone went dead.

Haley fell to the couch, tears rolling down her cheeks. For several minutes she huddled there, trying to get control of herself. She couldn't let this man, whoever he was, get to her. She had a job to do. But it was difficult this morning to get control as she was not only frightened, but physically and emotionally fatigued.

She must have sat there at least ten minutes when the phone rang again. She let it ring several times before she found the courage to pick it up, fearing it was her stalker. Finally, when it persisted, she answered. "Hello," she said in a voice that must have sounded exactly like she felt.

"Haley! What's the matter?"

Welcome relief washed over her. "Nat, I'm so glad it's you. I've had the most horrible night. And this morning's no better."

"I'm coming over," he said, knowing that would make him late for an appointment at his office. But he didn't care. He wanted to be with Haley.

"No, that's not necessary," Haley said. "Just hearing your voice has already helped."

"What happened?" he asked. "I can tell by your voice that something's wrong."

"I'll be fine," she said, not wanting to burden him with her troubles at the moment. She was just grateful to know he cared enough to call. She was already starting to get a grasp on things. "I've got to get to the office. Call me tonight, will you?" she asked.

"I'll do more than call," he promised. "I'll come by."

"Please do," she said.

"Are you sure you don't want me to come right now?" he asked.

She'd like nothing better, but she said, "Don't be silly. I'm fine, Nat. Thanks for calling. Your timing was great."

What did she mean by that? he wondered. "Haley, will you tell me about it tonight?" he asked.

"I will," she promised. She suddenly found she wanted to talk to Nat, to confide in him while being held securely in his arms. But for now she had to get to work and solve this case, and it had to be the best work she'd ever done as a prosecutor. Rob Sterling's life depended on her, ironic as that seemed. "Yes, I promise I will," she added.

"See you tonight then," Nat said cheerily. A moment later he hung up.

Haley hurried and finished getting ready for work. She drank a glass of juice, but skipped breakfast. Nat's call had made her feel secure. She was so grateful to him. This would be a productive day after all.

She rushed to her car and swung open the door. Haley stopped and stifled another scream. There on the seat, looking up at her, was an enlarged photo of her kissing Nat at the intersection several blocks away.

She hesitated, not wanting to even touch it, but she also didn't want to sit on it, so she took it gingerly by the edge and tossed it to the far side of the passenger seat, face-down. The back contained what was now a much-too-familiar scrawl of words. She forced herself to read them.

> *You are pretty when you sleep. But don't kiss no white man again.*

Haley shivered uncontrollably in the cool fall air as she started her engine. She offered a silent but desperate prayer for strength. Then as she began to drive off, something happened inside of her. The fear she'd been experiencing began to recede, and in its place came anger and determination. She would not be terrorized by this stalker, whoever he was, and she'd beat whoever he was working for.

She had a gun permit, and she knew how to use a pistol. She'd buy one today and carry it with her. She would not be defeated by terror. She could be as strong as any man William might hire in her place, she convinced herself. In her emotional high, she almost began to pity the man who was stalking her.

Only almost. Her fear had receded, but it was not entirely gone. And that was all right with Haley. A little fear would keep her cautious. She offered another silent prayer of thanks and continued toward the office with renewed confidence.

* * *

William Montgomery received a phone call at his office only moments after his arrival. He was later than usual: he'd spent several minutes at home grooming the speech he was giving today, announcing his candidacy. He answered the phone with a confident voice, as he was brimming with confidence today.

"Hello, William Montgomery speaking," he said.

"William, you sound fit and ready to announce," Nat Turley said.

"You bet I am," William said cheerfully. "Did you have a good time with Haley last night?"

If only you knew, Nat thought to himself. "She's a nice girl," he said to the district attorney.

"I know that," William said with a chuckle. "But is she still okay with the case?"

"She wouldn't talk about it," Nat said cautiously.

"But I asked you to get her to talk about it," the district attorney reminded Nat. "I have to know day by day if she's in control of the case. The moment it looks like she's not, I'll pull her off, as much as I hate to have to do that. Did you learn anything at all?"

"Yes," Nat said, still determined to proceed very carefully. "This business of the stalker has her very upset."

"So it's a stalker now?" the district attorney scoffed. "Isn't that a bit extreme?" He was beginning to doubt the stability of his young star prosecutor.

"Possibly," Nat said. "A guy keeps showing up, a black man. She's sure of that even though she's never gotten a good look at him."

"Do I need to pull her from the case?" William asked. "I can't let anything screw this one up for me."

Nat wanted to say yes, to get Haley off the case, to give her relief from the demons who were pursing her, yet he knew how terrible she would feel if that happened. His feelings for Haley were getting in the way of his task. He decided to stall. When it was totally clear to him that it was driving Haley over the edge, when he was sure she wasn't really being stalked, just imagining it, then he'd recommend she be replaced. But it would be for her sake, not William's.

Or, he reasoned, if Haley clearly displayed any feeling of doubt over Rob's guilt, as that was what the district attorney wanted to avoid, then he'd report that. "Leave her be for now," he said. "I'll be seeing her again tonight, and I think I can get her to open up to me. I'll call in the morning."

"You do that," William said.

It sounded more like an order than anything else, and Nat found himself wishing again that he'd never gotten himself into this position. It was so very awkward. "Good luck at your press conference," Nat said before he hung up.

William thanked him and cradled his phone in his hand, staring at it for a while before hanging up. He'd liked to have had a stronger assurance that Haley really did have things well in hand before the press conference. Perhaps he'd just chat with her himself once more. He asked his secretary to have her come to his office. While he was waiting, he looked over the newly prepared information that lay on his desk, awaiting his signature. He would announce it at the press conference. He was charging Rob Sterling with engaging in terroristic threats. Haley Gordon was the victim. He had enough proof now to make a case against Rob, and even though it wasn't nearly as serious an offense as murder, it still made a statement about how he ran his office.

Of course, he'd have to assign someone other than Haley to prosecute, but that was okay. This case could move much more quickly and a conviction could be on the books while the murder case was still moving forward.

He was expecting another typed information, bringing charges against Raul Garcia, to be on his desk in a few minutes. He'd have plenty of fresh evidence of his strong stand against crime to mention at the press conference. Even a fellow attorney wasn't exempt when he crossed over the line. Now Raul was facing arson charges.

Just then William's secretary announced that Haley had arrived. "Send her right in," he instructed.

Haley walked in, still angry and determined. William rose to greet her and sat right back down, signaling for her to do the same. "How are you this morning?" he asked, trying to put her at ease.

"I'm doing just fine," she said stiffly.

"Good," he said.

Haley, still thinking of her stalker, said "I'm going to get him."

Before she could explain who she was going to get and why, the district attorney reached his own erroneous conclusion. "Good for you," he said. "That's what I want to hear."

But she had more to say. She wanted William to know that she was not going to let the threats get to her anymore. She'd find a way to deal with them. "Let me explain " she began.

But William had been reassured. He didn't have time to waste on chitchat this morning. The press conference was coming up. Nat had left him worried or he'd never have asked Haley to come in. "That's okay," he said with a wave of the hand as he rose to his feet, picking up the information he'd just signed charging Rob with new offenses. "I just wanted to make sure everything was going okay. And I wanted to show you this." He grinned and added, "I'd sure hate to be in Rob Sterling's shoes."

He handed the information to her. She read quickly, her heart sinking. But she tried not to let her emotions show. She couldn't believe William was actually bringing more charges against Rob. It was so unfair. But all she did was ask, "So who gets to prosecute this one? I don't suppose I can since I'm the victim."

"That's right," he said. "One of the other attorneys can handle this one. It's open and shut anyway."

Haley was thinking of the two thugs Sergeant Thomas and Detective Palmer had arrested. It was anything but open and shut in her opinion. She'd hate to prosecute a case on their testimony. But

William was a step ahead of her. "I was worried about this case. Those two who initially fingered Rob as the one whose orders they were following will have to testify. But the clincher is one of the sheriff's own men. A correctional officer overheard Rob telling someone on the pay phone in the cell block to go after you. And he has the details nailed down. It was undoubtedly one of those two we have in custody that he was talking to. I'd like to see that cocky Dan Smathers's face when he hears about this one. I could put our weakest prosecutor on this case and Dan would lose."

Haley could hardly believe her ears. William was so confident. Had she been wrong about Rob? *If another officer heard him giving orders . . .* Her thoughts trailed off as the district attorney took the information back and moved toward the door. Haley knew she was being dismissed. She also knew that the district attorney had misunderstood her earlier about who she was going to get, but she didn't care. She hadn't lied, he hadn't let her finish, and she felt more secure, at least for now. She let the unintended deception stand. Mentioning the stalker to William was probably a mistake anyway. Let him think she meant it was Rob Sterling she was going to get.

The district attorney followed her out of his office, and as she turned up the hall she heard him say to his secretary, "Is the information on Raul Garcia ready for my signature yet? I want to be able to say at the press conference that we've already charged him for burning down his own office to cover up his mistakes."

It was all Haley could do to keep from turning back. Raul Garcia was a fine and honest man. He had not set fire to his own office. Of that she was certain. What was William Montgomery thinking?

Becoming attorney general, that's what, no matter who he had to step on, she thought with disgust. And at that thought, she couldn't help but wonder about a deputy who would testify against Rob, one of his own colleagues. Haley didn't know who she could trust anymore.

Actually there was one person, and she felt warm all over as she thought of Nat Turley. She could almost feel his arms around her, and the power of his kiss left her weak just thinking about it.

* * *

Until he had it nailed down a little tighter, Sergeant Rex Thomas wasn't going to mention anything to Haley about the correctional officer who was claiming to have overheard Rob's orders to threaten her. If Rob had given orders to anyone, it would have been the man he and Kurt had arrested. The man who had finally admitted to fashioning the note and chucking it through Haley's window.

Rex knew it was only a matter of time before Haley heard, and he hoped it could come from him, not someone else. He didn't want to give her anything that was weak. Rex intended to question his suspect, and as soon as he'd finished with him, he'd have a visit with Rob Sterling. He could do that without having to seek permission from Dan Smathers now that Rob had so foolishly insisted on defending himself.

Kurt met him at the jail a few minutes later, and the two of them proceeded to question their suspect. "Who did you receive your instructions from about writing the letter to Haley Gordon and throwing it into her bedroom?" Rex asked.

"I told you I don't know who he was. All he said was that he was hiring me to do a job for Rob Sterling, a guy who was in jail for murder," the man insisted.

"Are you absolutely certain it wasn't Rob himself?" Kurt asked.

"'Course I am," he said. "I don't take collect calls, and that's the only way a guy can call out of here."

"But someone accepted one from Rob," Rex insisted.

"Not me, I'm a business man," the big Tongan said. "I make sure I get my money up front and I don't take collect calls."

Rex and Kurt gave up. They believed the man was probably telling them the truth, at least what he believed was the truth. They next asked for Rob to be brought up for questioning.

Rob shook both their hands. "Hey, guys, what can I do for you?" he said, a friendly smile on his face. He hoped Miss Gordon had sent them with some questions that would set them on the right path. They reminded him of his right to remain silent and to have counsel present during questioning before they asked him anything.

As Rex had expected, Rob said, "I'm my own counsel now. You know that. And I'll talk to you guys. What do you want to know?"

He was not only disappointed but upset when they asked him about his call to the outside hiring someone to threaten Haley. "What on earth are you talking about?" he demanded. "I did no such thing. I'd never do that."

"I have a feeling you might," Rex said, staring hard at Rob. "In fact, we have a witness who says he heard you when you made the call." He stopped and waited for a response, hoping for something revealing.

"I didn't do it," Rob insisted. "If someone says I did, he's lying."

Rex kept a stone face. "An officer overheard you," he said.

Rob sat back and said, "Aha." Then he smiled. "You're talking about a correctional officer by the name of Frank Rawlings," he said.

Rex was rocked. The response was indeed revealing. Frank had sworn that there was no way Rob knew he'd overheard him. "Yes," Rex said slowly, "that's who it was, and he's prepared to swear to what he heard."

"I'm sure he is," Rob said, thinking about the productive morning he'd had in the exercise yard with a handful of select prisoners, one of whom was a little fellow who went by the strange name of Skunk. He'd acquired the handle because of the problem he had with body odors. Rob didn't even know his real name.

"This really ought to worry you," Rex said seriously, attempting to get Rob to tell them more.

Rob just smiled more and then said, "Not really. I've got bigger things to worry about than that." He paused and studied the detectives for a minute. He knew them both and believed them to be honest and thorough. After a moment he said, "You men are both good at what you do. And for that I'm grateful, because I know you'll want to get to the truth of the matter here. I would suggest that you talk to an inmate that everybody here calls Skunk."

"What's his real name?" Kurt asked.

"I don't know it," Rob admitted. "But it won't take you long to find out. He's a little guy. Smells bad. Talk to him. But before you do, let me tell you about something that happened last night."

The two detectives listened as Rob told them about the whispering guard. After he'd recited to them what the cowardly officer had said to him the night before, he said, "I learned his name this morning. Now, talk to Skunk, but after you do, get him some protection, because Frank will have him killed if he finds out Skunk said anything."

"That's an awfully strong accusation," Rex said skeptically.

"So it is. But we all know there's nothing worse than an officer gone bad," Rob said pointedly.

Rex nodded, as he looked hard into Rob's unrelenting gaze. He was experiencing something he suspected that maybe Haley Gordon was going through. He found himself doubting Rob's guilt. There was just something about him. He tried to shake the feeling off, but it persisted. *But can we take the word of anything an inmate says?* he wondered.

"We'll talk to Skunk," Rex said. "But what makes you think Frank Rawlings would really do something so drastic?"

"It wouldn't be the first time," Rob said with a frown. "You don't really believe five men jumping me was just supposed to be a warning, do you?"

Rex and Kurt exchanged glances. "We'll be back," Rex promised. "Is there anything else you can tell us?"

Rob shook his head. Then Rex thought of something else he wanted to ask Rob. Mostly he wanted to gauge Rob's reaction. He hadn't planned to say anything about this, but the little doubts he had just experienced caused him to do so. "Rob, there's one more thing I'd like to ask. It's not related to what we've just been talking about."

"Ask it then," Rob said.

"We have another witness who's come forward. Claims your wife was seeing someone else," he said. "Could that be true?"

Rob lowered his head and rubbed his eyes, the first real emotion he'd shown since the officers came in. "I don't think she would ever have dated another man," he said.

Then he looked up and met Sergeant Thomas's eyes. "A lot of men wanted her. Some flirted with her. I suppose some might have even tried to get her to go out with them. But hard as it is for people to believe, she loved me. What else can I say?"

"That pretty well covers it. Thanks," Rex said. "We'll talk to Skunk now."

"Don't let him get hurt," Rob pleaded. "He's okay, you know. Better than most in here."

Rex Thomas was shaken now. Rob seemed so believable. But he'd have to see what Skunk said before he even considered going in another direction on this case. He did have doubts however. And he thought about Miss Gordon and what she'd said about searching for the truth. That's what he'd do.

CHAPTER THIRTEEN

After only five minutes of questioning, Rex and Kurt had some answers. Skunk was more convincing than they thought he'd be. He told them that he'd heard Frank talking to some other inmates, telling them there'd be a lot of money waiting for them when they got out if they'd take care of Rob Sterling. After that he'd started following Frank around trying to get as much dirt on the man as he could. After the beating had not succeeded the way Frank had desired, Skunk claimed he heard Frank rake Rob's assailants over the coals. Skunk said that Frank had told the inmates that he'd been simultaneously working on something else with some friends on the outside—that he was orchestrating a little more trouble for Rob.

Skunk had also lucked out one day on his way to lunch, accidentally coming upon Frank and the same inmates that had attacked Rob. When they thought he'd passed, Frank told them they had a job to finish. He realized it would be difficult now, but eventually they'd get another chance at him, and he warned them that they better not mess it up the next time.

"Will you testify under oath to what you've told us?" Rex asked.

"Of course. It's the truth," Skunk said. "That Rob, he don't deserve what's happening to him. Bad enough what happened to his wife, but this here's just got to be stopped."

"Don't you fear for your own life?" Kurt asked.

"Detective Palmer," the little guy said, "I done asked for what I'm getting. I ain't got no life left. I'm headed to prison. How long do you think I can take life in there? If these guys get me first, so what?"

Rex actually felt sorry for Skunk. And he couldn't see where Skunk had anything to gain by lying. It seemed to both officers that all he could get was hurt. They didn't know what Skunk had done that would get him sent to prison, as he was convinced was going to happen, but he seemed like a follower, not an instigator. After letting him go back to the cell block, Rex turned to his partner. "We better get him some protection, just in case he's telling the truth. If what he and Rob are telling us is true, then Rob could be right. Skunk might not last long as soon as they find out that he's ratted."

"*If* he's telling the truth," Kurt reminded him.

Sergeant Thomas looked hard at Kurt. "Do you believe him?" he asked.

Slowly Kurt nodded his head. "I'm thinking it could be true, what he's saying. And I believe Rob could be telling the truth, crazy as that sounds. Makes me feel like a traitor. You may want to have me taken off the case."

"Hardly, Kurt," Rex said. "I was beginning to think I was losing it myself. There's a possibility that we may have been on the wrong track all along. This is not going to be easy, but we'd better look into it, and if Rob and Skunk are telling the truth, then we've got to find out who's behind all this. There could be money, brains, and power. If Rob has been framed, then it's our job to figure out how and by whom."

Kurt nodded his agreement. "There's only one thing that would upset me more than an officer I know and have worked with going bad. And that's someone falsely accusing him of it. Let's go sit down with Haley Gordon and see if we can sort through this thing. We've got to decide what to do next. We can't go on wasting our time."

"And we'd better see about getting Skunk out of there. He won't stand a chance against those inmates that thumped Rob," Rex added.

The two men found the sheriff in his office a half hour later. What they had to tell him didn't surprise him. "I've been wondering about this whole thing myself," he said. "I better have a talk with Frank Rawlings today. And I'll see that Skunk is protected, just in case," he promised.

"Okay, but you might not want to wait too long," Sergeant Thomas said.

"I'll take care of it. In the meantime, you two get over to the district attorney's office. Tell Miss Gordon what you've been told, then get to work. But remember one thing, fellows," the sheriff said cautiously. "We could be wrong. Look for evidence both ways. If Rob is behind all this and is pulling strings himself, we'd look mighty silly if we got him off."

Their next stop was the district attorney's office. They asked for an audience with Haley. "She left a few minutes ago," they were told by Haley's secretary.

"Where was she going?" Rex asked. "We really need to talk to her."

"I'm not sure. She got a call from some woman, and moments later she came out, putting her jacket on. She said she had to run but that she'd be back. She seemed in quite a hurry. She has her cell phone. Give her a call."

They tried as they left the office, but Haley wasn't answering. All they could do was try later. "Let's go back to the office and go over everything again," Rex suggested. "Maybe looking at our evidence from a fresh angle will help us see something we missed."

* * *

Haley had steeled herself for this meeting, but she still wasn't fully prepared for the way Rob Sterling affected her when he walked into the tiny room where she was to have a face-to-face meeting with him.

She stood and extended her hand. He was tall and solidly built and had an aura about him that made her feel small in his presence. Surprisingly, it was a good feeling. Rob smiled warmly and gazed for a long moment at her with his bright green eyes. That's where she saw the pleading and the pain. He couldn't hide it. Her heart went out to him.

"Thanks for coming," he said.

"Your sister said it was urgent," Haley said as the two of them sat down across a small wooden table from each other.

"My sister thinks everything is urgent," Rob said. "She's more worried about me than I am."

"She seems like a nice girl," Haley said, trying to settle herself down for whatever the purpose of this visit turned out to be.

"She's the best," Rob said. "Jennifer and Tasha were good friends. In fact, it was Tasha that introduced me to Jennifer." He smiled and Haley relaxed a little. "I told her that it was silly when she lined us up, Jennifer being a former Miss Utah and all, and me being a confirmed bachelor."

"There must have been a spark there," Haley guessed.

"There was. I still don't know what she sees . . . saw in me," Rob said, and his green eyes reflected a terrible sadness.

"Rob," Haley said in a formal tone, "you don't have to talk to me, you know. What you say could be used against you."

"I know all that, Miss Gordon," Rob said. "But I asked you to come, remember? I have nothing to hide. If I have to go to prison for the rest of my life, so be it. That's not as bad as what happened to Jennifer." He choked up and was silent for a minute, looking away from Haley as he regained his composure. When he looked back he said, "Even if I get the death penalty, which I don't deserve, it won't be worse than Jennifer's fate. She didn't deserve the death penalty, but she got it, and without the benefit of a trial," he added somewhat bitterly.

"What can I do?" Haley asked, feeling quite ill at ease again in the presence of Rob's pain.

"Help me find out who killed her," Rob said simply. "I really don't care much what happens to me, but for Jennifer's sake, I want him caught. Whoever it is, he's out there somewhere laughing at us all." Rob looked at her sternly. "That includes you," he said. "He's laughing at you too. I know about the threats, and I'm so sorry, but I had nothing to do with that. I hope you can someday find it in your heart to believe me," he said.

Haley slowly nodded her head. "I'm beginning to," she admitted, knowing that if William Montgomery could hear and see her now, she'd be through.

"Sergeant Thomas and Detective Palmer were here this morning," Rob said.

"Oh, what did they want?" she asked, also wondering what they would think about what she'd just told Rob.

"They wanted to question me about hiring someone to threaten you," he said.

"And did you?" she asked, praying that she knew what his answer would be.

"Send threats?" he asked. "No, but I talked to them."

"Then who sent them?" she asked.

Rob looked at her for a long time, holding her attention with his eyes. Finally he said, "Whoever killed my wife did it. Talk to your detectives. I'm sure they can tell you more by now. But that's not why I asked you to come."

"Okay," she said, trying to relax but finding it impossible. "What do you want to talk to me about?"

"The preliminary hearing is coming up in just a few days," he said. "Are you ready for it?"

His question set her back in her chair. "I . . . I don't know," she stammered, confused why he'd ask.

Rob smiled. "That's better than what I was afraid I'd hear, Miss Gordon."

She cut in, "Rob, please call me Haley."

Rob watched her for a moment again. He couldn't help but notice how attractive she was. He wondered why she wasn't married. Then he pulled his thoughts back on track and said, "I want to waive the prelim, Miss Gordon."

"It's Haley," she reminded him. "Waive the preliminary hearing?" she asked, not having expected such a request. "Why do you want to do that?"

He smiled at her, and she found herself relaxing just a little bit. "I'm surviving in here, Miss Gordon."

"Haley."

He smiled briefly. "Haley, then. I'm not liking it, but I'm surviving. I know you've got all it will take to convince Judge Horton to bind me over for trial. I'd like to save you the trouble. Not that I'm guilty—because I'm not—but I need to know who did kill her, and why, and that will take some time." He paused, troubling her with those painful green eyes again. Then he added, "And sometime, if you're willing to listen to me, I'd like to explain a few things to you. I know the circumstantial evidence looks bad for me, but I've had a lot of time to think in here, and I have some ideas about what I believe happened."

"I'd be glad to listen," Haley said, trying not to sound like she was fully ready to believe him, although in her heart she knew she was. "How about if we talk about it right now?" she suggested.

"If you're sure," he said.

Before she could answer, a correctional officer came running to the room. "Back to your cell, Sterling!" he yelled. "Sorry, Miss Gordon, there's trouble. We'll get you out of here in a minute," he said to her as he grabbed Rob by the arm and ushered him unceremoniously from the room.

Rob's stomach twisted and he forgot all about Miss Haley Gordon and what he'd been about to ask her to do. Skunk was in trouble. He was certain of it. He prayed that he wasn't hurt badly as he was prodded quickly back to his cell.

Haley stood in the doorway and watched until Rob disappeared. Then she stared absently down the empty corridor. She could hear yelling farther back in the jail. She found herself trembling. Somehow, she had the distinct impression this all had something to do with Rob Sterling. She was determined to find out what the connection was to Rob before she returned to her office and considered what to do next. There would be no preliminary hearing it appeared. That would buy her time, and for that she was grateful. But time was still critical. She needed to find the truth, and it wouldn't be easy. She really had wanted to talk with Rob about his side of the story. Surely he could have helped at least point her in the right direction.

It was a good ten minutes before the same officer who'd rushed Rob away returned. "Sorry for the wait, Miss Gordon," he said. "There's been some trouble."

"What did it have to do with Rob Sterling?" she asked.

"Who said it had anything to do with him?" he countered a little too quickly and harshly, essentially confirming her suspicions.

"Well, you certainly were in a hurry to get him away from here," she said. "So I just assumed you must have thought he was in some kind of danger or something."

"No, nothing to do with him," the officer said. "It's just policy when there's a disturbance of any kind to lock the entire jail down."

That made sense, but she wasn't satisfied that it didn't somehow involve Rob. She got the terrible feeling that he was in danger, and it worried her a great deal. "What happened back there?" she asked.

"I'm not at liberty to say," the officer told her coldly. "I'll need to ask you to leave now. You may come back tomorrow and finish your business with Sterling. Things will be kind of tight in here for the rest of the day."

* * *

The sheriff wiped his brow. If he'd delayed even another few seconds, Skunk would have been dead. It was hard to believe this was happening in his jail. First the attempt on the life of Rob Sterling—and he was convinced now that it had been just that— then this. The attack against Skunk had just started when he and several officers had entered the cell block. Those inmates hadn't intended for Skunk to live. He would, but he was on his way to the hospital right now.

And then when he learned that the men who had nearly killed Skunk were the same ones who'd attacked Rob, he knew that he had a serious problem. When he considered what the two detectives had told him this morning, he was afraid that one of his own people was behind it. He had to find Frank Rawlings fast. Frank was off duty, but he was scheduled to come on that afternoon, so the sheriff figured he couldn't be far from his house.

* * *

Rex was surprised when he and Kurt were summoned to meet the sheriff at his office. "Drop whatever you're doing," he was told, "and you and Palmer get to the sheriff's office at once."

The call had come on his cell phone from the sheriff's personal secretary. And she sounded as if it were urgent. "I hope nothing's happened to Sterling," Rex said as he made an illegal turn and raced through the light traffic.

He and Kurt were both puffing when they entered the sheriff's office. They'd literally run after leaving their car. The sheriff was on his feet pacing when they rushed in. "Glad you made it so quickly," he said brusquely as the two of them skidded to a stop. "You were right. Skunk caught a knife, but he'll live. I got there just in time, and it missed its mark."

"Who did it?" Rex asked.

"Five men were involved," the sheriff said.

"Same ones who jumped Rob?" Kurt guessed.

"You've got it. I want Frank Rawlings in here as fast as you can find him. And I want the two of you here when I talk to him. He's got a lot of explaining to do." The sheriff handed the sergeant a slip of paper. "This is his address. I'll be here."

"What about the jail?" Rex asked. "We need to talk to those inmates."

"I've got it covered. You get Frank," the sheriff ordered.

"What if he refuses to come?" Rex asked.

"Then arrest him," the sheriff said calmly. "There's plenty to charge him with."

* * *

Another tense meeting was taking place at that very moment. It was in an out-of-the-way place—dingy, dirty, and hidden from public view. Dan Smathers was fuming. "I could have you locked up for the rest of your life," he said to the man he faced. "You've been fouling things up terribly."

"Not my fault," his contact said, his light gray eyes flashing with contempt. "Frank Rawlings is just stupid."

"It most certainly is your fault, Alex," Dan said, poking him in the chest with a finger. "You're the one who selected him. He was indebted to you, you said. That doesn't make any difference. I told you to get rid of Rob in the jail and to have him framed for the threats to the prosecutor, the Gordon woman. I gave you two ways to solve the same problem. You failed on both counts. You'd better begin repairing the damage right now. If my name surfaces in any of this, you know what'll happen."

His contact simply smiled. "Don't you threaten me, Mr. Hotshot Attorney," he said mildly. "You've got more to lose now than I do."

Dan grabbed the man by the shirt. That was a mistake. His contact was as skilled at street fighting as he was vicious. He caught Dan on the chin with his right fist, and followed that with a lightning left to Dan's right eye. Dan's grip relaxed, and his hand slipped from the man's shirt as a knee caught him in the stomach. A third punch sent blood gushing from his nose as Dan slammed into a hard concrete wall and then slipped slowly to the floor.

He fought to stay conscious, his head reeling and his vision swimming. His contact never moved while Dan gradually regained his senses. "Better wipe the blood off," he told Dan five minutes later. "You look a mess. And don't you ever lay a hand on me again. This little meeting is going to cost you an extra five grand."

Dan listened and fumed as he rubbed the sleeve of an expensive suit coat across his face, leaving it soaked with blood. He was angry, but he was also beginning to think again. There was a way to turn this little fracas in his favor. Dan finally spoke as he ruined the other sleeve of his suit coat. "Have a note on my door before I get home. A threatening one. This will need to be explained," he said, pointing to his battered face. "I'll stall to give you time. And make it convincing. Warn me that I better not get Sterling off, that sort of thing. And find Frank Rawlings. He cannot be allowed to talk with anyone."

"He doesn't know you're connected with me. And he clearly doesn't dare cross me. Quit worrying. He's no threat to either one of us."

"You may be right, but I'll feel better when I know it for sure, Alex," Dan snarled as he finally began to get to his feet. After steadying himself against the wall, Dan looked with loathing at the man who was his closest ally and worst enemy. "The police," he began again. "I have a feeling Sergeant Thomas might be getting wise to what's happening. Warn him off too. Anyway you like is fine with me, I just don't want to know when or how you do it."

Dan's middleman nodded, brushing his light brown hair back. The two stared at each other for a long moment. Then they parted, neither man uttering another word.

* * *

Rex's cell phone was ringing when he got back to his car. He looked at it before answering. It was Haley Gordon's number. They'd have to wait for their meeting with her. He answered the phone. "Hello, Miss Gordon," he said, trying to sound calmer than he was feeling.

"Sergeant Thomas," she said, speaking rapidly. "Something happened at the jail. I need for you to find out what it was," she said.

"Kurt and I are on an urgent assignment right now. I'll call as soon as we're finished. We have a lot to talk about," he said. *A lot more than you can even imagine,* he thought to himself.

Haley was thinking the same thing.

She looked at her watch and quickly reached for the radio. She turned it on just in time to hear the voice of her boss, silver-haired and silver-tongued, as he said, "I am announcing today my candidacy for the office of Attorney General of the great state of Utah."

Haley shook her head. She hoped he wouldn't say anything about Rob Sterling. But after a couple minutes of pure political rhetoric, he said, "My philosophy is to be tough on crime. Whoever breaks the law in this state will get the same firm and unrelenting prosecution as is currently the case right here in Salt Lake. I am not blind to people who think they might be protected by their station in life. You break the law, I'll go after you. Even police officers and attorneys are not exempt. My office, for example, will be seeking the death penalty against Rob Sterling for the cold and calculated murder of his wife. We have a solid case and intend to move quickly on it. In a related matter, I just this morning filed charges against a fellow attorney."

Haley couldn't listen to any more. She turned the radio off angrily. She knew that Raul Garcia was about to be dragged through the mud and she refused to listen to that.

* * *

Sergeant Thomas and Detective Palmer were also listening to the district attorney make his announcement. After he'd finished, Rex looked over at Kurt. "He might have been wise to have waited on that one."

Kurt agreed and then added, "I don't suppose he knows what happened in the jail this morning."

"I'm sure he doesn't," Rex agreed.

"What about Raul Garcia?" Kurt asked.

Rex turned right, passed a bus, gunned the engine, then said, "Framed, I would guess. This whole thing is getting more complicated by the hour. I think Montgomery is planning on Haley getting Rob the death sentence. I would hate to be in her shoes when he finds out it's not likely to happen."

It took several more minutes of daring driving before the two detectives reached the street where Frank Rawlings lived. They slowed down and Rex said, "Number 765 is what we're looking for."

He saw the number a moment later, and he also saw the warning glint of sunlight reflected off a rifle barrel. He gunned the car as a shot rang out in the peaceful neighborhood. Glass shattered and Kurt sank with a groan in his seat. Another shot followed as Rex had the car fishtailing up the street.

CHAPTER FOURTEEN

Haley did what she had planned not to do. She returned to the office without learning any more about the incident in the jail. She desperately wanted someone to talk to, to confide in. She wasn't close to any of the other attorneys, and they were all busy anyway. And her secretary wasn't always as careful as she could be about not repeating things she heard. It was nearly lunchtime, and Haley had already had a busy and stressful morning, and she'd missed her breakfast. She didn't look forward to having lunch alone.

She looked thoughtfully at her phone. Then she looked up the number to Nat's office. He was someone she could both confide in and have lunch with, she thought with a little smile. *If he's free . . .* She picked up the phone and began to dial. Then she stopped. She'd be seeing him tonight. She was no longer scared out of her wits, just frightened enough to be careful. He'd interpret a call from her now as an indication of terror on her part, and she didn't want that.

There wasn't much choice, she decided. She'd lunch alone. That decided, Haley grabbed her jacket and purse and headed downstairs. Her phone went off in her purse before she got out of the building. She stopped and pulled it out. Without looking at the number, she answered. "Haley, it's Rex," she heard instantly. "Could you meet me at LDS Hospital? My partner's been shot and we need to talk. I'm going there right now."

Haley felt a chill come over her, sapping some of her newfound strength. "How bad is he hurt?" she asked, almost not wanting to know.

"He'll live," Rex said shortly. "Meet me in the emergency room. I'll explain everything."

Haley agreed and went to her car instead of lunch. Things were getting awful. She wondered if the shooting had anything to do with the Sterling case. Deep down, she knew. There were some evil people involved in this case, people whose identities were a complete mystery. Kurt Palmer was just one more of a growing number of victims.

She parked and hurried to the emergency-room entrance. Rex was waiting for her. "Now can you tell me what happened?" Haley asked urgently.

"It's a rather long story," Rex began. "I called for you several hours ago, but you were out and not answering your phone."

"Yes, I saw your number on the phone. I'd been at the jail talking to Rob Sterling when they cut us off and took him back to his cell," she said. "I don't know what happened, but whatever it was, it caused the whole jail to get shut down and . . ." Haley trailed off as she realized that Sergeant Thomas was nodding his head. "You know about it?" she asked.

"Yes, and it all ties in with why we're here and Kurt's in there," he said, pointing farther back into the emergency room. "They're working on him now. I don't think he'll need to be admitted, but it will take a little while to patch him up. Let's find a place where we can talk privately."

They ended up in Haley's car. "Mine's out of service," he'd said about his car when they couldn't find a spot where they were confident they wouldn't be overheard. "I'm in a spare the sheriff let me take. It's kind of messy."

Haley told Rex what she'd learned from Rob. And to her amazement, he told her that he was sorry he'd been so stubborn. "We hate it when one of our own goes bad. And the evidence did point straight at Rob Sterling. I'm afraid Kurt and I allowed our anger at him to blind us. I'm convinced now that he's innocent," he said. "You can't prosecute him."

"What's changed your mind?" she asked.

"The truth, as you put it. Rob told us the truth, and so did a little guy named Skunk, who is also in the hospital," Rex said. He then took Haley carefully through the morning's events. "When we found that it was the same inmates that had attacked Rob and tried to kill Skunk, we figured that Rob had been telling the truth all along. The sheriff sent Kurt and me to arrest Frank, and that's when we were fired on. I called for help and was met by an ambulance. They loaded Kurt, and I met several other officers. We couldn't find a trace of the shooter.

There were witnesses, but all they could describe was the car. I have a feeling it'll turn up and there won't be a trace of evidence in it."

"What about this Frank Rawlings guy?" she asked. "Did anyone find him?"

"He's gone. His car wasn't there, and his clothes and a lot of personal belongings were cleaned out. We put out an all-points bulletin, but I'm afraid he's in hiding," Rex explained. "I think he knows we're on to him."

Haley started her car and let the heater run. It was uncomfortably cool. Haley was famished, but she said nothing. She knew that Rex Thomas hadn't had lunch either. She could wait if he could. "Someone is pulling Frank's strings," Haley said after it had started to warm up in the car. "The question is who?"

"Which is exactly what we'd hoped to learn from Frank," Rex agreed. "But if we can't find him, we can't question him." Rex sat thoughtfully for a moment, then he turned again to Haley. "Miss Gordon, if Rob Sterling didn't commit the crime, who did?"

"I don't know. I suppose Martin Ligorni should be considered a suspect, but I doubt if it was him. Whoever did it has some very frightening friends, and I don't think Martin would have those kinds of contacts," she said. She brought the detective up-to-date on her own problems. She mentioned the latest note, but she didn't tell him it was written on the back of an enlarged photograph that she really didn't care for anyone to see except Nat. "I call him a stalker now," she said.

"Which he is," Rex agreed. "We should be able to collar him, and when we do, maybe he'll talk. We've got to find someone who can get us on the right road to whoever is behind this whole thing. Let's go check on Kurt," he suggested then. "I don't want him to think I've abandoned him."

Kurt was in need of a few days off, but he was in good spirits when Haley and Rex joined him. Kurt's wife had come while Haley and Rex were talking, and she was fussing over him to no end. "He'll be fine now," Rex said with a grin. "Some of us had better get moving. There's still work to do."

Once again, Haley and Rex went out into the cool afternoon. "I'm without a partner, but I guess I better get after it anyway," Rex said.

"What's next?" Haley asked.

"I was thinking about a quick look at Rob's house. I want to look things over there with a new perspective," he said.

"I'll join you there," Haley said. "I just wish I could talk to Rob first."

"Why can't you?" Rex asked.

"The correctional officer there told me I couldn't see him until tomorrow," she said.

"Mind if I come with you?" the detective asked. "They won't keep me out."

They walked back toward their cars. As soon as Rex reached his, he said, "Let's meet at your office, frame a few questions, then we'll go to the jail."

She agreed and walked on. When she got to the office, Rex was waiting for her. "You're not going to believe the call I just got," he said.

"From whom?" she asked.

"Dan Smathers. He says someone wants him off Rob's defense entirely. He wants to see me right now," he said.

"I wonder if he'll mind if I come along?" Haley asked.

"I don't care if he does or not," Rex said. "Dan's not one of my favorite people. Let's go, but maybe if you don't mind, we can ride together. Then we can go over what we want to ask Rob and save ourselves some time."

They elected to ride in Haley's car. Haley automatically headed toward Dan's downtown office. "He's at home," Rex said. "I guess he got quite roughed up." He gave Haley an address in one of the more expensive areas of the valley.

Dan met them at the door. Haley gasped. One eye was swollen shut, his nose lay slightly askew, and he talked with a slight lisp. "Looks like you've had kind of a rough time of it," Rex said, trying to sound sympathetic but not feeling so at all.

Dan waved them in but did not invite anyone to sit. He simply stood in his grand entryway and said, "Rob Sterling seems to attract a lot of interest. Apparently, from what I hear, you've been warned to get off the case, Miss Gordon. And now someone wants me off as well. It's not going to happen. I didn't ask to help Rob. In fact, I resisted, but now I'm committed, and regardless of what he wants, I know what's best for him. If you think for one minute that this kind of thing will frighten me off, then you're crazy."

"You don't honestly believe I had anything to do with this?" she said, pointing to his battered face.

"Who else would want me to quit?" he asked, his voice getting lower, almost dangerous. He held out a single sheet of paper. "Read it," he ordered. "It's pretty self-explanatory."

Amazed, Haley took it and read while Rex, his face dark with rage, waited.

> *Mr. Lawyer, you better not get that killer cop off. Back off or I'll have more than your face messed up next time. You just let Miss Gordon do her job. She don't want you messing around no more. Rob will hang himself with the lady's help.*
> *A friend of the prosecutor.*

Haley handed the note to Rex. "This is preposterous," she said to Dan as Rex read. "I can't believe you'd think that I would stoop to such things."

"I can think what I like," he said. "Take that thing, Sergeant. I'm not intimidated by it. It took three of them to do this to me, but I'm packing my gun now, so it won't happen again."

As they left the house, having been more or less ordered to leave, Haley took one last look at Dan. "You are unbelievable," she said.

He responded with a snarl, "See you in court. Rob has a preliminary hearing on Monday. And I'll be there to back him up just like His Honor ordered."

She didn't say another word, but Rex did. "I suppose you reported this to the city police," he said.

"No, I figured you could do that," Dan said with so much contempt in his voice that it fouled the air. "I'm not too popular among your colleagues. I've shown too many of them how dense they are. I don't expect anything to be done about this, but that's all right. I'll watch out for myself." He shut the door with force.

Once again in the car, Haley said, "He reminded me of something in there."

"What, a mobster?" Rex asked.

Haley chuckled. "That too, now that you mention it. No, I had planned to buy a pistol today. With what happened to you and Kurt,

I really should. I do have a permit."

"No need to get in a rush," Rex said. "I have a whole houseful of guns. I'll lend you one. I think it would be a good idea. There's definitely danger around. As soon as we finish with Rob at the jail, we'll drop by my place. I can lend you whatever you need."

Haley got another call from Rob's sister as they were arriving at the jail. "Tasha, how are you?" she asked.

"I'm doing okay, but I'm worried sick about Rob. He wants to see you again first thing in the morning. They wouldn't let me visit him today, but he was able to call out," she said. "He wouldn't tell me what was going on, but something is. Can you go in the morning again?"

"I'm just going in right now," Haley reported.

"But they said no one could see him today," Tasha said. "They wouldn't even let Raul and Sperry in."

"I have my ways," she said, winking at Rex.

"He really wants to talk to Raul and Sperry. Could you possibly—" Tasha began and then stopped as if it would be too much to ask the prosecutor to do another favor for the accused.

But Haley knew what she wanted and whispered to Rex, "Rob's sister would like Raul and Sperry to talk to him today."

Rex smiled. "I could use a little more help," he said.

"Tell them to come to the jail in an hour. They'll let them in then," she said. She'd almost asked that they come now, but thought better of it. She wanted to ask most of the questions, and Rex had already helped her formulate them.

Rex called the sheriff right then and got his approval for the men to visit later, then he and Haley entered the jail. It was becoming a very familiar place to Haley. Almost too familiar.

* * *

Raul Garcia was a determined man. He knew that it looked bleak, but he was not about to be beaten. He was so glad he'd listened to that still small voice that whispered to him, or he might never have taken all the backups of his electronic files. But he had them, and he wasn't going to tell anyone that wasn't one hundred percent on his side. So far, only four people, including himself, knew about those backup discs. Of course, his secretary was there when he'd taken them, and he'd sworn her to secrecy. The next day he'd told his wife. And an hour ago, over lunch, he'd decided that Sperry Collier needed to know.

That came about after he heard the district attorney announce on the radio that he was running for attorney general. Sperry had heard it too and called Raul at his home. "This smacks of corruption," the rugged ex-cop had told him on the phone. "He plans to use you as a pawn in his bid for higher office. It's too bad all your files were destroyed. That one that was planted would have been nice to have."

Raul had surprised Sperry when he didn't immediately agree. Instead, he'd said, "Have you had lunch?" Sperry hadn't. "Then let's get together," Raul had suggested.

It was over lunch in a small restaurant that Raul had smiled and said, "I have all the e-files, and a copy of the hard file on the case that was planted in my office. The Office of Professional Conduct has the original of that one. I also have a handful of other files."

Sperry had responded with, "I underestimated you, my young friend. Let's have a look."

They did, and Sperry agreed with Raul that news of the files should not be spread any further at the present time. "Someone, the same person who burned your office, would probably do anything to destroy these if they found out about their existence. We can prove that your secretary didn't create this faked file," he said. "How someone accessed your computer is anybody's guess, but it's not impossible. In fact, it's done all the time by amateur hackers. The only thing we need to prove is that it's not her work or yours, and that will be easy. What we need to do now is make a careful list, with your secretary's help, of all the inconsistencies. And let's also make two more copies of the discs and put them in other locations, such as safety deposit boxes. Your future as an attorney is on these discs."

They made two copies, then the secretary took notes while the two men secured the others. After that, Raul and Sperry headed for the jail. Raul's defense was well underway; they needed to get to work helping Rob now.

* * *

"You do remember that I'm assigned to prosecute your case, don't you, Rob?" Haley asked. "And that anything you say can be used against you in court?"

"I remember," Rob said solemnly. "And I expect that you'll do what you feel is right. Somehow I get the feeling that the truth is more important to you than winning though." He looked her straight in the eye.

"It is," she agreed, exchanging a knowing glance with Sergeant Thomas.

"You don't object to my taping this interview, do you?" Haley asked.

"Of course not. Turn on your recorder," he said.

Haley's questions were specific. She began by asking, "How do you account for your keys being on the kitchen counter? Remember, you said you usually kept them in your car. And also, your prints were the only ones on them."

"The only thing I can figure is that I dropped them on the back porch or the sidewalk out back," Rob said.

Haley said, "Okay, so it's your contention that whoever killed Jennifer entered by the back door, not the front, is that correct?"

"Yes. Why else would they use the keys?" he asked.

Haley merely nodded. "You came in by the front door, correct?"

"That's right," he agreed.

"When you came home, the lights were on and the storm had passed," Haley said. Rob merely nodded and she asked, "So what was the flashlight from the cupboard near the back door doing on the living room floor with no prints but yours and Jennifer's on it?"

"I don't know. Maybe Jennifer was using it," Rob said. "But it only makes sense that someone framing me would ensure only our prints were on it."

"The flashlight wasn't near Jennifer's body," Haley said, making no comment on his observation, but agreeing silently that it did loom larger and larger as a possibility.

"I'd say in that case that it was clearly used by whoever came in while the lights were out," Rob said.

Haley nodded. "Did anyone but the two of you know where you

kept that flashlight?" she asked.

Rob had spent hours thinking about the evidence that was stacked against him. This matter of the flashlight was hard to explain. "Not that I know of," he admitted.

Haley and Rex glanced at one another. This was a solid bit of circumstantial evidence. It was the very thing the prosecution needed, and it would be hard for the defense to explain.

"Let's talk next about the lamp," Haley suggested. "How did the assailant knock it over?"

"He probably didn't," Rob responded. "That was a terrible storm that night. The wind was out of control. Whoever came in the back door must have left it open when they dropped the keys on the counter," he said. Rob suddenly looked as if he were getting sick thinking about it.

"I'm sorry, I know this is hard for you, Rob," Haley said.

"That's okay, Miss Gordon, let's keep going," he said.

Haley had been saving the next question; his reaction would be critical. All her growing conviction as to his innocence could be shot down if he didn't answer this next query correctly. Rex knew nothing of what she was about to ask, and his objective assessment of the way Rob handled his answer would tell her a lot. She decided to simply make a statement, then depending on how Rob reacted to it, she would follow up with a question.

"Tell me about your conversation with Trista Zippeta," she said mildly, feeling her palms beginning to sweat with the tension that was filling her.

Rob's only reaction was a puzzled look followed by one of deep thought. Haley waited, glanced at Rex, who was also puzzled, then asked, "You do remember her, don't you?"

Rob shrugged. "I'm sorry, if I should know her, I've forgotten. And it seems unlikely that anyone would forget a name like that. But maybe I have."

"If you forgot the name, you wouldn't have forgotten the woman," Haley said as relief flooded over her. "Green eyes, long lashes, hair almost as black as mine but cut short, inch-long fingernails, beautiful to a fault. Thirty-five or so," she finished.

Rob shook his head. "I'm sorry, Miss Gordon," he said. "I really don't have any idea what you're talking about. Is this someone I'm supposed to know?" Rob asked.

"Yes, according to her. She claims she has information that both she and her ex-husband, Jake, will testify to," Haley said, totally convinced that Miss Zippeta's story was another part of an ever-growing conspiracy against Rob. She'd let Rex or Sperry take a crack at the Zippetas.

"Is it bad?" Rob asked.

"Only if it's true," she said.

"What did this Zippeta woman say?" he asked.

Haley shook her head. "It doesn't matter right now. We'll get to the bottom of it. Now Rob, how do you explain why you were so late the night Jennifer died? You were much later than you normally were. And how could the assailant have known you'd be late?" Before he could answer, Haley added, "There's a lot of unexplained time between when Jennifer died, during the storm, and when you got home. Explain that, please."

Rob shifted in his seat. This was a tough one. He hoped he could make her see why he'd been gone so long without making him look more guilty than ever. He knew only too well that time spent alone, without a witness, made an alibi very difficult to establish.

CHAPTER FIFTEEN

"Anytime," Haley prodded gently.

Rob drew a deep breath. "This will sound stupid," he began in answer to Haley's last question. "But it's the truth. You want to know why I was so late getting home that night because you're looking for my alibi?"

Haley and Sergeant Thomas both nodded. "I drove up to Park City," he said.

"Why did you go up there?" Haley asked in surprise. He'd said nothing about Park City in his early statements.

"After I left the library where I'd been studying, I went to my car. There was a note in it from Jennifer. She wanted me to meet her in Park City. She said she'd already gone up there and would be at some restaurant I don't ever remember hearing about before. She gave me the address and everything. She said she had a surprise for me."

"So you went?" Haley asked, having a difficult time with his story. It seemed rather far-fetched.

"Of course I went," he said. "It was a note from my wife. There was no reason not to go. It may seem strange to you, but it's not to me. She used to leave notes like that all the time as a surprise. It had been several months since the last time she'd left one, but when I found it there, I didn't have any reason not to meet her where she asked."

Sergeant Thomas, experienced detective that he was, couldn't help but jump in. "Rob, how did you know the note was from Jennifer?" he asked.

"It was her signature and her handwriting," Rob explained.

"So you had no reason to think anything strange or out of the ordinary was going on?" he asked.

"Of course not. She knew I would probably be studying at the library that evening, and that's my usual study spot. And I'd told her that I'd be home by nine that night. It would have been nothing for her to have driven up to campus a little earlier and left the note. The only thing different about this time as opposed to earlier times was the location she'd chosen for us to eat. She'd always picked places here in the valley. But I didn't give that much thought. Park City isn't all that far, and it seemed reasonable," Rob explained.

"Where is the note now?" the sergeant asked. "If it's forged, we could prove that."

Rob looked embarrassed. "I threw it away," he said.

"Threw it away?" Haley asked a little sternly.

"I'm afraid so. How was I to know it would be important later on? After I'd driven all over Park City for a couple of hours, looking for Jennifer and her car and for a restaurant I'd never heard of before, I was getting worried and upset. I looked in a phone book at a phone booth and when I found that the place didn't exist, I was frustrated and decided to go home. So I wadded the note up and threw it in a trash can that was just a few feet away. I figured that she'd somehow made a mistake, that she'd been given some bad information by someone, and that she must have gone home herself. I knew she'd feel terrible about it because she was probably trying to . . ." He paused. "Because she probably wanted to have a nice evening together. I didn't want her to feel that way for long."

"Did you try to call her?" Rex asked slowly, confused by Rob's sudden sadness, but deciding to let it go.

"I did, from the phone booth I mentioned," he said. "But there was no answer. I figured she just hadn't gotten home yet."

"Don't you have a cell phone?" the sergeant asked.

"I do, but I'd forgotten it that day. I left it plugged into a socket in the bedroom."

"It wasn't there when we searched the house," Rex said.

"Then someone took it," Rob suggested. "Probably the killer. He probably thought someone would be able to use it for evidence at some point or something. I'm sure he was doing everything he could to make it look bad for me. And he did a good job." Then Rex said angrily, "He probably took it as a personal memento. Jennifer had painted a smiley face for me on the case. It was probably a sick thing he did to remind himself of what he'd pulled off."

Rex nodded. "Why didn't you tell us about the note that night?" he asked shrewdly. "We could have gone up there and recovered it. Your alibi would have been firmly established right then and you would have saved yourself a lot of trouble."

"I was so upset that I honestly forgot about it," Rob said. "I know that sounds stupid, but finding someone you love . . . dead . . ." He choked up, but finished angrily, "I couldn't think straight. And then you guys came on, accusing me until I thought I'd crack up. By the time I remembered what I'd done with the note, a couple of days had passed. Seemed to me like it would have only made matters worse for me to bring it up then, so I didn't, except to Raul, and I asked him not to mention it."

"Did he try to find it, even though a couple of days had passed?"

"He did, but I was so disoriented that night in Park City after driving around for all that time, that I couldn't remember for sure where I'd been. He found the place where he thought I might have used the phone, and there was a trash can beside the booth, but it had been emptied since I'd been there. He looked in it, but the note wasn't there," Rob explained.

"Did anyone see you that night that would remember you, or did you talk to anyone while you were in Park City?" Rex asked.

Rob shook his head. "No, so there's no way to verify my story. But it happened just like I said. Of course, we know now that Jennifer couldn't have gone to Park City. She must have been killed while I was driving up there."

As Rex was posing his questions to Rob, Haley had been thinking. "Rob," she began thoughtfully, "you believe that someone forged the note, don't you?"

"It's the only thing that could have happened," he answered. "I didn't look that closely at it, but it looked like Jennifer's handwriting. It was at least close enough to hers that it didn't stand out to me. Anyway, Jennifer had left notes like that for me a half dozen times or more since we were married."

Haley then asked, "So if she didn't put the note in your car, who did, and how did they get it in there?"

"You tell me, Miss Gordon," he said. "Haven't there been notes in your car lately?"

Haley looked at Rex, who was clearly thinking exactly what she was. "There have, and I don't yet know how anyone got them in there," she admitted.

"Could be the same person," Rob suggested.

Haley knew that Rob could be right. "One more thing for now, Rob," Haley began. "Can you think of anyone who would know that Jennifer occasionally left you notes to set up surprise dinner dates?"

"Of course," he said. "Tasha and her husband knew. They were even in on it a couple of times."

"Anyone else?" Haley asked. "Think hard."

"I can't think of anyone," Rob said after a few moments. "But I'll try to . . ." He suddenly stopped talking.

"What, Rob? Did you think of someone?" Haley asked.

"Yeah, possibly," he began slowly. "I could be remembering wrong, but that strange law student, that Martin Ligorni, it seems like he sort of walked up on me when I found a note last spring. That was a long time ago, but it seems like he was standing almost beside me when I opened the door and spotted it lying on the driver's seat, just like this last one was."

"Did you say anything to him? Show it to him? Anything like that?" Haley asked.

"I don't remember. The guy was always around. I can't imagine why I'd say anything to him about it, but I might have," Rob said.

"Could he have seen over your shoulder and read it or anything?" she asked.

"Could have, I suppose," Rob said.

"What did you do with that note?" Rex asked.

"I don't know. That was months ago. I suppose I might have tossed it across to the far side of the seat, or . . ." He paused. "Or I might have put it in one of my books."

"And if you did that, might it have still been in your book the next day?" the sergeant questioned.

"Yeah, I suppose so, but I don't remember," Rob said. "It was too long ago to remember the details."

Haley and Rex looked at each other. They both knew another visit with Martin Ligorni was in order. "We've got a lot of work to do, Haley,"

Rex said as he pushed back from the little table that separated them from Rob. "Thanks for your help, Rob. And you have helped a lot."

Haley agreed. She smiled at Rob as she rose and shook his hand. "We'll get to the bottom of this," she said.

"But not by Monday," Rob guessed.

"No, I doubt it," she agreed.

"That's okay, because like I told you before, I'll be waiving the preliminary hearing," Rob told them.

A few minutes later, Haley found the latest note intended to scare her off, planted inside of her locked car in plain sight of the jail. Sergeant Thomas looked at her and shook his head. "This guy knows what he's doing," he said. "Getting into cars is a snap for him. I think Rob Sterling very well might be telling the truth."

Haley *knew* he was. "Yes, he could be," she agreed.

Rex shook the note open and read it.

> *Forget about Sterling, lady, or you won't be in no condition to think about nothing.*

Haley shivered. But she fought off any panic. "About that pistol of yours," she said to Rex.

"We're going to get it right now," he announced.

Thirty minutes later, Haley and Rex pulled up in front of Rob's house. She carried her purse, which now held a neat little .38 snub-nosed revolver, with her into the house. She would not be caught without it from this point on.

* * *

The jail cell felt hotter than normal to Rob as he sat on his bunk thinking. Maybe he was just upset. The session with Haley Gordon had been unsettling in a way. She had asked him questions similar to ones he might have expected her to ask on the witness stand. And yet, in her black eyes he was certain that he saw both sympathy and belief. He prayed that it was so, for he needed her help. He also needed the help of Sergeant Thomas, and the officer's apparent change of heart gave Rob the most hope he'd had since the night he was arrested and brought to the jail.

So much depended on Miss Gordon believing him. Rob carefully thought over the interview. Had he forgotten anything he should have told them? Or worse, had he told them too much? He berated himself for not keeping the note. It would have proven invaluable. Then he berated himself even worse for not having told them that night about it. Rex Thomas was right. That note, with his own fingerprints all over it, written in someone else's handwriting, would have been good support for his claim that he was in Park City that night especially if they had found it on site where he'd said he'd left it.

Rob laid down on the hard bunk just as his name was called again over the intercom. He had another visitor. This time it would be Raul Garcia. He felt so terrible about the mess Raul was in, and it was all his fault. He wished there was some way he could help him, but he was dependent on everyone else now. He couldn't help a soul. With a sigh, Rob pushed himself from the bunk and prepared to meet his best friend.

Detective Sperry Collier was with Raul. Rob told them every detail of his visit with Haley and Rex. They were interested in everything he told them, but Sperry Collier came to a very important conclusion when he mentioned the letter that Martin Ligorni had witnessed Rob find several months ago. That man loomed larger and larger as a major player in the whole matter of the framing of Rob Sterling. And Sperry intended to find out why.

* * *

A thin cloud of dust had settled on everything in Rob's house. Things had been straightened a little, probably by Tasha, Haley assumed. But for the most part the house appeared as it had the first time she'd been in it. Haley stood just inside the door for a moment and let the atmosphere of the place sink in. There was a terrible sadness here. It was as real to her as the coolness of the afternoon. There was also an urgency that pulsed steadily through her bones. It was as though the house itself could not find rest until the horrible thing that had happened there was concluded and justice appeased.

Haley felt the same unrest—the one who had brought the sadness to this home, who had ended the joy of living that had once resounded in these walls, needed to be brought to justice. Rex was moving about, looking here and there, studying whatever it was that interested his well-organized mind. Haley forced herself to move, to follow Rex. As soon as she did, he began to talk. Haley tried to listen, but all she heard was the sound of his voice, not what he said. Her mind was filled with what Rob had told them, where he said he'd been that night, and what had caused him to go there.

A skilled attorney could make a jury see Rob's story as something akin to a confession of guilt. She could do that, if she were motivated, and if she wanted only to make a case against a defendant. But that was no longer what she was about. Instead there had to be a way to help his statement, and the other things he'd told her, work with the physical evidence that had been found in this house to expose the truth, to expose the person who had actually instigated such fear and sadness in so many people's lives.

Rex was no longer talking. Haley shook her head, trying to drive away the spell of gloom that was slowly taking hold of her. She cast her eyes his way. She was surprised to see the look that was on his face. She expected him to be impatient with her distracted state of mind, or to urge her to get moving and look for whatever it was that might be found in here and then get out. That wasn't what she saw. His face was more a mirror of her own somber feelings. When he spoke again, she heard more than words. He spoke with intense feeling. "There's more here than it appears," he said slowly. "The setup of the shooting, the timing of it all—something's not adding up. Everyone connected to this case is either having strange things happen to them or they're acting weird themselves. There's a lot of unexplained tensions and . . ."

Haley nodded. "Greed or jealousy," she said. "A lot of criminals act out of one of those emotions. Could there be someone else who was jealous of Rob besides Martin?"

"That could be," he agreed. "But who? And could it have been that whoever it was didn't actually intend to kill her? Maybe he was just trying to get something else from her. Could he have only meant to frighten her? That sounds like something Martin might do, but any number of people could have wanted something Jennifer or Rob had."

Haley was watching the detective's face. Behind his expression was a mind that was working methodically. She said nothing, letting him continue. He turned away from her and stepped silently to the sofa. He knelt beside it, then he sat near the end of it. As he got up, his head was shaking. He took hold of the lamp that stood in the spot Jennifer had at one time appointed for it. He laid it on the floor in the same position he'd found it that night. "Stand there, Haley," he said, pointing to the very spot that Haley had been carefully avoiding.

She moved there and stood in front of the rocking chair that sat empty. "Stand there and watch me," he said. "And think about what it would have been like if it was dark."

Rex backed into the kitchen, out of Haley's sight. A moment later he came out, walking slowly, his eyes shut, recreating the darkness of that fatal night. One hand, his right one, was stretched out in front of him, his index finger pointing toward the spot where Haley stood, the spot where Jennifer Sterling had died. The other hand was also held out toward her. He seemed almost to be counting his steps. One foot touched the lamp. He stopped then and opened his eyes. "If he had the flashlight in one hand, and it was on her face as he came in here, *and* he was carrying a pistol with the other, he could have tripped on the lamp," he said.

"Most likely would have done," she agreed. "And then he might have fallen into the arm of the sofa," she added as she studied the scene before her.

Rex stepped over the lamp and attempted to re-create the fall that could have occurred. When he flung his arm against the sofa, he said, "Bang."

"It might have been an accident," Haley said excitedly, her thoughts churning quickly.

Rex looked thoughtfully at her. "Maybe the intruder meant to harm her later, or in some other way, but not at that moment."

Haley nodded in agreement. "But who could the intruder have been?"

"That's what we've got to find out," Sergeant Thomas said. "If someone did accidentally kill her, then he could have decided to make it look like Rob had done it. And he wanted us to think it was planned, calculated, and intentional. Could he have wanted Rob convicted, even to get the death penalty, so no questions would be asked?" The sergeant paused, drawing conclusions. "He wanted to let the system commit murder for him so he could avoid the penalties of his actions that night."

"Is there someone out there who hated Rob that we don't know about? Or someone who had a great deal to lose and would have considered Rob to be the most convenient sacrifice?"

"Maybe. There is Martin. He's a weird one. But he doesn't seem to have the money to fund all these threats and so on, though maybe he knows someone who does. Or maybe he's the ignorant cover-up for whoever's hiding him. We need to know more about him. At any rate, whoever did this would have gotten manslaughter for what he did here, if we're right in the conclusions we've just drawn," Haley said.

"If it's not Martin, whoever he's hiding might have a lot to lose, or at least thinks he does," Rex said thoughtfully. "In fact, considering that we're being watched, stalked, even shot at, I'd say this person will do anything to keep us from finding out who they are."

They turned at a noise, and Haley let out a little gasp. There, standing just inside the door were Sperry Collier and Raul Garcia. They both looked very serious. "Have you two been there long?"

"Long enough," Raul said. "We've got to find out who did this. And we've got to be very careful."

"Very," Sperry agreed. "And we have a lot to do." He turned to Rex. "Sergeant, I'm sorry about your partner. Is he going to be all right?"

"He'll be fine, but I guess I'll be working alone for a few days."

"Could you use a temporary and unofficial partner?" the private detective asked.

"I'd welcome it," Rex said, "now that we all seem to be more or less of the same mind."

CHAPTER SIXTEEN

While Haley fixed dinner that evening, Nat puttered about the kitchen. He tried to help, but he really wasn't a cook. He also didn't want to sit alone in her living room while she worked. Nat initiated conversation, but this time he did so wisely. He talked about his day, how he'd spent much of it researching case law that pertained to the civil action he had initiated for a company his firm represented.

It sounded very boring to Haley. She was glad she'd chosen criminal law; it was more creative and less technical, at least it sounded that way. Nat didn't sound like it bored him at all though, so Haley tried to act like it was all quite fascinating. When the meal was cooked, he helped her dish it up and put in on the table, and they sat down to eat. Nat hadn't taken many bites before he realized Haley was a very good cook. And being a man who didn't have a clue about cooking and neither the time nor the interest to learn, Nat felt that it was a good quality in someone he might want to get serious with. There were a lot of things about Haley that he really liked. In fact, he thought he might want to get serious with her as soon as this Sterling case was over and the district attorney was off his back.

About halfway through dinner, Nat casually asked, "Have you ever met that deputy who was shot today?" Nat already knew that she worked with him. She'd be very surprised if she had any idea how much he knew about her. And he found himself wanting to know more, but on a personal basis.

"He was assigned to work with me on the Sterling case," Haley said.

"Wow!" Nat exclaimed. "Aren't you frightened? I can't believe the awful things that are happening to everyone involved in this case. How is he anyway?"

"He'll be okay in a few days," Haley said. "And yes, in case you're wondering, I'm frightened, but only enough to make me cautious." She thought about mentioning the gun she now carried in her purse, but decided that would only make him worry more.

Nat took a bite and chewed for a moment. Then he asked, trying to sound casual, but honestly fearing what her answer might be, "Have you had any more threats of any kind? I've been worried sick about you ever since that creep was outside last night. I wish I could have gotten a look at him."

Haley smiled at Nat. "You don't believe he was really there, do you?"

"You saw him," he said evasively.

Haley got up from the table. "Let me show you something, Nat," she said, "but please don't get too upset about it."

She had placed the photo in a folder and put it in her computer desk. She'd about given up on the police being any help since the notes never had prints on them, but she kept a file anyway. She carried the folder back to the table. "Yes, Nat, I've had another threat of sorts, two in fact. The first one is in here. I'll let you see it if you want to."

"Please," Nat said anxiously.

She handed the folder to him and watched his face as he opened it. If it was a dramatic response she'd expected from him, she wasn't disappointed. Nat was stunned speechless. He stared at the picture for almost a minute. When he finally looked up, Haley said, "Turn it over."

He did, and once more he was shocked. But after a few moments, his surprise turned to rage. "This has got to be stopped, Haley!" he exclaimed. "This man is following you."

"It appears that way," she said casually.

"Haley! You've got to take this seriously," he said. "You're acting like it's no big deal."

Haley smiled. "You're sweet, Nat. But you've got to remember, I've been living with this thing for days now. And I've had all day to think about this photo."

"Well, I've only had a minute, and I'm sick to death with worry for you, Haley. You've got to get that district attorney boss of yours to let you off this case."

"But I don't want off the case, Nat. Don't you see? That's what somebody wants, and if we cave in to every criminal out there who tries to intimidate us, then they'd all do it, and we would become totally power-less. We can't back down to this kind of thing, Nat. At least I can't."

"But—but this," he stammered, looking again at the picture of the two of them in an intimate embrace. "It's horrible."

"I think it's kind of cute, myself. Maybe you didn't like it, but I enjoyed that kiss a great deal," Haley said with a grin.

"It isn't funny," Nat fumed.

"Sorry," Haley told him, "but I'm not going to let myself get all worked up about it anymore. I've been terrified, but I've got a grip on myself now. Please don't worry."

"Well, I am worried. You said there were two today?" Nat pressed angrily. "What was the second one?"

"Oh, that. It was a note left in my car when I was parked in front of the jail. After Kurt had been shot, Sergeant Thomas and I went to the jail to question Rob Sterling. When we came out, my stalker had left it in my car."

"How in the world is he getting in your car?" Nat demanded.

"I have no idea, but he does it fast and efficiently."

Nat was so agitated that he pushed back from the table and started pacing the kitchen floor. Haley got up too. She took his hand and pulled him to a stop. She tugged him around until he was facing her. "I'll take care of myself," she said. "You've got to believe that."

Nat drew back and looked Haley right in the eye. "I'm beginning to care an awful lot for you," he said. "I just wish this case would get over with so we could spend some time together without having to worry about your well-being."

She touched a finger lightly to his lips. "It's okay," she said. "I'm beginning to care about you too, but I don't want you worrying about me."

"I can't help it," he said softly.

A few moments later, Haley, her heartbeat slightly accelerated, said, "Hey, dinner's getting cold. We better finish. I made some dessert too."

They returned to the table, and Haley, who'd missed both breakfast and lunch that day, ate voraciously. She scarcely noticed that all Nat was doing was watching her. When she finally did, she said, "Nat, you've hardly touched a bite since we sat back down. I was hoping you'd like it."

"Oh, I do. You're a great cook, Haley Gordon," he said. "And this is simply delicious. But I guess I'm not used to this cloak-and-dagger stuff you're involved in. My stomach is tied in knots. I'm sorry."

"Well, let's clean up then, and we'll hold dessert for a little later. If you don't mind, I'd like to tell you about my day."

"If it gets worse than what I've already heard," he said, trying to sound lighthearted while feeling anything but, "then I'm not sure I can take it."

"It's quite interesting really," she said.

"Not boring like my day," he said. "I'm sorry if I bored you to death."

"You didn't," she protested weakly. They didn't talk much for the next few minutes. Only when the dishes were in the dishwasher and the kitchen appeared reasonably presentable did they talk about Haley's day again. When they did, she found that there was an awful lot she didn't want to talk about, so she left those things out. She told him what she'd done, but not how sympathetic she'd become to Rob's cause.

However, as she finished, she did say, "This is no open-and-shut case, Nat. We have a lot of investigating to do."

Nat realized from what she'd said that Haley had doubts about Rob Sterling's guilt, and he could see a way that he might be able to protect her, to get her off the case without her knowing he'd had anything to do with it. He'd simply share his feelings with William Montgomery the next morning. He told himself he was doing it for her, to protect a woman he'd become very fond of. That was at least partly true.

It began to grow late, and they were both a little tired. Haley wasn't quite ready to say good-bye though, so she put on some music. Nat said, "You have good taste in music. I bought this CD just last week."

She was impressed that they liked the same kind of music. "I'm in a music club," she said. "I can't take time to shop for music, so they send me e-mails about the newest stuff in the genres I like."

"Hey, me too. I've bought most of my CDs that way for a long time," he said. "This is good dancing music, Haley," he ventured, "would you like to try it out?"

"I'm not very good, but I'd love to anyway," she said, and she spent the next half hour in his arms, moving rhythmically around her small living room.

"You do too dance well," he teased.

"Thanks. But I don't get much practice."

"That's hard to believe," he said.

"No, really, I don't go out much," she said.

"Maybe you'd like to go out a little more," he said, "if you don't mind my company."

"I enjoy your company very much," she said. They continued to dance and Haley began thinking about *how* much.

"I've got to go now, Haley," he said as the midnight hour approached. "We've both got to work tomorrow. Thank you for a lovely evening."

"I'll walk to your car with you," she said, picking up her purse.

"Do you need your purse to walk to my car?" he asked. "It's only a few yards away."

Slightly embarrassed, she put it down and said nothing, and Nat wondered at the strangeness of her expression. They strolled down the walk, their arms around each other, gazing in the dim light at each other's faces. When Nat looked away from her, he stiffened. "My Jag!" he exclaimed.

"What's the matter with it?" Haley asked as he let go of her and started to walk more rapidly down the walk. "Where did you park it? I don't see it."

"That's just it!" he thundered. "It's gone. I left it right here." He'd stepped off the curb and was stomping angrily on the pavement where he'd left his beloved gold Jaguar. This was more than he could stand. "We've got to call the cops," he said, starting back up the walk.

Haley followed after looking around nervously for any sign of her stalker. She couldn't believe someone had stolen his expensive car from right in front of her apartment. He raced to her phone, put it to his ear, then slammed it down. "There's no dial tone!" he exclaimed. "Your stupid phone's dead."

Haley grabbed her purse again, opened it, and reached inside. She had to force her hand past the secure feel of the small .38 revolver before she found her cellular phone. She pulled it out and handed it wordlessly to Nat. Within two minutes a squad car pulled up outside. As they took a report from Nat, Haley began to worry. He was so worked up over his missing car that she feared he was going to have a stroke or something. When she tried to calm him down, he rebuffed her. He was really upset about his car being stolen, but his rudeness seemed almost unnatural. She went outside for a moment to get over the frustration she was feeling over him. She carried her purse with her; the stalker very much on her mind.

She walked absently to her car and opened the door for no real reason. She just wanted to be away from Nat until he cooled down. She was actually a little hurt. His car seemed more important to him than anything else. Was it more of a status symbol to him than a means of transportation? She wondered about it as she found herself looking at still one more note.

Despite her resolve, she was shaking badly when she picked it up and read,

> *You don't listen, do you lady? Tell your white friend that he'll get his car back as soon as you get off the Sterling thing. There ain't going to be no more warnings. My boss has had it with you.*

Whoever this guy was, he'd just inadvertently admitted that he was working for someone else. And Haley wished she knew who. She tried to control her trembling as she shoved the note in her purse and shut and locked her car, thinking what a waste of time that was. This guy could get in it whenever he wanted.

Apparently his skills extended to gold Jaguars as well—security system and all.

She kept her hand in her purse as she walked quickly from her carport to the apartment. She went in, shut the door, and sat down across the room from where the two officers were still talking to Nat.

He looked up, and his face went white. "Haley!" he exclaimed coming to his feet. "What's the matter?" He dropped on the loveseat beside her and took her hand in his, searching her face tenderly. "You went outside alone. Why did you do that?"

She reached in her purse and pulled out the latest, perhaps the last, note from her stalker. She handed it to Nat, disappointed that she'd let her fear show. "It was in my car," she said.

Nat read it, shook his head fiercely, and looked up at the officers who'd both followed him across the room. "What is it?" they asked. "Another threat against Miss Gordon?"

Nat put his arm protectively around her shoulders and pulled her to him. "Yes, and a confession to a theft," he answered.

One of the officers reached for the note, and Nat let him have it. As the officers looked at the note, Nat said to Haley, "I'm sorry. I let things get out of perspective there for a little bit." She was feeling a lot better about him already. She laid her head on his shoulder and he said, "They'll find my car."

Haley felt even better at his last words. His Jaguar had just been downgraded to a mere car. And he actually seemed more concerned about her than it, at least at the moment.

The officers finished looking the note over. "We'll need to keep this," one of them said.

"Too bad we don't know who this guy is," the other one added. "But if we do ever find him, this note will tie him to your car."

Haley remembered her phone. "My phone line is dead," she said. "I can't help but wonder if it was intentional."

The officers said they'd check around outside. When they came back inside a few minutes later, they told Haley that the line had been cut. "Are you sure you want to stay here tonight?" one of them asked.

"I'll be okay," she said, trying her best to put on a brave face.

The officers left, and Nat held Haley for several more minutes. Finally, he said, "Haley, I'm scared to death for you. Tell your boss tomorrow that someone else will have to take over Sterling's prosecution. It's the only way you'll be safe."

"I can't," she moaned sadly. "I just can't."

"Haley, I really would like my Jaguar back too. The thief said in his note that he'd let me have my . . ." He trailed off at the look Haley gave him.

"Do you honestly believe he'll give your car back if I go off the case? Think again," she said as she struggled from the now confining feel of his arms and stood up. The car was a Jaguar again. Somehow that hurt. "The kind of guy who threatens women and steals cars doesn't keep promises. Come on, Nat," she said, "I'll give you a ride home. You could stay here, but the neighbors would talk." She forced a grin.

"And we wouldn't want that," he said, also trying to be lighthearted when there was absolutely nothing to be lighthearted about.

"I'll call a friend of mine to come and get me. I can't let you drive home alone after you let me off."

Nat borrowed Haley's cell phone again. "Hi, it's Nat," he said a moment later. "I'm sorry for calling so late. I have a little problem. Can I talk to Steve?"

Nat waited for a couple of minutes. "I think I must have woken them up," he whispered to Haley. "His wife's getting him." Then just a moment later, Nat said, "Steve, I'm sorry to disturb you. I had dinner with a friend tonight, and someone stole my Jag while we were inside."

He stopped. It was clear that his friend had something to say about the loss of Nat's valuable car. "Yes, I reported it, and the cops have been here," he said. Then, after another pause while his friend talked, he added, "I hope so." Then he gave Haley's address and said, "I'll be waiting inside. I sure do appreciate it."

After disconnecting, he handed the phone back to Haley. "You'd better get this plugged in and charged. You don't want the battery to go dead while your other phone's out of order." She took it and he said, "I could sure use some of that pie you baked while we wait for my ride. Steve won't be long."

Twenty minutes later, when a knock came on the door, Haley opened it to a gorgeous blond who said, "Hi, I came for Nat." Then she turned to Nat. "Steve asked me to come get you," she said. "He got an ambulance call just after you phoned. Hope you don't mind."

Nat minded, all right, but how was Steve to know.

This must be Steve's wife, Haley concluded. Without any introduction, Nat headed for the door. "I'll call tomorrow," he said to Haley.

"Hi, I'm Haley Gordon," Haley said to the blond, annoyed that Nat had forgotten his manners.

"Oh, sorry," Nat said, his face scarlet. Haley stared at his expression for a moment. *This girl is not Steve's wife,* Haley decided as she felt a stabbing pang of jealousy and hurt. "Haley, this is my friend's sister, Susie Powell."

"Hi," Susie said as she took Nat possessively by the hand and tugged him toward the door. "You must be the attorney he's been helping." Nat didn't correct her.

Haley's evening had just spiraled, crashed, and burned. *What does that blond siren mean by "helping"?* Haley wondered. The blond ushered Nat through the door ahead of her as she said, "Nat, darling, I hope they find your Jaguar."

And what does Nat think he is doing? Haley finished silently as the door shut abruptly.

CHAPTER SEVENTEEN

Haley had given very little thought to the case during the night. The sleepless hours had been spent carefully removing Nat Turley from her mind. She wanted nothing more to do with him, and by the time she walked into her office that morning, she thought she'd successfully ruled out any further contact with him, social or otherwise.

However, the feelings she had been developing toward him were not so easily expunged. So she did what she'd taught her Sunday School students to do when evil thoughts entered their minds—she thought about the words to a hymn or a scripture every time her mind reverted back to Nat.

Haley got further help in not thinking about Nat from the district attorney later that morning. He didn't call her to his office; he came to hers. Without preamble, he said, "I'm thinking about pulling you from the Rob Sterling case."

Fire shot from her eyes, and she surged to her feet. "You can't do that!" she protested.

"I can do as I please," he said mildly, ignoring her anger. "I'm the boss here, remember?"

She dropped her voice a notch and tried to extinguish the fire he'd stoked in her already fevered mind. "Please," she said. "I've been working so hard on this case." She was very careful not to let any of her recent conclusions slip out.

"I know you have, Haley, and I deeply appreciate your efforts, but I intend to win this case. I'm concerned you have doubts or fears that are affecting your investigation. And I'm worried about your safety. Besides, I need to keep my promises to the public, and I can't do that and worry about you at the same time—too many special interest groups," he joked.

Haley kept her mouth shut after that. He was thinking only of himself. And Rob Sterling's life was nothing compared to the prestige of being attorney general, and who knew what after that. *Governor perhaps?* she thought bitterly.

"I'm really only thinking of you, Haley," he said. "You have the ability to win this case. I have no doubt of that. But you can't win it from the grave."

She was shocked. "From the grave?" she asked, her voice rising again.

"Yes, from the grave. I don't want to win this case at the expense of a bright young attorney like yourself. If your life is in serious danger because of this case, I simply can't take a chance, as badly as I hate to have someone else take over at this point."

Haley again gained control. "Mr. Montgomery, I can take care of myself. I have reason to believe the threats have stopped now. I have not received any today. And I'm prepared to defend myself if I have to."

"But you're a woman, and that's not fair to you," the district attorney said.

"I am an attorney, a very able prosecutor, and my gender has nothing to do with this," she said sharply. "Nor does my race," she added just for spite.

The district attorney wisely pulled back. He knew better than to use gender as a threat. "I like you, Haley, and I don't want to see you hurt," he said. "Are you sure you're okay with it?"

"I'm positive," she said.

"Okay, for now you may keep on it, but you be careful," he said. "I really want you to be with me when I get to the state capital."

"Thanks," she said, so relieved that she had to suppress the urge to cry.

"Are you all ready for the preliminary hearing?" he asked. "It's set for Monday, isn't it?"

"It is, and I'm ready," she said. She almost told him that Rob was going to waive the preliminary hearing, but he wasn't going to do it until that morning in open court, so she decided to leave well enough alone.

After he'd left, she did let herself break down for just a moment in the privacy of her office. But then she pulled herself together and thought objectively about the threats she'd received. The district attorney didn't know about some of them, certainly not the most recent. She hoped he didn't find out, or the next meeting they'd have would probably have a different outcome.

Haley pulled out her growing file, and as she opened it, she had a terrible thought. What if she did get taken off the case? The information in this file was very dangerous to Rob Sterling's future. In the wrong hands it could very well convict him. She was learning the truth, and the truth was in there, but a prosecutor who wanted to could twist the facts and make Rob look guilty.

The decision that Haley reached next surprised her. Everything in that file must be copied and kept at home. She wasn't completely sure why she felt so strongly about it, but she did.

Haley received calls from Sperry, Raul, and Rex that morning. They were all working hard to find the evidence they needed to back up the conclusions they had all drawn the day before. And it was not going well. Martin Ligorni had dropped out of law school, she learned from Rex. He still had his apartment, but he hadn't been seen by the neighbors since the day after they'd discovered the pictures of Jennifer Sterling plastered all over his apartment.

"I really would like to know if that note that Rob had in his law books is in Martin's apartment, but I also know that we don't have enough to get a search warrant to take a look," Sergeant Thomas told her. "I'm worried. Just like Frank Rawlings, Martin seems to have vanished. But unlike Frank, who I believe has been killed, Martin probably thought we were about to arrest him for murder and simply fled. We probably should have arrested him for something just to keep him around, but it's too late now. But we'll keep looking."

"Yes, we should have made sure he couldn't leave. But it's too late to worry about that now. Why don't you talk to the manager of the apartments," Haley suggested. "Make sure that if they decide at any point to rent it out to anyone else that they let you know. If they collect his belongings, then maybe we can find a way to have a look."

Rex agreed to do that.

When Detective Collier called, he told Haley that he'd talked to Ann Denton, the other secretary in the office where Jennifer Sterling had worked before her death. "She seemed really nervous today. Said she'd been mistaken. There was nothing going on with Jennifer and

Dan Smathers. She says to leave her alone, that she has nothing further to say," he told her.

"Witness tampering?" Haley asked.

"Looks like it," Sperry agreed. "Anyone who might be able to help seems to be either disappearing or changing stories."

"Check with that other woman, Trista Zippeta, and her ex-husband. See if their story is still holding together," Haley suggested. "If it is, let's figure out a way to find out what really happened with them."

"I've been kicking around an idea," Sperry said. "I'll talk to you about it later."

"Good, let me know how it goes with her," Haley said. "And with the ex."

As for Raul Garcia, he'd told Haley he was scheduled for arraignment on Monday on the charge of arson. "And get this, Haley," he said bitterly. "It's been scheduled at the same time as Rob's preliminary hearing, only in a different courtroom."

"Who's going to represent you?" she asked.

"I'll do it myself," he said. "At least at this stage."

"What have you heard from the Office of Professional Conduct about the complaint against you?" she asked.

"There'll be a hearing in two or three weeks, I'm told. I don't have a date yet. The law clerk that is conducting the investigation had something come up in his personal life that delayed things. They didn't tell me what it was, but the delay's okay with me," Raul said. "I could use a little more time to get prepared."

Haley wished him good luck and hung up. Moments later she got yet another call. "It's from a man, but he won't give his name," her secretary said.

She suspected that she knew who it was, and he was the last person on earth she wanted to talk to right now. Nat had reduced her to ashes last night. *But what if it's someone who has information that might help Rob?* she thought. She'd just have to hope it wasn't Nat.

It was.

"Haley, I can explain," he began desperately. "Please, over lunch. It's not like it looks."

"No thanks," Haley said and softly put the phone down.

She didn't need any more pain. And yet, what if she really had judged him wrongly? But she'd seen Susie and how possessive she was. And Susie knew about her: *the attorney Nat was helping.*

"Stop it!" she said aloud. "Forget him." She was worried someone had heard her and she glanced around. Only her office walls heard her. And they, at least, wouldn't help or hurt her by knowing her true feelings.

Haley walked to a small restaurant several blocks from her downtown office. She walked rapidly, trying her best to dispel her pain and grief. She had a lonely but excellent lunch and began the brisk walk back. She was so deep in thought that she didn't notice the gold Jaguar that pulled up to the curb. But she did hear the voice that said, "Get in lady, or I'll drop you right there."

She jerked her head around and found herself looking into the huge barrel of a pistol. The man holding it meant business, and he was driving Nat Turley's stolen Jaguar. She could either do as the man said—who she instinctively knew was her stalker—or die right there on a downtown Salt Lake City street. If she did what he said, she'd at least have a chance.

Haley got in, clutching her pistol-bearing purse tightly. At all costs, she had to keep that purse. The big man said, "This is the first smart move you've made since we met."

Haley was scared, but she was also angry, and her anger gave her control. "I wasn't aware that we'd met," she said icily. "Where are we going?"

He threw her a nasty grin and gunned the car into traffic. "It don't matter where we're going. What matters is what we're going to do when we get there."

Now she was afraid. The look he was giving her from the corner of his eye was something no woman ever wanted to see. "You and me," he went on, "are made for each other. We're even the same color."

Trying to be brave, she decided she needed to keep talking, to distract him. She'd shoot him if she had to. "Race has nothing to do with it," she said.

"Oh yes it does. You looked so stupid with that white guy. You know, the one that gave me this car." He was holding his gun with the barrel pointed in her direction. It didn't waver. She had to be very careful what she said and did. She might only have one chance and she couldn't blow it.

"The cops are looking for this car," she said. "It's only a matter of time, probably only minutes, and one of them will be following us."

"And if they do, they'll just have to quit following us, because if they don't, there won't be no black lady prosecutor no more," he said.

"You kill me and they'll kill you," she said.

"Shut up. I gotta concentrate on my driving. Don't want to attract attention by running red lights."

"Who are you working for?" she asked.

He turned his face toward her. "Rob Sterling, who else?"

"I don't believe it."

"Well, believe it or don't lady," the man said. "Makes no difference to me. I got what I wanted. I got my five grand, I got me a new Jaguar, and lady, I got you. That's all I wanted, and I got it. I don't care what happens to Rob Sterling. They can fry him for all I care."

She had him talking. She had to keep him talking. "Rob didn't hire you. Somebody else hired you on his behalf," she said.

"You're a smarter lady than I thought," he said with a grin. She shuddered at the way he grinned at her. "The guy that hired me, he's one tough dude. Ain't nobody messes with him. I tell you his name, and I might die, and I ain't about to do that, not since I got you, pretty lady."

As they rode, Haley had been working her right hand into her purse. Once it was there, she took hold of Rex Thomas's little pistol. *Maybe when we get to where we're going,* she thought, as her captor's large semiautomatic pistol remained pointed at her.

They made more turns than she could keep track of, but after about twenty blocks, he suddenly turned off the street on the west side of the city and pulled the Jaguar into an open garage. "This is where we're going," he said. "Don't give me trouble and I'll be gentle with you. I'm getting out first. You slide over and follow me."

It was now or never. Once he got Haley into that old house, she'd never come out alive. She was as sure of that as she'd ever been of anything. She moved the purse in front of her. "Get your hand out of the purse," he said as his dark eyes suddenly became very wide in the semi-gloom of the garage interior.

She shook her head. "I'd rather not," she said.

"You got you a toy gun in there?" he asked.

She was working the pistol into position in her purse. She was as calm as she could be. She knew what she had to do. "It's no toy," she said as she pulled the trigger.

The noise was deafening. The big pistol flew from her captor's hand. Blood spurted from both his hand and his thick arm. He began to howl and rolled from the car, leaving the keys in the ignition. Without waiting to see what he was going to do, she slid into the driver's seat as she pulled the still-smoking .38 from her purse, shifting it to her left hand. She started the engine, shifted into reverse, and gunned the engine, the whole time holding the gun toward the door of the house through which the big man had scrambled. The car roared into the street. She shifted gears and left a layer of rubber on the street. She hadn't gone a block before she slowed, watching her rearview mirror, and pulled her phone from her purse. She dialed 911, reported her location, and continued to drive.

A police cruiser appeared in moments, and Haley pulled over to the side of the road. The officers came running toward her. She dropped her gun back into her ruined purse and rolled down the window of Nat's car. She told the officers quickly who she was and what had happened. One of them spoke rapidly into his radio even as she heard sirens in the distance. "Are you injured?" one of the officers asked as she stepped from the car.

"I'm okay," she said. "But the guy who picked me up isn't."

"But you have blood all over you," one of the officers said.

Haley looked down and realized she was soaked with blood. "It's not mine," she said as the adrenaline began to wear off and she began to tremble. Then she thought about where she was and said, "Oh, no, I think I've ruined Nat's Jaguar."

The officers laughed and one of them leaned in and looked. "Not too bad," he said. "It'll clean up."

* * *

Sergeant Rex Thomas heard the radio traffic and turned in the middle of the street, heading north. It had only taken him a few seconds to put things together and realize that Haley was involved in the shooting that officers were responding to. He'd just picked up Sperry Collier and the two of them had been on their way to the home of Trista Zippeta.

That plan was quickly abandoned as the two worried men raced through the heavy city traffic. "Sounds like Nat Turley's gold Jag," Sperry said.

"Yes, and it was being driven by Haley's stalker," Rex added. "He must have kidnapped her. And from what they're saying about an injured suspect, I'd guess she used my pistol. I just hope he didn't use his."

Both men were relieved when they saw Haley a few minutes later. She was shaken up and covered in blood, but none the worse for wear. "They got your stalker," Rex told Haley after they'd parked behind the gold Jaguar.

"Is he okay?" she asked.

Rex chuckled. "I just talked on the phone with one of the officers at the house. He says you did a number on the guy's hand and his arm, but other than that he's okay. If he goes back to writing threatening notes though, he'll have to do it left-handed."

Just then another car came flying up the street and skidded to a stop across the road from where Haley stood talking to the officers. Nat jumped out and ran across the street. He didn't even look at his car. All he did was take Haley in his arms and hold her tightly, staining an expensive suit with the blood from her blouse. "Haley, I'm so glad you're okay. I was worried sick when the police called." He was almost sobbing, and all her anger at him drained away. He didn't say one word about his Jaguar. It really appeared as though it were her he cared about the most. And she finally broke down and cried, her tears wetting his suit coat.

"And Haley, about Susie "

"Not now, Nat," Haley interrupted through her tears. "Just hold me."

CHAPTER EIGHTEEN

The district attorney's office was buzzing when Haley returned late that afternoon. Everyone was amazed at the way she'd handled her stalker. Even the district attorney seemed pleased with her. "Haley, I owe you an apology," he said. "I seriously underrated you. It sounds like you handled yourself very well."

Haley was rather embarrassed by the whole affair. "I only did what I had to do," she said modestly. "And if you want to know, I was scared half out of my wits."

William's booming laugh filled the office. "Well, all I can say is if fear gets that kind of result from you, I certainly won't worry about you anymore. Rob Sterling can start planning his funeral."

That is one of the cruelest things I've ever heard, Haley thought to herself as she restrained from letting the district attorney know how monstrous she thought he was. Even when he was paying her a compliment, her respect for him continued to plummet. She began to wonder if she really wanted to work for him when he went to the attorney general's office, *if* he did.

"Oh, and Haley, I got a call from an attorney by the name of Nat Turley. I know you know him. He seems like a nice guy," William said. "He called to tell me how grateful he was to you for getting his car back for him. I told him I'd tell you."

"Thanks, William," she said. "But I really wasn't thinking about his car. It was my life that I was worried about."

"As I am. Keep up the good work, Haley," he said. "I've got a press conference to hold in a few minutes. You're welcome to come if you'd like. I'm sure you'll be asked about. If not, I intend to let the public know how proud I am of you and the work you do in this office."

After the district attorney had left, Haley wondered how much political publicity he was planning to milk out of what had happened to her that afternoon. It really made her angry that he would use something so serious to further his own ambitions, but it seemed that was exactly what he planned to do.

* * *

Sergeant Thomas and Detective Collier had to wait several hours before the doctors would let them talk to Haley's abductor. And when they finally were admitted to his tightly secured hospital room, he refused to say anything to them except to tell them he wanted an attorney. They could see that he wasn't going to be much help, at least not yet. They both knew from experience, however, that once he was closer to going to prison for a very long time, that he would probably become more cooperative.

Handwriting samples found in his house were already at the lab for comparison with the threatening notes Haley had received. But from preliminary examination, there was very little doubt that he was the author of all of them. They would just have to be patient. Enough pressure later on might bring some positive results.

As they'd waited to see the stalker, Sperry and Rex had come up with a strategy. They were determined to learn something of value from Trista Zippeta and her ex-husband. They decided that the next morning would be soon enough. Rex went home to spend some time with his family, but Detective Collier had other plans for the evening.

* * *

It was not Dan Smathers's practice to meet with his more seedy acquaintances at his office, unless of course he was defending them in a case. And it was never a good idea to meet with them at the same covert location more than once or twice. His recent meetings with such a man were becoming far too frequent, and it was becoming difficult to secure new locations. So he used an old one tonight—the very place where his contact had assaulted him. Dan Smathers was becoming more angry and nervous at the same time.

The contact had kept him waiting, and when the man finally appeared before him, Dan didn't wait long to snap angrily at him. "I'm paying you well," he said. "Why the screw up?"

They both knew what he was talking about. "My man got impatient," he was answered calmly.

"Yes, and he got caught. It's only a matter of time until he talks." Dan never took his eyes off the man as he addressed him. "He knows too much."

The other man snorted. "You're soft, Danny boy," he said sarcastically. "You carry too much fear. I'm disappointed in you."

"I didn't call you here to listen to your philosophical rantings," Dan said. "What do you plan to do about him?"

"I don't think it would be wise to tell you. You just keep the money rolling my way, and I'll take care of the details."

"You *are* going to see to it that no one talks to him, are you not?" Dan demanded.

"What can he say? He thinks Rob Sterling's hiding behind me. He has no idea it's really you who's paying him. You worry too much," the man scoffed. "You should be worried more about that skirt you're flirting with now, that Ann Denton."

Dan flared up. "She's none of your business," he said hotly.

"Ah, but she is. She knows a lot Danny boy. She knows about your dinners with Mrs. Sterling and who really paid the bill. But your partners don't know that, do they?" he asked slyly. "And if she got mad at you, she could make a lot of trouble, couldn't she? And even if she keeps her mouth shut, you really should be more careful about being seen with her. People might see you somewhere a little too nice and talk, you know. And it could lead to questions."

Dan was stunned. *How does he know so much?* he thought angrily. Now he had to wonder if the man also knew about the funds he'd been "borrowing" to keep up with his considerable expenses. If he did, he could do some real damage to Dan's future. *All the snake would have to do is send an anonymous note or make a short phone call,* Dan reflected in disgust, *and it could be over before I had a chance.* He finally said, "I've got things well under control with Miss Denton." He could only hope he was right.

"Well, one thing about it, at least the Denton girl's not married. Maybe you're getting a little smarter." The contact smirked. "Now is that all you called me here for, Danny boy? I hope it's not, because it's dangerous meeting so often, you know."

"No, it's not all. Where's Martin Ligorni?" Dan asked, ignoring the snide comment revealing how well the man had assessed Dan's behavior. *Detestable fool*, he thought angrily.

"He's a worm. Couldn't hurt you."

"But you gave him money—*my money*. Where is he?" Dan demanded angrily. "Or did you let him slip away like you did Frank Rawlings?"

Dan noticed just the slightest tic in his contact's grim smile. Suddenly he knew that his man was not in as complete control as he'd been assured. "You've lost both of them, haven't you?" Dan asked.

"Frank Rawlings is no threat to you, Danny boy," the contact said confidently. Dan hated it when he called him that, but there was nothing he could do about it.

"And Martin?" Dan asked, gritting his teeth against the pejorative nickname.

"He can't be far. I'll find him before the cops do."

"Ha! So you *have* lost track of him," Dan said grimly. "The cops had better not have him in hiding somewhere."

"They don't. And I'll find him first," he was promised.

"There's also Jake Zippeta," Dan reminded him. "Tell me his story is solid."

"He and his ex-wife are both greedy," the impatient man assured Dan. "They'll say what's needed when it's needed, if that prosecutor, Haley Gordon, does her job."

"She should have been spooked off by now," Dan reminded him. "If she stays with this case very far past the preliminary hearing, you'll be owing me a refund. She's too honest—no ambition for her own career. Someone else has got to take over the case, someone I can deal with. So you get her off the case soon or you'll wish you had."

"Don't try to threaten me, Danny," the man snorted. "One phone call is all it would take to set your own partners wondering what you're up to—not to mention the authorities."

Dan tensed. The contact was right, and they both knew it. "Just get her off the case."

"She will be," the contact assured him.

"Raul Garcia," Dan said.

"What about him?" the contact asked. "He's no longer a threat."

"I know. Good job for once. I want to see a good job with our note-writing lackey too. He knows who you are, and that could lead to me."

"No one will get to me, so you're safe," the other assured him. "I'll deal with my man."

The two men left, the contact first, followed by Dan. And from deep in the shadows of another abandoned building across the street, Sperry Collier watched, regretting that he'd been unable to get into the building where they'd met, close enough to hear what the two men had to say to each other. But he'd learned a great deal anyway. He'd had a feeling that it would pay to follow Dan Smathers tonight. He figured the capture of Haley's stalker would spur some action in her opponent if Dan were involved. And sure enough, Dan had hurried off shortly after dark to hold a furtive meeting with someone whose identity Sperry now had to discover.

Sperry followed the contact at a cautious distance. He was quite certain that whoever the man was, he was no novice. If Sperry was spotted, the man would be hard to follow or to find again. But the hardened private investigator also was not a novice. And he followed until the man pulled into a bar. He never got a good enough look to be certain he could identify him again. He was Caucasian, and that was all Sperry could be sure of. But after the man had been inside for awhile, Sperry wrote down his license number and a description of his car.

He doubted the license number would have the true name or address of Dan's contact, but he could at least check. It was another hour before he had the information he sought. It had been easy when he was a cop, but as a private eye, it always took some finagling to get the information he wanted. Sperry drove to the address listed for the registered owner of the car. To his surprise, he found a large home in a ritzy neighborhood. It probably wasn't the real address of the man who had met Dan that night, but Sperry decided to wait just in case he was wrong and the car appeared there later. To his surprise, it did, at about four in the morning. *At last*, he thought, *something concrete to work on.*

Sperry finally went home, moving noiselessly to avoid waking his wife as he got ready for bed. But all his care was wasted when the phone rang at five. He rolled out of bed, answered the phone, listened for a moment, then moaned.

The stalker was gone. He'd been busted out of the secure hospital room by an armed man wearing a mask. Sperry kicked himself for not staying near the bar and waiting for Dan's contact to leave. It was very likely that the man had something to do with the missing stalker. Sperry wondered if he was getting too old for this kind of work as he rolled back into bed. There was nothing more he could do that early in the morning. Rex hadn't seemed too worried, he'd just called to let Sperry know. Well, if Rex wasn't worried, then there was no use in getting himself all worked up.

* * *

Reporters flooded into the courtroom of the Honorable James F. Horton thirty minutes before court was scheduled to begin on Monday morning. Haley had arrived ahead of them. She always made it a practice to be to court ahead of time, even if she was forced to wait on the judge. She'd learned early in her career that most judges got very testy when they had to wait for attorneys.

She studied her case file as she waited, although Rob had assured her that he was going to waive the hearing. She was prepared just in case something went wrong. She occasionally glanced behind her. She'd also found it was a good practice to have an idea who was in the courtroom. Most of the reporters from the press she recognized, and several nodded or smiled an acknowledgment.

Court was scheduled at nine that morning. At ten minutes before the hour, Haley glanced back again and was surprised to see Nat Turley sitting in the back row near the door. He smiled and gave her a thumbs up. She smiled back but turned quickly to face the front of the room. Despite the warm reception she'd received from him after saving his car, she had remained firm in her resolve to break off their relationship. She had steadfastly refused to speak to him on the phone, although he had attempted to call her both on her cell and at her office several times. She didn't have the time or the emotional stamina to get involved in a complex relationship while she was working this case. The distraction Nat had already caused her was proof of that, she thought.

But sitting there now, thinking about him watching her, caused just the slightest softening of her heart. Maybe he did care more than she'd let herself believe. Maybe she should listen to his excuses about Susie the blond bombshell. Or maybe she should just keep Nat at a safe distance. *At least for now,* she decided.

In an effort not to give Nat the wrong idea, Haley didn't look back again, although she really did want to know who else might be in the courtroom this morning. She really needed to know; sometimes people who had a guilty interest in a case—those undiscovered by the authorities—made an appearance. It was sort of along the order of an arsonist who stood around watching the flaming evidence of his handiwork.

She found herself irritated at Nat for interfering. Of course, she knew that Rex Thomas would be coming in, and he would certainly keep an eye on the spectators. Sperry, however, would not show up because he was with Raul in a different courtroom that very moment.

A couple of minutes before the hour, two large deputies escorted the accused into the courtroom where he was seated at the defense table. Haley wondered where Dan was. The judge had clearly instructed him to be here as backup counsel. Maybe he hadn't learned the lesson about being late. But at exactly nine, just moments before the bailiff called the court into session, Dan, whose face still looked pretty bad, hurried in and sat next to Rob Sterling. The two exchanged glances, but that was all.

Judge Horton asked Haley if she was ready, and she said she was, hoping that she wasn't going to get surprised and have to present her case. Then he asked Dan if the defense was ready, but before Dan could answer, Rob spoke up. "Your Honor, if you will recall, I'm defending myself in this case."

The judge nodded and asked, "Are you ready then, Mr. Sterling?"

Rob answered immediately. "I have already pled not guilty in this case, and what I'm about to do is not to be construed as a change in my position. I say that, Your Honor, for the benefit of the press, not the court. At any rate, I have decided to waive the preliminary hearing today."

Dan's jaw dropped just the littlest bit and for the briefest moment, then he snapped his mouth shut. "Mr. Sterling, I would suggest you confer with Mr. Smathers about that decision," said the judge.

But Dan had recovered from his surprise and jumped to his feet. "Your Honor, I'm in total agreement with the defendant. We both know that there is no way we can present a case today that would overcome the state's burden of showing that a crime was committed and that it likely was the defendant who committed it. However," Dan added, scowling briefly at Haley, who was grinning to herself, "we'll be more than ready at trial and request a trial date be set for as soon as possible, if you will be presiding, that is."

"Well, since this hearing today has been waived, I see no reason that I can't handle the case at trial. We'll plan that way for now."

"Your Honor," Rob said, "I must again remind the court that I am representing myself. I can't stop you from letting Mr. Smathers sit here, but I don't need or want his help. However, I do agree that a date should be set for a jury trial no later than a couple of months away if possible." Rob hated to let it drag on that long. Sitting in that stuffy jail cell was already attacking his sanity, but he knew that he needed time, that he needed to give the detectives time.

"Miss Gordon," the judge said, "it appears that you will have it easy today. Will about two months or so give the prosecution time to prepare?"

"Maybe, Your Honor," she responded, quickly glancing at Rob, "but unless I can have an assurance that a continuance will be granted if I find that it's not sufficient time, I would have to object."

"Very well, you will have the continuance if you need it and if you make your motion at least three weeks before the scheduled trial date."

There was a shuffling of calendars, and finally the judge said, "It appears that the closest date I can give you is January second. Have any pretrial motions to me by the first of December," he said. "And Mr. Sterling, I would once again strongly advise you to accept the aid of Dan Smathers. You're in way over your head."

"Thank you for your concern," Rob said. "But I won't be changing my mind."

A moment later the judge rapped his gavel and swept himself from the bench, shaking his head as he left.

* * *

Proceedings were equally short a few doors down the corridor. Raul Garcia pled not guilty to the charge of arson and a preliminary hearing date was set a little over three weeks away. He too was advised to seek the aid of counsel, and the next case was called.

* * *

Haley smiled briefly at Rob as he was led away. He smiled back, and she couldn't help thinking what a gentleman he was. She had to help him.

She waited a few minutes for the courtroom to clear, noting that Nat had already left and hoping to avoid bumping into him. As she waited she thought about the stalker. She had panicked when she got the call from Rex, telling her that he had been taken from the hospital. But he assured her that he was certain that she had nothing to worry about. "I'm sure he won't be bothering you again," he'd said.

So Haley tried not to worry. She'd gained a lot of confidence in the sergeant, and if he felt that she was safe, then she'd try not to worry. She wondered if he knew more than he was telling her, but she guessed it didn't matter. Rex Thomas knew his business. She tucked the problem of the stalker somewhere in the back of her mind and gathered up her papers.

When Haley finally entered the corridor, Nat was waiting and took her immediately by the arm. "Please, Haley," he implored gently. "Give me a chance to explain. I feel terrible about what happened. I care for you a great deal. Please."

Haley, despite herself, felt her heart flutter, but she was still cautious. "Nat," she said, "I enjoyed the time we spent together, but I was hurt. I don't care to be hurt again, and the next couple of months are going to be very stressful for me. I can't afford to risk the added emotional stress you might give me."

"Haley, please. Meet me for lunch and just listen. Then if you still feel the same, I'll leave you alone," he promised, knowing full well that William Montgomery wouldn't like that at all.

Allowing herself to look at Nat's eyes was a mistake. "Okay," she relented, then added firmly, "but I'm buying my own lunch."

Nat's face lit up, and he applied gentle pressure to her arm. "You won't regret it," he said. "Thank you." Then he named a place. "Noon okay?" he asked.

"That will be fine," Haley answered, wondering what she had let herself in for.

CHAPTER NINETEEN

Nat had chosen the right profession. He was most persuasive. And that was even with a resistant and even slightly hostile audience.

"I can't believe that my best friend would do that to me," Nat was saying. He'd already explained that Susie was his friend's sister and that they had dated on and off for several months, but that she'd never really interested him. However, she felt differently and didn't want the relationship to end. "But Steve didn't know he'd get called out right then and asked someone else to get me," Nat said.

Haley nodded as she looked deep into Nat's appealing eyes. "She was quick to volunteer when his wife couldn't come because of the kids, I'm sure. Although it seems to me that Susie could have been the babysitter since she was staying with them for the night anyway. I wish you would have explained something to me right then. It would have saved me a lot of pain."

Leaning forward, Nat smiled and said, "I'm glad you feel strongly enough about me that pain was even possible, but I hope it never happens again. Am I forgiven?" he asked directly.

She found herself nodding in surrender. All the careful mental surgery she'd done had been for naught. *He's like an unrelenting tumor,* she jokingly thought to herself. "Of course you are, but you do realize how it looked to me?" she asked.

"I do. I did that night, but what could I do?"

Haley shrugged her shoulders and smiled.

"Saturday night the Lakers are in town playing the Jazz. I have two tickets. I'd be honored if you would go with me."

"Sounds like fun," she said.

* * *

"Did you patch things up with Haley?" William Montgomery asked Nat when they spoke on the phone that same afternoon.

"I did," he said.

"Good," William said. "I was surprised to hear that Sterling waived the preliminary hearing. I really wanted Haley to present her case, to get a feeling for how she's handling it. She must have been surprised when Sterling pulled that stunt," he said carefully.

"Oh, no, I don't think so," Nat said, falling right into the little trap the crafty district attorney had constructed.

"Oh, how's that?" William asked innocently.

"She didn't look surprised is all. And at lunch, she said something that made me think the defendant had already told her what his intentions were," he said. "I'm sure she could have proceeded and would have done very well," he added hastily, wondering if he'd said too much. The last thing he wanted was to hurt Haley.

"Dan Smathers must have told her," the district attorney said. "He probably wasn't happy to have to waive, though. He likes a good court scrap."

Nat chuckled. "You should have seen his face when Rob made his announcement to Judge Horton. It caught Dan completely by surprise. But he recovered quickly and tried to convince the judge that it was all his idea."

"I see," was the only comment William made to that revelation. He was not happy. Haley must have communicated directly with Rob Sterling, and that bothered him. He was afraid that Rob could be very persuasive, especially with a lovely woman like Haley who spent a lot of time alone. "Well, thanks Nat. Keep me posted," he said shortly, and the conversation was over.

William wasn't sure what it was, but something about this whole waiver of the preliminary hearing bothered him. He'd honestly thought that Haley was right on track after her close call with the man Rob had hired to stalk her, but his old nagging doubts had just resurfaced. Perhaps, he thought grimly, he needed to dig a little deeper in her handling of the case, discreetly of course, but thoroughly.

He gave it some serious thought for the next few minutes and then summoned Keith Breathwaite to his office. Keith was the prosecutor William assigned to handle the recently filed case against Sterling for initiating terroristic threats.

"What can I do for you?" Keith asked when he entered the district attorney's office. Keith was the oldest, most experienced attorney in the office. Nothing ruffled him. He just dug in and did his job. The district attorney liked him because Keith wasn't always particular about who got hurt. He just plowed ahead.

"When is Rob Sterling being arraigned on the terroristic threats charges?" William asked. "I want to keep this business of him hiring someone to threaten one of my attorneys moving in the courts as quickly as possible."

"It's scheduled next Monday, a week from this morning," Keith responded.

William scratched his chin, then he said, "It may be a bit premature, but I'd like you to subpoena the jail's visitation records from the day Rob was jailed through . . ." He stopped and seemed to calculate for a moment, then he said, "We can just as well make it right up through today."

Keith didn't question why. That was one of the reasons William liked him so well. He wasn't the brightest attorney in the office, but he was loyal to the boss.

"I'll get right on it," he promised.

"I will want to see who visited Rob, the time and day of their visits, and when he had multiple visitors," William instructed him.

The list might actually shed light on whom Rob was using to generate the threats, but that wasn't what the district attorney wanted it for. He wanted to know if Haley had been to see Rob Sterling, and if so, who might have been with her.

He liked Haley, but if she was in any way compromised on this case, he'd roll her off of it so fast she'd wonder if she'd ever been on it. Nothing and no one would stand in his way for higher political office.

"I'll see to it," Keith said again.

"Thanks. And Keith, not a word of this around the office. I don't want Haley Gordon to know you're after that record."

"Whatever you say," Keith agreed, but his eyebrows raised slightly. He liked Haley. He hoped that the district attorney wasn't going to cause her problems. But he dismissed that thought almost as fast as it had come. The district attorney liked Haley too. She was one of his favorites. *He'd never do anything to hurt her,* Keith thought to himself as he turned away.

* * *

The weather was getting very cool. October was fast coming to a close and winter was approaching. Sperry and Rex were getting cold sitting in the car with the engine off. But they were rewarded for their patience that evening when Trista Zippeta's car finally pulled into her driveway. She got out and pulled her coat tightly around her as she hurried to the house, a small bag of groceries in one arm. The detectives waited until she'd had time to get her coat off before Sperry got out and approached her door.

Rex waited in the car, listening to the small device that would record every word that Sperry and Trista said. They were quite sure that she was lying about her ex-husband's relationship with the late Jennifer Sterling, and they intended to find evidence to that effect.

When Trista answered the door, Sperry said, "Mrs. Zippeta?"

"I'm Mrs. Zippeta," she said, "but I'm not interested in whatever it is you're selling."

Sperry already had a foot in the door. "I'm not selling anything," he said as he simply pushed his way inside. "I'm here to offer you some money."

Trista was instantly interested. "Money?" she said.

"Yes, and all you have to do is convince your ex-husband to testify in court that he never knew Jennifer Sterling, let alone dated her," Sperry said. "Now that shouldn't be hard."

Mrs. Zippeta hesitated just long enough to convince Sperry that both she and Jake had received money from someone for doing the opposite. Finally she said, "I couldn't do that. We already told the prosecutor about it."

Sperry shook his head. "I'm here to make you a better offer to change your story. We both know that it is a *story,*" he said shaking his head as if to portray a sense of shame on her behalf.

Trista was acting very nervous and kept glancing at her watch. "Are you expecting someone?" Sperry suddenly asked her.

"Uh, yes," she said. "My ex-husband is supposed to be coming by to pick something up. I'm expecting him any minute."

"Oh, good. I'll just stick around then," Sperry said with a hearty chuckle. "We can settle this thing today and save me the trouble of returning."

Sperry began to walk around the room, looking at the paintings on the wall as if they were quality art, which they weren't. They were about as artful as her bright purple fingernails. He also examined a vase of imitation flowers. It was perfect for what he needed. He had a very small microphone in his pocket, and he needed the opportunity to put it someplace where it wasn't likely to be spotted.

Trista followed him around, but after a couple of minutes, she said, "Would you like a soda or something?"

Perfect, he thought. That would get her out of the room for a minute or two. That was more than enough time. "Sure, do you have Seven-Up?" he asked.

"Would a Sprite be okay?"

"Yes, that'd be fine."

She left the living room, and Sperry immediately secured the microphone in the flowers. He didn't know how often she dusted them or how long he'd need to leave the bug there, but it needed to be where it would be almost impossible to see. It took him a minute to accomplish the task. As he finished, he heard a car pull into the driveway. He quickly stepped over to the sofa and sat down. A moment later the door opened and a man with slicked-back dark hair stepped in and called out, "Hey babe! I'm home."

Trista came quickly from the kitchen with Sperry's Sprite in her hand. "Ah, Jake, I have company," she said with special emphasis on the *I*.

Jake looked quickly in the direction of the sofa. Sperry was already getting to his feet. He'd checked the court divorce records for the state earlier and couldn't find any record of their divorce. However it could have been done out of state, so that hadn't been conclusive. But he was pretty sure now that Jake and Trista were still very much man and wife. Their actions had just confirmed it. But for the sake of the little recording device in the car outside, he said, "Your wife was just getting me a soda. She told me you'd be home soon and that I should wait so I could discuss my business offer with the two of you."

Jake wasn't sure what to say. He looked at Trista with a question on his face. She tried once more to undo the damage already done to their story. "I explained that you were coming over to get something. He wanted to talk to both of us, and it's saving him the trouble of having to go to *your place.*"

Jake cleared his throat and shifted his feet. Sperry didn't wait for him to find words to reinforce his wife's facade. "Let's sit down, all three of us, and we'll talk about my offer."

No one moved. So he said, "Fine, we can discuss it standing here just like we are. You see, Jake, your wife and I were talking about the story the two of you are being paid to relate. You know, the one about Rob Sterling and his wife. I'm referring, of course, to the late Jennifer Sterling. I'm here to make you a better offer. I'll pay you more than our friend is paying, and all you have to do is tell the truth. Now that's a pretty good deal, isn't it? You only have to admit that the two of you are married and that you've never even met Jennifer Sterling, and I'll pay you more than he is for lying."

Now Jake realized what was happening, and his face went white. "You get out of my house," Jake said fiercely. "You're trespassing."

Sperry laughed. *"Your* house," he said. "Not *her* house?"

"Just leave," he ordered again. "We don't know nothing about what you're talking about."

Sperry shook his head sadly. "I'm afraid it's not going to be that easy. You can either do it my way, or I'll make sure the prosecutor knows that you two are still married. She'll be furious, and instead of benefiting financially as I've proposed, you could well be facing charges and likely some lengthy jail time."

Sperry moved toward the door. "I'll let you two talk it over. I'll be back. Have a figure in mind if you want to do business. I may even consider dropping the testifying thing. All you'd have to do is stay away from court when Rob is tried for murder. That's easy enough now, isn't it?"

When Sperry got in the car with Rex a minute later, the sheriff's deputy was grinning from ear to ear. "You handled that like an old pro," he said.

"I am an old pro," Sperry reminded him cheerfully.

Then the two of them turned their attention to the little receiver and speaker they had running. Jake Zippeta was saying, "How did he find out that we're still married, that's what I'd like to know? We weren't even married in Utah, and we could have gotten a divorce anywhere. He's gone to a lot of trouble to make sure we're still together."

"What's worse is that he knows who paid us," Trista said.

Sperry slapped his thigh in laughter, and Rex pumped his fist triumphantly. "All I called the guy was 'our friend,'" Sperry laughed. "They were so nervous they didn't know how to respond."

The detectives listened again. "We better see how much we can get out of him then leave the state," Jake suggested. "We aren't safe here now. Even if we don't agree to do like this guy asks, our contact would somehow figure out that somebody's onto the lie—our testimony would be worthless to him then."

Trista said, "How much should we ask for?"

"Well, let's see, we already got five grand from the other guy. And he was going to give us ten thousand more after court. So why not tell this guy twenty thousand? We can always take less if we have to," Jake suggested.

"Too bad this isn't completely legal," Sergeant Thomas said, patting the small device that continued to record on the seat between them. "I'm afraid it would be thrown out of court if we tried to use it. And we didn't have enough information to get a court order."

"True, but the Zippetas don't know that. I think it's time for me to return. Let me have the tape and that small cassette player," he said. "I think we've about got this loose end tied up."

Just to be on the safe side, the detectives slipped another tape in the recorder after taking the used one out. Then Sperry loaded the little tape in a miniature cassette player, which he then slipped into the pocket of his sports coat. "I shouldn't be long," he said as he got out of the car.

A few minutes later Sperry was drinking the Sprite he'd never gotten around to before, and he was talking business with Jake and Trista. "All we have to do is not do anything?" Jake asked.

"That's right," Sperry said. "Of course, I'm not too sure how your friend, you know, the fellow that gave you the five thousand, will react to this. He can be very dangerous. Three men who were on the take from him have already disappeared."

Sperry was of course stretching things a bit, but essentially it was true. Martin Ligorni was certainly missing, although Sperry was quite sure he was gone on his own accord, and he was also sure he could find him. The stalker had been taken by force from the hospital, and Frank Rawlings's whereabouts were anybody's guess.

Trista began to tremble. "How did you know it was five thousand that we were paid?"

"Oh, I know lots of things," Sperry said smugly. "Of course, I also know about the ten thousand you haven't collected."

The two glanced at each other. They both looked like they might be on the verge of a breakdown. "We'll take your money and leave," Jake said. "We were getting tired of Salt Lake anyway."

"I'll bet you were," Sperry said. "So, we won't have to worry about you coming to court and telling your little story?" he asked.

"If you pay us twenty thousand dollars we won't say another word," Jake promised.

"Twenty thousand!" Sperry thundered. "You already got five. You should be glad you can keep that."

Jake put on a hard face, but the sweat on his brow and shaking of his hands told Sperry it was all fake. "Ten thousand, and you've got a deal."

Sperry walked over to the fake vase of flowers. "You get to keep your five," he said as he reached down and plucked the little microphone out. "And I won't say anything to the D.A. about this."

"How did . . . that?" Jake stammered and then simply shut his mouth and sank back on the sofa.

Sperry pulled out his little cassette player. He turned it on and let it play for a moment. Then, as the pathetic couple sat in abject silence, he turned if off and said, "Do we have a deal? You keep the five thousand, I keep the recordings. Oh, there is more," Sperry added ominously, as he waved the little microphone in the air. "I'm still recording. There's a whole crew right outside the door. You do understand that, don't you?" They nodded.

Sperry then spoke directly into the little microphone. "I am Private Investigator Sperry Collier." He added the date and time, then he asked, "Do you understand that we are being recorded, Mr. and Mrs. Zippeta?"

"Yes, we do," Jake said.

"Do you, Mrs. Zippeta?"

"Yes," she agreed.

"Good. Just for the sake of clarity, Mr. Jake Zippeta, did you ever meet Jennifer Sterling?"

"No," he said softly.

"A little louder please," Sperry said.

"I didn't know her."

"Did you, Mrs. Trista Zippeta?"

"No," she said.

"And the two of you are still married?" Sperry asked.

"Yes," Jake said.

"Do you agree, Mrs. Zippeta?" Sperry asked.

"We are still married."

"That will be about all," Sperry said. "You two could be in a lot of trouble, so I would suggest that you don't try to pursue the lie anymore." He paused, then asked, "Would you mind stating the name of the man who paid the two of you to lie about an affair with Jennifer Sterling?"

"He never told us his name," Trista said. "But you know it anyway."

"Thank you both," Sperry said. "I hope I don't have to bother the two of you again."

Back in the car a minute later, Rex was laughing again. "The last part of that, the direct confession, is legal and admissible in court if needed for a rebuttal."

"They'll never testify," Sperry said with conviction. "In fact, they'll be gone by morning or I miss my guess."

"That was pretty smart how you did that," Rex said.

"You learn a few things over the years," Sperry responded modestly. "Let's get this tape copied and give one to Haley. It would make her day I think."

CHAPTER TWENTY

Sperry Collier got a call from a colleague in Colorado early Tuesday morning. The message he was given cleared his sleepy head, and he urgently rolled out of bed, kissed his wife, and told her he'd be in touch but that he'd be out of town for a day or two. He'd let her know when he'd be back. Then he packed a bag, got in his car, and began a long drive. He didn't want Haley or Rex to know where he was going or what he was doing. But remembering the call from Rex at five the other morning, he grinned and called the detective up.

"Sorry to wake you up," he said.

"I'll bet you are," Rex said with a groggy chuckle. "What's up?"

"I'm heading out of town," Sperry said. "Something's come up. I'll be in touch as soon as I get back. In the meantime, maybe you could brief the prosecutor on the Zippeta matter."

"I'll wait until a more sane hour to do so," Rex said. He knew from the tone of Sperry's voice that it would do no good to ask him what he was doing. He figured it had something to do with the Rob Sterling matter, and Sperry would tell him when he felt the time was right and not one second sooner. *After all,* Rex thought to himself, *I haven't been exactly candid over the fate of the stalker.* Nor did he plan to for many weeks to come. Some things were better left buried for a time.

* * *

Haley spoke briefly with Sperry by phone on Tuesday morning as she was getting ready to drive to the office. "I'm out of town and will be for a few days," he told her. She asked him if it had to do with the

Sterling case or if it was for Raul Garcia. She could feel his smile over the phone as he said secretively, "There's just something I need to do. I hope you can get along without me until I get back."

Haley asked Rex about it over lunch, and Rex said that he didn't know and that they would just have to keep working until Sperry got back. Then he said, "I need to bring you up-to-date on the matter of Trista Zippeta and her husband."

"Ex-husband," Haley corrected.

"Husband," Rex said firmly and smiled at Haley's reaction. Her face had lit up like it was the greatest news she'd ever received.

"It gets better," he told her, and he pulled his little cassette player from his pocket and handed it over to her. "Keep the volume down," he said, "and put it right to your ear. I don't want anyone eavesdropping."

She looked around as if there might be someone nearby that shouldn't be. But seeing no one suspicious, she did as the detective instructed. Rex had set the message to start right where he identified himself, the admissible stuff was all she'd hear. She was both relieved and incensed after listening to the short recording.

"Let's get a warrant," she said. "They should go to jail for this."

Rex shook his head. "We can get the warrant if you like, but I went by their house this morning. They must have left shortly after Sperry and I were there last night," he said.

Haley studied the officer's impassive face for a moment, then she said, "I take it there's more that I probably don't want to hear."

Rex answered by saying, "The Zippetas are no longer a problem. We can sure put a warrant on NCIC, and maybe someday they'll get picked up somewhere. But until they do, we can quit worrying about them."

* * *

Dan knew that Haley Gordon had to be taken off the Sterling case. But he was losing faith in the blackmailing, money-hungry, snooping fiend who was his main contact. He decided to leave him out of it this time and take the direct approach. From a pay phone a hundred miles from Salt Lake City, Dan called the office of District Attorney William Montgomery. He attempted to disguise his voice when a receptionist answered. He was quite sure she wouldn't have any idea who he was, but he had to be certain. "I have a message for William Montgomery," he said.

"He's in. I'll transfer your call," the woman said helpfully.

"That won't be necessary. Just tell him that Haley Gordon is working hard to get Rob Sterling acquitted. Tell him that as a voter, I don't want to see that happen. If he allows that woman to continue with this case, I'll hit the press with what I know and start a backlash of voter disapproval. If I have to do that, Mr. Montgomery will never get elected attorney general. Did you get all that?" Dan asked.

She got it all right, and as soon as the caller had dropped the line, she hurried into William's office. She knew he was alone because Keith Breathwaite had just left. William looked up from the documents Keith had delivered. His face was gray. And she knew that meant he was angry. Very angry.

She hated to make it worse, but she felt that the message couldn't wait. "Sir," she said rather timidly.

"What is it?" he snapped. "I'm rather busy here."

He seldom lost his temper with her. Whatever he was reading had him very upset. She braced herself and said, "I just got a call from someone who would only identity himself as a voter."

That last word sparked the district attorney's interest. He looked up and asked, "What did he want?"

"He asked me to give you a message."

"Then give it to me," he ordered.

The woman turned, shut the door, then said, "He wants Haley Gordon taken off the Rob Sterling murder prosecution," she said.

The gray of the district attorney's face turned a shade darker. "Did he give a reason?" he asked.

She nodded and told him what had been said, including the threat to go to the press. The district attorney rose to his feet like an erupting volcano. "That does it!" he roared. "Get Haley in here!"

That was not at all the reaction the receptionist had expected. She'd been afraid the district attorney would try to track the caller down and order him off the back of his outstanding young prosecutor. She was shocked that William was angry at Haley.

With trembling hands, she lifted her headset a minute later and punched in the intercom number to Haley's office. "Mr. Montgomery would like to see you immediately," she said, and before Haley could say anything she put the receiver down and fled to the ladies' room to avoid seeing Haley.

When Haley arrived at the district attorney's private office, his receptionist wasn't there. The woman's usually pleasant voice had been tight just a moment ago, and now she had slipped conveniently away from her desk. Haley's stomach rolled. *This could be it,* she thought as she opened William's door and walked calmly into the face of the storm.

"Shut the door," William ordered.

She did so and then stood near it, watching her boss. His face was gray, and the veins stood out on his thick neck. She felt his wrath even before he unleashed it on her. She decided to stay near the door so she could just leave if it got bad.

Haley waited as William shuffled some pages on his desk. When he looked up, fire was shooting from his eyes. "I gave you the best case this office has had all year," he hissed. "And what thanks did I get?"

She didn't know if he expected an answer, but there was no way to answer a question like that anyway, so she said nothing.

"That's what I thought," he said. "Well, I'm pulling you from the case as of this moment. Give the entire file to my secretary. I'm afraid that I'm the only one that can rescue this case from the mess you've got it in. From this point on, Haley, you will get the smallest, most unimportant cases that I can find for you. I thought I could trust you. I've never been so disappointed in my life."

He was still looking at her, and she was gazing steadily back. She should be angry, she realized, shout at him, demand an explanation, but all she felt was calmness and relief. She didn't know why, as this left Rob on his own to fight one of the most ruthless prosecutors in the state, but she did.

"That's all," William said.

But Haley really was curious, so she calmly said, "I suppose you have a reason for doing this to me."

"You bet I do!" he roared. "Working with the opposition. Covertly meeting with the defendant. Turning the voting public against me."

"The opposition?" she said.

"Sperry Collier and Raul Garcia for starters. Who knows who else. And don't deny it. I have the jail visiting logs right here," he said. "You're dismissed, Miss Gordon, and don't expect to go to the attorney general's office with me. It won't happen."

Haley looked at his angry face for one more moment. Then as she finally felt her own temper rising, she satisfied it by saying, "I don't expect either of us to go there, sir. The people of this state aren't that dense."

"Get out of here before I fire you for insubordination," he threatened.

"I have not been insubordinate," she said. "But you won't have to worry about firing me, because I quit. You'll have my resignation in writing within the hour. I'll clean out my things and be out of your hair before the end of the day."

"You can't quit!" he thundered.

"I can," she said. "It would be foolish of me to stay."

"I won't accept your resignation," he threatened.

"It won't matter, because I'll be gone anyway," she said. "You just want to keep me around so you can control me. Forget it, sir. I won't be controlled by anyone."

She'd had enough. The door was right where she wanted it, and she simply opened it and walked out, closing it behind her. The receptionist was at her desk again. She looked relieved when she saw how calm Haley was.

"Is everything okay?" she asked.

"Just great," Haley said with a smile. "He can't control me anymore."

Without further explanation, Haley left the receptionist trying to figure her comment out and returned to her office. As she walked by her secretary, she signaled for her to follow. "I'll be leaving today," she said. "But right now I'd like you to take the Sterling file down to William's personal secretary, if you don't mind. He'll be handling that prosecution himself," she said when she got an extremely quizzical look from her secretary.

Haley was glad she'd copied the file, because she knew that Rob would need it if he was to have any chance at all against William Montgomery.

When her secretary got back, Haley had already typed her letter of resignation. She was just folding it when the young lady said, "So why is he taking that case? He's rusty, isn't he?"

"He's still very good," Haley corrected her.

"What's he going to have you do now? That's all you've worked on for weeks," the concerned secretary said.

"It won't be up to him anymore," Haley said. "Would you take this to his secretary? Have her give it to him right now. Then I'd appreciate it if you'd come back and help me pack my things."

The young woman's mouth dropped open. "You're leaving!" she exclaimed and tears began brimming in her eyes. "Oh, Miss Gordon, you can't go. I love working for you."

"And you have been great as well," Haley said sincerely. "But sometimes people just have to move on. And this is one of those times for me."

* * *

Nat was busy with a client when William's call came. He told his secretary to tell William that he'd call him back. But William wouldn't be put off. So Nat apologized to his client and asked him to step out for a minute. "This is urgent," he apologized, "and it's very sensitive."

When he picked up the phone, he was caught entirely off guard. "Thanks for nothing, Nat," the district attorney's voice boomed. "You were to let me know if anything was going wrong with the Sterling case, and you did no such thing."

"But I did, sir," Nat objected, wondering what was happening. He'd never heard William Montgomery so angry.

"You told me she was afraid, but she had more guts than you'll ever have," William said offensively. "And I asked you to tell me if she was in any way beginning to doubt her own case. You didn't warn me at all, and all the time she was consorting with the defense."

"With Dan Smathers?" Nat asked in total surprise.

"No, you fool, with Rob Sterling himself. She's been to see him at the jail and has been working closely with a private investigator who was hired by Rob. You should have known and should have told me," William said.

"I'm sorry, sir, but I had no knowledge of this. I guess she was keeping me in the dark," Nat said even as he thought about her attitude toward the case. He was glad she was off the case, though, and he was off the hook.

"Next time I need a favor, I hope you can do a better job," William said.

"I did the best I could, sir," he responded, but the line had gone dead.

* * *

The Salt Lake County sheriff was not one of William Montgomery's fans, so when the district attorney called and gave him an earful over the shoddy work of Sergeant Rex Thomas, he wasn't particularly impressed or worried.

"I want him off the Sterling case," the district attorney demanded.

"Oh, and am I taking orders from you now?" the sheriff asked sarcastically.

"If you know what's good for you, you'll do as I say," William fired back.

"Thomas will work where I tell him to," the sheriff said, not at all intimidated.

"Well, he'll be without my support then," the district attorney announced, "and he won't be allowed in my office. I'm taking over the prosecution of your former deputy myself. And I'll use an investigator from my own office from this point on."

The sheriff was curious. Haley Gordon had seemed so on top of things, and the courage she'd displayed just a few days ago had impressed him a great deal. "Why is Haley Gordon no longer prosecuting the case?" he asked.

"Because she's incompetent," the district attorney responded. "I fired her."

William Montgomery slammed down the phone, so angry that he didn't realize the damage he was doing to his fledgling campaign for attorney general.

Within minutes, the sheriff had located Rex Thomas and asked him to come to his office right away. When Rex walked in the sheriff said, "I guess you know about Haley Gordon."

Rex went pale. "No, has she been hurt? I just had lunch with her a few hours ago and she was fine then. In fact she was in a great mood."

"Physically, she's okay, but I just got a call from William Montgomery. He says he fired her and that he wants you off the Sterling investigation."

"Oh," Rex said. "I suppose it was bound to happen."

The sheriff was caught short by that reply. "I thought she was a tough prosecutor."

"She is," Sergeant Thomas said. "But she's also an honest woman and one who seeks the truth. I've learned a great lesson from her, Sheriff."

"Oh, and what's that?"

"She reminded me that when I investigate a case, I should keep an open mind. You confirmed that when we discovered the problems with Frank Rawlings, if you recall. She was the first to figure out that Rob might have been framed. And it turns out she was right."

"Would you like to explain what else you've learned?" the sheriff asked.

Rex did just that, and when he was through, he said, "I think I can find out who did it, and I'd like to be able to keep working this case until I get it solved and proven. But you do need to know that it may mean I'll end up testifying for Rob against William Montgomery."

"I've been expecting that, so you go for it, Rex," the sheriff said. "You have my complete support. And as soon as the doctor releases Kurt to return to work, you'll have him to help you again."

"Thank you, sir," Rex said. "And I'd appreciate it if you'd keep our conversation confidential. This thing could get ugly."

"It already has," the sheriff reminded him. "You haven't told me who you think did it, by the way."

"I don't know for sure yet. But I'm convinced it's either a powerful person or someone with powerful connections. He's got to be behind all the threats against Haley Gordon *and* Dan Smathers."

"That seems strange," the sheriff said.

"It should be very clear soon," Rex promised. "Very clear."

* * *

"You have a visitor, Rob," a correctional officer told him.

"It's not visiting hours," Rob said. "Am I special or something?"

The officer smiled. Since the disappearance of Frank Rawlings, the officers in the jail were treating Rob with respect. And he was always polite and deferential to them. "It's an official visit. The prosecutor wants to see you."

Rob followed the officer up the corridor and into the room used for attorneys and other official visitors. Haley was already in the room, and she stood and smiled when Rob walked in. "Call when you're finished," the officer said, and he shut the door behind him as he left.

"To what do I owe the pleasure of this visit tonight?" Rob asked with a smile as he accepted her outstretched hand.

"I have some news," she said as she sat down opposite him at the table.

"Oh, bad news or good?" he said as his pulse quickened. He didn't need bad news. This place was getting to him.

"I'm not sure," she said with a grin. "I won't be prosecuting your case anymore. The district attorney is taking it over himself."

"Oh," Rob said as his face fell and he slumped in his seat. "That's bad news," he said morosely. "Really bad. He wants me convicted so he can climb the political ladder. He's made that quite clear to the press."

"Exactly, and that's why he bumped me off the case. It seems that he found out I wasn't convinced of your guilt. He told me I was through."

"Is that true?" Rob asked.

"Which? That I believe you're innocent, or that I'm through?" she asked.

"Well, I meant do you believe me? But I also wonder what you meant by through,'" Rob said.

"Yes to the first question. I believe you, Rob. And as for the next question, he told me I could only prosecute the insignificant little cases that didn't matter much," she said.

"Oh, I was hoping you meant you were leaving the prosecutor's office," Rob said.

"And why would you hope that?" Haley asked.

"Because I would beg and plead for you to represent me, Miss Gordon."

"Haley," she corrected.

"Haley," he said hesitantly, feeling that he was violating professional protocol. "Anyway, I don't have much, but I'd pay you for the rest of my life if I had to. I want Jennifer's killer found."

"So do I, Rob. And I want your name cleared," she said. "If you're asking me to represent you, I accept."

"But if you're still prosecuting, it would be a conflict," he said.

"I'm not. William only wanted to control me, so I submitted my resignation."

"Then you're hired." Rob's face lit up as he spoke. "We can do this," he said enthusiastically.

"We'll need a lot of help, but yes, we can do it," Haley agreed.

The officer opened the door. "Sergeant Thomas is here, Rob. I'll have him come in when Miss Gordon is finished."

"Send him in now," Rob said. "If it's okay with Miss Gordon."

"Haley," she reminded him.

Rob was happier than he'd been in a long time. Granted, the level of happiness he'd experienced before Jennifer's death was something he felt he would never have again. It just didn't seem possible. But it didn't matter anyway. They'd find whoever did this to her, and he could rest knowing justice had been served.

"He may come in," Haley agreed, watching the change that was coming over Rob Sterling. He was really quite a guy, she decided.

When Rex entered the room, he first said hello to Rob, then he turned to Haley. "I'm so sorry. The sheriff told me about the district attorney firing you."

"Is that what William is telling people?" she asked.

"He told the sheriff that," Rex said.

"He'll live to regret it," Haley said, and she really meant it. "He's lying. I resigned."

"What are you going to do now?" Rex asked Haley.

She smiled and turned to Rob. "Meet my new client," she said.

Rob suddenly became very sober. "Could you handle two clients?" he asked.

"I will represent you on the terroristic threats case too, if that's what you mean," she told him.

"That too, but I'm concerned about Raul. He's lost so much trying to help me," Rob said.

"I'd love to, and as soon as we get his matter cleared up, and I'm confident we can," she said, hoping that were true, "then he can be co-counsel, if you don't mind."

"Great," Rob said. "Will you let him know?"

"I'll call him at home tonight," she promised.

CHAPTER TWENTY-ONE

Raul's face lit up when Haley asked him if she could help him clear his name. She'd decided to talk to him in person. He was at home with his wife and children when she'd knocked on their door at about eight that evening.

At first he was angry at the news that William Montgomery had pulled her from Rob's case, but now he was excited as he realized what that meant. "For the first time I think Rob has a fighting chance of winning," he said.

"All the evidence against him was fabricated," Haley told him, "but skillfully done. Our work is cut out for us." Then she brought him up-to-date on the case. "But I'm not really here to talk about Rob's defense. He asked me to help you get yourself cleared so that the two of us could work together against the district attorney."

The two attorneys worked until nearly ten going over Raul's defense. "This won't be too bad," Haley said at last. "I think we can make a good case just using the fact that the planted file is so inconsistent with all the other files on the computer."

"No one knows I have the backup files yet," Raul said.

"And that's good. It would be best if we kept it that way for the time being," Haley agreed.

"Where are you going to set up office?" Raul asked. "It seems that you're in the same predicament as I am now."

"I guess I'll work from my apartment for now," she said. "What are you doing about space for your practice?"

"Same thing," he said. "Although there isn't much practice at the moment. My secretary comes here and we work in my study. It's crowded, but it will get us by until I can find permanent space, or until I'm sure I'll even need it."

"You'll need it," Haley said confidently. "We'll get this taken care of very soon."

Raul's wife came into the living room and said, "You two might want to watch the news. They said Mr. Montgomery held a press conference today and that he was going to announce some changes in his office, particularly as it pertains to the prosecution of Rob Sterling."

"Do you want to see it?" Raul asked, concerned about her feelings.

"I do, actually. It'll be interesting to see how he tries to gain political ground at my expense."

Haley felt very much at ease in the home of Raul Garcia and his family. She accepted a dish of ice cream as they all watched the news together. It felt good to be in a real home with such a nice family. Haley really hadn't thought much about being a wife and mother herself. Her career had always come first. Even after joining the Church, marriage had seemed a remote thing to Haley. She wasn't sure there was anyone for her.

At least she'd thought that until Nat had come along, and then she'd allowed herself a few stray thoughts about someday settling down. But she'd have to see about that. She was a long way from getting serious about him. There had already been a lot of bumps along the road. Time would tell, she decided, but she knew she wouldn't rush into anything with Nat.

The news was rather boring this evening, until William Montgomery appeared. His silver hair was flawless, and his silver tongue was at its smoothest. "I'm sorry to have to announce the departure of Haley Gordon from this office," he said.

Raul and his wife both glanced at Haley. She just smiled and said, "Not as sorry as he will be . . . I hope."

"Miss Gordon has enjoyed the complete confidence of this office until today when it came to my attention that she was intentionally compromising the state's case against the former deputy sheriff, Rob Sterling, who now stands accused of murder," William was telling the TV camera. "It has been the clearly stated position of this office that we were seeking the death penalty for the murder of former Miss Utah, Jennifer Sterling. The evidence against Mrs. Sterling's husband is overwhelming, and for some reason as yet unclear to me, Ms. Gordon was attempting to alter the evidence.

"I apologize to the citizens of Utah and once again declare firmly that the case against Mr. Sterling for the horrendous crime of which everyone is aware will be vigorously prosecuted. In order to minimize the damage done by Ms. Gordon, I'm going to personally handle this case myself from this point on. Again, it was very difficult to ask for the resignation of someone who had so ably represented my department in the past."

"What a rotten thing to do!" Raul finally exploded. He'd heard all he could stand without saying something.

William wasn't through though. He fielded questions, and in response to one about Haley's future plans, he said, "I have no idea what she plans to do. However, this office is looking closely at her actions in respect to this case, and we have not ruled out the possibility of either criminal charges or a complaint to the Utah State Bar. Let me be clear, though, that there is no animosity on the part of anyone in my office against Ms. Gordon. She was personally threatened in the most vile manner, stalked, and actually taken at gunpoint—her life threatened by a man we believe to have been hired by Rob Sterling. She acted bravely through all of that, but it appears to me that it affected her judgment very seriously when it came to how she was handling the case. Whether that rises to the point of further actions being taken against her remains to be seen. I sincerely hope it won't come to that," he concluded with an appropriately sober face.

"You praised her highly just a few days ago," a reporter reminded the district attorney.

"And appropriately so," William responded. "But again, what effect the series of events she was subjected to had on her mental stability is unclear. I must remind you, however, that my position is this: I will not tolerate crime at any level. And those people—police officers, attorneys, and others—who are entrusted with important responsibilities in safeguarding the lives and freedoms of the citizens of this state are not exempt when they stray from what is legal and ethically right. As district attorney, and if elected attorney general, I will not step back from that position. That is my promise to the citizens."

Raul turned the TV off. "That was rather lengthy," he said. "They certainly let him take his shots at you."

Haley merely nodded. She was stunned at the vehemence with which the district attorney had attacked her. However, it also reinforced her resolve. He was vulnerable and perhaps didn't realize it. But she would not back down. The truth, if not public opinion, was on her side.

Haley isolated herself from everyone except those she was working closely with for the following few days. Detective Rex Thomas was busy every day and kept her posted on his progress. Raul Garcia and his secretary spent many hours with Haley as they carefully prepared his defense to both William Montgomery's criminal charges and the complaint to the Bar. Haley intended to win the criminal case at the preliminary hearing. And she hoped that she could get the complaint to the Bar dismissed shortly after that, as the same evidence applied.

Private Investigator Sperry Collier returned from wherever he'd gone, saying nothing about his activities. But he also went to work on both Raul's and Rob's cases.

Numerous calls from the press reached her home, but Haley refused to comment on her resignation. The last thing she wanted to do right now was enrage her former boss even more. She'd take him on in court where facts and legal precedent would rule, and where political rhetoric had no home. Eventually, she hoped to let the public know the truth about William Montgomery before they made the mistake of elevating him to an even more powerful position than he presently held.

But now was not the time for her to say anything. The futures of Rob Sterling and Raul Garcia were in her hands. She had to concentrate on what was best for them, not for herself or even for the citizens of the state.

Nat Turley called and told her how sorry he was and how low-down the district attorney's behavior was. He confirmed their date to the Jazz game. She was polite to Nat and looked forward to their date, but something about his tone bothered her.

* * *

Rob was isolated from society, but not from the news. He was incensed over the treatment Haley Gordon had received from the district attorney. And not a single word of rebuttal from her had been aired. He didn't know if it was because she had refused to speak to the press or if they simply hadn't asked for her side of the issue.

Either way, it was grossly unfair, and it angered him. He admired Haley Gordon for her courage. She'd impressed him right at the first as someone who was not affected by her own importance, but rather as someone who cared about people and how they were treated. He'd judged her correctly, although those very qualities had caused her great pain. Rob couldn't believe how many people his predicament was hurting.

There had been days when Rob had sat in his lonely jail cell and felt sorry for himself, for the legal plight he was in. Other days he could think of nothing but the terrible and senseless loss of his lovely wife. At times he'd wondered if it was even worth the fight to defend himself. He was so alone without Jennifer, and too many powerful people had seemed firmly aligned against him.

But now he was determined. Whoever orchestrated this mess didn't care who was hurt, or how badly, as long as he remained untouched. That angered Rob. He hoped that those faithful people who were now working so hard on his behalf could figure it out. He prayed for them constantly, even more than he prayed for himself. Rob wanted the truth exposed, and even if it cost him everything he had in this world, it would be worth it.

On Saturday morning, Rob was doing what he did every morning for at least an hour. He was reading the scriptures. He was studying the book of Job in the Old Testament. He realized that Job had suffered a lot more than he had, but it was still easy to draw a comparison. As he read, he was inspired to do as Job had done and put his trust in the Lord. Not that he hadn't done so already, but he knew that his faith was not as strong as it could be.

Rob read on, then he sat the book on his bunk and thought about something in his situation that was quite different from Job's plight. Job's friends had not been faithful to him in his misery. He'd even been encouraged to curse God and die. Rob thought about his own friend, Raul Garcia. Not for one minute had Raul given up on Rob. Instead, he had helped to find new friends, and they were all giving their best efforts in his behalf. His sister and brother-in-law had also offered what means they had to aid Rob, even though they knew it could cause them to be estranged even further from Tasha's parents.

Tears of gratitude moistened his eyes. Those who were his true friends were ready and willing to make great sacrifices for him— already had, in fact.

Then he thought of the many others who hadn't so much as written to him or visited him in jail. Some had, and their support was helpful, but many had not. In particular, he thought of his parents and Jennifer's family. He hadn't heard a word from any of them. Apparently they had chosen to believe the worst about him. They hadn't even consulted him about Jennifer's funeral, which the police hadn't allowed him to attend. He felt somewhat betrayed, but he harbored no animosity toward any of them. He felt that his charity had been strengthened while in jail. He did wish they'd give him the chance to explain his side of the tragedy, but apparently that wasn't going to happen anytime soon. Maybe someday.

Then he thought about his little Sunday School class. He loved them. But he wondered what they were thinking of him. He supposed they also felt betrayed. He hoped it hadn't affected their budding faith in the Savior.

Rob picked up his Bible again and began to read. Then he was called over the intercom. He had a visitor. His sister, he supposed. He put his scriptures away and waited for the cell door to open.

He was surprised when they directed him to the attorney visiting area. And his heart lifted considerably at the sight of Haley Gordon. Her skin glowed this morning, and the smile she greeted him with was infectious. Her dark eyes practically sparkled as she took his hand and shook it.

"You're in a good mood this morning, Haley," he said.

"I've just been with a group of the most delightful kids I've ever met," she said.

"Oh, who's that?" he asked.

Haley beamed. "You'll probably be surprised by this, but your Sunday School kids came to see me today. They brought me a dozen red roses," she said, wiping a tear from her eye.

"Why would they do that?" Rob asked in amazement.

"This is their second visit. I didn't tell you about the first. They came to my office awhile ago and more or less demanded that I quit *persecuting* you," she said.

Rob began to laugh. "That's great," he said. "I was just thinking about them, and I wondered what they thought about me now."

"They love you, Rob. And when they found out that I was no longer *persecuting* you, they came to see me again just to thank me. I hope it's okay with you, Rob—what I did, I mean."

"What did you do?" he asked curiously.

"I told them I was on your side now, and they went wild. We can't lose with those great kids on our side," she said. "When this is all over, I want to invite them all over for dinner and ice cream. They are such an inspiration."

"May I come too, providing I'm out of here then?" Rob asked.

Haley grinned. "Of course. It wouldn't be right if you weren't there." And she was surprised at the sudden intensity of her feelings. She wanted Rob to be there. She wanted Rob to be her friend. Haley sharply cut off her thoughts. They were leading nowhere, and she thought sadly of Jennifer Sterling. Haley couldn't help but feel all the more determined as she thought of Rob's deceased wife and how horrible it was that she was deprived of Rob in this life, and he of her. It was so unfair. Jennifer had been so lucky to find Rob and win his love, and then she'd lost everything.

Rob noticed the change that came over Haley and asked, "Are you all right?"

"I'm fine, Rob," she said, embarrassed that he'd noticed she'd been distracted. "I was just thinking how unfair it is that Jennifer is gone and you're in here. I'll do everything I can to see that justice is served. I promise I will."

"Thank you," he said sincerely. "I know you will." He asked her politely to sit down and then did the same himself. "So how is Raul's case coming together?" he asked, and they got down to business.

* * *

The gold Jaguar shined inside and out. There was not so much as a trace of the stalker's blood left on the leather seats. Nat parked his treasured car and got out, looking up the walk at the apartment of the woman he also treasured.

And had betrayed, although he was blind to that. He had carefully justified his every move and felt very little guilt. She was safe now, and he could get serious about courting her. Rob Sterling's case would no longer come between them.

A moment later he knocked on the door. She nearly took his breath away as she invited him in. Her long black hair was brushed loosely over her shoulders. She wore a white cashmere sweater that made the brown of her skin shine with luster. The black pants she wore fit nicely, accentuating her tall, slim figure. Haley was a knock-out tonight. Nat could hardly wait to escort her to the Delta Center where heads would turn and stare with envy.

The Jazz were in good form that night, but so were the Lakers. It seemed to Nat that Haley was enjoying the game. To his enjoyment she even cheered a little, though Nat decided it wasn't in her nature to be too vocal. Nat got carried away, though, and Haley found herself almost as entertained by his actions as she was by the game.

In the end, the Jazz won by a couple of points. Nat was worn out from the tension, and Haley was ready to go home. But, being worn out didn't curb Nat's hunger, so they had dinner before he took her back to her apartment.

On her front steps, Nat lingered, holding Haley's hand and looking fondly into her eyes. He wanted this relationship to be right back where it was before Susie interfered. He was quite sure it was going there. He took Haley in his arms and kissed her. She responded, and he was so pleased that he failed to recognize the bit of hesitation in her kiss.

After the kiss and a lingering embrace, he gazed once again into her eyes. She seemed happy, and he was confident that he was winning her back.

Haley could read Nat's feelings in his sparkling blue eyes. But as she gazed into them, she found her mind wandering. She pictured green eyes. Eyes filled with pain. Eyes she wanted so badly to help restore to their former sparkle.

"Do you plan to look for work soon?" Nat asked, hoping to lengthen the evening with Haley.

"I'll probably just go into private practice," she told him. She really didn't want to tell him that she had her first clients. "It's getting late, Nat," she said abruptly. "And I'm tired. It's been a hard week." She suppressed a yawn.

"I'm sorry," he said. "I just hate to leave."

She smiled at him and accepted another date for the following Friday evening. Nat finally left, thinking that he had a future with this gorgeous woman now that William Montgomery was out of the way.

* * *

Dan Smathers's meeting with his contact was held late at night this time. Both were increasingly afraid of being seen together. Dan was optimistic tonight, and he'd hesitated to call this meeting, but there were some things that he needed to know to set his mind more at ease. He hated to keep using his contact, especially after he'd successfully gotten Haley Gordon pulled off the case without the man's help.

Dan was pleased that he now had William Montgomery himself prosecuting Rob Sterling. That was perfect. William was not particularly concerned about the truth. Like Dan, he mostly liked to win, and with his bid for attorney general now public, he especially wanted to win this case. Dan was feeling quite secure, except for one or two nagging things.

That was where the contact came in. "Hey, I did my job," he said. "Garcia is in trouble over his head, and Haley Gordon is no longer prosecuting. You have a man after your own heart doing it now."

"True, but I'm worried about the guy you had sending Haley the threats. Where is he?" Dan demanded.

The man shook his head. "Always worrying, Dan. There's no need. I have things well in hand," he said.

"Where is he?" Dan repeated through gritted teeth.

"Hey, man, I can't tell you that," the man answered, his eyes flashing in the semidarkness of the room. They were hidden deep in an abandoned building on the outskirts of the city. "I've told you I took care of it, that's all you need to know."

"Okay, where is Martin Ligorni? Mr. Montgomery is going to need him in court," Dan said.

"Don't worry, he'll be there," the contact promised.

Reassured on that point, Dan still had to address one more thing. "What is Haley Gordon up to now?" Dan asked.

"You're not going to like this. She's been visiting Rob Sterling at the jail. I think she's on his side now."

He's right, Dan fumed angrily. The last thing he needed was Haley helping Rob. It could mean that the judge would dismiss him entirely, and he had to keep his fingers in that pie. He had to keep *some* control.

"What do you want me to do about it?" the contact asked.

Dan calmed down and thought about it for a moment. "If we attack her again, it won't look good to the public, and it might actually hamper William Montgomery's image," he said thoughtfully. "Furthermore, it'll be hard to convince anyone that Rob is behind it this time. Leave her alone for now. I have a better idea." He shared his idea quietly, the whispered plan barely audible beyond a few feet of their conversation.

"Can do," the contact said. "You've got this one in the bag. Rob Sterling will be convicted and you can get back to chasing other men's wives."

Dan wanted to smack the arrogant man in the face, but he knew he'd end up the worse for it. So he simply smiled and said, "I'll be counting on you."

CHAPTER TWENTY-TWO

There wasn't a single judge in the Matheson Courthouse that Haley hadn't appeared in front of. She knew them all and was delighted that it was Judge Sherry Shelby that was presiding over the preliminary hearing for Raul this morning. Judge Shelby was extremely fair and compassionate. Haley silently prayed that she could convince the judge to throw out the case on Raul Garcia today. It would be such a waste of everyone's time to let this unjust accusation linger any longer.

Haley was nervous but confident as she reviewed her trial plan. She had some surprises for the prosecution. Sperry Collier had been very thorough. She hoped she could feel anywhere near as prepared for Rob's trial as she was today for Raul's preliminary hearing.

Raul had been looking around the courtroom as the public crowded in. He nudged Haley on the arm. "The Office of Professional Conduct is well represented here today," he said. "Both the fellow that's been conducting the investigation and the director of the office are here."

"Good, that's what we want," Haley said. "Maybe we won't have to present this twice."

When Keith Breathwaite walked in a few minutes later, he spotted Haley sitting beside Raul and blanched. Haley smiled at him, stood, and stepped over to the prosecution table. "You could save yourself a lot of embarrassment and move to dismiss right now," she said. "I know who subpoenaed those visiting records from the jail, and I don't like it. Someday you've got to learn to stand on your own feet instead of letting William do it for you. You could begin by ending this little facade right now."

Haley knew that he wouldn't dismiss, that he didn't dare, because he needed his job. And she didn't want it dismissed today anyway. It would only mean having to make the case later, which would just take a lot more time.

"I don't think I should do that," Keith said.

"All right," Haley said. "Good luck. You'll need it today."

Haley's presence at the defense table unnerved Keith a little bit, and as he put on his case, he didn't do as good a job as he was capable of. But in fairness to him, the best he had was José Ramirez, the man who'd complained to the Bar against Raul, and whose credibility Haley was prepared to tear to shreds. Keith also had the chief arson investigator who testified where and how the fire started, and the investigator from the Office of Professional Conduct to testify to the file on Mr. Ramirez. But their testimonies only supported Mr. Ramirez's, so theirs would be moot points by the time she was finished.

Haley kept her cross-examination to a minimum, but she did ask José Ramirez what he knew about computers.

"I don't know anything about them," he said.

"Are you telling this court," she asked, pointing toward Judge Shelby, "that you couldn't possibly break into a computer's secure files?"

"I couldn't even turn a computer on," he answered. "It's not my thing."

Haley asked the court's permission to call José at a later time if she needed to, and the judge granted it. When Keith rested his case, Judge Shelby looked impressed with the evidence he'd presented. She quickly denied Haley's motion to dismiss, which Haley and Raul both expected. It was just protocol.

Then it was Haley's turn. The nervousness was gone. She was ready to attack the state's case. "I call the defendant, Raul Garcia," she said.

After Raul was sworn in, Haley quickly dispensed with the questions about how he was employed and so on. Then she asked, "Mr. Garcia, were you retained to represent Mr. José Ramirez in a wrongful termination case against a former employer?"

"No. I've never even met Mr. Ramirez," Raul responded.

"You heard him testify today," Haley said. "Are you suggesting that he perjured himself?"

"That's exactly what I'm saying," Raul answered, his eyes flashing.

"Do you have any idea why he might do that?" Haley asked.

Keith Breathwaite was on his feet objecting instantly. "Calls for speculation by the witness," he said.

"I'll withdraw the question, Your Honor," Haley said. Then she turned back to Raul and asked, "You've seen the file that Mr. Ramirez purports to be a file created by you and your secretary about his case, have you not?"

"I have," Raul answered.

"And did you and your secretary make that file?"

"No, we did not," Raul answered.

"Then can you explain how it got into your filing cabinet and how an electronic file was created when a password was needed to enter the program where you keep those files?" Haley asked.

"I can't, but I do know that someone other than us created those files."

"Mr. Garcia, you have examined the file very thoroughly, have you not? Both the hard file and the electronic file?"

"I have," he said.

"And have you compared them to your other files created in your office as to style, format, type of papers that are there, unusual spelling errors, and so on?" she asked.

"I have," he answered.

Keith stood up. "I object, Your Honor. Testimony has already been given that the files, all but this copy that was taken by the investigator from the Office of Professional Conduct, were destroyed in the fire."

The judge turned to Haley, who said, "Your Honor, if you will allow me to proceed, I'll be able to establish that all the records were not destroyed."

Keith turned red. "How can you do that?" he demanded.

"Your objection is noted, Counsel, but I am going to allow Ms. Gordon to continue. You'll have the opportunity to cross-examine," Judge Shelby said.

"Thank you, Your Honor," Haley said, then she turned again to Raul. "Would you tell the court what records were not destroyed and how that happened?"

Raul then explained that he and his secretary had made backups of all the electronic files and that he'd made a copy of the hard file of the one purported to be that of José Ramirez. He explained that he'd had two copies of the CDs placed in safety deposit boxes, and that he kept one at home. He further explained why he'd taken that precaution. "I was of the opinion," he said, "that if someone could break in once, they could do it again. I even took several other files home for the very purpose of comparing them with the one that was planted in my office."

Haley smiled and glanced back at Keith, whose face showed exactly what she'd expected it would—worry.

Haley then produced the files and the backup discs and had Raul identify them. Then she asked him to explain what he'd found in the comparisons. "First, I always put my written notes in the file," he said. "You'll see that all of these files have several pages of written notes. The file of Mr. Ramirez has no handwritten notes of any kind."

Raul went on to point out numerous things in the Ramirez file that did not exist in the other files. He also pointed out that there was nothing in the Ramirez file bearing his signature, and yet every one of the other files had several pages with Raul's signature. He then attacked numerous spelling and grammatical errors in both the e-file and the hard copy.

After leaving that area, Haley asked Raul about his concerns over fingerprints. "Did you ask anyone to take fingerprints the afternoon before the fire?" she asked.

"I did. I called the office of a private investigator I had retained to help me in the Rob Sterling murder case. He wasn't in," Raul explained, "and his secretary told me that she didn't think he provided that kind of service."

"So you dropped the matter?" Haley asked.

"For then," he said. "I intended to talk to Detective Collier the next morning about it, but of course, by then it was too late."

"Did you think to ask the police to come and do it?" Haley asked.

"I thought about it, but no one seemed to believe anything I said after the fake file showed up. So I figured it would be a waste of time," Raul said.

Finally, Haley asked Raul if he had set the fire or asked anyone else to do it. He told the court that he had not.

On cross-examination, Keith Breathwaite tried to attack the validity of the records Raul had claimed to have removed from the office.

"Ms. Haley has subpoenaed three of the clients whose case files I took home," Raul said. "I suppose you can ask them. Their signatures are all there in those folders."

Keith tried several other tactics, but it got him nowhere. Finally, he gave up. Haley then called Raul's secretary, who basically verified what Raul had given in his testimony. Keith didn't even attempt to cross-examine her.

Then Haley called one of Raul's former clients, who verified that the file was in fact a correct file. Again there was no cross-examination by the prosecutor. Finally, Haley called the manager of a local computer company, Snappy Computer Service, and asked him if he knew Mr. José Ramirez.

"I do," he said. "He used to work for me."

"Used to?" Haley asked. "Under what conditions did he leave your company?"

"I fired him," he said.

"And what did you fire him for?" Haley asked.

"He was hacking into our confidential files," the manager said.

Keith again declined to cross-examine the witness.

Then Haley said, "I'd like to recall Mr. Ramirez to the stand."

José had been excluded from the courtroom and did not hear the testimony just given. He strode confidently to the stand. Judge Shelby said, "You are still under oath, Mr. Ramirez."

Then Haley asked José if he'd ever been employed by the Snappy Computer Company.

He hesitated before saying, "Not that I remember, but then, I've worked lots of places, and I don't remember them all."

"If I show you your employment records there, would it help refresh your memory?" she asked.

"I don't know. Maybe I did work there for a little while," he said.

Haley asked a flurry of questions that José answered haltingly. Finally, she turned to the Judge. "Your Honor, I'd like permission to call witnesses for the purpose of impeaching the testimony of this witness."

Keith roared to his feet with his objection, but the judge simply said, "He's close to having charges ordered by this court already, Mr. Breathwaite. You'd better sit down and listen."

Haley was prepared, thanks to the work of Detective Sperry Collier. She called a teacher from José's high school, a Mrs. Jenson, who testified that he was one of the sharpest students she'd ever had in her advanced computer class. Haley had also learned something else of great interest. Martin Ligorni had been in the same class. She was going to investigate any possible relationship between the two men later. "Do you know if he ever attempted to break a password and get into a secure file?"

"I watched him do it one day in class," Mrs. Jenson said. "He'd been bragging to some of the other students who told me he was breaking into school files. I didn't believe he could do it, so I asked him to try to get into a program of mine that had a password. It took him ten minutes, and he was in."

Keith had to do something on cross-examination. He stood and asked, "You've had many students over the years, haven't you?"

"Many," she agreed.

"And you can't remember all of them, can you?"

"No, but I remember José very well," she said, and Keith sat down with a long face.

The judge asked, "Did you intend to call more witnesses in reference to this impeachment matter?"

"Yes, I have three more," Haley said.

"And they will all testify to similar things?" she asked.

"Two of them will. The other will testify to another matter," Haley answered even as she wondered what kind of fool would hire the same man for all three attempts to discredit Raul. She was grateful that such a fool existed though, for it was making her job easier. She also found herself hoping that the same fool was the one trying to frame Rob. She couldn't help but wonder if such shoddy work could be Martin's. After all, he wasn't practiced in subtlety, as he'd demonstrated with his decorating tastes.

"What is the other matter?" Judge Shelby asked. "I will allow you to call the witness only if I need details."

"I will show that Mr. Ramirez was convicted of arson when he was eighteen," she said.

"That's good enough for me," the judge said sternly. "You won't need to call your other witnesses. This defendant has clearly committed perjury. Bailiff, take the witness into custody. He is in contempt of this court."

"Your Honor," Haley said, "I would respectfully request that Mr. Ramirez be protected. I'm also going to be representing Mr. Rob Sterling in the matters that are pending against him, and several potential witnesses in that case seem to have vanished. I would like this man available for questioning as a hostile defense witness in Mr. Sterling's murder trial."

The judge said she'd see what she could do, then Haley said, "I'd like to renew my motion to dismiss the charges against the defendant."

"Your motion is granted. The charges are dismissed," she said, and as she rapped the gavel she adjourned the court.

Haley shook Raul's hand. He said, "Thank you, Miss Gordon."

Haley smiled and said, "I didn't do anything really. You could have done it yourself. You and Sperry did all the legwork. All I did was ask the questions."

Keith Breathwaite stepped over and said, "Congratulations, Haley. Now I've got to go back and face the old bear."

Haley said, "I'm sorry, Keith. Good luck. If William gets on you too hard, you might tell him that I said he's next."

"You've got guts, Haley, I'll hand you that," he said. "But why would you want to defend Rob Sterling?"

"Because he's innocent," Haley said. "Which is not true of your star witness here. By the way, I'll be watching, and if charges aren't filed promptly against Mr. Ramirez, I'll see to it that the press gets right on it. And you can tell the district attorney I said so," she added.

Keith gathered up his papers and began stuffing them in his briefcase. Haley watched him for a minute, then she said, "I know you're handling the terroristic threats charges against Rob. I also know that you don't have witnesses who you dare put on the stand. I would suggest that you—"

"Don't worry, Haley," he interrupted. "I'll either be ready to make a case or drop the charges."

"You might want to run it by Mr. Montgomery," she suggested.

Keith snapped his briefcase shut. "You embarrassed me today, Haley," he said. "And if it was anyone but you, I'd be angry. But I'm not so stupid that I'll let you do it to me again. If the evidence isn't there, the charges will be dropped. And frankly, if William wants to fire me, I guess he'll just have to do it. I won't make it as easy on him as you did," he added. "I won't resign."

The director of the Office of Professional Conduct joined them. He said to Keith, "Sounds like that might be a wise decision. Miss Gordon here knows her job." Then he turned to Raul, who had also been listening. "Mr. Garcia," he said, "we apologize for the inconvenience you've been through. I'll see to it that the complaint against you is dismissed."

"And if we ever find out who was behind Mr. Ramirez in this whole affair, and if it's an attorney, I can assume he or she will be made to account?" Raul said with just a touch of bitterness.

"If it's a member of the Bar, you can certainly assume that." Then he turned back to Haley and said, "You did an excellent job here today. And in case you're wondering, the district attorney has not as yet filed a complaint against you."

Haley shrugged. "I hope he doesn't," she said, and turned and walked from the courtroom.

CHAPTER TWENTY-THREE

The district attorney called another press conference the day after Raul's charges had been dismissed. He reiterated his hard stance against those who treat the law with impunity. Haley listened to the press conference so that she could attempt to keep up with his thinking. With a sober face he apologized to the public for his office's failure to convict Raul Garcia of arson. "Mr. Garcia has gone free, and the blame must fall on my office. With the departure of Miss Haley Gordon, much of our evidence disappeared, and she was able to manipulate the evidence to fit her own agenda. She blindsided the prosecutor from my office and used twisted logic in convincing the judge to dismiss the case."

Haley couldn't believe his gall. And when he went on, it got worse. "This office is shocked and disappointed that Miss Gordon would take facts learned in preparing for the prosecution of this case, as well as others, and contort them to defend men she had once been sworn to prosecute. A sheriff's deputy who has sided with Miss Gordon in the attempt to upend the prosecution is no longer involved in the case. Investigators from my own office are busy reconstructing the evidence so that we will be ready to go to trial the first week of January," he said.

He still wasn't through. "I once again pledge that I will personally do everything I can to ensure the conviction of Rob Sterling for the murder of his wife, Jennifer Sterling."

Haley had braced herself for the district attorney to announce some kind of action he would take against her. So far he hadn't done that. But the day after the press conference she received a copy of a motion that had just been filed by the district attorney. William was making his first move. He was asking the court to order Rob Sterling to accept Dan Smathers as counsel and not to allow either Haley Gordon or Raul Garcia to be associated in any way with the defense. He cited a conflict of interest on the part of Haley, stating in his motion that she was too emotionally distraught to properly assist the defendant in the preparation and presentation of his defense. He also stated that it was unheard of for an attorney to work for the prosecution and then switch to the defense. It created a cloud over the legal process that was unfair to the taxpayers of the state, he argued. In the case of Raul Garcia, he alleged that the attorney's competency and integrity were in doubt.

Judge Horton scheduled a hearing on the motion for the next day. He appeared to be angry and told William that his motion was both unusual and out of place. He allowed brief arguments on both sides before making his ruling. Haley spoke in behalf of herself and Raul, who was also present. She stated that she was both qualified and willing to represent Rob. She also argued that Raul's name had been cleared and that the district attorney was bordering on slander in the things he said about Raul.

Dan Smathers was there and simply said that he had been assigned as backup counsel and that he was willing to continue if the court directed him to do so. *What I really want,* he chuckled smugly to himself, *is to make sure that nothing gets out of my control, and that no one brings up my relationship with Jennifer Sterling.* The court then asked Rob for his position on the matter, reminding him that he'd earlier elected to handle his own defense.

Rob said that he had asked Haley and Raul to represent him and that he would assist in his own defense. He further stated that he didn't trust Dan Smathers and that if he were allowed to be part of the defense team, he would be ignored by the defendant.

Judge Horton then ruled, "Ms. Haley Gordon, assisted by Raul Garcia, will be allowed to continue as defense counsel. Mr. Smathers, the court thanks you for your efforts, but having considered the feelings of the defendant, and upon being convinced that the other attorneys in the case, particularly Ms. Gordon, are well qualified, it appears that your services are no longer needed, and you are excused by the court from further service."

Dan didn't like the turn of events, but he reminded himself that he could protect his reputation with his firm in other ways. And Rob *would* go to prison—he'd see to that. Dan felt confident that no one else was quite as smart as he was. He'd learned how to manipulate people and keep them under control, a skill he was finding particularly useful with Ann Denton. He smiled at how well she was cooperating with him now.

William Montgomery then stood and said, "Your Honor, with all due respect, I'd like to ask that you recuse yourself from this case."

Judge Horton's face reddened slightly, then he said, "Put your motion in writing and have it to me by first thing Monday morning. I'll have it considered."

* * *

Nat was rattled and almost ashamed to pick Haley up for their date that afternoon. He thought about calling her and making an excuse, but he couldn't make himself do it.

He kept thinking about the call he'd received just minutes before leaving the office. William Montgomery had renewed his request for Nat to pump Haley for information. He used the guise that Haley couldn't give Rob the kind of defense that every defendant deserved. "The court needs something solid to go on before he'll order her to step down as Sterling's counsel," William had told him.

Nat had been entirely taken aback. He didn't want to provide any more of the kind of help William Montgomery demanded. Haltingly, he said, "I think it would be best if I didn't do that at this point. Miss Gordon has become very important in my life, and with the relationship that has developed, it simply wouldn't be right."

There was a tense pause, and Nat half expected the phone to blow up in his hand. His respect for William had all but disintegrated. The way he had treated Haley and the things he'd said about her to the press were outrageous.

Finally William spoke again. "That's a very foolish decision, Nat," he said. "But I'll give you the chance to reconsider. And while you do that very quickly, let me remind you that any relationship you have with Haley would certainly be gone if she were to find out that you had been reporting to me all along."

Blackmail. It was a lowdown, dirty trick, but the district attorney had him. Nat couldn't let Haley know what he'd done. He also didn't want the senior partner in his own firm to hear from William. The two were old friends, and William could affect his position in the firm. So Nat said, "All right, I'll let you know what I learn."

"That's better, Nat. You have a great future ahead of you," William said condescendingly, then hung up before Nat could say another word.

So with that weighing heavily on his mind, Nat rang Haley's doorbell.

The evening went reasonably well, although Haley thought Nat seemed rather withdrawn at times. She attempted to get him to talk about his work, wondering if something was going on there that had him worried. He said he didn't want to bore her with his job. He'd rather talk about hers. She had mentioned what a difficult week it had been for her, particularly that afternoon when William had made quite pointed personal attacks against her in court.

"But I'm going to stick with this case, and I'm going to beat my old boss," she said with such feeling that Nat's own guilt deepened. He didn't know how he could ever betray her again. She was such a good and beautiful person.

As he walked her to her door late that night, he said, "Haley, I've enjoyed your company more than ever tonight."

Haley found the statement a little odd considering how quiet he'd been. But he seemed sincere, and she put her arms around him when they reached her door. "Thank you, Nat," she said. "It has been a rather nice evening."

She kissed him tenderly, then on an impulse, she said, "Would you like to come in for a few minutes?"

I certainly would! he thought, hoping to talk about anything but their work. So for the next hour they listened to soft music as they sat side by side on the sofa, her hand in his. They talked about their respective childhoods. Nat was amazed when he learned of the terrible home life she'd lifted herself from, and his affection and admiration for her grew even more.

And Haley got Nat to talk about his own work a little more than he had before. It still sounded boring to her, but she could also see that what he was doing took both intelligence and a great deal of skilled legal work. She was quite impressed, and they enjoyed a very relaxed and pleasant hour together.

As Nat was leaving, he suddenly turned to Haley and said, "Why don't you come to my ward with me on Sunday? I'd like you to meet some of my friends there."

Haley was nowhere near ready for that. She wondered how she could gracefully decline. She asked him what time his meetings were. To her relief they started the same time her ward did. So she made the best excuse she could think of. "I just can't Nat. I have my little Sunday School class. I've got to be there for them."

"It won't hurt them to have a substitute just one Sunday," Nat said defensively.

"Maybe sometime," she hedged, "but not yet. You've got to give me time. I don't want to be rushed in our relationship."

Nat tried to be understanding, but it hurt him a little. When he left, their earlier romantic mood had dimmed. But he didn't blame Haley. He blamed William Montgomery. He knew he hadn't been himself that evening because of William's demands, and he felt that if he had, Haley would have been more receptive to his invitation.

* * *

Another judge ruled before the end of the day on Monday that Judge Horton did not need to recuse himself from presiding over the Sterling murder trial. And Judge Horton had his clerk notify both the district attorney and counsel for the defendant of the decision.

Once that issue was settled, Haley and Raul, with the help of Rex Thomas, a much-recovered Kurt Palmer, and the ever-aggressive Sperry Collier, began to put together their defense. They met daily as the day for the trial drew ever closer.

Haley also spent an increasing amount of time with Nat, and they talked a lot about her case. And Nat, even though he hated it, faithfully reported to William. But his information wasn't very helpful to the district attorney, who frequently grumbled at Nat, telling him he could do better.

The preliminary hearing on the charges of terroristic threats came around at last. The district attorney's office had delayed it once, and they'd tried to convince the judge to continue the hearing again for another couple of weeks, but Haley was there, and she was ready to fight. She strongly opposed a continuance, and the judge ruled in her favor. So Keith Breathwaite argued that two key witnesses had disappeared, but that when they were found, the state wanted to be able to file the charges again.

Haley argued that they'd never had a case in the first place, and that the charges should be dismissed without prejudice. "I was the victim of the attacks," she said. "And I don't feel that my client had anything to do with it. The state is only harassing the defendant by continuing to hold this ludicrous matter over his head."

The judge stated that he was ready to conduct the preliminary hearing, and ordered the state to proceed. Keith was then forced to admit that he wasn't prepared. The judge gladly dismissed the charge against Rob without prejudice, meaning that the matter was over; the state could not file again. Once more, Haley had defeated her former colleagues, and she'd done it with very little effort. But the big fight was ahead, and Haley had seen enough these past few weeks to realize that it was going to be tough. William Montgomery didn't play by the rules, and she would have to be on her toes every minute if Rob were to be freed of the charges he was facing.

* * *

Winter didn't wait for Christmas. It roared into the state a few days before Thanksgiving. A blanket of snow covered the area. Roads were a mess, and accidents kept the police and medical emergency people busy day and night. The weather was cold, and it kept the snow on the ground.

But while the rest of the city prepared for the holidays, Rob was unaffected by the dramatic change in the weather or the festive climate that accompanied it. The climate never changed in his dank jail cell. He did the only thing he could do—he waited. Haley and Raul reported to him regularly, though, and Rob looked forward to those visits. His best friend had found new office space and was trying to rebuild his practice while spending as much time as he could on Rob's case. But he admitted to Rob that Haley was the more capable of the two in the type of case they were fighting.

Rob was just grateful for Raul's assistance to Haley. And her visits lifted him a great deal as well. Not only was she a talented attorney, but she was quickly becoming a very good friend. Most of the time they were together it was all business, but at times she'd sit back and they would just visit. He found those minutes to be the only cheer in his life. They helped him get through the long and boring hours alone in his cell. Regardless of the outcome of his case, Rob didn't look forward to the time when he would no longer see Haley Gordon. As much as he tried not to admit it, she'd begun to fill a painful and empty hole in his life—he needed a friend and a compassionate ear.

* * *

Dan Smathers no longer had any official ties to the Rob Sterling murder case, but he had a lot at stake if Rob were acquitted. If William Montgomery lost his case, the police might begin probing the facts for reinterpretation; and there were individuals out there who, for spite, would drop hints about Dan's involvement with Jennifer. Of particular concern was his contact. He needed the man's help now, but once the case was closed, the contact would be a liability that Dan couldn't afford. And Dan couldn't help but wonder how many of those people his man had enlisted over the weeks might actually know who was paying the bills. Alex had promised to keep it confidential, but Dan knew that promises meant nothing to the man if there was something to be gained in breaking them.

Dan's personal life consumed him, even when working on other cases, and in mid-December, in the middle of a partners' meeting, Ralph Hacking suddenly said, "I'm concerned with the quality of your work lately, Dan." Others echoed his concern. Then the senior partner added, "I don't know what's bugging you, but you'd better grab yourself by the bootstraps and pull yourself out of it. You're not getting enough billable hours to justify your salary."

Dan began to seethe, but he didn't want it to show. He knew that Ralph was right, but Ralph had no idea the pressure he was under. "Sorry," he said, trying to sound contrite, "I didn't realize. Give me more work and I'll do it."

"You have plenty of work, you're just not putting in the time for your clients. Snap out of it, Dan, or we'll reconsider what you're making here," he said.

Ralph Hacking was getting quite elderly, but the fire that had made him a highly successful trial attorney had not dimmed. Dan knew he meant business. And the senior partner could not be dealt with through threats. Dan knew he better get to work or his position would be in jeopardy. Slightly disgruntled, he tried not to worry about the things his partners didn't know, like how much they were really paying him. He could never let them figure that one out. But that night, he again met with his contact rather than work on his cases. "The trial starts in just over two weeks," Dan said. "Are you ready to put our plan into motion?"

"You're wasting my time," the other said. "Unless you have something new to discuss, this meeting is over already. I have better things to do than listen to you grumble while I'm freezing my tail off."

Dan thought quickly. Then he said, "Haley Gordon might be getting too comfortable. Give her something to distract her. I don't care what it is, except that it can't be threats this time. But distract her some way."

"I'll give it some thought," the contact said.

"Give it some action," Dan ordered.

"Whatever you say, boss," his partner answered sarcastically. Then they left each other. The meeting was over.

* * *

Sperry Collier was better equipped now, but he was also freezing. Here it was, almost Christmas, and he was out in the cold and the dark, following a man he was fast learning to despise. But as Dan left, Sperry's interest shifted to the man he'd been meeting with.

Sperry couldn't help but offer a prayer of gratitude for technology. From his vantage point a hundred yards away, Sperry was able to both see the contact clearly, despite the darkness, and snap photos of him without the use of supplemental lighting. This was the first time he'd gotten a good enough look to enable him to begin the process of establishing the man's identity. He knew where he lived, although he'd never seen the man outside of his mansion except when he was in his car. The man always drove straight into his garage and shut the door before he got out of it. And seeing him inside the car had proven impossible. The contact had darkened windows that the cops didn't seem to notice, and he was nothing more than a shadowy form behind them.

The property was listed in a woman's name that, as far as Sperry could discover, didn't exist. The license plates on the car "belonged" to a company that again didn't seem to be real. It was all very frustrating.

But Sperry had finally gotten a look at the man. If he could just find a way now to listen in on one of the conversations between Dan and the contact, he'd make some real progress. The technology to do so was out there, but it far exceeded Sperry's budget. *Well,* he decided as he watched both men drive away, *I can at least find out who the guy is.*

Sperry spent the next day looking at hundreds of mug shots. It wasn't until late afternoon that he finally spotted a picture that could be his man. The basic shape of the face was right, but that was about all. The contact's hair was thinner now and cut much shorter. And if this was the same man, he must dye his hair, as the man in the mug shot was very blond. The contact had brown hair. He also wore a short beard, while the man in the photo was clean shaven. The photo was ten years old, so age would have changed him quite a bit. Sperry jotted down the name and continued to look at more pictures. But he found no other photos that were even close.

The next day, Christmas Eve, Sperry poured over court records. Gradually he began to put together a profile of the man the mug shot labeled Alexander Addison. He went by several aliases. The most common were variations of what was believed to be his birth name; Richard Addison and Alex Harrison were just two examples.

Sperry just couldn't be sure he had the right man. Nothing in the emerging profile was consistent with the large house in the expensive neighborhood. The man had been convicted previously on charges of burglary, armed robbery, drug trafficking, and extortion. He'd done time at the state prison for some of those charges. But it was one final charge that interested Sperry the most: a murder charge that showed an arrest date nine years earlier, but did not show a conviction, which meant he'd been acquitted.

Then Sperry found what he was looking for. "Good heavens," he whispered. The defense attorney in that murder case had been none other than a much younger but very aggressive Dan Smathers.

Convinced now that he had the right man, Sperry began to search out the names of defense witnesses listed in the record of the murder trial. Ten years was a long time when it came to searching for people with questionable backgrounds. But if Sperry could just find one who would talk, he might be able to learn something about Alexander Addison that would prove helpful. The fact that Dan and Alexander were meeting as they were was very significant, but he needed more information.

The Christmas season made it hard to devote the time needed to digging into Addison's past. Sperry wanted to spend time with his family. So, as much as he hated to, he put off the search for known associates of the man he'd come to think of as the contact.

CHAPTER TWENTY-FOUR

Christmas was also a difficult time for Haley Gordon, but for different reasons. Christmas was a time for families. It was a time to celebrate the birth of the Savior in the company of people one loved. It was not a good time to be alone. And alone was exactly what Haley was. She got up early Christmas day just because she always got up early. She had decorated her apartment with a small tree, and around it were the six presents she had been given.

The biggest Nat had given her before leaving, and Haley knew it would be something expensive because Nat liked expensive things. Even before becoming a successful attorney with a lucrative practice, Nat had enjoyed all the money he'd wanted. He'd been raised in a wealthy home and had never known what it was like to want something he couldn't buy.

That was not the case with Haley. In fact, it worried her that she and Nat would have very different—too different—perspectives on what role money was to play in family life, that is, if she ever decided to become serious with him. Her background also helped her be less concerned with problems relating to money. She'd learned that things always worked out the way they were meant to if one just lived right and had faith. That was why she wasn't stressed now that she had no income, only what Rob intended to pay her, and she wasn't sure he could ever pay her anything. Haley didn't care. She didn't know that she'd ever accept anything from him anyway, even if he could pay. Haley had scrimped and saved even when receiving a good salary. She could live modestly for a long time on what she had put away.

The way Nat threw money around bothered her. She couldn't help but wonder if that was one of the things that was holding her back from developing a deeper relationship with him. She looked at his present for a moment, then picked up each of the others, one at a time. Raul and his wife had given her something. Rex and Kurt had gone together on a small present. Sperry had sent her a small package in the mail. Her former secretary at the district attorney's office had come to her house the night before and delivered what Haley was quite certain was a book. She picked up one more present. It was from her Sunday School class. Her eyes became moist as she gazed at it. She almost opened it, but finally set it back beside the others.

There was a knock on the door. Haley got to her feet and went over. She couldn't imagine who might be there. When she opened the door, there was no one standing there, but there was a young teenage girl jumping in a car that was pulling away from the curb. She didn't get a good look at her and couldn't imagine why she would have knocked and then run. It was then that she noticed two brightly wrapped packages at her feet.

She smiled and picked them up. Maybe there were others who hadn't forgotten her. She carried both packages inside before she looked them over closely. Each had a typewritten label with her name on it. But the gift wrapping was different on both, as were the labels.

Feeling just a little uneasy, she shook both of them. Nothing rattled. She held them to her ear. *Nothing ticking,* she thought, smiling at her runaway imagination.

But after setting both beneath her tree, she felt a prickle of fear raising her skin. She forced herself to pick them up again. There was simply nothing to indicate who might have given them to her. But the only person she'd seen was a young girl, and as she looked at them now they seemed harmless. But were they?

She thought about calling Rex or Sperry, but it was Christmas; this was not the time to be bothering them with her little mystery. It would probably turn out that the gifts were from some of the kids in the ward or her home teachers, or something like that, and then she would feel foolish. Those days of terror she'd experienced while being stalked had affected her more than she liked to admit, she decided. But surely that was over. The stalker was gone. *Probably dead,* she assumed, since no one seemed to know what had happened to him. *There's nothing to be nervous about,* she told herself again.

Haley placed the packages beneath her tree and took her time with her breakfast. One of her few Christmas traditions was to prepare herself a lavish breakfast. The phone rang while she was still cooking. It was Bishop Coffman's wife. "Haley, we'd be honored if you'd have dinner with our family this evening. If you don't already have other plans, that is," she said.

Haley smiled to herself. The bishop's daughter had put them up to that, and she couldn't say no. Nat was out of town and wouldn't be back until the next day, so she was all alone. He had felt terrible about leaving, he'd told her, but he had a sister in Michigan who had insisted that he come there for Christmas. Haley had also encouraged him to go as well. And he'd finally agreed and flown out on the twenty-third.

So why not join the bishop's family tonight? she reasoned. "I'd love to," she told the bishop's wife. "What time would you like me to come?"

"We'll eat at six. Why don't you come about five and you can visit with us beforehand."

"What can I bring?" Haley asked.

"Just yourself," she was told. "We'll see you at about five then?"

"Yes, and thank you so much," Haley said.

She had been planning a short visit to the bishop's home anyway, as she had small gifts for each of the members of her class. She'd hoped to deliver them Christmas afternoon. It had seemed like a good way to while away the hours. And she loved those teenagers.

Haley had managed to use up well over an hour by the time she'd fixed breakfast, eaten alone, and cleaned up the kitchen. She then took a long and leisurely bath. An hour later she was dressed, her long black hair brushed until it shined, and her makeup, what little she used, was applied. She once again approached her little pile of gifts.

But she still didn't feel like opening them. So she got out her scriptures and read for another hour. She studied every account of the Christmas story, read about the Savior's appearance to the Nephites, and even spent some time studying the prophecies of Christ in the book of Isaiah.

Finally, she went to her tree with the intention of opening her gifts. It had never been particularly fun for her to open gifts. As a child, she'd rarely had any, and when she did, it was nothing but a token from one of her parents trying to make up to her for the lack of love they gave her. And anyway, part of the fun of receiving gifts was having someone else to be there when they were opened. But this is how it had always been for Haley, and probably always would be, she thought a little sadly.

Then she pulled herself together and debated over which to open first. She pulled the one from Nat close to her, fingered the ribbon, then decided to wait. She picked up one of the unlabeled ones. She again felt a prickle on her skin. *That's it! I will not be intimidated!* she thought. That one would be first. She recklessly tore the wrapping free to find a small box inside. She peeled back the tape and found another, even smaller box. She opened that one and picked up the card that lay on top of still another tiny package. Her hands were trembling as she opened the card.

> *Merry Christmas, Miss Gordon,*
> *Thank you for taking care of our teacher. We love him and want him back. They won't let us send anything to him, so we wondered if you would tell him that we are thinking about him and praying for him. We know they let you see him. Oh, and tell him we bought him a present too. We'll give it to him when you get him out of jail.*

It was signed by every one of the young people from Rob's Sunday School class.

Haley sat and cried. Those young people had just demonstrated for her what Christmas was all about; it was about love. And they were depending on her to convey that love to Rob. She could, and would, do that for them.

She wiped her eyes and finally pulled the last box from the package. She opened it and gasped. Haley had some background in jewelry, and the little necklace that lay folded in the box had cost those kids more than they could afford. It was a simple gold heart on an intricate gold chain, and it was beautiful. Rob's Sunday School kids must have pooled every dime they could find to buy this gift for her. Now she couldn't fail them.

With the children on her mind she opened the present from her own students next. It was a book by the prophet, and each one of the kids had signed their name inside the cover. She would treasure this book for the rest of her life. She read from it, skimming the pages at random for several minutes.

Haley opened the gift from Nat next. It was a sweater. An extremely expensive sweater, as predicted. And when she shook it open to hold it up against her, a small box tumbled to the floor. She smiled as she opened it. Another necklace. Pricey, very beautiful, but somehow it just didn't mean what the one the kids had given her did. She felt guilty as she put it back in the box and stacked it neatly beneath her tree again.

She continued slowly through the few remaining gifts. She left the other unidentified one for last. She reached for it, but her hand strayed to the gold, heart-shaped necklace from Rob's students. She picked it up and went to a mirror, where she put it on. The gold gleamed beautifully against the rich brown of her skin. It was a lovely gift.

As she admired it in the mirror, a thought came to her. She wasn't the only one alone today. So was Rob Sterling. And it didn't have to be that way. Impulsively, she picked up the card his students had written to her, stuffed it in her briefcase, grabbed a coat and her purse, and headed for the door.

The drive to the jail was slow even though traffic was light. It was snowing hard, and the roads hadn't been plowed. Haley felt sorry for the poor road workers who would have to leave their warm homes and their families and come out in this terrible storm.

When she arrived, several people were surprised to see her at the jail, but they didn't hesitate to call Rob up to see her. "You take as long as you like," she was told.

Haley was excited when Rob walked in, and a shiver ran up her spine, surprising her. Even in that horrible jail garb he was a handsome man. And he was very surprised to see her.

"Haley, it's Christmas," Rob said. "You didn't need to come today. You should have stayed home with . . ." He stopped and gave her a sheepish grin. He didn't know a lot about her. She was single, he knew that, but as for her family and her past, he knew nothing.

Haley smiled, and Rob felt his heart lift. "I should have stayed home with my dog?" she asked. "Is that what you were going to say?"

"Uh, yeah, I guess so," he said.

"Well, I couldn't do that, because I don't have a dog," she said with a grin. "I'm alone today, and I just thought that since you were too, maybe we could spend a little time together. Then we wouldn't both be alone."

Haley suddenly felt very awkward. The smiling man whose face she was gazing up at seemed like more than a client at that point. Perhaps he *was* something more than a client. Maybe this hadn't been such a good idea. Maybe she should leave now.

"Maybe we could sit," Rob said. "I don't have much to offer, but you're welcome to what there is," he said, pointing to the hard chair she'd sat on several times before. He took his usual place across the small table. "What a beautiful necklace you're wearing," he said. "Someone important must have given that to you for Christmas."

She fingered it. "It is beautiful," she said. "And it is from someone important."

Of course a woman as striking and wonderful as Haley has a boyfriend, he thought. He was surprised she hadn't married years ago.

"Can you tell me who the important person is?" he asked, knowing it wasn't any of his business, but feeling compelled to ask.

"Actually, it's from several important people," she said. "And they asked me to tell you, the next time I saw you, that they also had a gift for you, that they were saving it for when you got out of here. I decided that I should come tell you today. They also asked that I tell you that they love you. It really couldn't wait since today is Christmas."

Rob was puzzled. He couldn't imagine who might have sent a gift to Haley for him. He only had his sister, and she and her husband were coming this afternoon. "Who is it from?" he asked.

Haley smiled and said, "It's from the kids in your Sunday School class."

Rob lit up. "Really?" he asked.

"Really," she said.

"Wow, that's great. I can't believe they're still thinking of me." His face fell a little then. "So that's why you came?" Rob asked, feeling a little disappointment.

Haley's gaze was arrested as she looked into his eyes. That was not the main reason she'd come today. She couldn't lie to Rob. "Truthfully, no," she said. "It could have waited. I wanted to see you."

"Oh, has something come up?" he asked, the smile entirely gone from his face now.

"No, there's nothing new on your case. And I didn't come to talk about that anyway."

Rob's eyes strayed to the briefcase that Haley had placed on the floor beside her chair. "Then why the briefcase?" he asked.

"Because I wanted to show you the card from the kids. Just in case you didn't believe me. I figured if I had it in my briefcase, I wouldn't have to explain it to the officers," she said. She turned and retrieved her briefcase, opened it, took out the card, and handed it across the table.

Rob read, his eyes moist. He swiped a hand across his face and handed the card back. "Thank you," he said. "Thank you for coming, and thank you for letting me read the card. If you see them, tell them I love them too."

Haley still had the briefcase on her lap. She pulled out a yellow pad and a pen and slid them across to Rob. "Why don't you tell them?" she suggested. "You write it and I'll see that it gets delivered."

Rob wrote a full page, then he handed the pad to Haley. "Read it, and tell me if that's okay," he said.

Haley did as bidden, and then she looked up and into Rob's green eyes. To her surprise, they didn't seem as sad as they had. The expression of love from his little Sunday School class had lifted his spirits.

And had she helped? She hoped so.

For well over an hour, Haley and Rob just talked. He asked her about her past and listened intently as she gave him more details than she'd ever given anyone. She wasn't sure why she talked so freely, but she felt more open with him. They also talked a little about what he was going through—the guilt over how he and Jennifer were acting the weeks before her death, his fears about Jennifer's behavior. He also told her he'd been given a measure of peace in the matter. Both of them were touched to hear of each other's struggles, and there was a comfortable silence for a few moments.

Haley finally cleared her throat. "I better not test the good nature of the staff here," she said at last as she looked at her watch. "It's noon. They'll be calling you for lunch."

"I could miss that," Rob said. "What I wouldn't give for a good home-cooked meal."

"When you get out, I'll make you one," Haley said. "I'm not a bad cook."

"Is that a promise?" Rob asked.

"Two actually," Haley responded. "I promise I'll help you get out of here, and yes, I'll cook you that meal."

* * *

Haley enjoyed the time with Rob so much that she hadn't thought anything about her other Christmas presents. The drive home took even longer than the drive to the jail despite the fact that snowplows were working hard on the roads. The snow was falling so fast her windshield wipers couldn't keep up, and she had to drive very slowly.

When she finally got home, there was over a foot of fresh snow on the lawn in front of the apartments, and it was still coming down hard. Haley stomped her feet and brushed her coat off before stepping into the apartment. After leaving her boots at the door and hanging her coat up, she walked back to her living room window and gazed at the white wonderland that was in the process of being created outside.

The phone rang, and she reluctantly turned from the window and answered it. "Haley, it's me, Nat. Merry Christmas."

Hearing his voice should have been exciting. But instead, it had the same effect on her as a pin on a balloon. She sunk wearily into a chair and said, "Hi Nat. Thanks for the sweater and necklace. They're beautiful."

"You're welcome," he said. "They didn't come cheap. But you're worth that and a lot more."

It would have been far better if he hadn't said that. The world wasn't about money. At least hers wasn't. A couple of hours in a stuffy room in the county jail, doing nothing but talking to a prisoner who had nothing to give but a little time, had lifted her spirits and cheered her heart. Talking to Nat about how much she was worth to him monetarily was almost more than she could take right now.

Nat didn't sense her mood and went on. "What about the other present I sent you?" he asked. "Did you like it?"

"What other present?" she asked. "I only gave you one, you shouldn't have given me more."

"I can afford it," he said. "But didn't the other one come? I sent it a couple of days before I left. I'm sorry if it didn't come."

Then Haley remembered the other present, the second one without a return address. "Did you put your return address on it?" she asked.

"I can't remember. I might not have," he admitted. "I was in a hurry. But when you open it, you'll know it's from me. It'll really give you a kick," he said. "I'm sorry it didn't get to you by Christmas."

"But it did," Haley said. "I got it this morning, but I haven't opened it yet. I didn't know who it was from, and I saved it until last."

"When did you open the others?" he asked.

"I got up early," she said. "I didn't have many, but I opened them hours ago."

"That's why I sent you another one," he said. "I knew you wouldn't get many gifts, and I hate that for you."

That comment really annoyed Haley. Did he think receiving gifts mattered that much to her?

"It's really all right," she said a little stiffly. "Christmas isn't about receiving gifts anyway. It's about love and giving and remembering the Savior."

"I know that," he said. "I'm one of those who likes to give, especially to a wonderful woman that I am very fond of and miss a great deal. Hey, where have you been? I've been trying to call all morning," Nat said.

"I went for a drive," she answered evasively.

"But it's snowing hard there," Nat said. "I talked to my mother a little while ago, and she said she hasn't seen such a storm in years."

Haley wasn't about to let Nat pursue the issue of where she'd been. It wasn't something he'd understand. So she said, "It's really quite beautiful out. And I drove slowly. Hang on while I grab your present. I'll open it while you're on the phone."

She propped the phone between her ear and her shoulder and began to tear the wrapping off the gift. "You won't believe what I sent you," Nat said. "I had a hard time finding just the right one."

"I'm sure it'll be lovely," she said as she finished removing the paper. She was down to the box now, and she had to tear the tape loose. It was taped quite tightly. At last she got it off and opened the lid. She reached in through the wadded paper the gift was couched in and picked up what felt like a plastic bag. She pulled it out.

Haley screamed and dropped both the phone and the gift. In a heavy, clear plastic bag was a human hand. It had been severed at the wrist.

"Haley, what's the matter?" Nat was shouting into the phone.

Haley wasn't hearing him. She was sick. This was the most horrible thing anyone had ever done to her. She ran to the bathroom and threw up. For several minutes she stayed there. She finally washed her face and then carried a towel back into the living room and threw it over the bagged hand.

She then heard Nat's voice on the phone. She picked it up without listening to a word he was saying. "That is the sickest thing anyone has ever done to me," she shouted. "I don't ever want to talk to you again. I'll send your necklace and sweater back."

Nat was saying something, but Haley didn't want to hear it, and she simply cut off his call. Then she sat and sobbed for a long time. Finally she knew she had to get control of herself. She was confused and sick and bitter. Why Nat would do such a despicable thing was beyond her imagination. She thought she knew him. But clearly she didn't.

The phone rang. She ignored it and let it ring until the answering machine picked up. It was probably Nat. She didn't care if she never talked to him again. She waited a few minutes, then placed a call. "Sergeant Thomas," she said after she had Rex on the line. "I'm so sorry to bother you on Christmas, but the most terrible thing just happened."

CHAPTER TWENTY-FIVE

A whole slew of cops came to Haley's apartment. Every scrap of wrapping paper, the box and the bag and its unspeakable contents were taken into evidence. Mixed with the paper used as stuffing in the box, one of the officers found a card with a handwritten message on it. He showed it to Rex.

"This is sick," Rex said as he held it so that Haley could read it. The note read:

> *I just thought you could use another hand in your coming trial. You can't win it on your own.*

There was no signature.

After that, Rex made Haley repeat every word Nat had said in their conversation, as nearly as she could recall, anyway. Nat called twice more that afternoon, but they let the answering machine take his messages.

"We'll take the tape from your machine," Rex said. "There may be something of importance there."

Haley merely nodded. She was feeling very strange. She wanted to talk to Rob, of all people, to confide in him. She wasn't angry at Nat, just very confused and horribly disappointed.

Rex was deep in thought. "This is troubling," he said. "How well do you know this Nat Turley guy?"

"Apparently not as well as I thought I did," she said.

"Do you know his family?"

"No, I've never met any of them. The only person I know who's connected with him in any way is an old girlfriend," she said. "Or a current one," she added as an afterthought.

"Haley," Rex said as he watched the woman he'd come to both respect and admire struggle with her emotions, "were you in love with Nat?"

That was easy to answer. "No," she said. "But I thought I knew him pretty well."

"I see. Did he know you weren't in love with him and might he have been angry about that?" he asked.

"I don't know, Rex. I'm just all confused right now."

"When is he coming back?" he asked.

"Tomorrow night," she said. "If the airport's open, that is." The storm's intensity, if anything, had increased. And as the snow continued to fall, the wind had picked up. A fierce blizzard was in progress all along the Salt Lake valley.

Rex scratched his chin. "Why would he care about the Rob Sterling trial?"

"He's always asking me about how the case is coming," Haley said. "But it always seemed like he was worried about me. I think he thinks I'm in over my head."

"Or is he somehow connected with . . ." Rex didn't complete his thought.

Haley completed it for him. "Could he be connected with our investigation? Is that what you were going to ask?"

Rex nodded. "It's worth checking out. I'll get on it tomorrow."

The officers finally left at shortly after four in the afternoon. Exhausted, Haley lay down on the sofa, and before long she was asleep.

She awoke to the ringing of the phone. Groggy from her nap, she picked it up without thinking. She had been determined to not speak with Nat, no matter what.

"Haley?" a familiar voice asked. "Are you all right?"

"I'm fine, Bishop," she said as her head cleared and she looked at her watch. It was nearly six. "Oh, I'm sorry," she said. "I'm late. I fell asleep."

"That's all right. We were worried about you traveling over in the storm. We were afraid something had happened."

"Something did," she said.

"Are you okay?" the bishop asked.

"I'll be all right," she said. "It was nothing really."

"My wife nearly has Christmas dinner ready. Would you still like to come over?" he asked. "We'd love to have you. In fact, we'll come pick you up if you'd rather not drive, although the storm finally seems to have passed over."

It was dark outside, and Haley stood and moved toward her window. The snow was deep. She wondered if she'd still be able to get her car out. "I can drive," she said. "It may take me a few minutes to get my car out of the carport though."

"You stay put," the bishop said. "My daughter and I'll be there to pick you up in five minutes."

He was there in exactly that. Haley invited the two of them in. She still needed to clean her face, apply a little makeup, and change her clothes.

The bishop sensed that something was very wrong with her and asked, "Haley, you said something happened. Is it something I could help with, even if it's just to listen?"

Haley wanted to talk about it with someone, and her bishop seemed like a good choice. "Yes," she said. "I'd like to talk about it."

The bishop turned to his daughter. "Would you go start the car again?" he said. "We'll just be a few minutes."

"Thank you," Haley said to the girl as she left. "This really won't take long."

She then told the bishop of her relationship with Nat and then about the grotesque package he'd sent. He listened patiently. When she'd finished, he said, "Haley, are you sure it was from him?"

"Who else could it be from?" she asked. "He admitted he was sending me something he'd had a hard time finding, and he told me that it would really give me a *kick*. That seemed like such a strange thing to say. And when I found out what it was, I suppose you could say that it *kicked* me."

The bishop was very serious. "Yes, so you said. But what if his package really hasn't come yet?" she asked.

Haley threw a hand to her mouth. "I never thought of that!" she exclaimed. "Oh, Bishop, what if I've wrongly accused him?"

"You may not have," he said. "But if it wasn't from Nat, who was it from? You've been through a lot lately. I think it might be well if you didn't stay here alone tonight. In fact, we have a whole empty apartment in our basement. Why don't you pack a few things and come stay with us for a few days?" he suggested. "My wife and I talked about it earlier, when the thing with the stalker was going on, but then it came to an end, and we didn't say anything. But with what's happened here, we'd feel much better knowing you were safe with us."

Haley didn't argue. She knew that she'd be terrified of Nat if he showed up again, and he surely would. And if by some small chance it turned out not to be the package he sent . . . well, that was too terrible to think about. So the bishop and his daughter helped her pack a couple of suitcases. They even carried her computer to the car, and Haley took her complete file on Rob Sterling. As she left the apartment, she felt more at ease.

"We'll get your car tomorrow," the bishop said as they put the last of Haley's things in the van. "You can work right out of our house for as long as you like."

Haley was just settling into the seat of the bishop's van when her cell phone began to ring in her purse. She dug it out, hoping that Nat hadn't decided to call that number since she wasn't answering her apartment phone. But when she looked, the number on the phone was Rex's. She quickly answered.

"Haley, you're not going to believe this," the detective said in a surprisingly cheerful voice. "That hand isn't real. It's wax."

"Wax?" Haley asked.

"Yes, like from the wax museum in Hollywood."

"But it looked so real," she said.

"It had us fooled too, until we got to the lab and pulled it from the bag," he said. "I hope that makes you feel a little better."

"It does, but it's still a sick thing to do," she said. "It also begins to make some sense though. Nat said I'd get a real kick out of it, and he said he had a hard time finding one. I can imagine!"

Rex laughed. "Well, I just thought you ought to know." His voice became more serious, and he added, "I still intend to see what I can learn about Nat. That really is a warped thing to do, fake or not." A few moments later he hung up.

"What was that about wax?" the bishop asked.

"That hand, it was wax. It wasn't real," she said. "I guess I've overreacted. I just didn't know Nat had such a twisted sense of humor."

Bishop Coffman looked briefly over his shoulder at Haley. "If it was from him," he said. "Remember all you've been through," he said. "I hope you'll still stay in our apartment. I just have this feeling that you have some difficult days ahead."

"Thanks, Bishop, I think I'll still take you up on your offer," she said.

* * *

Haley called Rex, Raul, and Sperry the next morning. She explained where she was and why. "I don't plan to do anything but sit here and work on the trial plan," she said to Raul, who was the last of the three she talked to.

"I can't come until tomorrow, but I'll be over to help then," he said. "I've got a couple of ideas I'd like to run by you."

After Haley talked to Raul, the bishop's wife took Haley to her apartment. It was late morning because Haley had wanted to wait until the mail was delivered before she picked up her car. The driveway had been cleared and the nearly two feet of snow that had fallen were piled at one end of the parking area.

The mail was there, along with a slip notifying her of a package waiting at the post office. Haley's heart sank. What if she had been wrong? What if the package waiting for her there was from Nat? How could he ever forgive her? *Especially when he finds out I thought it was real,* she thought. *But then, it was intended to look that way,* she told herself.

Haley was shaking as she took the package. There was no return address, but Haley's address was written by hand, and there was no mistaking Nat's long, sweeping penmanship.

Haley felt terrible. She couldn't believe the mistake she'd made. How could she ever make it up to Nat? She wouldn't blame him if he never forgave her. Then she had a terrible realization. Rex was busy right now looking into Nat's past. She hurried to her car with the package and called Rex as soon as she was out of the cold and had her engine running.

Rex didn't seem too surprised when she told him about the package. "I've been doing some checking. There is no connection between Nat and Dan or Nat and Martin. But Haley, I'm afraid I do have a little bit of news that concerns me."

"Not about Nat, I hope," she said. "I've thought enough bad things about him already."

"It is," Rex said. "Has he ever said anything to you about William Montgomery?"

"I don't think he even knows him," Haley said. "He sure has been angry with the way William treated me though. Nat even said that it would be disastrous if William was elected attorney general."

"I see," Rex said. "So it would surprise you if I told you that William and Nat are not only acquainted, but that they're old chums."

"I don't think that's possible," Haley said.

"It's not only possible, it's true," Rex told her firmly. "And it seems that William helped Nat out a couple of times. Apparently William even helped land him his job. They say Nat owes William big time."

This news seemed somehow worse to her than the wax hand. Nat hadn't been honest with her. However, Haley wasn't sure she'd ever find out from Nat why he'd never told her about his friendship with William. She was afraid that he'd never talk to her again.

* * *

Nat had thought of nothing all Christmas day but Haley's terrified screams, the long period of time that had elapsed before she'd finally picked up the phone again, and then of the angry words she hurled at him before cutting him off. She had failed to answer any of the dozen times he'd tried to call her back. And she hadn't responded to any of his messages.

He couldn't make any sense of her strange behavior. How she could have reacted the way she did to his gift was not only absurd, it was preposterous. He didn't sleep all night, and the next morning he called the airline and succeeded in getting a standby seat on an earlier flight. His luck had held, and he'd gotten on the plane. So it was midafternoon instead of midnight when his plane landed at the Salt Lake International Airport.

Nat grabbed his bags and rushed for his gold Jaguar. From the airport, he drove directly to Haley's apartment. UPS had left a package on her step. He picked it up as he waited for her to answer her door. It had a regular UPS label, but there was no return address.

Nat got an uneasy feeling as he rang the doorbell again and again. When he finally gave up, he walked around back to see if her car was in the carport. If it was, he'd know she'd seen him through the window and wasn't answering. If it wasn't, he'd come back later. It was not there. Nat started to walk the shortest shoveled route back to his car when he realized that he still had Haley's UPS package under his arm.

So he returned to her door. As he sat it back on the step, a voice called out to him, "Are you looking for Haley?"

"I sure am," Nat said, turning toward the source of the voice.

"She's not here," a bulky neighbor on the porch of the next apartment announced. "She left last night with a couple of big suitcases, her briefcase, and her computer," the lady said. "She came back today and got her car. If you talk to the manager, I think you might find out where she went. I saw them talking before Haley left with her car."

Nat picked up the package again. If Haley had gone somewhere, she wouldn't get her package, and it might be important. He walked quickly to the manager's office. But he learned nothing from her. So he went to the apartment of the woman next door to Haley's.

"The manager doesn't know where Miss Gordon went," Nat said. "Could you tell me what kind of car she left in last night?" It might give him some clue as to who picked her up. He thought it might be Sergeant Thomas's patrol car.

The woman favored Nat with a secretive smile. "It was a blue minivan. I took down the license number. With all the troubles that Haley's had lately, a person can't be too careful."

She recited the number to Nat, who jotted it down. As he turned to leave, the woman said, "Lovely car, your gold Jaguar. I'll bet Haley loves to ride in it, Mr. Turley."

"She does," he said, wondering how she knew his name. But he didn't wonder for long—women like her just knew things about their neighbors. *And so much for "being careful,"* he thought wryly. *I could be a serial killer for all she knows, and she just gave me Haley's contact info!* Nat shook his head in disgust.

It took Nat half an hour and several phone calls, but he found out who the registered owner of the car was, and it was only a few minutes after that before he pulled up and parked on the street. *If Haley's here, her car's either in the garage or behind the house,* he decided after looking around and discovering that a driveway led around to the back.

He knocked on the front door and was admitted by a teenage girl with short brown hair. "I brought a package by for Haley," he said. "A belated Christmas present. Would you tell her I'm here? I'd like to give it to her myself."

The girl asked him to come in, then disappeared down a hallway. A minute later, she came back. "Are you Nat?" she asked.

"I am," he replied, fully expecting to get no farther than he was right now.

But the girl smiled and said, "Haley asked me to show you the way to the apartment downstairs. She's staying with us for a few days."

Haley greeted him with an apology. "Nat, I'm so sorry. I feel like such a fool. I don't know how you can ever forgive me."

"Quite easily, I'm sure," he said. "But it would be nice if you would explain what happened. I've done nothing but worry since you screamed."

"How come you're here so early?" she asked as she led him into her temporary quarters. "I thought your plane came in at midnight."

"I changed flights," he said. "I had to get back and see what happened to you. You can't imagine how worried I've been."

"I'm so sorry, Nat. And I'll understand if you never forgive me."

"Whatever it is, I'll forgive you," he said. "Just tell me what happened."

"I accused you of the most horrible thing," she said. "I feel like such a fool."

Nat took Haley by the hand and pulled her around to face him. "Let's start this with a proper greeting," he said as he laid the package he'd been holding on the edge of the sofa, and then pulled her close, enfolding her in his arms and seeking her lips.

Haley hadn't the will to resist. She felt horrible for falsely accusing him, but she didn't enjoy his kiss. There was just too much strain there. She'd been so terribly wrong about the package she'd opened, but there was still the matter of William Montgomery that was eating at her.

"Not another gift," she said after he'd finally released her from his embrace and picked up the package he'd carried in. "You really shouldn't have. Just this morning I got the one you sent the other day. I haven't opened it yet. I didn't think I should. After what I have to say, you'll probably want it back."

"No, this was a UPS delivery that was sitting on your doorstep," he said. "When I found out you'd moved, I thought I better find you and bring it here."

Haley picked up the newest package and began to examine it as she asked Nat, "How did you find out where I was?"

"Your neighbor, a big woman who seems to know everything," Nat said with a chuckle. Haley tore off the outer wrapping of the UPS package.

"Wouldn't you know it. I guess I better call her. I really didn't want to be found so easily," she said as she began trembling.

"Haley, what's wrong?" Nat asked in alarm.

"This package. It's just like the one I opened yesterday," she said. "The one I thought was from you."

"Oh, I see," Nat said. "It wasn't something you liked."

"It was horrible. And I was so stupid, I actually thought it was real and that you'd sent it. I don't want to open this one," she said. "We should just give it to the police."

Nat took it from her. "Nonsense," he said. "I want to see what's inside."

Nat, over Haley's continued objections, opened the package and she braced herself. Whatever was in there, she would not scream, no matter how real it might appear.

And she didn't, but Nat's face went a pasty white when he pulled out a heavy plastic bag with a hand inside. "Is there a note?" she asked as calmly as she could.

Nat's hands were shaking so badly he dropped the bag, and as he fished for the note he also dropped the box. As calmly as she could, Haley knelt on the floor and found the card inside the box. She read it out loud to Nat who was now sitting on her sofa, his head in his hands, staring with fixed eyes at the terrible thing on the floor.

Haley read,

> *I'm so sorry. I should have sent you both hands at once. You will need them if you think you're going to get*

Sterling off on the murder rap. Give it up, Miss Gordon.
You can't win.

Nat looked up. "This is what was in the other box?" he asked.

Haley was so ashamed. "It was. I'm so sorry, Nat," she said again.

"You thought I'd send you a . . ." he couldn't finish.

"You don't have to forgive me," she said. "I'd try to explain, but I'm afraid you'd never understand."

"I might forgive you, Haley, but you're right, I'll never understand," he said. "You thought I'd sent you the hand of some dead person."

"It's not real," she said. "It's wax."

"No, this one's real," he said. "Just look at it."

"It's wax," she said calmly.

"But you thought I'd sent you . . ." Nat stopped and looked at Haley like he was seeing her for the first time. "You thought I'd do something like that?!"

Haley felt even more embarrassed at his reaction. But all of a sudden the thought hit her. She did know someone who was deranged enough to do something like that—Martin Ligorni! Suddenly Haley wanted to get back to her case. In an attempt to end her visit with Nat so she could start work on tracking down where the hands had come from, she decided to bargain with Nat in order to clean up the misunderstandings in their relationship as quickly as possible. Before she could change her mind, she acted on the thought. "I'll make you a deal, Nat. If you'll forgive me for thinking you sent that horrible . . . *thing* . . . to me, I'll forgive you for not telling me about your chummy relationship with William Montgomery."

Haley had expected a reaction, but she was shocked when Nat's pasty face went beet red and he uttered an expletive she thought she'd never hear from him. "He told you, didn't he? Montgomery told you."

It dawned on Haley that there was a lot more to this thing with Nat and William than she'd even guessed. She intended to find out what it was. She thought Nat might be vulnerable now if she could just make him think she knew something she didn't. "Why don't you tell me all about it," she suggested with a stern face. "I'd like to hear it from your lips. Then we can forgive each other."

Nat hung his head. "I had to, Haley. You don't understand what he's done for me, how good he'd been to me. I'd never have gotten a job with such a respected firm if it hadn't been for him. I owed him."

She said nothing, and in the silence, Nat's guilty confession came out, how William had asked him to date her and to keep him informed of how the case was going. He tried to justify himself by telling Haley that after he'd gotten to know her, he'd held a lot back from William, because he'd become so sincerely interested in her. Nat went on explaining how relieved he'd been when she quit the district attorney's office. "I thought he'd leave me alone after that. I was so glad, because then I could spend time with you on my own terms, not his. But then he called again, and he wanted me to spy on you as you got Sterling's defense ready. But I didn't have much to give him, and he got angry. And so I guess that's why he told you," Nat moaned. "I'm sorry, Haley. Please forgive me."

Haley just looked Nat calmly in the face. She'd been commanded to forgive, but she would never trust him again. She didn't even care now if he forgave her. He could just take his unopened gift and leave as far as she was concerned.

And that is exactly what he did.

CHAPTER TWENTY-SIX

The wax hands, it turned out, had been stolen from a business in California that made such things for Hollywood movie makers. "I think this was meant to rattle you," Raul Garcia told her as they worked together on the plan for court. "Did it work?"

"I'm fine now," she said. "But it did shake me up at first. I wish they could have traced the purchase. I can't help but wonder if California is where Mr. Ligorni's disappeared to."

"Well, we're sure to find him sooner or later, and then we'll haul him in. But, well, you don't think what he might still do to terrorize you might distract you—if it was him, I mean?" he asked.

Haley put down her pen and looked Raul straight in the eye. "Do you think it's affected me too much to continue?" she asked, her voice tinged with a hint of anger.

"I'm just asking," he said. "I don't mean to offend you. But you've got to remember that Rob Sterling is my best friend."

Haley forced herself to relax. "I'm sorry, Raul. He's my friend now, too. I've learned what a great guy he is. And I intend to see that he gets acquitted. I promise you that nothing will stand in my way. Is that good enough?"

"It's great by me," Raul said slowly. He hadn't failed to catch the expression that had crossed her face when she'd called Rob her friend. Then he smiled and said, "Sorry I brought it up."

"It's okay. Let's forget it and get to work." She smiled back, failing to see the realization that had dawned in Raul's eyes.

* * *

At that same moment, the investigative arms of the Sterling defense team were also sharing equally revealing information with each other. The trial was to begin the following week, and both detectives had kept some vital information back from each other and from Haley. Both had good reasons, but as the trial approached, Rex in particular had begun to doubt the wisdom of keeping his secret from Haley. So he'd decided to mention it to Sperry and see what he thought.

Sperry simply listened, smiled, and said, "With what you've done and what I've done, Haley should have all she needs to clinch this thing." And he went on to amaze Rex with an accounting of his own actions.

Now they were debating what to do. Each had a witness tucked safely away. Each of the witnesses could provide evidence that could prove fatal to the district attorney's case against Rob. Neither detective wanted his witness disclosed to the prosecutor, even though they knew he had the right to know, because they knew Montgomery was unethical. They were rightly concerned he would demand immediate access and would intimidate the witnesses into either refusing to testify or, worse yet, into changing their testimony to benefit the state's case. They were also concerned about the trial being delayed if Haley insisted on disclosing the identity of the witnesses to the prosecutor. Montgomery might successfully argue to the court that he would need more time to assess the testimony and what effect it might have on his case.

They finally decided that they had to tell Haley and Raul and let them decide if they should tell Mr. Montgomery. But they would also discuss what they could do to assure that he would not be able to damage the testimony of either witness before they got them on the stand.

* * *

Haley hung up the phone and turned to Raul, "That was Sergeant Thomas. He says that he and Detective Collier have something they need to tell us. It's critical, and it can't wait."

"I sure hate to stop what we're doing right now," Raul said. "Can't they wait until this evening?"

"I don't think so. They'd like us to come to Sperry's office right now. Rex said that what they have could make or break our case."

Thirty minutes later, Haley and Raul were listening to the detectives' stories. They looked at each other and frowned. Haley spoke up when the men had finished. "Why didn't you tell us before?" she asked. Haley was upset. "I can't believe you would both keep such vital information to yourselves."

"We were afraid you'd feel like you had to tell the district attorney, and we all know what he could do to these two if he had time to work them over before trial," Rex explained.

"Let me explain something to the two of you." Haley said. " In the *Rules of Criminal Procedure* is a little rule known simply as 'Rule Sixteen.' It is the rule on discovery, the rule that provides what information the prosecution may have, and vice versa, that must be given promptly to the opposing side." As she said it, she tried hard to keep her anger in check.

Both detectives nodded. They knew the rule. Haley went on, "The rule specifically requires that we, the defense, shall disclose to the prosecutor any evidence we have that relates to alibi. Among other things, that's what we have here, is it not?"

They both agreed that it could be. "And if that doesn't cover it adequately, the rule further tells us that we have a duty to let the court decide if evidence we have should be provided to the district attorney if he needs it to prepare his case." She paused, then asked, "Have I stated it about right?"

"Yes, Haley, you have," Rex agreed sheepishly. "But prior to today, you didn't have this information, so you're off the hook. Correct?" he finished with an impish grin.

Haley couldn't help but lighten up at that comment. "Up until now, I suppose so, and there's certainly nothing that would have required you to tell me if you felt you had reasons not to, but I think it's pretty clear that I have no choice but to talk to William at this point. If we put those two on the stand without William having had a chance to fully investigate their claims, he could ask the judge to keep the testimony from the jury, and the judge would do just that," she said. "Is that right, Raul?"

"It is," Raul agreed firmly. "We have to let William know. And we better do it today, or we're almost sure to see him ask the court to push the trial to a later date, and he'd get it. We can't let Rob rot in that jail for another month or two because of this."

The detectives both exchanged chagrined expressions, but Haley smiled encouragingly. "Hey guys, don't feel bad. You've probably done the right thing. And talk about great investigative work. I'm proud to have you on my side. Thank you so much. Rob will be grateful too."

"Can you make it work?" Sperry asked.

"We've got to," she said firmly. "If you'll let me use your phone, I'll get the hard part over with right now. I'll talk to William."

"Would you mind if I record your conversation with him?" Sperry asked. "It might be good to have it on record if the district attorney decides to give you a hard time, or even if he simply badmouths you."

"That's fine. Set it up, and I'll make the call," Haley said.

A couple of minutes later, William Montgomery came on the line. "Are you calling to throw in the towel?" he boomed. "You really should get out while you can and save what little dignity you have left, Haley. If you don't, it could well be the last case you ever try."

The men could tell from the frown on Haley's face that the recording had been a good idea. She sat and listened while he ranted on. Finally, she broke in and said, "William, if you'll listen for a minute, I called for a purpose. I have come up with a couple of witnesses. I thought I should let you know."

William cut her off with a laugh. "Bring them on, girl. I'll tear them to shreds in court," he said.

"You don't know that. I haven't even told you who they are or what they plan to say," she began.

"Save it, Haley. You're wasting my time. See you on Monday, unless you wise up before then," he said, and the phone clicked rudely in her ear.

Haley was grinning. "Sperry, I owe you. Don't let this recording get lost. William will rant and rave when he finds out who we have waiting in the wings. And he'll probably deny he and I ever had this conversation. But we did, and our witnesses will be allowed to testify."

Haley had Sperry play the tape back for the sake of the others. When it had finished rolling, Raul said very seriously, "This should be a lesson to all of us. Power can obviously be intoxicating—the district attorney seems to have lost the ability to reason. William's ego just gave us the break that will win this case for us, and he doesn't even know it."

Of course, there were also things *they* didn't know. Things that fell outside even the jurisdiction of "Rule Sixteen."

* * *

The rest of that week was extremely busy. Haley and Raul both traveled out of state to interview their potential new witnesses. For Haley, that was a most uncomfortable thing about the trial, but she wasn't about to let her own discomfort affect Rob's future.

When she returned, she went immediately to the jail. Haley looked forward to those visits. Since Christmas day, her time with Rob had been nothing but business. But despite that, she found her feelings for him growing. She knew it was foolish, but she couldn't help it. The only way to stop it from happening would be not to see him at all. And that would have to wait until the trial was over and he was free to again pursue his own life. Anyway, she didn't feel that expressing her uninvited emotions would be appropriate for a long time to come—if ever. All Rob needed or wanted right now was a friend and a good defense team. So she'd just have to deal with the frustration. Right now the only thing that really mattered was achieving justice for Rob.

He was smiling when he joined her in the familiar little room. He shook her hand, and he held it slightly longer than was customary. "How did it go?" he asked after they'd both taken their places across the table from each other.

"Very well," she said.

Rob sighed. "They'll both come through for me?"

"They will, despite the fact that they are both justifiably frightened."

"What did they tell you?" he asked.

She told him, and he looked very grim momentarily, then hopeful.

* * *

Sperry Collier knew who the contact was, but even though he'd spent many tedious hours keeping him under surveillance, he'd learned nothing more that was helpful. As the date for trial approached, he had the feeling that he'd need to be ever more diligent. Something was going to happen, he just didn't know what.

* * *

Bad weather delayed the beginning of jury selection by several hours. Another storm moved in that morning just in time for the commute, and it snarled the traffic. Over half of the large group of potential jurors were late, some by as much as three hours. One never made it at all. He ended up in the hospital from injuries he'd gotten when another driver slammed into his car at an intersection. Even Judge Horton had trouble getting to the courthouse. He was nearly an hour late, and that was something he prided himself on never happening.

The delay kept Rob sitting nervously in a small holding cell while Haley anxiously awaited his arrival at her table. Even though he was the accused, and she was supposed to support him, she drew strength from his presence. When the judge finally arrived, they brought Rob in. For the trial they had allowed him to dress in a suit. Haley watched him as he was escorted across the front of the courtroom. There was just something about that man that she really liked. Even though he was justifiably nervous, he still had a smile for her. Rob touched her heart in a place where no one else had. She wasn't quite sure what to do with those feelings.

Rob didn't help any when he sat down next to her, squeezed her hand beneath the table where no one could see, then leaned over and said, "If you can talk as good as you look, Haley, we've got it in the bag." He then gently let go and faced the front of the room. She knew that he meant her confident air and professional I-mean-business attire, but the compliment sent chills up her spine anyway.

When the proceedings finally began, William Montgomery delayed things again by asking for a recess. He'd hired another attorney to assist him since all the attorneys in his office were busy with cases. He blamed the congestion in his office on Haley. He hadn't yet been able to replace her. And he had found someone to assist him just the evening before. "But he needs another day, Your Honor," William said, "to clear his calendar."

Haley ignored William's jabs at her, knowing it was probably obvious to everyone there that the state simply wasn't ready. She stood and opposed his motion. "This has not been an easy morning for any of us to get here," she said. "But we *are* here, including the potential jurors. Mr. Montgomery has had adequate time to obtain whatever *help* he needs since I resigned from his office. That was weeks ago."

The court agreed, and Montgomery then asked for a brief recess, which the court granted. Fifteen minutes later, they began. William had an investigator at his table, but no other attorneys had joined him.

The jury selection process ate up the rest of the day. It was obvious to Haley and Raul that William was causing delay after delay. They knew that he was wanting whomever the other attorney was to help in the selection process. By the end of the day, he seemed to have gotten his way, for little progress had been made.

The next morning, with improved weather, court started on time. William still had no co-counsel, but he seemed to be fine with that. Ten minutes later, it was clear why. The other attorney walked in and sat down beside William.

Haley couldn't believe her eyes. William Montgomery had hired her only other enemy on the face of the planet. Dan Smathers cast a wicked smile in Haley's direction and then ignored her from that point on.

The day was consumed by the continued process of selecting a jury. William whispered to Dan constantly as he scrutinized the potential jurors. The day ended with the task still uncompleted, and just before leaving the bench, Judge Horton looked directly at William and said impatiently, "We will have a jury seated before noon tomorrow."

And that they did, to the benefit of the majority of those involved. Now Haley could only hope that the six men and six women who had been selected would see things their way. Haley smiled at Rob after the last juror had taken his seat. "We have the advantage, you know," she said. "We have the truth on our side."

CHAPTER TWENTY-SEVEN

William Montgomery had done a masterful job during his opening statement. He outlined the state's case against Rob, and had the jury heard nothing else, Rob would most certainly have been convicted. Haley had kept her statement brief. She had mostly just explained to the jury that they shouldn't place too much on what the prosecutor had stated. "We'll be able to show that the evidence he has mentioned is seriously flawed," she concluded.

Then it was time for the meat of the trial to begin. The prosecution was ready to start calling witnesses. Haley and Raul had been provided a list of those potential witnesses by the prosecution. They had carefully planned how to cross-examine each one of them.

The first witness the district attorney called was Sergeant Rex Thomas. Rex testified to what had been found at the scene the night of Jennifer's death. William asked his questions in such a way that everything Rex said cast Rob in the worst possible light. Rex answered truthfully, knowing that Haley would give him the chance to expand on cross-examination.

"Sergeant," she began when her turn came, "you testified that the only fingerprints on the keys to the back door—the door the killer may have entered through—were those of the defendant. Is there any way a person could have held those keys to open that door without leaving prints, or without smudging those already on them from previous use?"

"Yes, it's simple, really. First, of course, you wear a pair of surgical gloves. Then you leave no prints there or anywhere else in the house," he said.

"Objection!" William thundered. "Non-responsive. He's speculating about things that haven't been asked."

"They will be, Your Honor," Haley said, "but if you'd prefer that the witness wait, it's fine with me."

Judge Horton looked over his glasses at Rex. "Stick to the question asked, Sergeant," he said. "You may proceed, Counselor."

"Would you demonstrate for the jury how a person wearing surgical gloves might hold these keys?" she said, handing Rex the ring of keys that William had just introduced into evidence. "And could you show us how one might unlock the door without smudging any prints that may already be on it?"

Rex held Rob's key by the edge, using the key ring to supply leverage, and showed how it could be done. Several members of the jury nodded as he did it. Haley then had Rex demonstrate why it was similarly logical that no prints but Rob's and Jennifer's were found on the flashlight. Next, she asked him about his testimony regarding his questioning of the defendant that night. He'd earlier testified that Rob said very little to them and did not state an alibi at that time. William had not allowed the detective to refer to his later questioning of Rob. But Haley did. And Rex testified that Rob later stated that he'd gone to Park City after finding a note he believed to be from his wife. "It was in the car and was a request that Rob meet her at a restaurant in Park City."

"So contrary to the impression you left when being questioned by the district attorney, the defendant did in fact state to you where he had been at the time of the crime?" she asked.

"That's right," he said.

Haley then had him testify to Rob's explanation for why he didn't ever meet her that night and why he'd thrown the note away. Then she asked Rex to explain where Rob told him the keys to the house, those now in evidence, were ordinarily kept.

"He kept them in a compartment on the driver's side door of his car," Rex said.

"And did he tell you when he last saw them there?" Haley asked.

"He thought he'd put them back in there the previous night after using them."

"When you asked him how they came to be in his house when he got home that night, what did he tell you?"

"He said that he must have dropped them accidentally on the porch or the sidewalk. He couldn't be sure."

Haley knew that this was one piece of testimony she couldn't do any more with. She was certain that Rob had dropped them, as he speculated. *I'm glad I've got better explanations for the other evidence,* she thought as she prepared to ask her next question.

"Did Mr. Sterling have an explanation for how the keys came to be on the kitchen counter just inside the back door?" she asked.

"He told me that whoever killed his wife must have left them there after using them to open the door."

"Now, Detective, can you tell the jury where the defendant told you that he and his wife normally kept the small flashlight that you found on the living room floor, the one we just discussed in regard to fingerprints?" she asked.

"He told me that they kept that flashlight in a kitchen cupboard right next to the back door," he said. "It's right above where we found the keys."

Haley noted the nods of several jurors. Her job was to make the jurors see reasonable doubt in the prosecution's case. She may have successfully begun that process just now, at least, she hoped she had.

Haley had Detective Thomas testify in detail to some of the things Rob would testify to later if she decided to have him take the stand, which was very likely. She did that because she wanted the jury to already have the explanations in mind as they considered the matters other prosecution witnesses would likely testify to later. She accomplished presenting a believable reconstructing of events, in Rob's favor, despite a constant barrage of objections from the district attorney.

Haley reviewed several other things Detective Thomas had said, not to discredit him, but to give him a chance to propose other possibilities than those the prosecutor had allowed him to mention. Despite several more objections from William, Haley felt she'd scored points with the jury. However, there was much of what Rex had testified to that would have to wait on explication until she could produce her own witnesses that would provide clarification and reinforcement of the defense position.

Another prosecution witness that afternoon discussed in detail the blood-splatter evidence from the scene, showing the position of the weapon when it was fired. William tried to point out that the defendant had been kneeling beside the sofa when he fired the fatal shot. But on cross-examination, Haley got the witness to admit that someone who was approaching in the dark and stumbled over the lamp could have accidentally fired the shot as his arm struck that of the sofa.

Haley glanced at Dan while the expert was testifying and was interested to note the look of shock on his face. It was only there for a moment, but she suspected that she'd hit on something he already knew about that night.

William produced witnesses about all kinds of forensic matters, which meant very little on their own, but which he attempted to use to show Rob was the guilty party. They included blood that matched Jennifer's that was found on Rob's clothing, the make and caliber of gun used, the fact that Rob had once owned a gun of that caliber, and the time of death of the victim. Finally, on the third day of prosecution testimony, the fifth day of the trial, William produced witnesses who he claimed would establish motive.

Haley couldn't believe that he would actually call Ann Denton, the secretary who had worked with Jennifer, but he did. The young woman testified that a number of men were always going into Jennifer's office and taking her to lunch. When Haley questioned her, she tried to get her to name some of the men, but she said she didn't know who they were except by sight. Then Haley tried a long shot and asked if any of them were in the courtroom that day. Without batting an eye she said, "No."

Haley knew she was lying, but let it go. William got up and asked her to state once again if Jennifer had been seeing other men, and she said she had been.

Two other people testified that they had seen Jennifer with men other than Rob, but Haley simply let their testimony go. The weakness in these testimonies was that no one had testified that Rob had knowledge of these alleged improper dates. Haley smiled when William said that he was still attempting to find a man who had given earlier statements that he had personally dated Jennifer and knew that Rob was aware of it. But the man seemed to have moved and they couldn't find him. He promised to keep trying and said he would use him in rebuttal to the defense's case after the witness was located. Haley would be surprised if they ever found Jake Zippeta, and if they did, she would have a huge surprise for Mr. Montgomery.

Haley stood and objected to the reference William made to Jake Zippeta and asked that the jury be instructed to disregard it. The judge sustained her objection. Just then, an investigator from William's office rushed in. The two conferred for a moment, then William turned back and dropped a bomb on Rob, Haley, and Raul. He said he had just received some information that he'd like to present. The judge called the attorneys to the bench. "What is this in regard to?" the judge asked softly so he couldn't be heard by the rest of the audience.

"Motive," William said with a snide grin directed at his former star prosecutor. "A half million dollars' worth of motive."

"What are you talking about?" Haley demanded.

"Life insurance. Rob took out a life insurance policy on Jennifer the week before her death in the amount of a half million dollars," William said.

"I'll need to see the evidence," Haley said as she felt a terrible sinking in the pit of her stomach. "And I'll need to interview your witnesses."

"I could save us all some time and have my witness on the stand in five minutes," William said.

Haley was suddenly suspicious. "You just found out about this and yet your witness is ready to testify?" she asked. "I don't think so."

The judge intervened. "I'm going to adjourn for the day. Give Miss Gordon everything you have. We'll start again on Monday, unless you need more time," he said to Haley. "That will be all for now."

William scowled at Haley. He'd tried to pull a fast one on her and get an undisclosed witness on the stand. She'd stopped him for the time being, but now she had to find out what was going on with the insurance policy. Rob had some explaining to do.

As soon as Haley returned to her seat, Rob leaned over and asked, "What was that all about?"

"I'll meet you at the jail in a few minutes," she said. "We need to talk."

Court was adjourned for the day, and Rob was led away feeling somewhat alarmed, but trusting his attorney completely. "I'll see you," he said with a forced smile.

As soon as Rob was out of the room, Haley descended on William. "If I can prove you learned this one minute sooner than you just told the judge, I'll make you wish you'd never met me," she fumed.

"I already wish that," William shot back. "You have become a great disappointment to me."

"By the way," she added, "I hope the information Nat Turley gave you was good because there won't be any more. He and I won't be seeing each other again."

Haley could see by the district attorney's reaction that he was unaware his little information-gathering scheme was over. Well, he knew now. "Okay, give me what you have," she said. "And I want it all."

William handed her a copy of the insurance policy he'd referred to. She barely glanced at it. "Where's the application?" she asked.

"Oh, that, it's here somewhere. Oh, yes, here it is," he said. *He had a copy prepared, he's just being a jerk,* she decided.

"They just gave me this," he said. "The agent's name is Bradley Owens. And his address and phone number are there on the policy."

"That's good, but since he's here, I'd like a minute with him right now," she said.

"Oh, I think he's gone already. He came prepared to testify, but he's a busy man. See you Monday, Haley," he said and curtly turned his back on her.

It was clear that Montgomery figured this would stall the trial as it was doubtful that she could find this Bradley Owens on the weekend. She was fuming when she returned to the table where Raul was just gathering things up. Haley briefed him on what had just transpired. "I'm going over to the jail to meet with Rob and get his position on this," she said. "He didn't by any chance mention this to you, did he?"

"He didn't tell me he'd purchased any life insurance on his wife, that's for sure. What he said was that he was *considering* getting a policy on *himself.* I don't remember ever hearing him mention one on Jennifer," Raul said. "I need to get home if you can handle this with Rob by yourself. One of my boys is having a birthday today, and I'd like to spend a little time with him."

"No problem. I'll let you know what I learn," she said.

Haley had to wait for a few minutes while an inmate count was completed in the jail. When Rob finally came in, she could see that he'd been worrying. "What's happened?" he asked.

"Sit down, and I'll tell you," she said as she opened her briefcase. She found the papers William had given her, then she said, "This is about a life insurance policy on Jennifer that William claims you bought the week before her death."

Haley was watching Rob's face closely. He was clearly surprised. "Life insurance on Jennifer?" he said. "I never bought any such thing. Why would I do that? The only thing I did about life insurance was talk to an agent about a policy on myself. But I'd never finished taking care of it."

"When was that?" Haley asked.

"Probably about a week before Jennifer died. But we never even talked about one on Jennifer."

Haley opened the papers William had given her. As she turned the policy itself toward him, she said, "This is the policy. It says here that Jennifer is the insured and that you are the beneficiary. It's for a half million."

"What!" Rob exclaimed. "That's impossible." He looked quickly through the pages. "I didn't sign anything, Haley. They've made this up."

She then handed him the application, which was all typed up and had a signature at the bottom. "Do you remember signing this?" she asked.

He shook his head. "Oh, no!" he groaned.

"You did then?" she asked, terribly disappointed. "This isn't forged?"

"No, but it's all my fault," he said. "I signed a blank form. I was supposed to call him in a few days and let him know how much we had decided on for the policy. He said he'd fill it in and get it approved as soon as I called."

"Did you ever call?" she asked.

"No, we hadn't ever decided before Jennifer was killed," he said.

"What was your agent's name?" she asked.

"Uh . . . he was a really old guy. I remember telling Jennifer that it seemed kind of strange buying life insurance from a man who had one foot in the grave," he said. "Fred! His name is Fred Owens."

"Fred, not Bradley?" she asked.

"Bradley's his younger brother. I'd never do business with him. You've just got to look in his eyes to see why," Rob said.

Haley could see a conspiracy unfolding. She had to find Fred Owens. The last thing she wanted was to have Bradley on the stand.

"All right," she said, "I'll get to work on this over the weekend. Oh, did you ever give them any money?"

"No, none," he said.

"Good. This is all a hoax," she said. "We'll take care of it."

"Thanks, Haley. I don't know what I'd ever do without you," he said.

She wished he wouldn't ever have to, but she banished the thought quickly from her mind.

* * *

Dan Smathers was not invited to the second meeting in as many weeks of the partners of Hacking, Kirkwood, and Smathers. It was held Friday evening at a location outside of the firm's office. Ralph Hacking had some disturbing information for the others. He'd quietly had an audit conducted when he noticed the amount of money coming in through Dan's account. "His secretary has been embezzling," he told the others. "And the amounts are quite staggering."

"How much is missing?" Jim Kirkwood asked.

"We won't know exactly until we can interview his clients and look at their records," Ralph said. "And I think we need to do that right away. But so far, in just a quick look at the past year, it's over a quarter of a million dollars."

"How long has this been going on?" another partner asked as he wiped the sweat from his face.

"Three or four years," Ralph disclosed.

"Has the secretary been confronted?" still another partner asked.

"No, but she'll probably be here in a few minutes. I took the liberty of inviting her here under the guise that there was to be a little party in her honor. If she comes, we'll confront her together."

She came, and within minutes, she'd admitted what she'd done. But then she stunned everyone but Ralph Hacking when she said, "I was told to do it by Mr. Smathers. Most of the money went to him."

Ralph had suspected as much. That's why he'd left Dan out of the meeting. He suggested the police be called, shook his head, and adjourned their meeting.

* * *

A couple of hours later, Rex Thomas got a call from a detective of the Salt Lake City Police Department. "Hey, Rex," he said, "isn't that wormy Dan Smathers working with the district attorney in the case against Rob Sterling?"

"He is now," Rex said.

"Then I think you'd be interested in tagging along with me tonight. We'll be conducting a search of Dan's house. His secretary just fingered him in an embezzlement case from his own law firm," the detective said.

Rex's partner was out of town, so he excitedly dialed Sperry's cell phone. Sperry picked up right away. "Hey, if you're not busy, you might want to be around tonight. There's something going down of interest to both of us."

But Sperry spoke very softly into the phone. "Can't tonight. I'm onto something. I'll call you in the morning."

Rex was intrigued, but both men knew better than to talk of sensitive matters on their cell phones. So they both went their own ways that night, each wishing he knew what the other was up to.

* * *

Sperry was tailing Dan Smathers. He took pictures and wrote down license numbers. Dan met three men, each separately and at different locations. And he handed something in an envelope to each of them. Money, Sperry assumed. At this point that wasn't important. What Sperry needed was to find out who the men were. Before the night was over, he knew, and it was big. He couldn't wait to share what he'd learned with the rest of the defense team.

* * *

Dan was not at home when a dozen officers knocked on his door. When he didn't answer they forced their way in as allowed by the search warrant they'd obtained. They were looking for evidence of embezzlement—secret bank accounts showing large amounts of cash deposits, or anything else that looked like potential evidence.

They found nothing. Dan Smathers was more careful than they'd figured he would be. But the search was not an entire flop. Rex found something they were *not* looking for. In a drawer in Dan's bedroom there was a cell phone. On the front of the case someone had painted a smiley face.

How Rob Sterling's cell phone came to be in the bedroom of the man who was now assisting in the prosecution that could send Rob to prison for the rest of his life, or even to his death, was a mystery worth looking into. He took several pictures and then collected the phone and put it in an evidence bag.

"What are you taking that for?" the police lieutenant in charge of the search asked.

Rex said softly, "It would be better if all the officers don't know this just yet, but this phone was last seen in the bedroom of Rob and Jennifer Sterling the morning before she died. It's Rob's phone."

The significance of that revelation was not lost on the officer. When Rex explained that he'd collected fibers from the murder scene the night of Jennifer's death, they agreed that the search should include the seizure of samples of Dan's clothing. But to make sure the evidence seized wouldn't be thrown out in court, they decided that it would be wise to get another search warrant, one that specifically allowed a search for evidence relating to the death of Jennifer Sterling.

CHAPTER TWENTY-EIGHT

The office of the district attorney consisted of a group of dedicated men and women who were committed to fighting crime. Many were career prosecutors. But for the most part, they were an honest and hardworking group of attorneys.

But corruption was also breeding more corruption in the office as well, and among the group committed to riding the coattails of the boss to bigger and better things was an individual who'd been called into the office that night to assist in the preparation of the search warrant on Dan's home. He stayed in the office while he waited to hear what happened at the search. In the meantime, he called William and informed him, and William came down immediately. A disaster was unfolding, and he had to take immediate steps to stop the case against Dan from going any further.

When the officers returned for a second search warrant for the same home, William was waiting for them. Rex knew a change of plans was necessary, and he whispered to the lieutenant that this was neither the time nor the place to begin the process for that new search warrant. So the request wasn't made. But William still aimed his fury at Rex Thomas, accusing him of trying to derail the Sterling trial by throwing mud at Dan Smathers. "And as we can all see, there was no evidence," he said.

Rex eyed the lieutenant. They had the stolen cell phone, and William didn't know that. So they better let well enough alone. The lieutenant nodded his silent agreement. "Sorry sir," Rex said, feigning humility. "I guess we were wrong."

After leaving, Rex again called the cell phone number of Sperry Collier. "Sperry, are you still tied up?" he asked.

"In a way," Sperry said. "Actually, I'm overwhelmed. I need help."

"The same's true here," Rex said. "But I'm free for the moment. Can I meet you somewhere?"

Sperry named a location. "But hurry, and come discreetly."

Rex walked up to Sperry's car a few minutes later and tapped on the window. It was bitter cold, and he'd left his car a block away. Sperry turned and saw him, signaling him to get in.

"What's up?" Rex asked.

Sperry told him. "I've been tailing Dan Smathers. He's a busy man tonight. And I'm worried about what Alexander Addison might be up to."

Rex knew all about Addison, but they hadn't been able to find enough evidence to do anything but worry. That he was connected with Dan was clear, and both detectives were convinced that Alexander was the man who had given orders to the stalker. Through small clues here and there, they were sure he had something to do with the strange behavior of the law student Martin Ligorni as well. And they also believed he'd played a major role in the actions of the corrupt and now missing correctional officer, Frank Rawlings.

Rex said, "We better get some reinforcements. Dan's home was searched tonight for evidence of embezzlement from his own law firm."

"Did they find any?" Sperry asked.

"No, but I found Rob Sterling's missing cell phone. We can tie Dan to Rob's house now. And if we could get a warrant to search his house again, to take his clothing for example, I think the lab could prove that he was in Rob's house. All they need to do is find matching fibers to those we vacuumed up from beside the sofa, and we've got him. A match of fibers is definitely possible unless he's thrown that clothing away."

"Then let's do it," Sperry said. "What are you waiting for?"

"I was going to, but William Montgomery showed up and I decided not to tip my hand. The city has an officer sitting over there, just to make sure Dan doesn't show up and start moving his clothes out."

Sperry chuckled and Rex glanced at him. "So what exactly are you doing now?" Rex asked the PI.

"Dan won't be moving anything out of his house for a little while at least." He chuckled again. "As we speak, Dan's in the third house on the right side of the street," Sperry said. "I'm just waiting for him to come out."

"Do we know who lives there?" Rex asked.

"I have no idea."

"There's a car in the driveway," Rex said. "Would you like me to get a license number?"

"That would be great. I drove by, but there's mud on the plate. And I didn't dare leave my car for fear Dan would come out and drive off and I'd lose him," Sperry said.

"While I'm out there freezing, would you call this number?" Rex asked. "Lieutenant Grover with Salt Lake City is already calling together some officers. Ask him to send a couple of officers to take your place here. I'll be right back."

Rex had just squatted down behind the car in the driveway when he heard the front door open. He slipped quickly around to the side of the car and ducked down. He heard voices. One was Dan's, the other was a woman whose voice he instantly recognized. Dan was speaking. "I'll send you some money. But get out of town tonight. Call me tomorrow and let me know where you're at."

"But Dan, I don't want to, " she began.

"Just do it, Ann," Dan broke in, and he started walking toward the driveway.

A moment later the door to the house slammed shut. Dan walked within a few feet of Rex who had shuffled silently to the front of the car, then he turned rapidly up the street, got in a car parked there, and drove away. Sperry slowed down but Rex waved him on. They didn't want to lose Dan now.

Rex then cleaned off the front plate of the car, jotted the license number down, and hurried back up the street to his own car. He was shivering when he got in and started the engine. He was quite sure he knew who the woman in the house was, but he needed to be positive. So he called in her license plate number on his cell phone.

Within a minute, Rex had his answer. He'd been right. Her name was Ann Denton, the woman who'd testified that Jennifer was seeing other men. She'd been jealous of Jennifer, and she was clearly involved with Dan now. Although Haley had gone easy on her in court, she'd told Rex that she might call her again later. *Dan must have thought about that possibility,* Rex thought now. *It's clear Dan wants her where she can't be found.*

Another call to Sperry confirmed that he was still following Dan, heading south on State Street. "I'll be relieved shortly," Sperry said. "I'll meet you back at the sheriff's office. Lieutenant Grover will meet us there. So will your boss."

"Have you talked to Haley?" Rex asked.

"No, I tried to call earlier, but there was no answer on her cell phone."

"I'll try to get hold of her. If I have to, I'll swing by the place she's staying at. She needs to be there when we meet with Grover and the sheriff."

Haley answered her phone. "I'm at Bishop Coffman's house in the apartment here. I've been looking at obituaries in the newspaper files on the Internet."

"Find anyone you know?" Rex asked with a chuckle.

"No, but I think I've found a missing insurance agent," she said.

"Ah," Rex murmured. "Can you meet me at the sheriff's office?"

"Sure, but what's happening?" she asked.

"A lot. See you as soon as you can get there," he said. "Oh, and Haley, do you know anyone in the district attorney's office who would come meet with us without telling William?"

"I think I could persuade Keith Breathwaite. William's embarrassed him enough already that I think he'd like to redeem himself with the rest of the staff."

"Call him. Get him there if you can. But we don't want William to know. Not yet anyway."

* * *

The sheriff looked to Rex to take the lead in the meeting. "Time is of the essence," Rex was telling the assembled officers as Haley and Sperry walked in. Haley's eyes were sparkling and her face was shining despite the lateness of the hour. Rex could tell that Sperry had filled her in already. So he just said, "Welcome, Counselor. I was just ready to brief everyone on what's going down."

"Thanks, Sergeant," she said as she sat down next to Sperry and glanced around the room. There were at least twenty officers, some from the police department, others from the sheriff's office. Kurt Palmer, who had just gotten back from out of town, was seated next to Raul Garcia. She hoped Raul had enjoyed some quality time with his son before they called him. Then she caught Keith Breathwaite's eye. He gave her a thumbs up and smiled awkwardly. She gave him a little wave and turned her attention back to Rex.

"We don't know where Dan Smathers is heading, but it could be to a meeting with a man he represented years ago, a man he's been spotted with twice in the past few weeks by Sperry Collier. His name is Alexander Addison."

Several officers murmured. They knew of Alexander's reputation.

"Mr. Breathwaite is here representing the district attorney's office. He's given us the go-ahead to pick both men up if in fact they do meet up somewhere. Two units, four men, are tracking them right now," Rex explained. "If they happen to go to the location that Sperry is most familiar with, we'll learn a lot. Sperry got permission from the owners of that particular building to place some recording devices. We may get lucky and have unsolicited confessions before the night's through.

"You see, we have reason to believe that this Alexander Addison is the middle man for Smathers. That is, he's the one we believe has been arranging such things as the threats against Miss Gordon, the fake hand deliveries to her, the bribing of Jake and Trista Zippeta, the disappearance of Frank Rawlings, the framing of Raul Garcia, and the fire that destroyed Raul's office. The list goes on, but you get the idea. His home will also need to be searched. Dan either has something on Addison, or Dan is paying him a lot of money. The man Miss Gordon winged," he said with a grin, "had been naming Rob Sterling as the person behind what he did. The same was true of the man we arrested for the Garcia fire. We now believe Mr. Addison was the one naming Rob.

"That brings me to the next item. Smathers's own firm accused him of embezzling firm money tonight. And I'm talking large amounts. Some of you were involved earlier this evening in the search at his house. Other than finding the cell phone we believe was stolen from Rob Sterling's house the night of his wife's death, we struck out there," Rex said.

"However, we believe we can still track down some evidence pointing to where he's been stashing the stolen money. We're hoping that Mr. Breathwaite will approve a search warrant for the home of Miss Ann Denton as soon as we're through with this briefing. Ann is a young woman who worked in the same office with the late Jennifer Sterling and at first told us that she'd seen Jennifer with Dan Smathers. Her behavior led us to suspect jealousy there. And when her story changed and she testified differently in court, we really wondered about her motive. Dan Smathers just left her home a few minutes ago. I was just outside when he left, and he instructed her to leave town before the night was over and said he'd send her some money.

"Anyway, there could be some evidence in her house that would be helpful," Rex suggested. "Now," he continued, "let me explain a couple of other things for those of you here who don't know what we think happened with Jennifer Sterling." He went on to explain their theory on Jennifer Sterling's death. "First of all, we believe that Rob Sterling is the wrong man. I'm convinced that Dan Smathers killed Jennifer Sterling."

There was a buzz through the room. Rex waited until it quieted down, then he said, "However, we have information indicating it was an accident of sorts, and we can get into the details of that later."

After explaining how they also needed to get fiber samples from Dan's clothing, he looked at Haley. "Miss Gordon, I think you've learned something tonight as well." He grinned. "Haley's been on the Internet looking at old obituaries," he told the others.

She smiled and everyone turned her way. "This afternoon in court, William threw a curve at us. He said that he had proof that Rob had purchased a half-million-dollar life insurance policy on his wife the week before she was killed. He gave me a copy of the policy. I talked to Rob Sterling about it early this evening. He claimed that he had been working with an agent by the name of Fred Owens. He even signed a blank application that Mr. Owens was to fill out after Rob and his wife decided on an amount. The witness Mr. Montgomery is planning to call is Fred's younger brother. They operated an office together. Rob says he would never do business with the younger brother, Bradley. But when he cracked a joke about buying life insurance from a man who was so old he had one foot in the grave, it made me wonder," she explained.

"Thus the obituaries," she went on with a grin. "And bingo, Fred died a week after Rob went to jail. Convenient, huh? I'm sure we have only to look a little deeper and we'll find a Smathers and Bradley Owens connection. And since the district attorney was foolish enough to enlist Dan's aid, my guess is that we'll find that either Dan or Mr. Addison helped Bradley Owens out financially."

"Thanks, Haley. So there's something else we need to follow up on. There are also a couple of surprises that we have for Mr. Montgomery. We'd planned on giving them to him in court, but depending on how things go the next few hours, we may not wait. Oh, and there are three jurors who need to be picked up tonight for questioning. They all accepted packages from Dan Smathers earlier. Sperry, if you could give us their names and addresses." Sperry did so and then Rex said, "Okay, now let's get some assignments made. What we can't do tonight, we can finish in the morning. They're all yours," he said, indicating Lieutenant Grover and the sheriff.

Before assignments could be made the report came in that Dan Smathers had met up with the contact, Alexander Addison. They were using a location where they'd met before, the very one where voice-activated recording devices awaited their visit. "Rex and Kurt, come with me!" Sperry shouted. "I know the place. But we'll have to hurry."

"What about the search warrants?" Keith asked as they started away. "I'll need affidavits."

"That can wait. Let's have someone pick up Miss Denton. Maybe she'll even give consent," Rex said as he shrugged into his coat.

The sheriff took over as Rex left, and Haley listened quietly as men were dispatched to various locations around the valley.

* * *

The lunch tray that was picked up at Rob's cell was still full. He hadn't eaten much. Ever since Haley's visit the night before, he'd been a bundle of nerves. He had great confidence in Haley, but he kept worrying about the life insurance policy. He'd foolishly signed the blank application. What if Fred had filled it out with Jennifer's name instead of his? Or what if Bradley had somehow gotten hold of the file? Or what if . . . His imagination was driving him nuts. The thought tormented him that if he was convicted, Jennifer's killer would go free, all because he'd done something dumb like that.

An officer appeared at his cell door. "Put these on," he said to Rob as he handed him his suit and dress shirt.

"Why?" he asked. "It's Saturday. They don't hold court on Saturday."

"I don't know why," the officer said. "I was just told to have you up front in your suit by one o'clock this afternoon."

Rob's stomach began to roll. Something was up, and he couldn't even make an educated guess at what it might be. When he was ushered out a few minutes later, the sheriff himself greeted him. "There's going to be a little meeting in my office in a few minutes. You need to be there," the sheriff told him.

"What's it all about?" Rob asked. "Am I being accused of something else now?"

"Just be patient, Rob. You'll see."

The first face Rob saw as the sheriff steered him into his large office was Haley's—smiling, radiant, and beautiful. She rushed over to him, took hold of his manacled hands, and said, "Can we get these off now?"

The sheriff grinned and said, "Sure can."

"What's going on?" Rob asked as Haley sat down and signaled for him to sit next to her.

"We're going to have a meeting," Haley said.

"I already know that," Rob responded gruffly. "What kind of a meeting?"

Just then Raul, Rex, Kurt, and Sperry entered the room. They all spoke to Rob and Haley, and before Rob had time to renew his question, the district attorney came in. He was the only one who was grim, and Rob couldn't help but be encouraged by that.

"I'd like to know what in the world is going on here?" William demanded.

"Just sit down, William, and you'll see," the sheriff said.

They all sat around a small conference table. The sheriff sat at one end. The other end was open. William moved toward that chair, but the sheriff said, "No—there'll be use for that one in a moment. Why don't you sit here across from Miss Gordon?"

William did as the sheriff asked, but again he demanded, "What is this all about? Haley, why can I feel your sly hand in this?"

She smiled pleasantly as Rob bristled beside her. "You're a smart man," she said. "I did call this meeting."

William started to speak again. "Wait just a minute, William," Haley said. "You asked a question. I'm about to answer it. You were a decent man until you decided to run for attorney general. Since then, you've allowed yourself to fall into a trap. I wanted to give you the chance to save face today. At three this afternoon, Judge Horton and his clerk will be in his courtroom to listen to my motion to have Rob's case dismissed. I have every reason to believe he'll grant my motion."

"It's more likely that he'll have you committed," the district attorney snapped.

Sperry Collier spoke up. "Mr. Montgomery, we all argued against this but being the kind of person she is, Haley insisted that you be given a chance to hear us out now. Please refrain from further insults."

Rob was watching Sperry as he spoke. He could see that the man was seething. He looked dangerous in fact. William could apparently see that as well since he said, "All right, what do you have on your mind, Haley?"

"I was hoping that after what you're about to hear, you'll want to make that motion yourself. It'll give you a chance to redeem yourself with the rest of your office as well as the public. But that'll be up to you."

"I did retain co-counsel. Why isn't he here?" the district attorney asked.

"Dan's in jail " Haley began.

"What?!" William thundered, coming to his feet.

"Sit down, Mr. Montgomery, and I'll explain. That's part of what we wanted you to hear this afternoon. There is some information that I intended to use in court that you know nothing about."

"Then you can't use it," William said. "There are discovery rules, you know."

"And you waived," Raul spoke up.

"I did no such thing," he argued.

Raul pointed to a small cassette recorder that was sitting in the middle of the table as Haley said, "First tape, please."

Sperry punched the button that started the tape rolling. When the district attorney heard his own voice, he demanded that the device be shut off. "You're devious," he hissed. "Okay, so you made me angry before you offered to tell me about them."

Haley just shook her head. Sperry said, "Let's forget this. He's not worth saving."

"No, we'll move ahead," she said. "Okay, William. Dan's in jail for embezzling money from his own firm."

"I already—" William began, but then Sperry caught his eye, and he slammed his mouth shut.

Haley continued as though there had been no interruption. "He'll be facing other charges as well, and I think you should be the first to name them when you hear all that we have to tell you."

She looked at the sheriff. "Is Mr. Ligorni out there?"

"He is," the sheriff said.

"Would you have him brought in?" she asked.

Rob was sitting quietly, though he felt like he was walking through a land mine. He hardly recognized Martin Ligorni when he was shown into the room. His face was clean shaven. He had lost weight, and his eyes were sallow. "This is Martin Ligorni," Haley said. "He and Rob were in law school together."

"I know who he is," William said.

"Good. He tried to get away from here and succeeded. But Detective Collier, with the aid of some colleagues from out of state, tracked him down. He's decided to tell the truth now. He's made a full statement that you're welcome to read at your leisure, but for now, I've asked Martin to just favor us with a few highlights.

"Tell us, Martin," Haley said, "about your attraction to Jennifer Sterling, the former Miss Utah."

"Rob stole her," he said, his eyes flashing hatred toward Rob.

"Okay, let's skip ahead," Haley said. "You knew that Jennifer left notes for Rob in his car, didn't you? Notes that asked him to meet her at different places for dinner?"

"Yeah," he agreed.

"And you took one from one of his books in class, didn't you?"

"Yeah, last spring," he admitted.

"And did you copy her handwriting and write one yourself just before her death?"

"Yeah."

"What did it say?"

"It said for Rob to go to a restaurant in Park City to meet Jennifer."

"What was the name of the restaurant?" Haley asked.

"I can't remember. I made it up," Martin confessed.

"And what did you do with the note?"

"I was going to stick it under his windshield wiper, but then I noticed that the window on the passenger side was down just a little bit. So I shoved it through."

"Did it land on the seat?" she asked.

Martin nodded.

"When was this?" Haley asked.

"The day somebody killed Jennifer," he said.

"Why did you leave the note?" Haley asked.

"So I could go watch Jennifer through the window and be sure Rob wasn't there," he said, his eyes starting to brim with tears.

Haley turned to William, who, for a change, seemed to have nothing to say. "Maybe I could summarize the rest," she suggested.

William nodded sullenly. "Martin went to Rob's house. He saw a man inside, heard a shot, and then saw Jennifer lying on the floor inside. The man left about then, but he couldn't tell who it was. Though he later said it was Rob after a man offered him a thousand dollars to say so."

She turned again to Martin. "Is that about right?"

He nodded.

"Did you want to ask him anything, William?" Haley asked.

The district attorney shook his head.

"Next one," Haley said.

The sheriff had the stalker brought in. Haley shuddered when she saw him. Rob put his hand on hers, and she quickly gained control. Sperry Collier said, "This man has also given us a statement. For reasons I think you can understand, I'll just tell you quickly what he told us. By the way, when he was taken from the hospital, it was actually Sergeant Thomas who arranged it. He's been under federal protection ever since. He was working for a man by the name of Alexander Addison. Mr. Addison paid him large sums of money to do a variety of tasks for him. They included threatening Miss Gordon, kidnapping her at one point, bribing Martin, and so on. He was told by Mr. Addison that he was doing all this for Rob Sterling. Is that right, sir?" he asked.

The stalker nodded. He was then led out as the sheriff finished with, "Of course he was presented the evidence confirming that Dan Smathers was actually his employer. Okay, now we come to Dan himself and Alexander Addison. Next tape please." Sperry started the next recording.

Rob could hardly believe what he was hearing. And William looked like he wished he were a mouse so he could quietly slip out.

The recording had been made late the previous night. And it was obviously without the knowledge of Dan or Alexander. A heated argument was taking place. Alexander told Dan that he owed him a lot more money. "That insurance agent wants fifty grand," Alexander said on the tape.

"He got ten," Dan said. "That's it!"

They argued about that for a while, with Dan finally agreeing to pay him another fifteen thousand dollars. Then Dan said, "I took care of several of the jurors myself. That cost me nearly a hundred thousand."

"I could have taken care of it for a lot less," Alexander said. "It serves you right for trying to do my job for me."

The tape went on, and after a while, Alexander said, "I'll need another fifty grand for myself."

"You've been paid too much already," Dan growled.

"I want more, Dan, or I tip the cops off to who really murdered Jennifer Sterling," Alexander said.

"It wasn't murder. You know that. I didn't mean to kill her. The gun went off when I tripped over that lamp."

Rob gripped Haley's hand so tight it hurt. She looked at him. His eyes were filled with tears. She wanted to hold him, to comfort him, but all she could do was cry with him, which she had begun to do.

Sperry shut the recorder off. "There's more," he said. "But I think you get the picture, Mr. Montgomery."

The district attorney nodded. "I'll make the motion to dismiss the charges against Mr. Sterling," he said. The source of disgust in his voice was unclear—battered pride maybe, or shame for letting pride take him where it did. Either way it moved him from his seat and out of the room without another word.

* * *

That evening on the news there was a lengthy story about the arrest of Dan Smathers and the release of Rob Sterling. Rob and Raul sat in Raul's comfortable living room and watched.

There was also mention that the distinguished district attorney, after announcing that the charges against Rob had been dismissed and that Dan Smathers would be arraigned on a variety of charges that Monday, had made another announcement.

"For personal and health reasons, I am withdrawing from the race for Utah attorney general. I also regret that I will not be able to complete my term as district attorney. I'll be resigning effective the first day of February," he said. There was a pause, then William added, "I regret having to make this decision, as I could have done a great deal for the state of Utah."

Rob turned to Raul. "Man still has his pride."

"Yes, sad though," Raul said.

"No apology for what was done to you, I see."

Raul just shrugged his shoulders. "I'm fine," he said. "He was just trying to do his job."

"I expected you'd say that," Rob told him. "You're too much, buddy."

Raul looked over at Rob and grinned. "I'm getting my practice back," he said. "What's Mr. Montgomery got now?"

"I think he should have extended an olive branch to Haley too. The least he could have done was offer her a job at his office again," Rob added.

"That would have been too much like an apology," Raul said as he and Rob turned back to the TV. The camera remained on Mr. Montgomery as he brushed back his silver hair, then turned and walked briskly away.

"I suppose the public will form their own opinions as to why he *suddenly* had health and personal problems," Rob remarked.

"Yes, most people will see through what just happened," Raul agreed.

EPILOGUE

Two Months Later—

The group of young teenagers ate every morsel Haley had cooked. She'd fixed a big meal too. Of course, Rob Sterling ate more than he was used to, surprising himself with his own appetite. He'd finally gotten that promised home-cooked meal.

"Are you going to go back to law school?" a young man asked.

"Yes, but not for a while. I still need a little more time to recover," he said. "It takes a lot of concentration to go to law school, and I'm not ready for that yet."

"Why did you sell your house and move out of our ward?" he pressed.

"I couldn't ever live there again," he said. "There were too many memories. And I couldn't find an apartment in the ward."

"We've missed you, Brother Sterling. Are you going to buy a new house in our ward so you can be our teacher again?" one of the girls wanted to know.

"Actually, I hope I can find one here eventually. I've missed you guys, too," he said. "But I've had a lot of expenses and it'll be some-time before I can afford a new house."

"Oh, did you have to pay a lot of your money to Miss Gordon for helping you?" she persisted.

"Well, actually, no. She wouldn't take anything," Rob said as he flashed Haley a grin.

"Why not, Miss Gordon?" the girl asked her. "You earned it. You did an awesome job."

"Thank you, but for some things, you just can't take money," Haley tried to explain.

That didn't make sense to the well-dressed young woman, but one girl spoke up slowly, pushing her thoughts past the barrier of a difficult learning disorder she faced. "Some . . . sometimes p-people d-do things for other people . . . because they l-love them," she finished triumphantly.

Haley looked at Rob and wondered if someday that could be the case. She. was just about to correct the girl when Rob caught her eye. Haley paused, recognition sinking in. Then she realized that even though it might be a long road getting there, she had just caught a glimpse of what that day might look like.

ABOUT THE AUTHOR

Clair M. Poulson spent many years in his native Duchesne County as a highway patrolman and deputy sheriff. He completed his law enforcement career with eight years as Duchesne County Sheriff. During that time he served on numerous boards and committees, including serving as president of the Utah Sheriff's Association and as a member of a national advisory board to the FBI.

For the past twelve years Clair has served as a Justice Court judge in Duchesne County and currently represents the Justice Court judges of the state as a member of Utah's Judicial Council.

Church service and family have always been priorities for Clair. He has served in a variety of stake and ward callings, and he and his wife, Ruth, an accomplished piano teacher, have five children and nine grandchildren. Clair also does a little farming, his main interest being horses. Both Clair and his wife currently help their oldest son run *the* grocery store in Duchesne.

Clair has always been an avid reader, but his interest in creating fiction began many years ago when he would tell bedtime stories to his small children. They would beg for just one more "make-up story" before going to sleep. *Conflict of Interest* is Clair's ninth published novel.